PRAISE FOR
ONE SNOWY NIGHT

"Heartfelt and homespun! Curl up under a quilt and escape into this hopeful read."
—*New York Times* bestselling author Lori Wilde

"Stitched through with heart and hope, *One Snowy Night* is a story that will renew your faith in love, family, and the possibility of fresh starts. In short, this is the novel we all need right now."
—*New York Times* bestselling author Marie Bostwick

"Pulls readers into an enchanted frozen land filled with people with warm hearts. So curl up with your favorite quilt and read Patience Griffin's newest book."
—*New York Times* bestselling author Jodi Thomas

PRAISE FOR THE OTHER NOVELS OF
PATIENCE GRIFFIN

"Griffin's lyrical and moving debut marks her as a most talented newcomer to the romance genre."
—*Publishers Weekly* (starred review)

"Griffin gets loss, love, and laughter like no other writer of contemporary romance."
—*New York Times* bestselling author Grace Burrowes

"A captivating story of four friends, two madcap romances, an idyllic Scottish town, and its endearingly stubborn but loyal inhabitants. . . . Witty, warmhearted, and totally charming!"
—Shelley Noble, *New York Times* bestselling author of *A Resolution at Midnight*

"Griffin has quilted together a wonderful, heartwarming story that will convince you of the power of love."
—Janet Chapman, *New York Times* bestselling author of *Call It Magic*

"A life-affirming story of love, loss, and redemption. . . . Griffin seamlessly pieces compelling characters, a spectacular setting, and a poignant romance into a story as warm and beautiful as an heirloom quilt."
—Diane Kelly, author of the House-Flipper Mysteries

"With the backdrop of a beautiful town in Scotland, Griffin's story is charming and heartwarming. The characters are quirky and wonderful and easy to feel an instant attachment and affection for. Be forewarned: You're likely to shed happy tears."
—RT Book Reviews

"Definitely a 'must read' for any woman with romance in her heart."
—Fresh Fiction

"[I] laughed, cried, sighed, and thoroughly enjoyed every word of this emotional story set in a small coastal village in Scotland."
—The Romance Dish

"A heartwarming romance series!"
—*Woman's World*

"A fun hop to scenic Scotland for the price of a paperback."
—*Kirkus Reviews*

"Draws the reader into life in small-town Scotland. [Griffin's] use of language and descriptive setting [made] me feel like I was part of the cast."
—Open Book Society

ALSO BY PATIENCE GRIFFIN

Kilts and Quilts Series

To Scotland with Love

Meet Me in Scotland

Some Like It Scottish

The Accidental Scot

The Trouble with Scotland

It Happened in Scotland

The Laird and I (novella)

Blame It on Scotland

Kilt in Scotland

One Snowy Night

Patience Griffin

JOVE
New York

A JOVE BOOK
Published by Berkley
An imprint of Penguin Random House LLC
penguinrandomhouse.com

ISBN: 9780593101476

First Edition: March 2021

Printed in the United States of America
1 3 5 7 9 10 8 6 4 2

Cover art © Anna Kmet
Cover design by Judith Lagerman
Book design by Alison Cnockaert

For BrendaRae and Wanda

Thank you, BrendaRae, for opening up your home and chauffeuring me all over Alaska. You're not only a terrific tour guide but an amazing quilter!

Wanda, thank you for answering the call of adventure again. We have had quite a few over the years, from Girl Scout campouts, to Maine, to Puerto Rico, to Scotland, and most recently to Alaska. You are my favorite travel buddy!

Serenity Prayer

God grant me the serenity
to accept the things I cannot change;
courage to change the things I can;
and wisdom to know the difference.

Chapter 1

THIRTY-FOUR-YEAR-OLD HOPE McKNIGHT tried *not* to watch the clock, which hung on the dingy blue wall of her minuscule living room. But it was impossible to keep from glancing at it every other second. She turned and gazed out the frost-covered window into the pitch-black of night and shivered before peeking at the clock again.

Ten thirty.

Ella should've been home from the football game an hour ago. Calling and texting her daughter's cell phone hadn't eased Hope's worry, as Ella hadn't responded.

Hope always agonized over Ella's safety when it snowed, even when it was only a dusting. Sweet Home was remote, with winding roads leading in and out of the town, population 573—Alaska Native people, transplants, and multigenerational Alaskans like herself—and Hope knew better than anyone how treacherous the roads could be. Plus there was a deeper threat hanging over their little house. For the past two Friday nights, her sixteen-year-old daughter had staggered in the front door, clearly drunk. Hope felt defeated . . . and guilty. Lecturing Ella from birth about the pitfalls of alcohol—even being the head of the local chapter of Mothers Against Drunk

Driving—hadn't prevented her daughter from getting caught up in Alaska's number one pastime.

Is Ella doomed to repeat my mistakes?

Hope tried to shove the thought from her mind, but she couldn't stop feeling—down to her bones—that Ella's drinking was inherently her fault.

Hope glanced at the car keys hanging on the hook by the front door. At least there was that: Ella wouldn't be driving. But that didn't mean she wasn't getting a ride home with another inebriated teen.

To stop fretting, Hope pushed herself off the couch to rearrange the furniture in her living room, anything to occupy her mind. At one time she'd thought about getting a degree in interior design, but that was before. And because her living room was tiny, the rearranging took no time at all. She needed something else to keep from going crazy with worry. She strode to the closet and pulled out a rucksack. "I'll start packing without her," she said to the empty house. Every year they took several snow camping trips in the thick forests surrounding Sweet Home, where Hope could test Ella's survival skills.

Hope's gaze traveled to the clock once again. Yes, according to the experts, only five percent of what people worried about actually happened. But Hope knew that danger lurked around every corner, ready to ruin lives. She was living proof of how a good life could turn awful in an instant. And how, once things went bad, there was no way to turn back time and recapture the joy she once had. When her parents named her Hope, they'd made a grievous error . . . because she had none. She hadn't been prepared for what life had thrown at her. Her *job one* now? To prepare Ella for what lay ahead, good or bad.

She went to Ella's room and unearthed her daughter's backpack from beneath a pile of clothes. As an exhausted and overworked single parent, she'd thrown in the towel about Ella keeping her room picked up. In the vast scheme of things, an untidy room wasn't important. Having the skills to make it alone was. Knowing how to survive in the wild was key, too. Their camping trip would only be two days—Saturday and Sunday—the first days Hope had had off since September.

She dug past the second layer of clothes on the floor but couldn't find Ella's wool socks. Just as she was going to look in her daughter's closet, Hope's phone rang. She raced for the other room and caught it on the tail end of the second ring, knowing it had to be Ella.

"Where are you?"

But Hope was wrong. It was Piney Douglas, the closest thing she had to a mother now. Not that she didn't love Piney, but Hope's heart sank. *Where are you, Ella?*

"Where am I?" Piney chuckled. "I'm in my drafty apartment above the Hungry Bear"—the grocery store–diner where Hope worked. "Where else would I be?"

"I thought you were Ella." Hope could've added that Piney might've been anywhere, even the cabin next door to Hope, where Piney's boyfriend, Bill Morningstar, lived. Bill was known throughout Sweet Home for making Alaskan quilts.

Piney clucked. "Ella's fine. I'd know if something was wrong."

Hope sighed, thinking of Piney's crystals, tarot cards, tea-leaf readings, and other psychic stuff. Bill thought Piney's belief in the spirit world was complete rubbish and didn't seem to think twice about voicing his opinion. But Hope had to admit that at times Piney had an uncanny ability to know what was up with Ella, and thus decided that Piney was an intuitive. Piney maintained that she was more in touch with the universe than regular folks because she was born on the summer solstice. She certainly looked like Mother Earth—her gray hair curled at her shoulders, her Bohemian skirts flowing about her, and her wise smiling face, as if she were privy to the world's inner secrets. A self-proclaimed hippie, Piney had arrived in Alaska in the seventies, searching for the truth, traveling and sleeping in her converted blue school bus, way ahead of the current tiny home movement. Piney and her thirty-four-year-old daughter, Sparkle, had lived in that blue bus until just a few weeks ago, when two suits from Juneau had arrived, asking to purchase the bus for the state capitol as part of a pioneer sculpture. Piney took the money, telling everyone she'd outgrown the bus. But Hope knew money was tight since Sparkle's emergency appendectomy. It was perfect timing, too, as the apartment above the Hungry Bear had been vacated the week before.

"Keep your chin up, buttercup," Piney said. "Don't let your negative thinking carry you away. Besides, I'm calling to see if you know whether the rumor is true."

Once again, Hope glanced at the clock. *Ten forty.* Maybe she should call the Alaska State Troopers to find Ella. "What rumor?"

"Mr. Brewster heard at the bank that Donovan Stone is coming home."

It felt like a lightning strike. Hope couldn't breathe. Couldn't think either. "Donovan? Here?" *What am I going to do?* She hadn't seen him in seventeen years, not since his grandmother's funeral . . . where he'd told Hope he never wanted to see her again. And he hadn't.

The front door creaked. For a second, Piney's call kept Hope from being able to move. But as Ella tripped on the threshold, Hope yelled into her phone, "Gotta go." She lunged for her daughter, breaking her fall and keeping Ella's head from hitting the corner of the side table.

Ella's response was to laugh as she went down. "You should see your face!"

Hope didn't think it was funny. "Where have you been?" She kicked the door shut with her foot. Winter was just getting started, and the baseboard heaters were expensive to run.

Ella stopped laughing. "Chill, Mom. I was just out with friends." Her words were slurred, and her breath smelled of cheap wine.

A smell that brought back awful memories.

"Who drove you home tonight?" Hope hadn't heard a vehicle. "Were they drinking, too?"

"I walked home from Lacy's."

"The trail through the forest?" Hope glanced out the window to the black sky beyond. "Did you have your flashlight with you?"

"I was fine," Ella said. "I didn't need my flashlight. I know my way."

But Alaska was dangerous!

Sweet Home wasn't Anchorage, but someone could've kidnapped Ella and Hope would've never seen her again. Or Ella could've fallen into the river. Or she could've encountered a late-to-hibernate bear!

Hope got to her feet and helped Ella to her feet, too. "We're going to talk about this tomorrow. I know you're sad about Grandpa's passing—"

Ella swayed from side to side. "Don't bring Grandpa into this. He has nothing to do with *anything*." She wobbled into her room.

Hope followed and caught the door before Ella slammed it shut. Hope's heart was heavy, so very heavy, as she watched her teenage daughter stagger across her room and fall into bed. Hope plodded over to Ella and pulled off her boots. "I think your drinking has everything to do with Grandpa's death."

Death was such a harsh word, but it had been harsh for Hope to see her dad lying in that casket, felled by a heart attack. There hadn't been time for her to fall apart, though. Hope had to keep it together for Ella. Remain strong. Even when she felt her life coming apart at the seams. Sometimes it was best to focus on the small things.

Hope laid a hand on her daughter's arm. "I couldn't find your warm socks." She congratulated herself for coming up with something so benign.

Ella rolled her eyes. "Please don't start lecturing. They're at the bottom of my closet. I'll pack in the morning, all right? And yes, you've told me a hundred times to take care of my feet, especially during winter." She rolled away, burying her face in her pillow, which muffled her voice so she sounded a bit like Charlie Brown's teacher. *It can mean the difference between having a good time and losing toes.*

Hope wasn't deterred, only determined. Determined not to waste these two days off from her job at the Hungry Bear. Determined to teach Ella how to start a fire with wet wood and no matches. Mostly, she was determined to get Ella out of the funk she'd slipped into. They both were still reeling from the loss. She'd love to coddle her daughter, but that would be a disservice. "Listen, the world is harsh. It's my job to teach you survival skills." Things Hope had been forced to learn on her own, when she had to grow up all at once.

Ella sighed heavily, as if having a mother were the most annoying thing. "You've told me a million times: 'We're all alone in this world. I better be prepared to fend for myself.'"

"It's nice to know you've been listening. I'll see you in the morning." Hope started to leave, but Ella grabbed her hand.

"Stay. Tell me a story." Ella had switched gears again, from cranky teenager to affable angel. She'd always loved stories.

"Which one do you want to hear? The one where I stared down a bear?"

"No. I want to hear about Aunt Izzie."

Have people been talking? Has someone said something to Ella about Donovan returning to town? "You haven't asked about Izzie in a long time."

"I know. I want to hear about her now." Ella reached over the side of the bed and pulled a ribbon from between the mattress and box spring. "I found this ribbon to tie on the Memory Tree."

Hope reached out and ran her fingers over the ribbon. "We can do that on our camping trip, okay?"

"Sure," Ella said.

Hope had started the Memory Tree after Izzie died. It was the same mountain hemlock where Donovan, on Izzie's eleventh birthday, had carved her name—*Isabella!*—declaring that the tree was now hers. She'd been thrilled. After Izzie's death, Hope had started visiting the tree, bringing trinkets, things Izzie might've liked, to decorate it. Over the years, the two of them had continued the tradition, as Ella had enjoyed finding new treasures for Aunt Izzie.

"Go ahead." Ella closed her eyes, as if ready for a bedtime story.

Hope understood. Only the two of them were left. When Ella was little, Hope had started telling her stories about Izzie. It was one of the ways Hope kept her sister alive, and a way for Ella to know her namesake. Hope's mother had hated that she'd named her child Isabella after her dead sister, telling her it was cruel, making Mom despise Hope more.

Izzie was always a clear image in Hope's mind and she never tired of talking about her. "Izzie was just a little thing with a big personality. Even though she was six years younger than me, she tried to act like we were the same age and wanted to do everything I did. Because your grandmother worked nights in the ER, I babysat her a lot. It was fun. I taught her so much, from how to say her ABCs to how to tie her shoes. When we'd go with Mom to the Sisterhood of the Quilt stitch-ins, Izzie and I would set our sewing machines side by side and make all sorts of things from the fabric the Sisterhood would give us. Like matching pillowcases for the bedroom we shared, and blankets for Izzie's stuffed animals. We used to play Barbies together, bake cookies, and I really didn't mind if she tagged along with me and my friends." *Most of the time, anyway.* Donovan and his brother, Beau, were great about letting Izzie hang out with them, too.

"I know that stuff already. What happened to Aunt Izzie?" Ella said.

"You know what happened," Hope answered. "She died."

"You've never told me *how*." The whine in Ella's voice almost stopped Hope. But for the first time, it felt like the right moment. Sharing the sobering story would be one more way for Hope to atone for what she'd done to Izzie and their family. Tonight, especially tonight, Ella needed to hear it.

But it was hard to lay open the gaping wound of what had ruined Hope's life. How *she* herself had ruined it. How it'd been no one's fault but her own. "This isn't easy for me, Ella." She took a fortifying breath. "I really need you to pay attention and take everything I'm going to say to heart. Okay?"

Ella sighed. "You're being dramatic."

"No, I'm not. I'm going to tell you how it is. How it *was*." She started at the beginning of that awful night. "It was New Year's Eve. I was at a party, celebrating with my friends."

Hope left out the part about Donovan, how they'd fought that night. How her friends had encouraged her to dull her anger and disappointment with alcohol after he'd dropped the bomb that he was going to stay in Alaska for college, not go to Boston like they'd planned. Maturity and years of adulting had Hope seeing things differently. She understood now why he couldn't turn down a full ride, when every penny counted at his dad's house. Yes, Hope would leave out Donovan when telling Ella the story, but she wouldn't shy away from her guilt in the tragedy. "I had a few sips of wine from one of those red Solo cups."

"So what? A few sips won't kill you, Mom," her inebriated daughter countered. "I drank more than that tonight and I'm fine."

"Yeah, sure, you're fine. I should've videoed your swan dive through the front door a few minutes ago. Even a few sips of alcohol can impair your reflexes." *When you need them the most.* It had been that way for Hope. She'd been lucky when they tested her blood alcohol level and it was under the legal limit.

Hope moved closer. "Scooch over so I can tell you the rest." She sat beside Ella on her twin bed. "While I was still at the party, my mom called from the hospital, telling me to pick up Izzie from a sleepover, because she was complaining of a stomachache."

"I bet you didn't want to leave your friends," Ella said.

Guilt covered Hope, wrapped around her like a familiar,

well-worn robe, the tie in the middle squeezing her stomach until it hurt.

It was true. Her senior year, she'd begun resenting how much of her time wasn't her own, how she had to drop everything to take care of Izzie. Izzie wanted her to play like they used to, but Hope only wanted to spend time alone with Donovan. After being best friends their whole lives, Donovan had finally stopped serial dating every girl at Sweet Home High and saw Hope as more than a pal. If Hope had known sooner that going out with Jesse Montana—tight end on the football team and good friend of Donovan's—would wake Donovan up, Hope would have accepted Jesse's offer a few years earlier. Apparently, Donovan didn't have a clue that Hope had loved him since the first day he'd moved in next door.

"Mom? Mom! You're doing what you always do when you talk about Aunt Izzie," Ella said.

"What?"

"Zoning out. Get back to the story."

It wasn't just a story to Hope. She'd lived it. And now she had to make her daughter understand how life could go wrong in an instant. She dropped into lecture mode. "My mom always told me not to drink, to stay away from alcohol. Working the night shift in the ER, she saw the disastrous outcomes of drinking and driving—mangled bodies, loss of life." It hurt to say those words, but Hope was doing penance. "At the time, I didn't think it was a problem to have a few sips. I didn't know I was going to be driving right after. But I was the one with the car keys and I shouldn't have drunk at all." Also, Hope never understood those who couldn't have fun without knocking back a few. Donovan was one of them. She'd loved him, but she didn't like that he drank so much, and so often.

"So . . . you picked up Aunt Izzie . . ." Ella had missed the point completely.

Hope sighed, feeling defeated, but plowed on anyway.

"The point is, I should've listened to my mother and stayed away from alcohol."

Ella rolled her eyes. "Enough with the sermon, already. What happened next?"

"I yelled at Izzie for being a nuisance. For faking being sick." Hope had railed on her little sister, telling her that she'd ruined her night. Hope would never forget how Donovan had reached over and laid his hand on hers. *Don't take it out on Izzie. I know you're mad at me.*

"Then?"

This was the hardest part, recounting those horrible details. "There was a snowplow in the other lane."

"Was it snowing hard?" her daughter asked.

"Not when I'd left home, but by the time I left the party, visibility was horrible, nearly a whiteout." Donovan had offered to drive, but Hope wouldn't let him. He'd had too much to drink. Sixteen-year-old Beau was three sheets to the wind, too. It was left to Hope to get them all home safely.

"But you've driven in snow your whole life. What's the big deal?" her daughter prompted.

"There was a moose. He charged into the road in front of the snowplow." Hope took a deep breath to get the next words out. "The snowplow hit the moose and sent it flying toward my side of the road. I hit it. The moose flipped backward and crushed the back of my car." If only she'd had better reflexes to swerve and miss the bull. The biggest *if only* of her life.

Hope didn't remember too much after that, only what the snowplow driver had told her and the state trooper at the hospital. She'd often wondered if she could've saved her sister if only she'd been prepared—stopped the bleeding, kept Izzie from going into shock. It was one of the reasons Hope was adamant about teaching her daughter survival skills, beyond hunting and fishing, although those things were very important, too. Alaska was wild and anything could happen.

"I don't know why Donovan and I were brought to the hospital first."

"Who's Donovan?" her daughter asked.

"Nobody," Hope said quickly. "I was dazed from the accident and only had a broken arm." Donovan had just cuts and bruises. "Even though I confessed right away to my mom that I'd had some wine, she didn't yell at me but was only relieved I was okay." Beau arrived in the next ambulance and was pronounced dead on arrival. "When Izzie was wheeled in on the stretcher, she looked so small and broken. She only lived an hour before dying." Hope would never forget seeing her mother collapse with grief beside Izzie's hospital bed. "And that's why I'm head of MADD in our area," Hope finished, though the story was far from complete. She left out the part where her mother never forgave her. How her parents split up over Izzie's death, motivating her father to move to the North Slope. How it was her mother who brought MADD to their borough, and then on her deathbed insisted that Hope take over.

Hope had been looking off into space but glanced down at her daughter now.

Ella's mouth was open, making her look completely stunned. "You were driving the car? *You* killed Aunt Izzie?"

It was an icy knife to the heart, but it was true. Hope nodded bravely. "Yes. I'm responsible for my sister's death."

"That sucks . . ." Ella shook her head. "I can't imagine. How did your mom take it?"

"Badly."

"You would've grounded me forever. Whatever happened to your mom? You and Grandpa never talked about her."

Hope definitely wasn't ready to get into that. "She got sick—cancer—and died a few years later." Mom had been livid when Hope got up the courage two months after the accident to tell her that she was pregnant. *It's a slap in the face*, her mom had said. *Haven't you hurt this family enough?* When baby Ella was born, Mom pretended her granddaughter didn't exist. After her death, Dad had moved back to Sweet Home, continuing to work on the North Slope and commuting home on his weeks off, which eased Hope's load of raising a child alone. But now he was gone, too.

Ella looked stricken, then turned to face the wall. "Mom?"

"Yes?"

"What if you die, too?" Ella's voice was strained.

Hope understood. They didn't have anyone now, now that Dad was gone.

She wanted to tell her: *There are worse things than death.* Like being disowned at seventeen by your own mother and being forced from the house, alone and pregnant. Whenever she thought about that dark time, Hope tried counting her blessings. She owed Piney so much: for supporting her emotionally, for giving her a job and letting her stay with them in the bus until Mom died and Dad moved back to Sweet Home.

But all she said was, "You know how hard I try to be prepared for every contingency." Hope wanted to reiterate how important it was that Ella be prepared, too . . . for accidents and to go it alone. If Hope had been prepared seventeen years ago, she might've handled her mother's rejection better, instead of letting grief and depression nearly consume her.

Maybe it was time to tell Ella more of the truth. How Donovan and Beau had been in the car that night. How her mother couldn't stand to look at Hope after she'd killed her sister. Maybe the truth would scare Ella *straight*.

But Ella had fallen asleep.

Hope brushed her daughter's dark blond hair from her face. The same color hair as Ella's father, a father she'd never known. Hope had been sure she'd never have to tell Ella about Donovan. There was no reason to. But apparently, Donovan was returning home.

Hope turned off the light and left Ella's room, feeling drained. She'd spent the last seventeen years feeling tired. Exhausted to the bone.

She didn't have the energy to finish packing for their camping trip tonight or to worry about Donovan coming to town. She shuffled to her ten-by-ten-foot bedroom. She didn't turn on the lights but slipped off her slippers and jeans before climbing into bed, leaving on her turtleneck and kuspuk, a kind of loose Alaska Native hoodie. She threw her coat over the bed, too. Anything to keep warm tonight.

Before she fell asleep, Hope knew her eleven-year-old sister—*dead eleven-year-old sister*—would come to her in her dreams. Izzie had visited her on and off for the last seventeen years. But since Hope's daughter had started drinking, Izzie had visited nearly every night. Her sister was always sparkling, almost glowing. Hope didn't shy away from her sister's pop-ins, as they comforted her in ways the town's platitudes never had. Her sister would be wearing the same red moose flannel pajamas she'd worn on the night Hope had picked her up from the sleepover. But instead of covered in blood, the pajamas would be clean and new. Hope never told anyone about the dreams, which seemed so real.

For dreams they must be.

The first time Izzie had visited Hope was two days after she'd died. Her sister hadn't been chatty then but sat cross-legged on the floor beside Hope's bed, something she'd done a million times in real life. But this time, she stared off into the distance, looking lost. When Hope called out to her, Izzie had shaken her head, as if she didn't want to talk. But these days, Hope couldn't get her to shut up. Eleven-year-old Izzie, still in her little-girl body and her moose pajamas, spoke as a woman who'd lived a lifetime and had plenty of advice to give. Hope welcomed seeing her sister. It was hard to imagine that Izzie would've been twenty-eight a few months ago. If only Hope hadn't killed her.

Hope closed her eyes, and before she'd really drifted off to sleep, Izzie appeared, sitting at the foot of Hope's bed.

"Piney certainly threw you for a loop." Izzie had a twinkle in her eye, as if she were having fun, stirring up trouble. "Didn't you ever suspect Donovan might come back after his grandfather died?"

"I suppose." Since Charles Stone had moved away seventeen years ago, the news of his death took nearly a month to reach Sweet Home.

Izzie reached out as if to pat the quilt covering Hope's legs but withdrew her hand before touching it. "Do you think he's coming back to reopen the hardware store and lodge?"

A Stone's Throw Hardware & Haberdashery had been everything to this town when Hope was growing up. Her dad had worked there on weekends sometimes. And the lodge, well, Hope loved going to Home Sweet Home Lodge with her mom and Izzie, when the Sisterhood of the Quilt gathered for their monthly get-togethers. But that had been then.

Hope shook her head. "No. He wouldn't reopen his grandparents' businesses. He's probably just coming to Sweet Home to sign papers at the bank, probably get a real estate agent, too . . . if I had to guess."

Izzie slipped off the bed and put her hands on her hips. "Are you finally going to fess up to my namesake—my niece—and tell that child that Donovan is her father?"

Hope shivered. She couldn't imagine telling anyone the truth. Though all of Sweet Home must have a clue.

"No. I'm not going to tell Ella about Donovan. I told you before. Ella thinks her father was an oil worker who lived in the Yukon, that he died in a work-related accident before she was born."

"Are you at least going to tell Donovan that my niece belongs to him?"

"No!" Hope couldn't. Donovan had been crystal clear at his grandmother's funeral. *I never want to see you again.* There had been such vehemence in his voice.

Her last act of love was to respect his wishes. Besides, she didn't want him to hate her more than he already did.

"Donovan might be coming to Sweet Home, but the fact is, my know-it-all little sister, I don't plan to see him at all."

DONOVAN STONE DROVE the several hours from Anchorage to Sweet Home feeling numb. Not from the cold, or the snow that littered his windshield, but because he couldn't wrap his head around his grandfather being gone. Grief was only part of the problem. In his will, Grandpa had left Donovan both the hardware store and the lodge. *Why?* Donovan hadn't called Sweet Home *home* since he was eighteen.

For the last month, he'd put off coming to Alaska. But if he wanted to sell the properties, he had to see them first and meet with the real estate agent with whom he'd set up an appointment for tomorrow. The sooner he got things wrapped up here, the sooner he could get to Florida.

It'd been a long time coming. Donovan had served his country by way of the Marines, then given his all to his business, which meant he'd had little time for family. To be fair, he'd flown Dad and Grandpa from Florida, where they'd retired, to visit him in San Jose for every holiday. When Donovan had sold his Silicon Valley consulting company, he'd promised his dad that he'd relocate to Florida. But he hadn't moved quickly enough, and now Grandpa was dead.

Donovan drove around the final bend in the road and there sat Sweet Home. The new snow was plowed off to the sides, but that was the only thing he recognized. All the charm from the town was gone—the streets were deserted and most buildings were boarded up, but all of them looked battered, beaten, and run-down—including A Stone's Throw Hardware & Haberdashery. It made Donovan sick. With paint faded and the windows dark, it felt like the hardware store was dead, too, just like Grandpa.

Something caught Donovan's attention out of the corner of his eye. He saw a rack, then the beast coming toward him. He slammed on the brakes and veered to the side. As casual as could be, a moose strolled into the road. A moose acting as if he were trying to get a better look at the businesses—the Hungry Bear Grocery-Diner, the bank, the nailed-up medical clinic, and the churches—Baptist and Catholic—on either end of the town. Moose sightings were normal in Alaska, and Donovan should've prepared himself for it. But he hadn't.

Seeing the huge bull was a disturbing reminder of why he'd left, and immediately, he felt the pain of losing his kid brother again. Beau had been Donovan's best bud, best cohort in mischief, and best confidant. The two of them had been closer than most brothers. It seemed wrong, so wrong, that Beau's vibrant life had been cut short at sixteen.

At the tail end of that gut-wrenching memory stood Hope. Hope, who had been his whole world. But that was before she killed Beau, and before Donovan left for good.

Although he was back now, he knew there was no chance of seeing her. Hope had always wanted to explore the world, starting with college in Boston. She was probably living somewhere in Europe by now.

He thought about their last fight, when he told her how his dad had convinced him that it was best for the family if he took the full ride he'd gotten to the University of Alaska in Anchorage.

Two hours later, the fight was pointless. Beau was gone. And a week after that, Donovan dropped out of high school and put Sweet Home in his rearview mirror for good. Or so he'd thought.

He pushed all the dark memories away. He never let himself think about Hope or the good times they'd shared together. He'd done fine without her for the past seventeen years. He'd even conquered his drinking problem, one day at a time. The ninth step in the program said he should make amends. He'd made amends with everyone else, but he wasn't ready to take that step with Hope. He couldn't forgive her, let alone ask her to forgive him for leaving. No matter how he looked at it, it was best if Hope wasn't still in Sweet Home.

Donovan didn't stop at the hardware store or anywhere else in town. Instead, he drove straight through, not wanting to speak to anyone who was left. Surely, being back in the familiar surroundings of his grandparents' lodge would help acclimate him to being plunged into his past, plus help him get used to the far-north weather in the privacy of the lodge. He was freezing.

But three miles later, he was disappointed once again. Seeing the neglected condition of the lodge and the three surrounding cabins was like taking an ice pick to his heart. If his grandparents were still alive, they'd be devastated at how the pride of the borough had decayed into a shabby mess. His grandparents had always kept Home Sweet Home Lodge in pristine condition, making sure the exterior was welcoming for guests and for the women of his grandmother's monthly Sisterhood of the Quilt gatherings. He chuckled derisively. "Now it's not even fit for the Addams Family."

Donovan fought the urge to turn the rental car around and drive back to Anchorage. Instead, he pulled the car around the circular driveway and parked near the door. As he got out, a 4×4 truck pulled in behind him. At first, Donovan assumed the driver was looking for a place to turn around, but then the vehicle stopped and an old man eased out of the truck. He didn't immediately walk Donovan's way but reached back into the vehicle, pulling something out and holding it in his arms. Two seconds later, Donovan recognized both the man and the "package."

Mr. Brewster waved his free hand. "I saw you driving through town and decided to bring you a present."

"Nice to see you, Mr. Brewster. But that doesn't look like a present. That looks like a dog." A puppy. A very small puppy, but definitely a Bernese Mountain Dog. Donovan used to earn extra cash helping Mr. Brewster with his prize Berners, especially when there was a new litter.

Mr. Brewster handed over the puppy. "I brought you this runt. I don't have time for him, as he's not worth anything to me as he is. He's not thriving, and I remember how, back in the day, you had a soft spot for the sickly ones." He patted the pup in Donovan's arms. "Thought you could do your magic with this young'un."

"I-I—" Donovan tried.

"You always wanted a Berner for yourself. Now you've come home at last, he can keep you company while you fix up the place."

Donovan went speechless, unable to tell Mr. Brewster that

he had it wrong on all accounts, except for how he'd wanted a Bernese when he was a kid. Dad had said no, not out of meanness, but because he had his hands full with the pups he had already, as he put it. Donovan understood better now that Dad really had a lot on his plate—working full time, raising him and Beau all alone. Donovan's mom had walked out on them when Donovan was only six. *Carrie Stone ran to places unknown* was what he heard one of the women of Sweet Home say about his mom. He didn't know where his mother was . . . and he didn't care. She'd left him a couple of legacies that he fought against every day: alcoholism and the urge to run when things got tough.

When Mommie Dearest left, he and Beau started hanging out with Hope, their next-door neighbor. Hope scolded and mothered them, as if she'd known exactly what they needed. To be fair, he and Beau helped the then-prissy Hope toughen up, playing war in the woods behind their houses and later hunting, fishing, and foraging in the forest.

Mr. Brewster was walking away quickly, waving a hand over his shoulder. "See you soon. Call me if you need help with the hardware store."

Donovan got the sneaking suspicion that the old man was trying to coerce him into staying. But it just wasn't happening—runt or no. Donovan no longer called this place home.

He looked down at the dog. "What am I going to do with you?"

The helpless furball gazed back, wagging his tail a mile a minute and staring up at him with unadulterated love in his eyes.

Donovan hadn't seen that kind of adoration since he was a teen. Instead of a dog, it was Hope who'd been looking at him then.

Man, he needed to stop thinking about her. Yes, every now and then in the last seventeen years, she'd crossed his mind. Maybe once or twice a day. But since his grandfather died and the will had been read, Donovan couldn't keep thoughts of Hope from constantly popping up. The way her dark hair framed her pixie face, her taking-it-all-in brown eyes, and her indelible smile. *Except after the accident.*

The puppy slobbered on his hand. Donovan frowned at him, but the darn dog just gazed back lovingly.

"Let's go inside." Donovan walked up the scraped walkway, wondering who had shoveled the snow. Before digging the key out of his pocket, he set the dog on his feet. "Make your business here. Nan wouldn't care for a pup peeing in her house." But Nan had been gone a long time. Remembering brought on the guilt for what he'd done to his grandmother—leaving her when she needed him most.

The dog stood in the snow, appearing shocked to be exiled from Donovan's warm arms. The pup looked up at him with pitiful eyes.

"Don't give me that look. Be a man." Donovan shook his head. "I mean, be a big dog, Beau." It had just come out, his brother's name, and it rocked Donovan. "I really am rattled, aren't I?" He stared at the dog a little longer. "I'll call you Boomer for now. And whoever your new owners turn out to be, they can rename you whatever they like."

Little Boomer took a leak, then stumbled back to Donovan, looking ready to get lifted out of the snow and snuggled back in his arms. After he picked him up and before he could put the key in the lock, another vehicle pulled up. It was Rick Miller, Donovan's platoon mate, friend, and business manager. Rick had seen Donovan at his worst and at his best. Donovan trusted him like no other.

Rick unfolded his large frame from the truck, ran a hand through his short black hair, and then gave a low whistle. "Dude, you should've said something. This is some view." He turned around in a circle, taking in the woods, the mountains off in the distance, the river running behind the lodge, and the frosted meadow to the west.

The river he and Hope used to fish in, the woods they'd played in. A knot formed in Donovan's chest, and he pushed away the warm memory of his nearly perfect childhood.

He cleared his throat when he realized Rick was studying

him. Donovan pointed to the path leading to the back of the lodge. It had been shoveled, too. "There's more. The river has some of the best fishing in the borough."

"Show me," Rick said enthusiastically.

"This way." Donovan tucked the dog inside his coat, not wanting the pup to catch a chill. Which was ridiculous, as Berners were made for this weather. He glanced down at Boomer's head poking out and saw that the pup had already fallen asleep.

Rick slipped his messenger bag under his arm and pointed to the dog. "Who's your pal?"

"Boomer. An old friend of my grandfather's brought him by." But Donovan couldn't keep him. These types of dogs loved hard work and cold weather. It would be cruel to take him to Florida to laze around the pool.

Rick rubbed Boomer's head as he stepped around Donovan, heading to the back. "Come on. Show me this river before I freeze." Rick had grown up in Louisiana with his grandparents. He'd spent two years in the oil fields before joining the Marines.

Donovan caught up with him just as Rick started to climb the stairs to the porch.

"Be careful," Donovan warned. "Looks like there's dry rot. It's probably not safe after all these years."

Rick jumped up and down on the step he'd landed on, testing it. "This one seems fine." He kept climbing and Donovan followed him up the rickety steps.

When Rick reached the top, he stopped and stared at the view. "I know you want to sell, but this place could be a gold mine. I could see fishermen paying a bundle to stay here." He glanced back at the structure. "After you fix up the exterior, of course."

Donovan grunted. He had no intention of fixing up the place, beyond making it sellable.

"Listen to me. I'm your business manager, remember? This place is cash in the bank." Rick looked at him then.

"You've been searching for a new venture. I believe you've found it."

"Yeah, I don't know." But Donovan did know. He'd said good-bye to Sweet Home, and he'd meant it. He was the kind of guy who never looked back. Being back in Alaska caused ancient history to resurface, making him wish for a handful of Rolaids.

"I know that look. You're going to ignore me and my excellent advice, even though you know I'm right."

Donovan frowned. "Let's get inside, so I can sign those papers." He unlocked the French doors using one of the keys that the attorney had given him when the will was read. Donovan pushed open the doors and then walked into the past.

The massive dining table stretched horizontally in front of him, covered with a sheet. In fact, all the wooden furniture was covered with sheets, but he knew, by heart, every piece underneath—the dish hutch that rose to the ceiling, the side table with drawers for the tableware, the upright piano that was probably out of tune by now, and the long bar, where Nan had hosted her famous yearly Wines of Alaska tastings.

Donovan pulled out the waking puppy and set him on the floor.

Rick followed him inside. "Wow. I expected the place to be empty. But you could move right in."

Donovan slid the sheet from the dining table and pulled out two chairs. "Have a seat while I see about getting the heat going." But he hadn't thought to have the utilities turned on, which seemed like an important oversight now, especially since October felt like full-on winter. It might not have done him any good anyway. After seventeen years, he certainly didn't want to flip a switch before having the furnace checked out. But maybe he could start a fire in the large hearth, which could heat a good portion of the downstairs.

Beside the fireplace he found tinder, seasoned wood, and matches that looked like they'd been placed there just this morning.

Boomer toddled into the open living room and looked up at him.

"So, pup, do you think the wood was left here by the same person who shoveled the walkway for us?"

In answer, the dog yawned and collapsed at Donovan's feet.

Donovan stacked tinder and logs on the grate, struck a match, and watched while it took off. When he was sure it was going, he secured the screen in front of the hearth before picking up the dog and heading back to where Rick had spread the documents on the table.

"I've liquidated assets, as you requested," Rick said. "Instead of buying a place in Florida, though, my advice is for you to sink the money into this place."

Sink was probably right. "You're sounding like a broken record, Rick." Donovan handed the dog off to him. Then, with pen in hand, he sat down in front of the papers.

"After you get those signed, I'll take them in to town to mail them. I assume there isn't a fax machine anywhere."

"There may not even be a post office in Sweet Home anymore either. It used to be in the hardware store." It was starting to dawn on Donovan how not having the hardware store might've affected the residents of Sweet Home. He tried to remember which nearby towns might have a post office. Even the closest might be an hour away.

Rick pulled out his phone. "I'll do a search."

Donovan anticipated the frown on his face. "No service?"

"Not a single bar," Rick said.

"What did you expect? It's the wilds of Alaska."

The wind whipped outside, and the puppy whimpered. Rick handed the dog back. "Are you puppy-sitting, or do you own him?"

Donovan grunted again, not really having an answer for his friend. "Drive back to town to see if you have any cell service, or you can ask at the Hungry Bear where to mail those."

"Okay. Will do. By the way, I didn't see a hotel on the

main strip, if you can call it that," Rick said. "Is there a B-and-B in town?"

Donovan motioned to where they were standing. "As far as I know, this is the only B-and-B for miles." He hoped there were beds upstairs for them to sleep in and quilts to crawl under, or they were going to be freezing tonight—something else he should've anticipated.

"Do you need anything while I'm in town?"

"No. I'm good."

"I'll be back," Rick said, in his best Schwarzenegger voice, as he walked out the front door.

"Fine." Donovan wanted to explore the rest of the house alone anyway. He glanced down at the sleeping runt, who was keeping him company whether Donovan wanted him to or not.

But the moment he heard Rick pull out of the driveway, Donovan thought of two things he needed. One: find out how to get the gas, electric, and water reconnected. Two: Boomer would need dog food.

"You'll need a bed, too, because I won't share mine." He frowned down at the pup. "Let's take a look at the lodge first. Then we'll head into town."

The dog squirmed, so Donovan set him to his feet. Faltering some, Boomer followed Donovan from the dining room, down the hall, and into Nan's spacious sewing room, which had easily accommodated all the members of the Sisterhood of the Quilt and their sewing machines. But now the long tables sat empty, devoid of sewing machines, notions, and fabric. Everything else was in its place—a stack of patterns on a side table, a scattering of pincushions, and some dust-covered scissors. The floor was still littered with fabric scraps from one of Nan's sewing sprees. The white walls had gleamed back then but were dingy now. The love and laughter from this room were just a faded memory, too.

He and Beau had always been welcome when the Sisterhood of the Quilt gathered, as the motherless Stone boys needed some mothering, according to the ladies—but it had felt a bit like smothering. The two brothers had been taught, under duress, how to use a sewing machine while both of them complained loudly. But they'd made superhero capes and had learned how to hem their own jeans. Nan would laugh, reminiscing about how she'd made Grandpa learn to sew before she agreed to marry him. *Charles, you need to learn to take care of yourself. In case anything ever happens to me.* At the memory, Donovan choked up. Something did happen to his grandmother—Beau's death. Grandpa spent long years alone after Nan's heart gave out. Heartbroken over Beau. At least now his grandparents were together again . . . in heaven.

And now, it was Donovan who was left alone. The pup at his feet growled. Okay, maybe not completely alone.

Next, they traveled to his grandmother's office, which had once been a closet. Like the sewing room, this room had been left untouched. Donovan sat in the chair and looked around, trying to see the things Nan saw when she sat here. But something was amiss. All the newspaper clippings tacked to the wall—articles about quilt shows, first-prize quilts, and fabric sale sheets—were placed neatly, organized, one against another. But over the top of these articles was an old newspaper clipping that had been tacked at an angle, making Donovan wonder if it had been placed there in anger . . . by his grandfather, after Nan had died.

Donovan pulled it from its place and read the headline: *MADD Expands into Sweet Home.* The article was dated six months after Beau's death. He skimmed the rest, seeing that Hope's mom had founded a chapter of MADD in their area. Not only that, but Penny McKnight had forced the city council to declare the town dry.

For a moment, Donovan couldn't believe Penny would start up MADD, because it felt like a slam against Hope. But he'd seen people do strange things when they were grieving. Just look at how he had walked away from his town, his family, and his friends without glancing back. Grandpa wasn't the angry type, but Donovan could imagine his grandfather pinning this article here in his grief, saying, *Too little, too late.*

Donovan tacked the newspaper clipping back on the wall, aching for a drink to dull his senses. Man, he really needed cell service to call his sponsor. He wondered if he'd have to make the long haul back to Anchorage just to catch a meeting.

First, though, he needed to head into town to get some dog food, the last thing he'd thought he'd be buying when he woke this morning. Begrudgingly he picked up the puppy and headed for the door. He was in no mood to be chatty, and once he got to town, he hoped like hell he didn't run into anyone he knew.

Chapter 2

HOPE TIED HER boots, pulled her parka over her polo, and then headed for the Hungry Bear. When Piney had texted this morning, telling her not to come in until three, anyone else might've welcomed the extra time off. Not Hope. The utility bill was due Friday and there wasn't enough in her account for the automatic withdrawal. After work tonight, she'd have to use the Hungry Bear's Internet to remove the autopay, then call the electric company to tell them she could make a partial payment and pay the rest later, something she'd done before.

Hope didn't begrudge Piney. October was the off-season. Actually, Sweet Home didn't have an on-season anymore. Not since the quirky A Stone's Throw Hardware & Haberdashery closed and people stopped coming to town to see it, and since Home Sweet Home Lodge stopped bringing in fishermen and outdoor enthusiasts, making things dire in Sweet Home during the winter. The Hungry Bear had to support three employees—Piney, Sparkle, and Hope. And with Sparkle's medical bills piling up from her surgery, things were rough at Piney's.

Hope had always gotten by before and she would this time, too. She let it go.

What Hope couldn't get over was how badly the camping trip with Ella had gone the past two days. It had been pretty much a bust. Her daughter wouldn't discuss her drinking problem or her grief over her grandfather dying. Yes, they'd enjoyed adding a string of used spools to the Memory Tree and sprucing up the branches where some of the ribbons had come off, or where past Christmas tree ornaments had fallen. And yes, Hope checked off some items from the list of things she wanted to teach Ella—starting a fire in less than optimal conditions, target practice with the .22 shotgun, and fishing for dinner in the river. But Hope had felt guilty for missing church. Father Mike didn't like Hope and Ella playing hooky, even though he'd gotten used to their camping trips. But mostly, Hope had felt distracted because of what Piney had said about Donovan coming to town.

The truth was, with Sweet Home being so small, it would be hard to avoid him. Nearly everyone came into the Hungry Bear for supplies or to have lunch in one of the booths in the front corner of the building. She would have to come up with a plan to avoid Donovan, if he showed up.

Hope entered the Hungry Bear and saw Sparkle waiting on two men, probably linemen, if the truck outside belonged to them. She waved to Hope.

Sparkle was anything but *sparkly*. She and Hope had been born the same day; Hope's mom and Piney had shared a room at Regional Hospital. Sparkle and Hope were never friends in school, as Sparkle had been super quiet, her strawberry-blond hair curtaining her face and her expressions. The kids talked about her behind her back, but she didn't seem to notice. For the last seventeen years, though, Hope had considered Sparkle her closest friend. Living in a bus with Sparkle and Piney had shown Hope that they'd all been wrong about Sparkle. She was quirky and funny when she felt comfortable enough to open up, and Hope couldn't imagine her life without her now.

"How are you feeling today?" Hope asked, referring to her recovery from surgery.

"Better," Sparkle said.

Hope touched her arm. "Don't overdo. Your mom and I can handle things down here. You know that."

Sparkle shot Hope one of her impish smiles. "I just don't want you two to replace me with one of the out-of-work lumberjacks."

"Not a chance."

Piney was waving Hope over to the cash register, where she was checking out Miss Lisa, one of the older women in town.

Miss Lisa grabbed Hope's arm, bringing her to a stop. "Did you hear Donovan Stone is coming back to Sweet Home?"

Normally, Miss Lisa's gossip felt harmless, but right now, it was a wallop to Hope's stomach. "Yes, I heard." She tried to keep moving, as if there were an emergency in the back, but Miss Lisa's bony fingers had turned into vise grips.

"You and that Stone boy were thick as thieves when you were children. Do you remember?"

"Yes, we were good friends." *Until I killed his brother.*

Miss Lisa gave her an exaggerated wink. "More than friends, weren't you?"

Hope pulled away. "Don't believe everything you hear."

Before Hope could sprint away, Piney must've taken pity on her and said, "Hope, I need you to work in the stockroom today. To figure out what needs to be ordered for next week."

Perfect! This would keep her out of view from Donovan, if he showed up, and of course, anyone else who wanted to speculate about who Ella's father was. But hiding in the stockroom wouldn't stop the tongue-wagging that was certainly going on around town. "Sure." Hope headed down the aisle toward the back of the store.

But Miss Lisa got in the last word. "If I see Donovan, I'll be sure to point him toward the Hungry Bear to find you."

What could Hope say? *Thank you?* This wasn't the first time Miss Lisa had embarrassed Hope. And just like that, Hope felt thirteen all over again, as that bittersweet memory came over her.

During a Sisterhood of the Quilt gathering, Miss Lisa had teased that Hope had a crush on Donovan, just because she was talking to him in the doorway. When Hope ran from the room, red-faced and on the brink of tears, her mom had followed.

"Don't let Miss Lisa get under your skin," her mother said.

"She has no right to say those things. She's so obnoxious."

"I know it seems that way, but you should feel sorry for her. She has no family—no kids, no husband. This community is all she has, and what seems like teasing or gossiping is just her way of connecting with other people."

"Tell her to stop!" Hope said.

"Here is what's good about Miss Lisa. She's an excellent quilter and loves to teach others. Ask her to show you how to hand-appliqué and I bet she'll be nice to you in the future."

Mom had been right. The next time Hope saw Miss Lisa, she asked for help on a Sunbonnet Sue quilt for Izzie. Miss Lisa had beamed and been a patient teacher to Hope. That connection had kept Miss Lisa in check even when Hope had turned up pregnant at seventeen. But apparently there was an expiration date on praising Miss Lisa's quilting abilities, because she seemed in rare form today. Hope's mom wasn't here anymore to make her feel better. And the Sisterhood of the Quilt was no more, too.

Hope stopped by the canned peas, turned around, and came back to the front of the store with purpose. "Do you still quilt, Miss Lisa? I remember your quilts were the most exquisite in the borough. I loved your Baltimore quilts. Do you still have them?"

Miss Lisa's brows knitted together and she looked sad. "I haven't quilted in years. My eyes don't work good anymore."

Hope felt sorry for her and took a step nearer. "I'd love to come over sometime and look at your collection." She didn't know where the offer had come from. Where was she going to find the time to pay a call on Miss Lisa?

The old woman perked up. "Would you bring your daughter with you?"

"Sure." If Hope could get her to come.

"How about tomorrow evening?"

"Let me check with Ella to see if she's free."

Miss Lisa dug in her purse and came up with a pad of paper. "Write down your number so I can call you in the morning."

Hope started questioning whether she'd done the right thing. But she took the paper and wrote down her number.

"Eighteen-fifty," Piney said to Miss Lisa.

Miss Lisa smiled brightly at Hope but spoke to Piney. "Hold my groceries. I need to get some more."

"Talk to you tomorrow." Feeling resigned, Hope walked away, kicking herself for taking on one more thing. She couldn't imagine a life where she had time for herself once in a while— to soak in the tub, read a magazine, or just time to daydream.

But the reality was she had inventory to count and a list to make for next week's order. She settled into her two-hour shift, alone in the back. An hour and a half later, Piney called on her phone.

"I need you to come to the front and watch things here. Sparkle isn't feeling well, and I need to get her upstairs. You can close up, can't you?"

"I'll be right there." Hope wanted to stay in the back. But being in the back room hadn't given her anxiety a rest. Instead, being alone gave her mind time to wander to old memories and good times with Donovan. Though her heart would like to see him again, she couldn't. It wasn't just that she wanted to grant him his wish of never seeing her again; she also didn't want him to see that she'd never become the person she'd envisioned for herself, that she'd never even left Sweet Home. Hope trudged to the front, passing Sparkle on the way.

"Sorry to take you from inventory," Sparkle said. "Mom insists she has to go up to the apartment with me. Between you and me"—Sparkle leaned toward Hope conspiratorially but winced from the movement—"I think Mom's feet are bothering her today."

"You go rest. I don't mind watching the front." As long as a certain person from her past didn't come in to haunt her.

Piney squeezed Hope's hand as she walked by. "See you bright and early in the morning."

"You bet." Hope smiled at Mr. Brewster, who was making his way to the front with a loaf of bread. "How are you today, Mr. Brewster?"

He grinned at her. "Better than I've been in a long time."

Hope wondered what was up with him. He was a nice man, but he never looked this happy. She took his money, stashed his bread in his reusable shopping bag, and wished him a good evening. Only twenty more minutes until closing.

There was a steady stream of last-minuters, picking up tidbits for tonight's dinner and tomorrow's lunch. At five to five, a tall man in a parka came through the door with a puppy peeking out of his jacket.

Hope reached forward to pet the dog. "Hey, cutie, what's your name?"

The man pushed back his hood and Donovan emerged. At least a version of the Donovan she'd known.

Donovan appeared as shocked as she was.

Every emotion hit her—surprise, happiness, regret, longing for the life she gave up long ago. And on top of everything else, utter embarrassment, as she was dressed in this-is-all-I-have-to-wear-as-I'm-out-of-clean-clothes-and-I'm-doing-laundry-at-Piney's-tomorrow.

Perhaps the greatest shock to her system was seeing that the boy she'd loved with all her heart had turned into a man. She barely recognized him. His smiling blue eyes had turned serious with worry lines beginning to show. His boyish face was serious now, too—rugged, with a shadow beard. He was handsome, knock-down gorgeous, while Hope had become a hollow shell of the girl she'd been in high school. It was humiliating.

For a moment, time stood still, some kind of game of chicken to see who was going to speak first. Donovan finally opened his mouth, but before he could say a word—and

Hope's ears were perked and ready to hear anything he had to say after seventeen years—the bell above the door jingled and Ella bounded inside.

"Mom, we're out of milk. Can you bring some home? I'm on my way to Lacy's."

Hope should've reminded her that it was a school night and to be home for dinner. Then on a much higher plane, she thought maybe she should've had the wherewithal to introduce the two.

Ella . . . this is your dad.

Donovan . . . your daughter.

But Hope could barely breathe, let alone speak. For the first time ever, father and daughter were in the same room together, sharing the same air, the same space. Hope couldn't wrap her head around it. Fortunately, her daughter didn't even look at Donovan. Which was weird, as Ella usually had a crazy radar for dogs and should've at least seen the puppy.

Ella just grabbed a Snickers and then the door handle. "Can you pay for this? Lacy's waiting." And she was out the door . . . *gone.*

Donovan was gone, too, down the aisle. Which was just as well. Hope had no words.

Piney came down the stairs. "Sparkle wants crackers." She stopped short. "What's wrong with you? You look as if you've seen a ghost."

Hope kept her eyes on Piney, while tilting her head in Donovan's direction. Her peripheral vision said he was making his way up front with a bag of puppy chow.

"You go, buttercup," Piney said. "I've got this."

HOPE IS MARRIED? It never occurred to Donovan that she'd find someone else. *Someone that's not me.* His stomach suddenly cramped as if he'd done a hundred crunches.

But he was being ridiculous. He'd dated a lot of women. No one seriously, though. No one who had been like Hope. No one he'd cared for as much as her.

And Hope has a kid? He just couldn't shake the feeling of regret that he'd missed so much. For all he knew, Hope had a slew of rug rats at home. By the looks of the daughter he'd seen—*a teenager!*—Donovan had probably only been gone two minutes before Hope got hitched.

She hadn't changed a bit. Except she was too skinny and had a worry line between her eyebrows. She'd matured from a pixie into a woman. Her dark brown hair was a bit longer—just past her shoulders—but still straight, still the color of hot chocolate. Back then, she'd dressed nicely, but her long-sleeve green polo with the Hungry Bear logo had seen better days and her jeans were very worn.

"Donovan Stone! As I live and breathe," Piney exclaimed. She might act like she wasn't expecting him, but Mr. Brewster knew, and if he knew, the whole town did by now.

"Hi, Ms. Douglas."

Piney air-batted him. "Stop with that nonsense. I'm just plain Piney."

There was nothing plain about her. She glowed in her yellow peace sign tee shirt and long psychedelic skirt.

"How have you been . . . Piney?" She hadn't changed much, either, just a few extra wrinkles, a few extra pounds, and her dark hair was gray now.

Piney raised an eyebrow. "I'm the same. I'm not the one who's been out in the world, making something of himself. I read about you in a *Forbes* article on Hope's computer."

Hope. There was that name again. And where had she gone while he was picking out dog food?

"Who's your friend?" Piney asked.

Donovan didn't want to talk about the dog. He wanted to talk about Hope. But Alaskans had a special relationship with their dogs. "Mr. Brewster brought this Berner by. I'm calling him Boomer."

She patted Boomer's head and laughed. "He's going to make a great work dog for you at the lodge."

Why did everyone assume he was staying? "Well, here's the thing—"

"I've got some chew toys in the back." Piney stepped from behind the counter. "You're going to need them. Follow me."

He did as he was told, but he planned on finishing his sentence before getting the dog anything else. "I'm only here to put the lodge and hardware store on the market."

"Oh, here they are." Piney handed them over as if she hadn't heard him. "I'd get him at least a couple." She glanced down at Donovan's feet. "You don't want to turn your fancy loafers into chewed leather, do you?"

Donovan took four, deciding not to waste his breath on convincing her of his intent. She'd figure it out—they all would—when he headed out of town for good. He frowned, wondering what he was going to do about getting Boomer a new home. The puppy whined.

"Can you ring me up while I take him out for a minute?" Donovan asked.

"Sure." Piney pulled a box of Greenies from the shelf. "You might as well get these, too. You're going to need these to help clean his teeth when he's a bit older."

"Fine." Donovan walked to the front and then out the door. Boomer took his sweet time finding the right place to take a whiz. The temperature was dropping and Donovan still had other things on his list.

The dog finished and Donovan picked him up, holding him like a football this time, and headed back inside.

Piney was bagging up his dog-related items. "We don't have single-use plastic bags in the store. You'll have to buy a few of these for your things. Hope makes them out of old shirts and jeans that folks in Sweet Home are done with. Would you like to choose your bag?" There was quite a variety—pink flowers, blue checks, camouflage.

"Whatever is fine."

Piney gave him the one with the pink flowers and a purple striped bag. He should've chosen.

And since Piney was pulling a fast one on him, he decided to pump her for information. "Who did Hope marry?"

Donovan figured it had to be a local boy. Maybe Jesse Montana? That was who she'd dated before.

Piney raised a knowing eyebrow. "That's really not for me to say. You'll have to ask Hope."

"But—"

"You better take some food with you. I have reindeer sausage left over from the lunch crowd. And some salmonberry pie. It's good. All the sweeter since I had to fight off a bear for those berries."

He was getting hungry. "I could just get some cheese and crackers."

"I won't take no for an answer." Piney was out from behind the counter again and heading for the diner part of the store. "Grab yourself a bag of chips to go with your dinner. We'll get you fixed right up."

Donovan acquiesced. "Do you have enough reindeer sausage for two hungry men?"

Piney looked around, as if someone else had snuck in the store without her seeing.

"It's my business manager—Rick. Didn't he stop by here?"

"Don't know. Maybe Sparkle or Hope took care of him."

"Anyway," Donovan said, "Rick is here helping me wrap things up." Maybe Piney would take the hint this time.

"Sure, I have plenty." She opened the lid of one of the steamers. "Forget the chips. There's a couple of baked potatoes in here. Just the thing for hungry men."

A hot meal did sound good. "Thanks, Piney."

She finished packaging up his dinner on paper plates covered with aluminum foil before walking back. As she got close, Boomer started sniffing, as if there might be a manly meal in there for him, too.

Piney grabbed the camo bag this time and put the plates inside. "I wouldn't give him any reindeer sausage, no matter how much he begs. It'll be too spicy for him."

Donovan looked down at Boomer. "Did you hear that? No reindeer sausage for you."

The dog looked away, as if pretending not to hear.

Donovan handed her his credit card. "Where does Hope live?"

"Why do you want to know?"

"Just curious."

"On Rescue Drive."

Where the cheap rentals and trailer park were. Donovan felt sorry for her that she'd married a man who couldn't take care of her.

Piney handed back his card. "You know we have grocery delivery, if you need it. Just give me a call." She passed him a business card.

"I'm not going to be here long enough to need groceries," he said, driving the point home.

Once again, she didn't respond.

Donovan gathered his homemade bags. "Thanks for dinner."

She laughed. "Don't worry. I put it on your card."

"I expected you would."

"See you soon," Piney said.

But Donovan didn't think so. He might be curious about what Hope had been up to, just to fill in the blanks. That didn't mean he wanted to come face-to-face with her again.

If he needed groceries in the meantime, he'd order them online and have them delivered from Whole Foods or something. He could even go a little hungry.

But when he got Boomer settled into the vehicle, he couldn't help but pull a U-ey and make his way to Rescue Drive. The cabins were even more run-down than he remembered, the trailer park more shabby, too. He shouldn't have come. It made him feel awful. He made his way back to the main drag and headed out of town, anxious to put Sweet Home behind him.

PINEY LOCKED THE door and watched through the window as Donovan and his dog got in the SUV. As she made her way upstairs to her apartment, a deliciously sneaky idea came over her. One that involved Hope, Donovan, and Ella.

It wasn't as if she'd had a clear vision. Except she could see that Ella's future was bright, full of happiness, and overflowing with love.

She stepped into her home and pulled out her phone.

"Hello."

"Hope? I need you to make an after-hours delivery. It just came in."

Hope paused on the other end and Piney could tell she was debating whether to ask if it could wait until tomorrow. But Hope never let her down. Still, just in case . . .

"It's an emergency," Piney lied. Most of the time, if it was truly an emergency and the store was closed, Bill would do the run for her. "Sorry about this. Bill's busy and can't do it." Another lie. Actually, Bill was ten feet away in the kitchen, just putting the finishing touches on a pot of caribou stew for Sparkle's recovery.

Hope sighed. "Sure. No problem, especially since it's an emergency. Where am I going?" The rustling on the other end told Piney that Hope was pulling on her coat.

"Home Sweet Home Lodge." Piney made sure to sound as innocent as possible, and saying the whole title made it sound like an official request.

"But he was just in the store!"

Piney noticed that Hope didn't use Donovan's name.

"He needs food to get him through, buttercup."

"I think you're up to something," Hope accused.

"Scout's honor. He needs food," Piney said, though she'd never been a scout.

Hope paused again, long enough that Piney was getting worried she would refuse.

"I could take the groceries," Piney said. "That is, if you think it's okay for me to leave Sparkle. You saw how she looked earlier." Yes, she'd played the guilt card. And yes, she'd rescued Hope earlier from checking out Donovan's groceries. But now that the initial shock was over, it was time for those two kids to kiss and make up!

"Fine," Hope said petulantly. "I'll be right there."

"See you in a few." Piney hung up.

"What are you up to?" Bill asked.

Piney jumped. "You scared me."

"I heard you. Do I need to make a delivery?" He was reaching for his coat, which was slung over her chair.

"No. You relax." Piney moved his coat and patted the recliner. "You put your feet up. You've been working hard in the kitchen." This seemed like a role reversal, but Bill was too strong and burly to be considered effeminate in any way.

Bill grumbled as he took his place in the chair. "I know you're up to something."

When he was settled, Piney leaned over and laid her head against his. He didn't like it when she told him how lucky she was to have him in her life, so she kept it to herself. Also she didn't mind that he never said how much he cared for her because he was the type of man that showed it, every day in the little things he did—a Comfort quilt for Sparkle's recovery, insisting on carrying the groceries up to the apartment for her and Sparkle, and fixing things around the store and up here, too. He was a grumbly old bear, but Piney loved him. She'd spent all these years, happy as a clam, without a man. But the last two years with him had been the happiest she'd ever known.

"Just give me a second. I'm going to run downstairs for a minute." She handed him the remote. "Turn on the news and I'll be right back to watch it with you."

He grunted something close to *okay*.

Piney hurried downstairs and grabbed one of her three grocery carts, filling it up with anything and everything nonperishable, as she suspected Donovan might not have the refrigerator running yet. The grapevine hadn't reported that the utility company had been out there.

She added up the amount and stapled a note to one of the bags: *On credit*. So he'd know that he wasn't getting a free lunch.

There was a knock on the store's door. It was Hope.

Piney turned off the lights, grabbed the bags, and unlocked the door. She walked out quickly. "Open the back."

"What's the rush?" Hope said.

Piney didn't want her to see which bags she'd chosen for this delivery. "I just want to get back to Sparkle."

Piney tried to ignore Hope's dagger-filled eyes. *Okay, she's not happy, but it's for her own good.*

Piney hurried to put the bags in the back and closed the hatch quickly so Hope wouldn't see them under the streetlight. It had been a long time since Piney had experienced this much fun.

"Isn't that Bill's pickup?" Hope asked, pointing to the evidence parked across the street.

"Bob Brewster picked him up and took him out to his place to fix one of the dogs' runs." Piney might be going to hell for lying so much in such a short period of time.

"What groceries could Donovan possibly need that he didn't buy an hour ago?" Hope appeared agitated with both her and Donovan.

Piney only wished she could go along to watch the fireworks. "Make sure he doesn't stiff you on the tip. He's loaded, you know."

Hope rolled her eyes, making her look exactly like her teenage daughter. She walked to the driver's side and opened the door. "I'll see you in the morning."

Piney would be eager to hear all about it.

But the truth was Hope never talked to anyone about Donovan. Not when he left. Not when she found out she was pregnant. There had been some speculation that the baby wasn't Donovan's at all. Hope went to stay with her aunt in the Yukon for a few weeks following Izzie's death. Over the years, Piney had overheard Ella tell her friends that her dad had been a Yukon oil worker who'd died on the job. But Piney never believed it. Ella was the spitting image of Donovan—his hair, his eyes. Ella even paced like Donovan did when she was telling a story. Piney would have liked to be there when Hope broke the news to Donovan about his daughter.

She chuckled as she went back inside the store. Yes, with Donovan back in town, interesting days were upon them. Piney would make the most of them, especially since Ella's bright future hung in the balance.

Chapter 3

HOPE STARTED HER vehicle and the trunk-open light flashed on. Grumbling, she hopped out to see what was wrong and found one of the bag handles hanging out. She opened the trunk to shove it back in and caught sight of which bags Piney had selected. One was made from Hope's favorite blouse from high school. The other from one of Hope's skirts. What was Piney thinking?

More accurately, what was Piney up to? She'd saved Hope from having to check out Donovan's groceries, but then did the ol' out-of-the-frying-pan-into-the-fire bit. Hope did not appreciate it.

She started the car and sat there for a moment, stalling. She'd been so relieved the awkward encounter was over, and now she was driving out to the lodge for round two?

Wasn't it just last week she'd decided to make a conscious effort to put the past behind her, and only look forward going forward? It was one of the reasons her favorite clothes from high school had been made into bags.

But now, her past was at the lodge. She put the car in gear, anxious to get this over with.

It started to snow, just a dusting, as it had seventeen years ago, when she'd driven Donovan and Beau to the New Year's

Eve party. Donovan's car had been in the shop, giving Hope the rare opportunity to drive them. She wished now that his car had been fine, or even better, that they'd never gone to the party at all. But she'd never wish away the one night she and Donovan had been intimate. Though people at church and throughout Sweet Home whispered behind her back and gave her sideways glances as her pregnancy started to show, it didn't matter now. Hope couldn't imagine life without her daughter.

It was moments like these she understood why her mother had hated Hope after the accident . . . for Hope had taken her child away.

She shook off her feelings of regret, guilt, and sadness.

How she wished for a simpler time. But happiness and contentment were always out of reach. She pulled away from the Hungry Bear.

The way her thoughts were bombarding her and how queasy her stomach felt, she was worried she might not make it out to the lodge in one piece. To calm her nerves, she turned on the radio, and providentially, one of her favorite songs was playing—Casting Crowns' "Voice of Truth." It always spoke to her, telling her not to be afraid. Peace filled the car and she made the rest of the trip without her hands shaking as she clung to the steering wheel.

The song ended as the lodge's circular driveway came into view. She was shocked to see more than one vehicle. There was an SUV and a truck. Confusion and panic washed over her, making her want to turn the car around and drive away. Who did Donovan have with him? *His wife?*

Adding to her discomfort, Hope had expected the place to be lit up, as it was back when Charles and Elsie Stone had run the lodge. But there was only a faint flicker of light coming from the picture window.

Frowning, Hope sat there for a long minute, contemplating what to do. Finally, she slipped from the car and went to the trunk. Using her cell phone as a flashlight, she rummaged through Donovan's bags, looking for evidence of a wife, girlfriend, or bimbo who might be in the house with him. But there were no fresh vegetables or fruits, no feminine products, just a load of junk food that guys usually bought. She glanced at the window. Wouldn't Donovan be keeping an eye out for his groceries, as was the case with most deliveries?

No shadow of a man was visible.

A huge part of her wanted to set the groceries on the front stoop, tap the doorbell, and run—an adult version of ding dong ditch. But Hope was no coward. She marched up the steps to the double front doors—trying not to care that she wasn't put together, like his wife probably was. Before reaching for the doorbell, Hope straightened her shoulders and took a deep breath. Instead of ringing the doorbell, she knocked.

She expected him to fling the door open, but it took a few minutes before there was sound on the other side. And when the door opened, instead of Donovan, a beautiful man in a parka stood there.

For a moment they both stood speechless. Finally, he smiled. "You must be Hope." He yelled over his shoulder, "Donovan! You have company."

"No, no." Hope thrust the bags at him. "I'm just here to drop off groceries."

Donovan must have been nearby, because he appeared at the beautiful man's shoulder, frowning at her outstretched arms with the groceries dangling from her hands.

"Here. Take them." Hope jiggled the bags.

"Take what?" Donovan asked.

"Your groceries." She did a mini thrust this time. Whatever she was doing with her arms, she was trying to compel one of them to take the food so she could escape to her car.

The other man held the door wide. "Come in to get out of the cold."

Donovan was shaking his head no, while the other man gently took her arm and pulled her inside.

"Let me take those." Mr. Kind and Beautiful gave her a

warm smile, the opposite of the Grinchy expression on Donovan's face. "I'm Rick, by the way. Rick Miller, Donovan's business manager. I'm sorry he's being so rude." Rick gave Donovan a pointed look before grabbing the bags and heading to the dining room table. "Go stand by the fire. You're shaking."

Yes, Hope was shaking, but it had nothing to do with the cold, and everything to do with the boy she used to love.

DONOVAN WAS SHOCKED for the second time in an hour. Why was Hope at the lodge? Was she trying to dig around in his life? "What are you doing here?"

Hope looked at him as if he were a bonehead. "I'm delivering the groceries you ordered."

"I didn't—" He stopped himself.

They stared at each other for a long minute, frowning.

"Piney," they said together, disgusted.

"What in the world was Piney thinking?" he said out loud, but mostly to himself.

Hope looked decidedly unhappy. "Half the time, I don't believe she thinks at all. She calls it instinct."

This wasn't the old Hope he knew. Old Hope would've smiled, especially where it concerned him.

For a second, he wished for the old Hope back.

But in the next second, he didn't. He was happy with his life . . . *without her.*

Boomer wandered over to Hope. She picked him up and held him close, like a security blanket.

Ludicrously, Donovan had a tinge of envy, wanting to be the dog.

Rick stood there with a goofy grin on his face, until Donovan gave him the look—like he better stop enjoying himself.

Rick took the hint. "I'll put the groceries away." He might as well have said, *I'll leave you two alone.*

Donovan scanned Hope, comparing his memory of young Hope to current Hope. Current Hope needed to eat more, smile more, and get more rest, if the dark circles under her eyes were any indication. What happened to her after he left? "So you're still in Sweet Home?" It was a leading question, but he wanted answers . . . whether she wanted to give them or not.

Her lips turned into a stubborn straight line, letting him know she wasn't going to respond. She pointed to the other room. "How does Rick know who I am?"

"Intuition," Donovan deadpanned.

"I don't think so," Hope said.

She was all attitude, no longer the sweet go-along-with-anything-he-said girl. And the weird thing was, he kind of liked her this way.

Hope straightened her shoulders and stared him down. "Where's your wife?"

Once again, she'd caught him off guard.

"I left her at home," Donovan lied, trying to be as brazen as Hope.

Rick hollered from the kitchen, "Don't let him fool you, Hope. He's not married." He stuck his head around the corner. "Never found the right woman."

Donovan raised an eyebrow at Rick. "I think you should go outside and check for bears. Take some food with you. They like that." Which reminded Donovan that he should pick up bear repellent if they were going to be here for a few days. Maybe a rifle, too. And Grandpa used to keep a soup can filled with marbles on the porch to scare them away.

"I'll pass," Rick said. "The kitchen is calling me."

"What's your dog's name?" Hope nuzzled the dog, not meeting Donovan's eye.

He frowned at his charge. "He's not necessarily my dog."

"Yes, he is," came from the kitchen. "And the dog's name is Boomer."

Hope smiled and pointed to the other room. "I like your business manager." Her face was contorted, as if she couldn't comprehend why anyone would need a business manager.

"He's worthless," Donovan said loud enough for Rick to

hear. "I really should fire him." Donovan moved closer to the fireplace, where Hope stood. "What's your daughter's name?"

She stared at him wide-eyed but finally answered, "Ella."

The name rocked him. "For Isabella?"

Hope nodded, this time with all the sadness in the world. "Yes."

He went to a safer subject. "How's your dad doing?"

Misery filled Hope's eyes and they began to mist. "He's gone. Heart attack, last month."

He reached out to touch her but stopped himself. "Oh, Hope. I'm so sorry. I didn't know."

She moved her head as if trying to shake off the grief. "I heard about your grandfather. He meant a lot to all of us. As did your grandmother."

For a moment, mutual grief filled the room. That one small connection felt like old times. Hope had always been so empathetic—issuing compassion as easily as if sharing a Ziploc bag of Oreos during lunch period. But they weren't kids anymore and he wasn't in the mood.

He stepped away. "Rick, what are you doing in there?"

A second later, Rick came into the room with a tray of chips, Pop-Tarts, and nuts, arranged like hors d'oeuvres.

"Are you kidding me?" Donovan exclaimed. The guy had been an elite Marine Force Recon and now he was acting like Martha Stewart.

Rick set the tray on the side table closest to Hope. "You have a guest. It's only right you feed her."

Hope did need to gain some weight. "Eat," Donovan said.

Rick sighed heavily. "Sorry about him. He usually has manners." He snatched a Pop-Tart before taking the seat across from her. "So Donovan tells me you were a better shot than him when you were kids."

Surprised, she glanced at Donovan for a split second before answering Rick. "I just have better depth perception."

"I'm the one who taught her how to shoot!" Donovan complained. He could've told her he'd qualified for Expert in the Corps, but he didn't.

Rick nudged the tray toward her. "Please have something. I don't like to eat alone."

Yeah, Donovan had heard his friend use that line many times on unsuspecting females. Rick oozed charm. And suddenly, Donovan got worried. If Rick spent too much time around Hope, she'd fall for him, like all women did.

"She better go." Donovan approached Hope, not to hug her good-bye but to take the dog.

"Yes. I need to get home." Reluctantly, she handed over Boomer before starting for the door.

"Hold up," Rick said. "Donovan will see you out."

Donovan gave Rick the I'll-set-you-straight-when-I-get-back look before handing the puppy off to him.

"Yeah, I'll walk you out," he said, following her. "For protection."

"I can take care of myself," Hope said over her shoulder.

"Humor me, then." Donovan hurried around her and held the door open.

"Suit yourself."

He walked her out to her beat-up Honda Civic. "It was good to see you." It wasn't, really. The encounter made him feel uncomfortable on so many levels.

"Sure." She knew he didn't mean it. "Good-bye, Donovan." Her words were firm and felt final.

Fine by me. He walked back to the lodge, shivering from the cold.

Rick was waiting at the door. "Now that girl is a good reason to stay."

For you or for me? Donovan shook the thought away. Long ago, he'd told Rick all about Hope, and he was certain Rick would never go after someone Donovan was interested in.

But Donovan *wasn't* interested. Not since the day Beau died. He walked into the kitchen and grabbed an unopened bag of Doritos.

While he pulled out a handful, he glanced down at a small slip of paper lying on the counter and picked it up. A bill from Piney. Figured. This whole debacle was costing him in more ways than one. Tomorrow, he'd have to go to the Hungry Bear to pay his bill, plus inform Piney that she'd better stop delivering groceries out to the lodge. And she better stop meddling, too. But he wouldn't admit how badly her delivery person had thrown him.

Donovan went back into the living room and sat on the dilapidated sofa.

"Hey." Rick set down his half-eaten Pop-Tart. "I'm going to throw some numbers together for what it would cost to remodel this place."

Donovan couldn't care less about crunching numbers.

Rick pulled out a pad of paper and wrote furiously, mumbling all the while. "You can use the winter to fix things up. Work on the inside." He looked up at Donovan. "Are you handy around the house?"

Begrudgingly Donovan answered, "I used to help my grandparents and my dad with stuff. So sure, I'm pretty handy." He'd helped his grandfather build the back porch, and when he was needed, he was happy to help the home-steaders around Sweet Home.

Rick tapped his list. "I'll drive to Anchorage tomorrow for supplies."

"Good. Can you bring back some groceries, too?" That way Donovan wouldn't be forced to go to the Hungry Bear.

"Shouldn't you support the local economy?" Rick said. "Besides being the right thing to do, it's a good business practice. It'll build up goodwill with the folks of Sweet Home."

"You don't understand," Donovan said.

Rick set down his pen. "Explain."

Because Donovan had shared so much with Rick, he was honest with him now. "It's Hope. It's too hard seeing her." *It's digging up old feelings—good times and grief.*

"Listen," Rick said, "this might be good for you."

"No. Don't start in on personal growth again. I've had a lot of it these last umpteen years in AA."

"It might be time to deal with Hope and your brother's

death, is all I'm saying," Rick said. "Maybe you should go with me to Anchorage."

Rick didn't have to say the rest: *You need to catch a meeting.*

"I will."

"Now, can we get back to figuring out what we're going to need in order to update the lodge?"

Donovan looked around with new eyes. "I don't know. Maybe we should get an interior decorator in here to update everything. For staging." Yes, restore the place for selling purposes only. The best time to sell would be late spring, not October with winter already here.

"Do you know anyone in town who could help with decorating?" Rick asked.

"We could ask the real estate agent." Courtney Wolf from high school. "Let's put that on our list of things to go over with her tomorrow."

Another idea popped into Donovan's head. If he wasn't going to put the place on the market until spring, maybe he should hold a couple of town events here, like Grandpa and Nan did when he was a kid. They would help raise the profile of the lodge.

It was Business 101 that turnkey income-producing properties enticed more potential buyers than a boarded-up, defunct old lodge would.

He picked up Boomer and set him in his lap. "My grandparents used to hold Sweet Home's Christmas Festival here, or at least part of it." He'd have to ask Piney or Mr. Brewster if the festival even existed anymore. "One of my grandmother's favorite traditions was to have a wine tasting on the first night of the festival, featuring only Alaskan wines."

"Then you're going to stay?" Rick asked hopefully.

"No!" Donovan hadn't really thought this through. "No. Not permanently. Maybe just through the Christmas Festival. Then I'll hire a manager to run the lodge until it goes up for sale in the spring."

"Okay then," Rick said.

Donovan glanced at the dining table, imagining all the

cookies and cakes and cheese and bread that it used to hold. "Re-creating my grandmother's wine tasting and hosting the residents of Sweet Home just one more time seems like a good way to honor my grandparents."

"I think so, too." But Rick was giving him a knowing look.

"Stop it. The wine tasting has nothing to do with Hope."

"Of course. I believe you." But Rick's words didn't match his face or his tone. "On a more serious subject: Are you sure a wine tasting is a good idea?"

"I promise, my sobriety is safe." Donovan appreciated how Rick helped him to stay accountable. "I've never been fond of the sweet fruit wines of Alaska." Then Donovan remembered the newspaper clipping tacked to the wall in Nan's office. "There might be one obstacle, though. If the town council still exists"—and he was pretty sure it didn't, with the town so small now—"I'll have to speak to them about lifting the ban on alcohol."

They spent the rest of the evening planning and strategizing how to pull off the wine tasting.

"Rick, I don't think we can get everything done in one afternoon in Anchorage," Donovan said. "When we head out tomorrow and when I have some decent cell service, I'll book us a couple of hotel rooms."

Rick pointed to Donovan's chest, where Boomer was fast asleep. "What about your buddy?"

Donovan ran a hand down the puppy's back. "He'll go with us. Everyone in Alaska takes their dogs with them everywhere. Even runts like Boomer."

Donovan glanced at his watch. "It's ten and I'm beat. I'm going to take Boomer out, then head up to bed. What about you?"

"I'll be up in a while. I want to make sure I have everything organized for tomorrow. I call dibs on the room with the king-sized bed."

"Go for it." Donovan planned to stay in his old room tonight, the one he and Beau shared whenever they slept over at Grandpa and Nan's. Rick would be proud that Donovan's personal growth would begin now by revisiting his past this way.

"Come on, Boomer," Donovan said, though the dog was already in his arms.

He walked out into the night and set Boomer on his feet. "So, little guy, you liked Hope?"

Boomer sniffed around, getting the hang of this bathroom thing.

"She liked you, too," Donovan said. "I could tell. She looked at you the way she used to look at me." With complete love in her eyes.

Now, Hope only looked shell-shocked . . . and more than a little worn out.

"You ready for bed?" He picked up the dog and went in.

As Donovan walked upstairs, he realized two things. Away from the fireplace, it was going to be very cold in the lodge. And Boomer wouldn't do well on the floor of an unheated home.

He frowned down at the pup. "I guess I'm not sleeping alone tonight."

Chapter 4

ON THE WAY home from the lodge, Hope had half a mind to drive to Piney's and give her what for. But then Hope remembered the gallon of milk Ella had said they needed. She pulled into the Hungry Bear and parked.

Using her key, she unlocked the door and went in.

"Well?"

Hope jumped. "Piney! You about gave me a heart attack." But as soon as Hope said it, the words made her sick because of her dad. "What are you doing, standing there on the steps?"

"I came down to set the alarm. I heard you pull up. You really need a new muffler."

"I know."

"So how did it go?" Piney asked.

Hope flipped on the lights. "You mean, other than Donovan hadn't really ordered any groceries?"

Piney winked at her. "Who said he didn't? Maybe it was a ploy to get you out at the lodge alone."

"He wasn't alone." Hope raised her eyebrows at Piney.

"Who was with him? I didn't see a wedding ring."

"A lot of men don't wear rings," Hope said, thinking of her father, who never wanted his ring to get caught in the equipment at work. "His business manager, Rick, is with him. Donovan said he didn't order any groceries and I believe him."

Piney laughed. "Always siding with that boy. Some things never change."

Hope opened her mouth but then decided it wasn't worth the effort. She changed the subject instead. "Ella said we're out of milk."

"You better take a package of cookies with you, too," Piney suggested. "You look like you're in need of some stress eating."

Hope pointed to the street. "I see Bill's truck is gone."

Piney peeked around her. "Huh. So it is."

"Bill was here earlier, wasn't he?" Hope said accusingly.

Piney smiled. "'Night, buttercup. Set the alarm before you leave."

"Fine. I'll see you tomorrow morning," Hope said, as Piney made her way back up the stairs.

Hope skipped the cookies—her billfold couldn't afford any sort of bingeing. She grabbed the milk, paid, set the alarm, and then headed to her car. But then she remembered she needed to get on the Internet to turn off autopay on her utility bill.

Fifteen minutes later, Hope was finally on her way home. When she pulled up to her tiny rental house, the lights weren't on, which meant Ella wasn't home yet either.

Hope went inside, made herself a bowl of off-brand Cheerios, and ate her dinner in silence. Next, she texted Ella and asked when she would be home.

The answer came quickly: Soon.

To pass the time, Hope pulled out her sewing machine and reached for the box of clothes on the floor of her closet. Everyone in Sweet Home contributed their no-longer-wanted items so Hope could upcycle them into bags for the Hungry Bear. Piney didn't charge the locals when they forgot their bags—unless they were perpetual abusers—but she did charge $4.99 a bag to those who didn't live in Sweet Home, for which Hope got two bucks a bag. She made most of her bag money during the summer months, though there was only a fraction of the tourists in Sweet Home compared to when she was a kid. Bag money became the emergency fund, stored in the coffee can on top of her fridge. Last winter, bag money had paid for Ella's two rounds of antibiotics when she'd gotten a bad case of strep.

Behind the box of clothes to upcycle, Hope spied the Rubbermaid container of Izzie's clothes. Mom had saved them and now Hope saved them, too.

Apparently, tonight was all about revisiting the past—seeing Donovan twice tonight, thinking about him ever since, and now the Rubbermaid container. She gave in to the urge, deciding it was okay to dredge up more crushing emotions, as she dragged out Izzie's clothes and pulled the container over to the couch.

Every dress and every blouse Mom had made for Izzie was in that container. Hope laid each piece on the floor, remembering the good times when Izzie was here—the apple dress she wore to the church picnic, her Brownie uniform, even the pink plaid blankie Izzie had dragged to bed each night and the Sunbonnet Sue quilt that Hope had made her. Hope then stood back and examined the collection. And was surprised when she saw what she'd done.

It was crazy, but somehow, Hope had laid out the items in the shape of Izzie's tree. A fat trunk center was made up of pants near the bottom, with shirts toward the top and their sleeves outstretched as branches. The blankie stretched out underneath as the ground. Hope could see how quilt blocks would fill in the tree. Emotions—good ones—flooded her, and it felt like kismet. All these years, she and Ella had contributed to Izzie's Memory Tree, and now it was time to make one of their own.

Hope went back to her closet and pulled down the shoebox that held Izzie's favorite things. She took hair bows, buttons, and a charm bracelet back to the "quilt" laid out on the floor and positioned the new items on the branches. When she was satisfied with how it looked, she grabbed her phone and took a picture.

Ella came through the door just as Hope was picking the clothes up off the floor and sorting them into lights and darks.

"What are you doing?" Ella asked.

"We're going to make a quilt out of your Aunt Izzie's clothes," Hope said.

"We?"

"It would be a fun project for us to do together." Hope pointed to the wall behind the sofa. "We could get it done and have it up by Christmas."

"I only know how to make grocery bags for Piney."

"It's time you learned how to make a quilt." There was enough fabric here to make an additional quilt—a lap quilt. With arms loaded, Hope headed to the washing machine in the kitchen. "Grab the darks and follow me in here."

"Do I have to?" Ella moaned, but did as she was told.

"I can't wait to show you the picture on my phone of what it's going to look like." She glanced at her daughter. "Are you hungry?"

Ella passed her a scoop of detergent. "I ate at Lacy's."

"Did you get any studying done?"

"Some."

Hope shut the lid of the washing machine and hugged her daughter—partly to see if she'd been drinking, yes, but mostly because Hope's heart was filled with joy. Then she smelled the strawberry wine on Ella's breath. She started to ask who had been buying it for her, but then Ella unexpectedly hugged her back.

"It's nice that you have a project," Ella said.

"*We* have a project," Hope corrected. She made a mental note to do some digging to find out who was buying alcohol for the kids in Sweet Home these days. Back when she was a teen, any number of twentysomethings were happy to pick some up in the next borough over for the price of a pack of smokes. Hope put her focus back on their quilting project. "Do you have any graph paper?"

"Sure. It's on top of my desk."

Hope went to Ella's room to retrieve the graph paper. Several of Ella's drawings were strewn across her desk. Seeing them always reminded Hope of Izzie and her artistic talent, too. While Hope was at it, she commandeered the colored pencils before running back to the kitchen to start sketching the quilt on paper.

She found Ella staring at her phone with a frown on her face. "I don't get it. This is supposed to be a quilt?"

"You'll see. After I get it drawn up." Hope took her place at their small dining table. "Sit with me while I work."

"I'm tired. I'm going to bed."

But as Ella walked away, she pulled out her phone. "Hey, Lacy." And went into her room.

Hope wouldn't be discouraged by her daughter's lack of enthusiasm. For the next hour, she sketched Izzie's Memory Tree quilt and colored it. She was happy with the outcome but was worried that her sewing skills were too rusty to pull off this quilt. Yes, she had sewn with the Sisterhood of the Quilt back in the day and then made clothes for Ella until Ella told her to stop, but she hadn't made a quilt since the Sisterhood had disbanded after the death of Elsie Stone.

Holding the drawing, Hope went to Ella's door and knocked. "Come out and see what I drew."

"I'm too sleepy."

Only moments before, Ella had been gabbing away on the phone.

"Are you sure?" Hope asked, knowing she sounded a little needy. Yes, she talked to people every day at the Hungry Bear, but things weren't the same as they were twenty years ago when Hope was growing up. She'd been part of a tight community then. Now, it felt as if there was no real community left.

"Leave the drawing on the table. I'll look at it in the morning."

"Sure." Disappointed, Hope went back to the kitchen, knowing she should give up and go to bed.

This was the main reason she'd stopped quilting . . . no one to share her ideas with. One of her favorite parts about quilting was experiencing it with others, from the initial concept to the final product. In this case, she only had a drawing, a skeleton of what the quilt would become. But she still had that urge to connect, something the Sisterhood of the Quilt had encouraged her to do at a young age.

She pulled back the curtain and looked out at the street. Bill's truck was sitting in front of his cabin. She ran to her bedroom window and checked there. Sure enough, Bill's lights were still on. Hope didn't let herself think about it, she just hurried back to the kitchen and grabbed the sketch off the table and her phone from the counter. She rushed to the front door and slipped on her coat and boots. Bill was the only quilter on the street and he was still awake.

There was no doubt about it, Bill was gruff. But Hope had gotten used to him. She'd also given him a pass because anyone who could quilt like he did and be so generous with his beautiful Alaskan quilts had to have a soft spot under all that grizzle. And Piney cared for Bill, which said a lot about him.

Hope's boots crunched in the snow as she hustled next door. When she got to Bill's porch, she hesitated. *This is stupid. It's late. Surely he doesn't want me bugging him.* But she was already here and his light was on. Finally she got up the nerve and knocked anyway, then waited nervously as she heard grumbling and shuffling on the other side of the door.

Bill slung it open and peered at her. "What do you need?"

"Can I come in? I want your opinion on something."

He stared at her for a long moment . . . with his usual frown deepening. Finally he stood back. "Well, since you're already here."

Hope crossed the threshold, looking around. Though Bill had lived in Sweet Home for two years, she'd never been inside his cabin. It was so small it made hers look like a sprawling ranch. It was just one room with a small kitchen area tucked at the back and a twin bed nestled into the front right corner. Bill's bulldog, Mangey, acted as if he were older than Bill, barely lifting his head an inch to stare at her before dropping it back down on the quilted dog bed at the foot of Bill's bed. The rest of the room looked like Elsie Stone's sewing studio at the lodge. Hope couldn't believe that Bill had a small longarm quilting machine taking up most of the left side of the cabin. The rest of what should've been the open area was instead filled with a large table holding a sewing machine at one end and cutting mats everywhere else.

"I love what you've done with the place," she said, smiling. "It's kind of a quilter's dream."

He grunted impatiently.

She handed over the drawing. "I don't know if you know this, but my sister died when I was seventeen. I want to make a quilt out of her clothes and this is what I came up with."

Bill pulled glasses from his pocket and put them on, making him look like Grizzly Adams getting ready for story time. He laid the paper on the table and, grabbing a pencil, immediately started making changes.

Hope stood back, trying to get a glimpse of what he was doing, but his hand covered his work.

Finally, he glanced at her. "The trunk is too short and the branches too chunky." He looked down at the picture again. "What do the fabrics look like?"

She pulled up the photos, then handed him her cell phone. "This is how I laid it out."

"You've got a good eye for color," he grumbled. He handed her phone back and then her updated drawing. "Anything else?"

Since she had already been bold enough to come over here uninvited, Hope pointed to the chair in the corner, which was neatly stacked with quilts. "I'd like to see your collection sometime."

Without answering, he walked to the door and opened it.

"Not tonight, of course," Hope said, backpedaling. "But sometime." She headed for the door, glancing at the drawing.

He had indeed made it better. *Much better.* He'd added half-square triangles where she had used only squares. And he framed the whole picture with Bear Paw blocks, alternating them with moose.

She stopped at the threshold. "Thank you for this. Good night."

He shut the door behind her without saying a word.

She hurried home, eager to redraw the quilt, incorporating Bill's suggestions. He'd made the picture more interesting, more Alaska-like, without taking away from Izzie's Memory Tree. She wondered what she could do to repay him.

At her kitchen table once again, Hope worked on the drawing until she could barely keep her eyes open. She finally put the colored pencils back in the box and stood, stretching. She treaded to her room and slipped on her blue flannel pajamas.

As she crawled into bed, she thought she'd be too tired even to pull up the kuspuk-inspired quilt that her mom had made for her when she was ten. Surprisingly, though, she lay awake. The awkward moments she'd shared with Donovan earlier flooded back to her. He had made her feel things she hadn't felt in years—or at least she'd been able to keep those feelings at bay while he was gone from Sweet Home. Was he also behind the burst of creativity she'd had afterward, ending her day on a higher note than expected?

"Hey." Suddenly eleven-year-old Izzie was sitting beside Hope, propped up against the headboard with her feet stretched out.

"I'm sleeping," Hope said.

"You're never too asleep to talk to me, though."

Hope rolled over to face her. "Okay. You're right."

Izzie slid down in the bed. "Tell me how it went with Donovan. Is he as cute as he was when I died?"

"Yeah. But he's definitely not a kid anymore. He's a man, Izzie."

Izzie rested her head on her hand and stared off into space. "He was awfully *fine* then." She dropped her hand and looked over at Hope. "Did you reconsider telling Ella the truth about her dad?"

It wouldn't hurt to be honest with Izzie, especially since Hope wasn't really having this conversation. "Yes. I did think about telling Ella when she came home tonight. But I'm not going to do it. Donovan said he wasn't going to be here long, so wouldn't it just hurt her?" And him. "Besides, if I told her now about who her real father was, Ella would never trust me again. I've lied to my daughter all these years and there's no way back from that."

Izzie sighed. "You might be right."

"I didn't expect you to agree with me."

Izzie shrugged.

They lay in silence for a long moment, before Izzie spoke again. "I'm glad you're doing something with my clothes. They were only taking up space in your closet. You have to admit space is a precious commodity in your tiny house."

"Yeah," Hope said. "I know."

"What took you so long?" Izzie asked, her voice taking on the tenor of that otherworldly wisdom of hers.

"Your clothes were incubating," Hope said. Elsie Stone used to say that about quilting projects that were set aside.

Izzie slid down farther until she and Hope were face-to-face. "You're not making any sense."

"It's finally the right time, is all," Hope said. "What did you think of the design?"

"Absolutely brilliant. I also think it's a good idea to have Ella help you with it." She paused, looking serious. "You know Ella is in trouble, right? She's too young to understand that Dad is happy in heaven and he doesn't want Ella to be sad over him."

"I tried to tell her," Hope said.

"But she doesn't hear," Izzie finished for her.

Hope got a crazy idea. "What if Dad visited Ella like you visit me?"

"It doesn't work like that," Izzie said. "Ella is going to have to walk through her pain. No shortcuts."

"I'm afraid there's going to be more stumbling than walking." Because of Ella's drinking.

"Everyone stumbles, Hope," Izzie said in her wise-woman voice. "What's important is whether you can catch yourself from falling. Or even better, if someone else is beside you, to steady you and help you to your feet again."

Hope knew the answer, but she asked the question anyway. "Like what you do for me?"

"Exactly," Izzie said. "And what you're now going to do for your daughter."

Chapter 5

WRAPPED IN HIS winter coat and reveling in the morning sun, Donovan stood on the porch with his cup of coffee as Rick walked to his car.

"I'll see you in a while," Donovan said.

Rick waved, started his car, and eased out of the circular driveway as Courtney Wolf—real estate agent and an ex from sophomore year in high school—pulled in. She glanced in her mirror and adjusted her blond poufy hair before sliding out gracefully.

"Hey, Donovan," she said in that breathy voice she used to get guys in high school, "how's it going? It's great to see you." She scanned him from head to toe, her smile widening as she scoured every inch of him.

He scooped up Boomer, using him for cover. "Hi, Courtney. Long time no see."

"Who was that leaving just now?" She motioned to the end of the drive. "He was a looker."

"My business manager, Rick Miller."

"Did he really have to run off like that?"

"We're heading to Anchorage right after you assess the property, well, both properties. Rick is driving into town to have some sandwiches made at the Hungry Bear."

"You know I always speak my mind," she said. "So tell me, what is it with you handsome men? Do you always run in packs?" She laughed. "With a last name like Wolf, you'd think I'd have better insight into men than most."

Donovan only nodded, where once upon a time he would've laughed right along with her. "Come on in and take a look around." He held the door open and she smiled at him as she stepped over the threshold.

Donovan decided it was best to set things straight with her from the start. "At first I thought I'd put the lodge and the hardware store on the market as is. But now that I'm here, I've decided to fix up the lodge to get a better price for it in the spring." He watched her reaction to see how disappointed she was that both properties wouldn't be listed now.

She smiled, seeming happy with the arrangement. "I don't expect anything to move until the spring anyway. You'll fix up the lodge, but what about the hardware store?"

He shook his head as he set Boomer in the box he'd made up for him using one of the towels from the downstairs restroom for padding. "The hardware store is too big of a project. For the lodge, though, I'd love a list of contractors who could oversee the remodeling, as I don't plan to hang around."

Her face fell at that.

"I promised my dad that I'd move to Florida," he explained.

"What about your place in San Jose?" Immediately, she looked embarrassed. "I Googled you. Something I do with all my clients." She stepped closer. "Especially ones I haven't seen since high school."

He could tell she was flirting with him and it wasn't completely unpleasant. Courtney was nice, her blond hair flawless and her green eyes incredible. But he wasn't really into the pageant type. Sure, he'd dated his share of beautiful women, especially when he needed some arm candy for events in Silicon Valley . . . but they'd only been concerned with getting their photo into magazines. Hope popped into his mind. He would've been proud to have someone like

Hope on his arm. She was genuine. At least that was the Hope he'd known seventeen years ago.

He pointed to the other side of the house. "Courtney, come take a look at the kitchen. I think it's going to need a lot of updates."

She followed him and started speaking as soon as her foot hit the linoleum. "A complete gut . . . down to the studs. A modern, professional kitchen from top to bottom would be a huge selling point. Everything updated, all personal touches gone. Sleek cabinets, professional-grade appliances, and maybe concrete flooring."

"Do you know any . . ." Donovan's eyes landed on the backsplash of handpainted tiles in the style of Dresden Plate quilt blocks, the tiles Nan had painted herself. He'd been going to ask Courtney about an interior decorator, but he didn't trust her. She'd probably volunteer herself. Courtney was all hair spray, fake nails . . . and she wanted to gut *everything* in the kitchen! He didn't want the lodge to be sleek or glamorous. His grandparents' lodge deserved an authentic Alaskan look—maybe tile in the kitchen, stained hardwood floors throughout, bearskins, and bright curtains. "Um, uh, do you know a good floor guy?"

"Sure. We'll tear up this dreadful stuff. Don't you worry." She glanced around at the walls. "Actually, you should paint all the wood in the lodge. It would give it the modern look it needs."

Donovan cringed. He couldn't paint the wood that had been felled from the surrounding forest. His grandparents would be rolling over . . . He wished he'd never called Courtney, as she was already putting herself in charge of what was or wasn't going to be in the lodge. He panicked. "Well . . . I know you have ideas, but we'll have to clear everything with my interior decorator first."

Courtney lifted one perfectly shaped eyebrow. "Oh? Who did you get?"

Now he was really in trouble. "The same person who did my apartment in San Jose." Which was a whopper. He and

Rick had decked out his bachelor pad, making it a man-cave dream—industrial, sterile . . . not Alaskan at all.

"Sure," Courtney said again. "I'll get him locally sourced swatches and tile samples."

"Her," Donovan corrected. He had no idea where that came from.

"Just let me know where to send them," Courtney said.

"I'll take care of it." Donovan just wanted this conversation to end. "Let's take a look at the back porch."

Courtney took measurements of everything and recorded them in a notebook. "I'll get you copies of everything I'm doing." When she wasn't flirting, she seemed very professional, and Donovan felt like the sale of the lodge was in good hands.

When he led Courtney into his grandmother's sewing studio, Courtney sighed and turned back to him.

"You know, I only came a couple of times with my mom to the Sisterhood of the Quilt, but I really liked it. At the time I chose to spend more time with my friends. I guess I just assumed the Sisterhood of the Quilt would always be around."

"Me, too."

Courtney gave him a sad smile, and in that moment, she seemed more real than he'd ever seen her. But then the moment was gone. "We'll have to think about how to stage the studio. It certainly can't be a sewing room. That would only appeal to a small subset of buyers. It's large enough to make it into an in-home theater with dark curtains to block out all the natural light from those large windows."

He felt another twinge of guilt—actually more than a twinge. The studio had been his grandmother's pride and joy. It was where the Sisterhood of the Quilt met. It was where laughter had reigned and memories had been made.

Courtney walked to the doorway. "Show me the bedrooms."

He took her upstairs and answered all her questions, while she jotted down the details of each one. There were a lot of rooms to cover in the main building, and then there were the three cabins outside, and she wanted to examine every one of them. Donovan was beginning to worry that Rick would think he wasn't going to meet him in town at all.

"How many acres with the property?" Courtney asked, looking at the view of the river out back.

"I believe a hundred," Donovan said.

"I'll check with the borough to be sure, and find all the boundary lines." She stopped and looked at him. "Do you want to go into town for lunch before we get started on the hardware store?"

"Actually . . ." Donovan made a show of looking at his watch. "This has taken more time than I expected. I'm supposed to be on my way to Anchorage with Rick by now. Is there any way we can reschedule the hardware store for when I get back?"

Courtney's pleasant smile faded. "I really can't do it tomorrow or the day after. I have appointments with clients outside of Fairbanks the next two days." She appeared conflicted. "I could try to reschedule with them."

"No. I'm not in a super rush." But Donovan could tell his dad was anxious to have him in Florida as soon as possible. Which brought up several more things he'd have to do to make things work, if he was going to put off selling the lodge until spring. Like finding that contractor, a manager to run the place, and a housekeeper.

"What about Friday?" Courtney offered. "Let's meet up for coffee at the Hungry Bear. Nine a.m.?" It was amazing how quickly she'd switched from conflicted to completely in charge and in control. "Is it a date?"

Not a date. Donovan didn't have the time or the inclination to do any *canoodling*—Nan's word—while he was in Alaska. "I can meet you Friday morning."

Courtney didn't linger but went to her car, as if afraid he might change his mind. Or maybe she was being considerate, understanding that he was late. "See you at nine on Friday at the Hungry Bear." She waved and got in her car.

But as soon as she did, he had a creeping feeling of doubt. *Hope.* Hope worked at the Hungry Bear, and seeing him with Sweet Home High's biggest flirt would certainly make her jealous.

But they weren't in high school anymore. They were adults now. They were nothing to each other. Just acquaintances. She'd had a whole life he knew nothing about. No way would she be jealous.

But the feeling still nagged that he would be doing something awful to Hope if he met Courtney at the Hungry Bear.

On autopilot, Donovan took Boomer's makeshift bed to the SUV and set it in the back seat. Next, he put Boomer in, then locked up the lodge, though Donovan doubted there was a need. Besides, it seemed that someone in Sweet Home already had a key. The same someone who had left seasoned firewood by the hearth. He wondered if it was Hope. He decided Piney would be the one to ask.

When he got into his vehicle, the sun came out, making the *Home Sweet Home Lodge* sign cast a shadow on the lodge in the shape of a cross. Donovan sucked in a breath. Though Beau and Nan had been on his mind nonstop, until this moment he hadn't thought to stop at their graves. "I know Rick is going to be anxious to get on the road, but I'm not going to put this off one more minute."

Sweet Home's cemetery was two miles from the lodge and one mile from town. The setting in the summer was quite beautiful with the trees towering over the resting places of the town's dearly departed. All through their teens Donovan and Beau had mowed the cemetery's lawn, helped dig graves, and even acted as pallbearers when needed. They'd gotten paid for the mowing, but the rest was in service to Sweet Home. The last two caskets that Donovan had carried had been Beau's and his grandmother's, memories Donovan usually kept buried deep. But he was going to drive to the cemetery just the same and have a long overdue discussion with his brother and say a quick hello to Nan.

Donovan pulled onto Cemetery Road, his heart heavy. The trees had morphed from skinny to thick, and there were more of them. The surroundings had changed but Donovan hadn't. He never got over missing Beau. The weird thing was he couldn't imagine now what it would be like to still have him in his life. Which only made this trip harder.

He turned onto the long driveway and found the place where they'd buried Beau and Nan, near the standing statue of the Bible. He glanced at the back seat, where Boomer was hanging out in his box. "I won't be long."

Donovan got out of the car and strode quickly to Nan's grave. "I wish I had flowers for you." He'd pick up silk flowers in Anchorage and bring them back later. Daisies had been her favorite. He stood over her grave for a long moment. "When the ground thaws in the spring, I'll bring Grandpa's ashes to Sweet Home and bury them alongside you, per his last request." Grandpa loved Nan so much. Donovan wondered what it would be like to share a life with someone he loved that much. He didn't see that in his future now. Now that it had all changed.

Next, he went to Beau's grave. He squatted down and wiped away the snow covering the words: BELOVED SON AND BROTHER.

"I'm going to bring flowers for Nan. I don't think you'd appreciate those. If I were still drinking, I'd bring you a six-pack."

The wind gusted and Donovan shivered. "There's not a lot to say. Hope's still here in Sweet Home, which is bizarre. And she has a kid. She named her Ella after Izzie. Her girl is a teenager, too. You know what that means, don't you? Hope got married right away. How could she do that? I thought I meant everything to her." He laughed mirthlessly. "I guess not."

There was no sign that Beau was even listening, but Donovan still had a lot bottled up that needed to be said. "All this time, I thought Hope had gotten out of town and gotten on with her life. But it doesn't seem like she has." He paused, gathering his words. "It's not that she looks unhappy. She just seems worn out. Remember how much energy she used to have? She's just not the same person anymore." He wouldn't tell his brother how he worried he might have something to do with Hope stalling out in her life. But maybe he was giving himself too much credit.

"Nothing's turned out like I thought it would. I thought we'd always live here in Sweet Home, you and me, pranking each other, even as adults, and teaching our kids the best ones. I couldn't see beyond that. It's weird, but in some respects, things are better than I thought possible. I have a boatload of money, more money than I ever imagined. I have the military to thank for that. The Marines gave me a career. I never knew how much I loved computers until they said I had an aptitude for programming and trained me. After I got out, I started my own consulting firm, and recently, I sold it."

Donovan stood to break the news to Beau, though he probably already knew. "Grandpa died. That's the reason I'm back here. It's been surreal, you know. I'm all alone. It doesn't feel right to be back in Sweet Home with all of you gone." His only consolation . . . Dad was still alive.

"Beau, I want you to know that I've never forgiven Hope for what she did to you. For cutting your life short." A part of Donovan knew it was ridiculous to defend his brother's honor in this way, but he couldn't help it. "And I never will forgive her, I promise."

Another gust of wind blew through, but this time, from the tree above, a truckload of snow tumbled down, bashing Donovan's head, almost like it was on purpose.

"What the . . ." Donovan looked up at the tree.

He spoke to the sky, the trees, to whoever, whatever. "I don't believe in signs!" But he could almost hear Beau telling him, *Get over it, bro. Leave the past in the past.* Something Rick had said a time or two over the years.

No, Donovan didn't believe in signs, but maybe just this once he would.

"All right, I'll forgive Hope." Or he'd try to. *In my own sweet time.* "But I'm not going to *tell* her that I forgive her." Hope didn't deserve to know.

"Just one more thing before I go," Donovan said. "I want to tell you that I wrote you while I was at boot camp." With no television, Internet, or phone calls, he'd had no distractions from his grief. And no alcohol, either, to dull the pain. "I really missed you, you know? I still do." He should admit the rest, too. "I also wrote to Hope. *Every day.* I pretended like none of this had ever happened, that she and I were still in love, and that you weren't here in the cemetery. Nan, too. That Sweet Home was still the way it was when we were young, happy, and stupid." Those were magical times, but the Disney movie was over, the reel destroyed. "I never sent the letters, obviously. She'll never know about them." They were hidden at home, top shelf in his closet. Out of sight, out of mind.

Now, here he was, standing in the cold—chilled from the snow pummeling his head—and admitting everything to Beau, and the pain was back in full force. And the strange thing was . . . the only person who might really understand what he was going through was Hope. The one person he could never open up to again.

HOPE STOOD LOOKING out the front window as the sun came out. It hadn't been out in days and she felt pulled to the Hungry Bear's storefront window, soaking up as much sunshine as she could.

She was also looking for signs of life. For the past three days, she'd expected to see Donovan in the store buying fresh meat and vegetables. *Man—no, men—cannot live on junk food alone.* But Hope hadn't seen him or Rick in the store. Or around town, for that matter. Had Donovan left Sweet Home without telling anyone good-bye? At least he should have had the courtesy to say something to Piney, for goodness' sake.

She shivered. Or had he been in an accident and was lying dead in a ravine somewhere? She sent up a prayer that Donovan was okay . . . wherever he was.

Hope had done her best to keep busy. After work on Tuesday evening, she called Miss Lisa to reschedule the quilt tour of her home because Ella was studying for a test at Lacy's. With all the studying Ella was doing, Hope expected good grades at report card time. She spent the evening alone, cutting apart Izzie's clothes for the Memory Tree quilt. On Wednesday, Hope took Ella to Miss Lisa's quaint house, as promised. Ella, surprisingly, enjoyed the visit, complete with tea, homemade pound cake, and oohing and aahing over the beautiful quilt collection. When they got home, Hope made a fresh stack of bags for the Hungry Bear, which meant cash for her next installment to the utility company. And last night, she cleaned her little house from top to bottom, wondering the whole time if Donovan was truly gone.

Yes, he probably was, but she stared out the window anyway, waiting for something to happen. The morning rush, which had ended an hour ago, had consisted of Mr. Brewster having a cup of coffee, while Paige Holiday, a friend from Hope's youth, ran in for two bananas and five pounds of flour.

Outside, Courtney Wolf pulled up in her red sedan. Not necessarily the person Hope wanted to see.

Courtney had dated Donovan in high school, and Hope pretty much had a problem with anyone who dated Donovan. That meant she liked very few of the women her age who remained in Sweet Home. Also, Courtney was too pretty, if that was such a thing. Her blond hair was always perfect and her green eyes were dazzling. Hope felt like an ugly duckling next to Courtney. It didn't help that she was always dressed nicely, like today. Hope looked down at her worn kuspuk. Piney had declared Kuspuk Fridays for all her employees. Hope really needed fabric to make herself a new kuspuk. But paying her utility bill came first.

As Courtney got out of her car, she waved to Hope, which was surprising. Hope half waved back. She was even more surprised as Courtney opened the door to the Hungry Bear.

She looked around and said, "My date isn't here yet. I'll sit in the diner and wait."

Hope looked out the window again, wondering who her

date might be. There were only a few bachelors left in town: Mr. Brewster, One-tooth Joe, and Crazy Lyle. The rest of the men were married. Except she had heard that Jesse Montana might be coming back to town. He was the only guy she'd ever dated besides Donovan. If she could call *one time* actually dating.

She glanced at Courtney as Sparkle set out two coffee mugs, filling one of them.

When Hope turned around, Rick was coming through the door. *Now, that makes sense.* Rick was as beautiful as Courtney. They would make the perfect couple.

Rick did go to Courtney and held out his hand, introducing himself, but he didn't sit. Instead, he went to the small counter and engaged Sparkle in conversation, though he was the only one speaking.

The door opened once again. This time it was Donovan.

Hope didn't have time to think before Courtney was motioning him to the diner side of the Hungry Bear.

"Hey, you," Courtney said. "Come have some coffee with me."

Hope should've been glad that Donovan was alive. She had a vivid and accurate imagination when it came to dismemberment and death. But dating Courtney? No! Just no!

Donovan looked at Hope, his expression something resembling an apology. At least there was that. Boomer was tucked into his jacket and she melted a little because Donovan had such a good heart when it came to animals. And once, a long time ago, he'd given his good heart to her. But having a date with Courtney Wolf under Hope's nose at the Hungry Bear erased it all.

As he walked past Hope, he mumbled something. It sounded like *No other place in town to meet.*

So maybe he wasn't trying to rub Courtney in her face. But she felt sick just the same. She looked around for something to do. Someplace close to the diner side of the building. She decided on the magazine rack. The latest *Real Men of Alaska*—a dating service magazine for the desperate—

needed to be straightened. Every woman within a hundred-mile radius had thumbed through the magazine, looking for Mr. Right or Mr. Grizzly. Maybe Hope should buy this issue to show everyone she had options. But she couldn't . . . the utility bill. She leaned over, trying to catch what Donovan and Courtney were saying without them seeing her, and she nearly tumbled over. Thank goodness Hope righted herself before they saw her as a jealous fool.

Now Sparkle was taking them each a muffin, although Courtney's sleek figure indicated she didn't touch white sugar. Hope wished she looked like Courtney. In high school, Courtney was a cheerleader and Hope was just herself, watching from the sidelines, while Donovan made touchdowns—on and off the field. But Hope always had one thing that Courtney didn't. Hope loved Donovan with all her heart, and she knew no one would ever love him as much as she had.

As much as she did, still. Which was just pathetic. She never dated. Even if she'd found someone decent, she wouldn't act on it. She knew what real love felt like and was certain that particular brand of lightning wouldn't strike again. Especially for her. She was destined to live out the rest of her days alone. Which was pitiable.

At least she had Ella.

A sudden fear came over Hope. Today was Friday, and Ella might be out drinking again tonight, even though football season had ended last week. She had no idea how to help her daughter. It seemed as if every parent in Sweet Home, and possibly all of Alaska, had at least one child who was drinking too much. The only thing she could do was to reason with Ella once again.

Courtney sneezed. Then she sneezed again and again. "Your dog's too close. I'm allergic," she said between sneezes.

Hope wasn't proud of herself for smiling over Courtney's affliction.

Donovan stood. "Rick? Can you take Boomer?"

"Sure." Rick came over and retrieved the dog.

Sparkle was fond of dogs and came out from behind the counter to scratch Boomer behind the ears. Rick smiled, as if it were his charm that had Sparkle opening up, something she seldom did.

Hope went back to arranging the magazines but realized she might have lingered too long because Donovan glanced her way again. She walked to the register, pretending to be arranging the bags this time.

Courtney pulled out papers and slid them to Donovan. They spoke for a couple more minutes, then Donovan downed his coffee and stood. Courtney did, too. Then they headed for the door, leaving Rick with the dog. It looked like Rick might be hitting on Sparkle, because she was looking down, smiling and blushing. The thought occurred to Hope that maybe Sparkle could be sparkly after all.

Hope looked out the window and both Courtney and Donovan were gone. Courtney's car was still there, so they must've left in Donovan's car.

It was a bold move, but Hope stepped outside, looking up and down the empty street. Donovan had disappeared. Again.

In an effort to forget him, Hope trudged back inside to work on next week's order. While she was at it, she pulled cans to the front of the shelves, trying to emulate the big grocery stores in Anchorage and Fairbanks.

She hustled to the front whenever the door opened and customers came in. The whole time, Rick hung out with Sparkle.

An hour after Donovan left, he returned . . . sans Courtney. Which made Hope exceedingly happy, though she really shouldn't care. But she wasn't going to be hard on herself; Donovan was the kind of guy you just don't get over. By the look on Courtney's face earlier, she hadn't gotten over him either. Which made Hope see Courtney in a different light, as they both were in the same boat.

Donovan glanced over at Hope before grabbing one of the shopping carts. "Rick, you want to help with this?"

"I can't. Sparkle and I are going to take Boomer for a walk."

"The runt is too little to walk," Donovan said.

"Then we'll just take him out for a break." Rick smiled at Sparkle, who was pulling on her coat. The way Sparkle was beaming at Boomer, Mr. Brewster might've given the puppy to the wrong person.

"I appreciate it," Donovan said to his friend. "I'll get the groceries." But he didn't immediately get to it; instead he hovered nearby, looking down the aisles. "Is Piney around?"

"She's busy," Hope said. Probably upstairs, doing her crossword while having a coffee. Like a good store clerk, Hope automatically said, "Is there something I can help you with?"

"No." He seemed determined on it.

"Fine. I hope you had a nice date." Hope decided to ignore him until he was ready to check out.

But apparently Donovan wasn't done with her. "It wasn't a date."

"That's not what Courtney said."

"She's my real estate agent. We met to go over what I need to do to the lodge to put it on the market." He frowned at Hope as if this were none of her business. "Then we looked at the hardware store so she could get it listed."

"Oh." Hope felt foolish. "Sorry." But she wasn't completely in the wrong since Courtney had led her astray. She shouldn't get involved but she couldn't help herself. "You better let Courtney know where you stand. By what she said to me and how she was acting all dreamy-eyed over you, she's picking out wedding bands."

Donovan raised an eyebrow, looking completely unamused.

Hope couldn't shut up. "I just don't want you to give Courtney the wrong idea, is all." *Because back in the day, I'd gotten the wrong idea and look how I turned out!*

As expected, Donovan's frown intensified.

Yes, Hope had gone too far. Donovan's affairs were none of her business. *Affair* being the operative word.

He didn't respond to her advice but kept his mouth shut and headed down the aisle where Hope had just organized the canned fruit.

At that moment, Piney came down the stairs, stopping near the bottom, as if beholding her kingdom. "Anything interesting going on down here?"

Donovan stopped pushing his cart and said, "Do you have a minute, Piney? I have a few questions for you."

Chapter 6

"SURE." PINEY LOOKED in Donovan's cart, as if checking for perishable items. "Let's sit in the diner."

"Yeah." Donovan parked his cart out of the way and followed Piney. He had to work very hard not to look in Hope's direction, something he'd been doing way too much.

As he approached one of the tables, Rick and Sparkle came in the front door. Piney looked floored, which was typical, as Rick had that effect on women.

Donovan took the lead. "Piney Douglas, this is my friend and business manager, Rick Miller."

"He can't live without me," Rick teased, smiling at both Piney and Sparkle.

"It seems that way," Donovan said. "We've been working together since the Marines, seventeen years now."

Piney stared at Rick, then at her daughter, with an eyebrow raised, as if to say, *Are you really buying all his charm?*

Donovan elbowed Rick to answer the unspoken question.

Rick held out Boomer for Piney to see and then handed him off to Donovan. "Sparkle was helping me with Boomer, Donovan's new puppy."

"As long as that's all she's helping you with," Piney said.

"Put a dog in front of Sparkle and that girl will go anywhere with anyone."

Rick laughed. "Good to know."

But Piney wasn't laughing.

Rick was handsome, and women loved him, but Donovan wouldn't call him a player. Rick just enjoyed the company of women. Later Donovan would talk to Rick about not messing with Sparkle's emotions. Sparkle was Piney's daughter, and Piney was one of Sweet Home's finest.

Back in high school, Sparkle wasn't the kind of girl who drew attention to herself. The opposite, actually. He remembered her wearing only black and gray. Not a goth girl, but one who wanted to blend into the scenery. She had straight, strawberry-blond hair that hung to her shoulders and a face full of freckles. Donovan noticed now that she was kind of cute. But in high school, no one seemed to notice her or talk to her. He was guilty on that count as well, as he couldn't remember them ever having a conversation, which seemed odd, since Sweet Home was the size of a postage stamp.

Sparkle wasn't Rick's type. Come to think of it, Courtney would be a better fit for Rick. For some reason, though, Rick had latched onto Sparkle and had gotten her to talk. Something Donovan hadn't seen when he lived in Sweet Home.

"You two go find something to do," Piney said. "On second thought, Rick, help Sparkle get ready for the lunch crowd. I need vegetables cut up." She glanced over at Boomer. "Don't forget to wash your hands before you touch anything in the kitchen."

"Nice to meet you, Ms. Douglas," Rick said, and then he turned and followed Sparkle into the kitchen.

Piney watched as well until they were gone. "Is that boy up to no good?"

"No, ma'am." Donovan would have to make certain of it.

"Do you promise that he's not toying with Sparkle, because she's an easy target," Piney said, glaring at Donovan as if to get the truth out of him.

"I promise," Donovan said. "Rick is a good man."

Piney switched gears, gesturing to where Hope stood at the cash register. "What's going on with you and her?"

"Nothing." Donovan started to point out that she'd sent Hope on a fool's errand the other night, delivering groceries to them. But Piney's motives were obvious.

"Donovan Stone, you owe that girl for the hell you put her through. Don't you forget that."

"What about the hell she put *me* through?" he asked.

For a long moment, he and Piney had a stare-off, but he caved first. He had too many questions for her, so he got right to it. "I found a newspaper clipping in my grandmother's office saying the town had gone dry."

"Your grandparents are sorely missed here in Sweet Home," Piney said with genuine emotion in her voice.

"I noticed the bar is boarded over and that you don't have any alcohol on your shelves," Donovan said. "I assume the town is still alcohol-free?" He noticed Hope was sweeping near the diner and he was certain she was trying to listen in.

"Why are you asking whether the town is still dry?" Piney looked at him as if he were being insensitive with Hope standing so near.

"I should've explained myself first. I want to bring back Nan's Wines of Alaska tasting for one last time. To honor her. I figured I would need to get permission to serve alcohol."

"From the town council," Piney said.

Donovan had assumed the town council was defunct. But odd things happened in Alaska and who knew who or what the town council consisted of now. As an example, Donovan had read a funny tidbit that Talkeetna had repeatedly elected a cat as mayor.

"Do you know when the town council will meet next?" Donovan asked.

"I'm on the council," Piney said without answering his question.

It wasn't surprising that Piney was a council member. She'd been here forever and the Hungry Bear was a hub—

especially now, with the hardware store closed. Certainly many town complaints were aired right here in the Hungry Bear's aisles.

"Can you add me to the agenda for the next meeting?" He and Rick would have to draw up a proposal.

"Certainly." Piney looked over at Hope with worry in her eyes, which made Donovan wonder if Hope had a drinking problem now and Piney was concerned for her sobriety.

"When is the next meeting?"

"The twenty-eighth," Piney answered.

"Thanks. Just a couple more things." Donovan retrieved the paper from his coat pocket, which had all his questions on it. "Oh, yes, I need an interior decorator, someone who has a good eye for what an Alaskan lodge should look like."

"Hope. She's your girl," Piney answered quickly.

Yes, Hope had liked moving around furniture and fussing with pillow placement when they were kids, but that was then. He put both hands on the table and leaned forward. "Hope's not my girl!" *Not anymore.*

There was a small gasp. Apparently, Hope was still nearby. But he didn't care. He wouldn't put himself through it—taking decorating tips from the person who'd killed Beau. But then he remembered his promise to Beau to at least try to forgive. *Man, this is going to be hard. A process . . . not unlike AA.* Beau couldn't expect him to forgive overnight, could he?

Piney just sat there with a pleasant expression on her face, as if she were enjoying the show.

He decided he'd ignore all the women in the Hungry Bear and plow forward. "I need a housekeeper, too. Before you say anything, don't suggest *her.*" He was sure Piney knew who he meant.

Piney nodded and motioned to the bulletin board on the wall. "In that case, put up a flyer. There's bound to be someone in Sweet Home who would be happy for the work."

"Thanks, Piney." Donovan rose, only then remembering his last question. "Do you know who might have shoveled

the lodge's walkway and laid firewood by the fireplace before I arrived?"

"Probably Hope."

Donovan frowned at Piney. "No disrespect, but you're
starting to sound like a broken record. I know for sure it
wasn't Hope." He knew one thing: Hope wouldn't go
against his wish for her not to have anything to do with
him again.

"It couldn't have been Sparkle," Piney countered. "She's
still healing from surgery. I could ask around."

"No. Don't. Thanks anyway. Boomer and I better get back
to picking out the rest of the groceries." He looked down at
the furball cuddled in the crook of his arm. He really liked
this dog and had to admit there was no way he could give
him up now. Mr. Brewster was a sly devil, but that didn't
mean the old man was right about Donovan staying on in
Sweet Home. He'd only be here long enough to get the work
done on the lodge.

And when Donovan saw Mr. Brewster again, he was going to ask about the shoveled walkway and the dry firewood.
Maybe he'd know who it was that Donovan should thank.

DONOVAN WAS WRONG. This one time only, Hope *had*
gone against his wishes. She'd been the one to shovel the
walk and to make sure that Donovan had good firewood. *It was
the least I could do.* Besides, she hadn't technically disregarded
what Donovan wanted from her, which was nothing! He hadn't
seen her do it and he'd never know it was her. She'd done her
elf's work the night Piney told her that Donovan was returning
to town. She hadn't intended to slip out and go to the lodge in
the dead of night, but after she woke up from her talk with
Izzie, she couldn't go back to sleep.

At the time, Hope wasn't completely sure that Piney was
right about Donovan coming home for a visit anyway. So she
had nothing to lose, except a few hours of sleep. She loaded her
hatchback with firewood, drove out to the lodge with her snow

shovel, then made fast work of the walkway, as there were only a couple of inches of snow. Next, she located the key that Elsie Stone kept hidden for the Sisterhood of the Quilt under the loose railing on the back porch, carried the firewood inside, and placed it by the large hearth in the living room, leaving newspaper for tinder and matches, too. It was weird to be back in the lodge. Such good memories from childhood, but terrible ones at the end. When she arrived home and fell into bed, she should've slept soundly, but she didn't. It wasn't Izzie who visited, but memories of Donovan.

Today, Hope had only caught a smidge of Donovan and Piney's conversation. But the whole town had to have heard him exclaim that Hope wasn't his girl anymore.

Donovan wheeled his shopping cart by her.

"Wait up." She pulled a fleece bag from the bottom of the shopping bag pile. Most bags were made from shirts, dresses, and pants, but this one had come from an old baby blanket. "Boomer will be more comfortable with a little padding. Put this under him." And then, because she was feeling sassy, she added, "We like all our customers to enjoy their visit to the Hungry Bear. Even the runts."

Donovan looked at her with a strange expression . . . like maybe she'd lost it? Or maybe it was surprise and appreciation? Who knew?

Finally, he said, "Thanks." He positioned the blanket in the bottom of the cart, then gently set Boomer on top before going on his merry way. Not that he seemed all that merry. More like confused. Or disgruntled. She had no idea anymore what was up with him, which was fair, since he didn't know anything about her either.

From her spot at the front, Hope watched as Donovan carefully positioned items in his cart, making sure not to bury Boomer. When the first cart was full, he returned for a second.

As he went to pull little Boomer from his makeshift bed, Hope said, "Leave him. I'll keep an eye on the small fry. He won't be in anyone's way here."

Donovan nodded. "Okay."

She pulled Boomer's cart behind the counter while Donovan rushed off to get more.

Rick and Sparkle reappeared, carrying stacks of packaged salads, and shelved them in the case on the diner side of the building. Rick touched Sparkle's elbow, said something to her, and then they came over to Hope.

Rick glanced in Boomer's cart. "What's going on here?"

"Babysitting," Hope answered.

Sparkle reached down and scratched the puppy behind the ears. "He's the sweetest thing I've ever seen."

Hope laughed. "You say that about every dog you meet."

Donovan maneuvered his cart back toward the front, looking ready to check out.

"Did he tell you about our trip to Anchorage?" Rick asked, smiling.

That saved Hope from trying to figure out where he'd gone. "Silent as the grave." *Oh, crud.* What a stupid thing to say. What was wrong with her?

Donovan frowned.

Rick didn't seem to notice her faux pas. "Anchorage was quite the adventure. We loaded up on stain for the exterior of the lodge. I'm hoping we get a few warm days. The lady at the store said it might get into the forties for a short period of time, which is all we need."

"Or she might've just been feeding you a line, hoping you'd clear her inventory this late in the year," Hope said teasingly but also because there might be some truth in it. Winter was here and the forties wouldn't be seen for many, many months.

"You might be right," Rick said with an *Oh, well* easiness. "Then we went to the furniture store." He turned toward Sparkle. "I bought a couple of large beanbags. You should come out to the lodge and watch movies with us tonight."

Sparkle dropped her head, looking embarrassed.

Donovan jumped in, as if to ease Sparkle's discomfort. "We bought a bunch of kids' movies. Christmas ones, too.

We thought it would be cool to stock up for the future buyer, for when families come to stay at the lodge."

The phone rang and Piney picked it up. "Hope McKnight, it's for you."

"Can you take a message?" she asked. That was when she noticed the confused look on Donovan's face.

"McKnight?" he asked.

Hope straightened her shoulders and dared him with her eyes to contradict her. "I kept my maiden name."

Rick laughed and laid his hands on their shoulders. "Looks like the two of you have a lot of catching up to do. Hope, you should come out for movie night, too." He looked at her with some pleading in his eyes.

Sparkle gave her a quick glance, too, as if to say, *I'll go if you go.*

But Hope didn't want to. It would be beyond uncomfortable.

"Bring your daughter," Donovan suggested. "I'd be interested in her ideas for what might keep teenage guests occupied."

Hope was more concerned about keeping Ella out of the lodge's wine cellar. "I'm sure she can't make it. A busy teen and all." She frowned. "But I'll come." For Sparkle's sake. And for no other reason.

Rick smiled broadly. "Also, it'll give you a chance to look around the place. Donovan said he was going to ask you to give him some decorating ideas."

Hope was shocked. Donovan looked shocked, too, at first, but then he seemed angry. Like he was going to plug Rick's mouth to keep it from running.

"I don't know anything about decorating." Which wasn't true. As a kid, she liked to pretend she was an interior designer. But now, who had time for fanciful things like decorating? Certainly not her.

"Donovan says you understand the spirit of Alaska better than anyone." Rick looked outside, as if Courtney might reappear and challenge him on the unfounded claim.

Piney came from nowhere and patted Hope on the back. "Then Hope accepts. She'd love to decorate the lodge."

Hope was speechless. But darn if she wouldn't find her voice and let Piney know that she didn't like getting thrown under the bus.

Piney pointed to the groceries. "How about I check you out? Hope, you sack."

"We'll get out of your hair." Rick ushered Sparkle back to the diner and they took a seat in a booth.

Happily, Piney rang up the groceries. "I appreciate you patronizing my store, Donovan. Especially since you just came from Anchorage."

"Happy to do it," Donovan said.

His sincerity made Hope's heart twitch, which was a shock unto itself. She'd come to accept that her heart was closed after many years of disuse. She'd been asked out by many of the lumberjacks who passed through Sweet Home, and before that by a few of her classmates before they'd married. She never had felt a thing, though. But something was happening now. And Hope was not happy about it. Opening herself up to feelings for Donovan now felt as reasonable as having open-heart surgery without anesthesia.

"What are you fixing for dinner, then?" Piney said. "I have a nice roast there in the meat case."

Donovan nodded. "That's a good idea. Do you mind wrapping it up for me?"

Piney motioned to Hope. "You take over here, and I'll be right back with that roast."

Hope grabbed the roll of aluminum foil and two cans of green beans and rang them up. "Do you even know how to make a roast?"

Some of the old mischief was visible in his eyes. "No. But I figured either you or Sparkle would." His expression became more serious. "Thanks for agreeing to come to the lodge tonight." Then he backtracked. "Not for me, of course, but for Sparkle and Rick." He gestured toward the diner. "That's something, isn't it?"

Rick and Sparkle seemed like an odd pair, but who could tell when a couple was going to click? Or unclick, as was the case with her and Donovan.

"I'm happy to do it. I'd do anything for Sparkle and Piney." They were the only family that she and Ella had left.

Except there were limits. Piney seemed hell-bent on forcing her and Donovan together. But there wasn't the slightest chance of that happening. That stupid nursery rhyme raced through Hope's head.

All the king's horses and all the king's men,
Couldn't put me and Donovan back together again.

Chapter 7

"WHAT'S GOING ON?" Ella asked. "Why are you getting dressed up? You aren't going to church for some reason, are you?"

Hope looked down at the dress she'd put on and groaned. She'd better go change. "I'm headed out to Home Sweet Home Lodge."

Ella's brow creased. "Why? That place is abandoned."

"The grandson of the people who owned the lodge is back in town to put it up for sale," Hope said.

"Then why are you going out there?" Ella asked.

"We were friends when we were kids," Hope explained as benignly as she could.

"Oh?" Ella's eyebrows rose to the ceiling. "Mom, do you have a *date*?" She seemed to think the idea was both funny and absurd.

"No, I don't have a date. Sparkle seems to have a crush on Donovan's friend Rick."

"Donovan? Why does that name sound familiar?" Ella asked.

"I don't know," Hope lied. She seemed to lie a lot to Ella, as far as Izzie was concerned. "Anyway, Rick invited Sparkle out to the lodge to watch a movie tonight. Sparkle won't go unless I go, too."

"You guys are acting like a bunch of freshmen."

"Would you like to come along?" Hope didn't know why she'd asked. Okay, Donovan had invited Ella, but maybe deep down she really did want Ella to get to know her dad . . . without there being a bunch of drama to go along with it.

"Sure," Ella said, surprising Hope. "As long as I don't have to wear a dress, too. Can I bring Lacy along?"

Safety in numbers. "Absolutely." Then a razor of panic slid through Hope. What if Ella figured out that Donovan was her father? She tamped down the fear; there was no way for her to find out. "Can you be ready in five?" Then, as an afterthought, she added, "Grab a couple of cheese sticks for you and Lacy. Dinner will be late." Hope was going to have to cook the roast while Rick chatted up Sparkle. At least the roast would keep Hope busy, which would ward off her feeling awkward around Donovan. She wondered if Elsie Stone's pressure cooker was still on the premises and safe enough to use after all these years.

"I'll go call Lacy," Ella said as she raced from the room.

Hope still needed to change back into what she was wearing earlier—turtleneck, kuspuk, and jeans.

Fifteen minutes later, they picked up Sparkle. Lacy was going to drive out later, as she had to finish her chores first.

Hope glanced over at Sparkle, who seemed as nervous as Hope felt. Ella had earbuds in and had no idea how tense the women were in the front seat.

"Thanks for agreeing to come along," Sparkle said quietly. "I know this has to be awkward for you."

"I'm happy to do it," replied Hope. Oh, she was definitely going to hell for all the lying she was doing.

"Why would it be awkward, Mom?" Ella said, surprising Hope.

"No reason," Hope lied again. "I thought you were listening to music?"

"I can do both," Ella chirped. "So . . . awkward, why?"

Sparkle quietly cleared her throat and Hope knew she was being nudged. *Fine!*

"Donovan and I were neighbors growing up. We dated for a brief time in high school." Then Hope added. "Ancient history."

"The Stone Age." Ella snickered.

The closer they got to the lodge, Sparkle seemed to squirm more. "Are you okay?"

Sparkle sighed. "I just can't believe Rick wants to spend time with me."

"I can believe it. You're a smart, beautiful woman, Sparkle, so I'm not surprised at all. The more important question is: Do you like him?"

"He's very . . . charming," she said.

"Well, this should give you an opportunity to assess him, not the other way around. Do you hear?"

"I guess so," Sparkle said.

"I know so," Hope said.

A few minutes later, they pulled up to the lodge and parked. All three guys came out on the porch to meet them— Donovan, Rick, and Boomer, who, of course, was in Donovan's arms.

Hope opened her door, but Ella scrambled from the car first.

She rushed up the porch steps, straight to Donovan. "What a cute dog!" It was like she was ten again. But teenagers could easily revert. Especially if it was her daughter and a dog was involved. "What's his name? Can I play with him?"

"Boomer." Donovan set him in Ella's arms.

Hope realized Sparkle hadn't budged. She looked too paralyzed to leave the car. Hope reached over and squeezed her hand. "We're just going to have a little dinner and watch a movie. If you decide you don't like Rick, then we'll leave. No harm done." But Hope couldn't imagine any scenario where Sparkle wouldn't like Rick. Hope had a good feeling about him, and her intuition was saying that Rick was one of the good guys. Rick had Donovan's stamp of approval, which spoke volumes.

Though Hope was a jumble of nerves, she felt like she had to be the strong one here and went around to the other side of the car and opened Sparkle's door for her. Sparkle took the hint and exited.

Hope slapped a neutral pleasant expression on her face. "I see my daughter Ella has commandeered your dog." Hope walked up to the porch, modeling for Sparkle how it was done.

Ella had Boomer in the driveway, playing a game of chase with him.

"I'm glad they're getting along," Donovan said. "Maybe she'll wear him out and he'll quit gnawing on my moccasins."

"Stop whining," Rick said. "I'll pick you up a new pair when I head back to Anchorage."

Hope got closer and noticed a good portion of one moccasin had been chewed away.

"Come on in." Rick held the door wide, smiling at Sparkle.

Sparkle glanced over at Hope.

Hope gave her an it's-all-good look, then waved at Ella. "Are you coming?"

Ella scooped up Boomer and ran for the porch.

As Hope neared the door, she became aware of a wonderful smell from inside the lodge. "You put the roast in?" She was speaking to Rick as she stepped inside, but it was Donovan who answered.

"We got the Internet," Donovan said. "I YouTubed it."

"Don't let him fool you, Hope," Rick said, shutting the door behind Ella and Boomer. "Donovan is a great cook. If it weren't for him, I'd be emaciated. I'm not sure what I'm going to do when he moves to Florida."

"I told him to move to Florida, too," Donovan said. "My business manager needs to be close to the business, right?"

"What's in Florida?" Ella asked, as she slipped off her snow boots and set them on the mat.

"My dad lives in Florida," Donovan said. "He'd be here with me now, but he's recovering from back surgery."

"Is he going to be all right?" Hope asked. She'd always liked Mr. Stone. And he was Ella's grandfather, something Hope had never considered before.

"He'll be fine. He's starting physical therapy next week. All this is bad timing."

Hope knew what he meant. With Charles Stone's passing this past month, she wondered if Donovan's dad had to miss the funeral. But she wouldn't ask.

"Where'd you get Boomer?" Ella inquired.

"Mr. Brewster. Do you know him?" Donovan said.

"Yeah. I help out sometimes at the kennel, especially in the summer."

Just like Donovan did.

Ella looked lovingly down at Boomer. "Is this the runt Mr. Brewster told me about?"

"The one and only," Donovan said.

Ella gave Boomer a little squeeze and then kissed his head. "I always wanted a Berner."

"Really?" Donovan glanced over at Hope. "Maybe your mom can get you one. Or your dad?"

Ella shook her head. "My dad's dead." She said it matter-of-factly, as if stating Boomer was a dog.

Izzie had had that kind of candor and it was surprisingly comforting to see it in her daughter.

Donovan, though, looked as if Ella's words had thrown him off guard. After a moment, he seemed to recover . . . sort of. "I'm sorry to hear about your father."

"No worries," Ella said. "He died before I was born." She glanced at Hope, but then she frowned. "Mom, why do you look so weird?"

"Nothing," Hope answered quickly and wrongly. "I mean, I don't look weird."

"Yeah, you do. You were weird at home, getting ready. And now you're starting to freak me out."

Hope shoved her hair behind her ears, something she did

when she was nervous. Thank goodness, Rick came to the rescue. "Everyone, go stand by the fire and get warm." He helped Sparkle off with her coat.

The visit was just getting started and Hope already wanted to head home. She realized then that "The Little Drummer Boy" was playing quietly in the background. She pointed to the air, as if she could touch the music. "Which one of you is in the Christmas spirit?"

"Guilty," Rick said. "I'm a sucker for the holidays. Since the stores in Anchorage were already gearing up for Santa, I took advantage and bought a bunch of decorations, too."

"Yeah, you can no longer park a vehicle in the garage. Packed," Donovan added, shaking his head. "Thanksgiving isn't even here yet."

Hope scanned the interior of the lodge. It looked totally different now than when she'd shown up with the grocery delivery, when the only illumination came from lanterns. Now, the overhead lights were lit, along with every lamp. This was how Hope remembered it, except there was no laughter resonating from the Sisterhood of the Quilt. Also, two large bean-bag chairs were parked in front of the television set, the same TV that had been there seventeen years ago.

Hope raised her eyebrows at Donovan. "I'm surprised that, being a man and all, you didn't upgrade to an eighty-five-inch flat screen while you were in Anchorage."

"It's on back order." Donovan stared at her for a long moment.

Thank goodness Rick jumped in, because Hope couldn't help but stare back.

"We went to the furniture store to buy new couches and chairs, but my man here"—Rick jabbed a thumb at Donovan—"couldn't make up his mind. I don't understand it. He had no trouble decorating his apartment in San Jose."

Ella plopped down in one of the beanbags. "I like them."

Donovan shrugged. "The industrial look in San Jose won't work for the wilds of Alaska."

"Need I remind you that you are *from* Alaska?" Rick

turned to her. "Hope, you have to help him. This place needs a woman's touch if he's going to turn a profit come sell day."

"What about Courtney?" Hope shouldn't have blurted that out. But now that she had, she waited, feeling morbidly curious to see how Donovan felt about the always-perfect-nearly-Miss-Alaska. It wasn't like she wanted Courtney to overhaul Home Sweet Home Lodge. Just the opposite. Hope just wanted to know if Donovan would fall for Courtney's womanly wiles like he'd done before. Before he and Hope got together.

Donovan's brows furrowed. "Courtney isn't exactly the Alaskan lodge type. Her tastes run closer to the big city than to Sweet Home."

Hope tried to keep her face from contorting, but her thoughts and emotions were definitely taking sides. He might as well have come out and said that Courtney would get along great in the big city . . . with him.

Ella grabbed a piece of cheese from the tray on the coffee table. "Why don't you just keep the place?"

"I can't," Donovan said, at the same time Hope said, "He can't."

She was so embarrassed. Even Sparkle looked embarrassed for her.

Hope walked toward the kitchen. "What else needs to be done? Can I cut up some veggies?" She tried to sound perky, but it was hard to sound upbeat when everyone knew she was pathetic.

Unfortunately, Donovan followed her into the kitchen. "You have a great kid. She seems to love Boomer."

"She loves animals," Hope said. *Just like you always did.*

Hope had a solution to keep them from being alone. "Ella, get in here and help."

"She just ran outside, saying her friend was here." Donovan pulled romaine from the refrigerator and a colander from under the sink. "The knives are in that drawer."

She wanted to snap at him, *I know where the knives are.* Back in the day, she'd spent almost as much time at the lodge as he had.

"Mom, Lacy's here," Ella called from the living room. A second later, she and Lacy were in the kitchen with them.

"Wow." Lacy stared at Donovan as if he were Chris Hemsworth. Then she spoke to him. "My mom's Aberdeen North. She said to tell you hi. She says that you, her, and Ella's mom went to high school together."

"Aberdeen," Donovan said wistfully, or at least that was how it sounded to Hope. "Yes, I remember her. You do, too, don't you, Hope? Aberdeen was a senior when we were freshmen."

"Yes, I know Aberdeen well." She didn't point out sarcastically that she still lived here, and that Ella and Lacy were best friends, which brought Aberdeen and her together regularly. "Aberdeen comes into the Hungry Bear every Saturday."

Lacy turned to Ella and grabbed her arm, but then glanced back at Donovan. "Your real dad is such a hottie! Why didn't you tell me he's still alive?"

"WHAT?" ELLA WENT cold, as if Lacy had pushed her into Icy Lake.

"My mom said that he"—she pointed at Donovan's chest—"is your *real* dad. That your mom had a thing with him in high school."

"You're lying, Lacy! My dad died before I was born. Mom said so."

"I'm not lying," Lacy cried. "Just repeating what my mom said."

Shaking, and knowing she was about to cry, too, Ella turned to her mom. "Is it true?" Her voice cracked.

Mom had gone sheet-white, as if all her blood had drained away. Fear gripped Ella. Her granddad had looked like that in his casket. Was her mom going to die, too?

Mom reached out a hand, but Ella backed away, wiping at the tears she couldn't stop.

"This isn't how I planned to tell you," her mom said.

Donovan dropped the colander and it clanked across the floor. "It's true?"

Well, at least Ella wasn't the only one who'd been left in the dark. But it didn't make her feel any better.

Her mom nodded at the guy who was supposed to be her dad.

"You lied to me," Ella heard herself screaming, though she felt outside of herself. Tears completely blurred her vision. She was pretty sure she was going to *hurl*. She tried to run from the room, but her mom grabbed her shoulders.

"Let me explain," her mom said.

But Ella didn't want to hear it. She jerked away and ran from the lodge.

"Wait up!" Lacy was running after her.

"No!" Ella didn't want to be friends with Lacy anymore. She'd done this because Ella had given her notes from history to Tad—Lacy's boyfriend. And she was just being nice! It wasn't like she liked him or anything. "You did this on purpose!"

"I didn't," Lacy pleaded. "I thought you knew. Why else would you be coming out to the lodge?"

That was a good question. But no way was Ella going back in there and ask her mom *why*. Why had she brought them here?

"Don't be mad!" Lacy was blubbering like *she'd* just been betrayed and not Ella. "You're my best friend."

Ella stopped running. She needed a Kleenex. Snot was all over the place.

Lacy caught up to her and took her arm. "Let's get out of here. We'll go to my house. My mom's on a date." She tugged Ella toward her car.

And Ella let her. What else could she do?

Mom was a big fat liar.

Grandpa was dead.

And even though Ella had apparently gained a father tonight . . . she had never felt more alone in her life.

• • •

DONOVAN BACKED INTO a chair and sat. Hope looked as pale as a ghost, nearly as upset and looking as awful as she had the night Izzie and Beau died.

Rick hurried into the kitchen. "What's going on? What's wrong with Ella?"

Donovan hung his head, feeling too shocked, too stunned. *I have a daughter?* "You tell him, Hope. In fact, tell us both how this happened." He looked up at her, just in time to see her anger rise to the surface.

"You were there, Donovan Stone!" She put her hands on her hips. "Or do I need to remind you of 'going all the way' with me?"

"How could you have told Ella I was dead?" Donovan just couldn't wrap his head around it. Any of it!

"What is going on?" Rick repeated.

Hope seemed to give up her holier-than-thou act and pushed past Donovan. "I don't have time for this. I have to find my daughter."

Donovan grabbed her arm. "Give her a minute to process." He certainly needed one. Maybe seventeen years' worth.

Hope glared at him. "You've been a father all of ten seconds and you're telling me how to raise my daughter?"

"Father?" Rick said. "What is she talking about, Don?"

Sparkle came into the kitchen and led Rick away. "Let me explain about Hope and Donovan."

Donovan felt defeated. "I wasn't trying to tell you how to raise Ella. I could just tell she needed some time to take this all in."

"She doesn't have time." Hope broke free. "You don't understand. I have to stop her." Then Hope was gone.

Donovan dropped into a kitchen chair and let his head fall into his hands. "Man. This is so messed up." He still couldn't comprehend why she hadn't told him he had a daughter.

But apparently he did have one.

He just didn't want to admit that maybe some of this was his fault.

HOPE PARKED HER car in front of the Hungry Bear and got out. She looked up and down the dark empty street, but there was no sign of life. *Where are you, Ella?* She wasn't answering her phone and Hope hadn't been able to find her at the usual spots. She'd knocked for fifteen minutes on Aberdeen's door, thinking the girls might've parked elsewhere and were drinking inside. But no such luck. No one answered.

Hope didn't know what to do. She texted Piney. Can I come up?

Piney pulled back the curtain from the front window and motioned her to come on in. Hope unlocked the door to the store, careful not to set off the noise-activated alarm as she quietly let herself in and made her way upstairs.

Piney was waiting in the doorway of her apartment. She put an arm around Hope's shoulders. "Get in here, buttercup. Sparkle called and told me everything. The herbal tea is steeping."

"Have you heard from Ella?" Hope asked anxiously.

Piney shook her head. "Not a word. Go sit down. You look as wound up as my yarn."

"I can't stay. I have to get home." But being with Piney felt like home. If only she could stay forever. "Ella is never going to forgive me!"

Piney took both of her hands and squeezed. "That's not true. Ella's going to be fine. I've seen it."

"I better go." Hope didn't have time for Piney's crystal-ball talk now. "I just wanted to make sure Ella wasn't here." And she'd thought seeing Piney would make her feel less frightened, but it wasn't working. "I'll see you at the store tomorrow."

"Get some rest," Piney said, as Hope left. But sleep would be elusive tonight until Ella was home, safe in her bed.

Back in her car, Hope tried to put the key in the ignition,

but her hand was shaking too much. "Pull it together, Hope," she said aloud. Ella was probably hurt somewhere, and she had to find her. Hope had to search each byroad—paved or gravel. She wouldn't give up!

A sudden crash of music from her phone startled her. It was Lacy's number! With fumbling fingers, Hope finally answered the call. "Ella?"

"No. It's Aberdeen."

Dread spread through Hope's body. *Ella has been in an accident.* "Is Ella all right?" But Hope's nervous system was preparing her, telling her that Ella was dead.

"Yes, of course Ella's all right. Sort of," Aberdeen said. "Lacy told me what happened out at the lodge. I'm so sorry. It's all my fault."

"What do you mean *sort of*?" Hope asked. "What's wrong with Ella? Did they get in a car accident?"

"No accident. I just got home from a date and found both girls in Lacy's room with a bottle of rum, drunk. I'm sorry about that, too. I need to put a lock on my pantry."

Thank you, God, for keeping them off the roads.

"I'm so glad they're safe," Hope said, feeling genuinely grateful.

"About everything that happened at the lodge, I never meant to cause you and Donovan trouble," Aberdeen continued. "I shouldn't have been gossiping on the phone with Lacy in the room."

You shouldn't have been gossiping at all! Hope kept her mouth shut, but it did bring up an important point. "How did you know Donovan was Ella's father? I never told a soul."

"Oh, Hope," Aberdeen started. "We *all* guessed. But if anyone dared mention it Piney shut us down."

"How?" Hope would like to have that kind of power.

"She warned all of Sweet Home that if we didn't keep our noses out of it, she was going to close the Hungry Bear . . . for good. We believed her." Aberdeen paused. "And since the town had just lost the hardware store, everyone did as she said. I remember my own mom getting onto one of her friends when she started to speculate about *who had knocked you up*. My mama's words, not mine."

"Apparently you forgot Piney's warning tonight," Hope said bitterly.

"I feel terrible about it," Aberdeen whimpered. "Please, Hope, know how sorry I am."

Hope couldn't say, *Oh, sure, it's okay. No harm done.* Because harm had been done. Irrevocably.

The good feeling of knowing that Ella was okay had faded, and anger had taken its place. *Tonight was supposed to be a drama-free night!*

"Can I speak to Ella?"

"If it's okay, Ella wants to sleep over," Aberdeen said instead. "Is it?"

No! It's not okay for Ella to sleep over! But Hope didn't want to make things worse. She'd always chosen her battles with Ella. Apparently, Hope had lost this one. "Let her know that I'll pick her up at ten in the morning."

"Okay." Aberdeen sounded hesitant.

Hope knew it would be early for the girls, but it was the best time for Hope, as she could slip away from the Hungry Bear for a midmorning break. Getting Ella alone in the car and taking a drive out to the cemetery would give Hope a chance to say what needed to be said. Explain all of it. Okay, not necessarily all of it, but enough for Ella to get the idea. She didn't want to demonize Donovan, who had been grieving back then, but she also didn't want to be the villain of the story. The truth was always hard to pin down. Between now and then, Hope prayed she'd find the right words that would help Ella feel better.

Hope should go home and get some sleep. Or work on Izzie's Memory Tree quilt. Instead her mind was filled with Donovan Stone. *No time like the present.* She put the car in gear and headed back to the lodge.

PINEY WATCHED HOPE drive away, knowing she had to do more. Bill would tell her that she should mind her own

100 * Patience Griffin

business and stay out of Hope's. But Hope was family. Ella, too. And it was time to make sure that Donovan was brought into the fold.

Absence did not, alas, necessarily make the heart grow fonder, but proximity did.

Unfortunately, Hope was going to get mighty uncomfortable while Piney fixed what the universe had messed up when little Izzie and Beau died. She should've hunted Donovan down after he left and told him Hope was pregnant. But she'd been there at Elsie's funeral when he'd told Hope that he wanted nothing to do with her ever again. And Hope had been so upset that it seemed wrong to interfere. But for Donovan's and Hope's sakes now, Piney would take off the kid gloves and dish out a dollop of tough love.

It wouldn't be easy.

But it would be worth it to have those two back together. She just prayed that Hope could forgive her for the lie she was about to tell.

Chapter 8

SLOWLY, HOPE DROVE along the curvy road leading out of town. The weather didn't have anything to do with her keeping her speed down; no, her snail's pace had everything to do with going back to the lodge, when she felt certain that Donovan must hate her. But if she couldn't talk to Ella tonight, then she would speak with Donovan. Explain. Answer his questions. Maybe even beg his forgiveness.

But the memory of standing near Elsie Stone's grave, Donovan telling her he never wanted to see her ever again, felt fresh. As new as the snow that was starting to fall.

Now that Hope knew Ella was okay, she felt bad for abandoning Sparkle. But hadn't Rick said he'd get Sparkle home? Hadn't Sparkle told her to go, giving her the nod of approval before Hope ran out? Her memory was clouded . . .

She had even more trouble thinking about what she was going to say to Donovan. Regret covered Hope and she swiped at a tear. If she'd told Donovan about Ella sooner, maybe Ella could've had a father all these years. But the truth was, Hope felt certain Donovan wouldn't have welcomed the news that she was pregnant. And who knew whether Donovan even wanted to be a parent now?

Should she ask him?

Once she got to the lodge, it took everything in her to leave the car and go to the door. It was even harder to knock.

When she finally did, Rick answered with Boomer in his arms. He pulled her in for a quick hug, as if he'd known her forever. "Are you all right? Sparkle and I were worried sick about you."

Hope wished her eyes weren't red. She had to keep reminding herself: *Ella is okay!*

"Is Donovan here?"

"The back porch," Rick said.

Probably cooling off. "Thanks."

Hope gave Sparkle a small wave as she walked through the dining room. Sparkle's eyes were filled with pity. That look was something Hope had become accustomed to from the folks of Sweet Home, but never from Sparkle. Stepping out on the back porch, Hope felt like she was about to face a firing squad.

Donovan was standing with his back to her, looking at the nearly frozen river.

"How's Ella?" He didn't turn around. "Is she okay?"

Well, she's drunk. But Hope didn't say that. "She's spending the night at Lacy's. Aberdeen called and told me." Hope paused. "Can we talk?"

Donovan shook his head, still not looking at her. "I'm not sure I want to speak to you right now."

Hope didn't blame him for being furious.

"Don't you have questions?" Hope said.

Silence. Hope waited. Just as she was about to leave the porch—and his life forever—Donovan turned around.

"Let's go inside to Grandpa's office and give Rick and Sparkle some alone time. I think we've aired enough dirty laundry in front of others for one night."

"You're not calling my daughter dirty laundry, are you?"

He ran a hand through his hair, looking defeated. Frustrated. Angry. "Of course not, Hope. I'm just a private person these days."

"Then you've been away too long. Have you forgotten that

no one gets true privacy here in Sweet Home?" She noticed that Donovan hadn't corrected her by saying, *She's my daughter, too.*

This wasn't going well.

Why had she come back?

Apparently, she was into punishment.

She followed him inside, then through the kitchen. It was as if Donovan was keeping her out of Rick and Sparkle's line of sight, sneaking her to Charles Stone's office because he was embarrassed by her.

The office looked like a time capsule, exactly how Charles had left it, neat, tidy, with everything in its place, the opposite of Elsie Stone, who liked everything out so she could see it—papers, fabric, patterns. Hope still missed her. All of Sweet Home did.

Donovan shut the door behind Hope. His features were hard, taut. "Why did you come back to the lodge tonight?"

"I told you, to answer your questions. I know you have to have some," she said honestly. Why else would she put herself through this?

"Okay." Donovan nodded, watching her closely as if she might try to steal something. "I'll ask the big question first."

Hope braced herself. "Fire away."

"How could you keep this from me?" His voice cracked. "Keep Ella from me?"

Hope sighed heavily. "I assure you, it wasn't deliberate. When I realized I was pregnant, it took a while for it all to sink in." Izzie was gone. Beau was gone. *You were gone.*

"But after it sank in?"

"I was in shock over losing Izzie and Beau. My heart was broken and I felt lost. You had been clear that we were through. You told me never to contact you again." *Don't call. Don't write. Don't ever do anything for me again. You've done enough.* She'd been one hundred percent certain he didn't want to be saddled with *her* baby. She could still see the hate in his eyes at Beau's funeral when he looked in her direction.

"Oh, come on, Hope! That's bull! You can't honestly think that I wouldn't want to know that we were going to have a child?"

She hung her head. "I was a mess . . . for a long time. Not thinking clearly, as I am now." She was too embarrassed to tell him that she'd barely been functioning back then and didn't know how to begin to explain that dark time to him now. And then the shame that followed. He'd gotten away from Sweet Home and made something of himself. She turned into a sub-par version of the girl he'd known. She couldn't tell him that her own mother had shunned her. How her parents divorced. How Piney had taken her in and nursed her somewhat back to life. Or at least woke her up and forced her to smell the coffee. That her former life was no more. No more Izzie, no more Beau. No more parents. No more stability. No more future. *No more you!* All of her energy had gone into surviving. Not trying to fix the past. She gave up hope of rising above like he had done.

He slammed his hand on the desk. "Why didn't anyone from Sweet Home reach out to me?" He clutched a stone paperweight and she was certain he was going to hurl it against the far wall. "I would've wanted to know!"

Hope was startled by his transformation. And only now was she starting to comprehend what she'd done to him. The time she'd stolen away from him to get to know his daughter. And the damage she'd done to Ella by not telling the truth. She wasn't going to make excuses anymore. Wasn't going to point out that she'd only been a scared kid. It didn't matter that she'd been sure *then* that he would've hated her for being pregnant. That was nothing compared to the hurt in his eyes *now*.

What in the world could she say to him? Okay, she would just give the facts and try to keep her crushed emotions out of it. Finally, she spoke. "I just found out tonight, from Aberdeen, why no one hunted you down and told you. It seems, back then, that Piney threatened to shut down the Hungry Bear if anyone gossiped about me being pregnant. No one was allowed to speculate about who the father was." Hope watched him. "I wasn't talking. I never told anyone that you were the father. Not even Piney or Sparkle."

"Fine, you didn't want me to know Ella. But why did you come up with this fictional father?" he ground out.

"Mom sent me away to Aunt Betsy in the Yukon." The evenness of her tone didn't betray the pain of the blow, when Mom had said Hope was to go with Aunt Betsy after Izzie's funeral and not come back. Hope had begged not to be sent away. Dad had begged, too. At least he'd convinced Mom that Hope could return after several weeks—not back home, but to Sweet Home. "I got back to Sweet Home just a day before your grandmother died." Hope hadn't even gotten to tell Elsie how sorry she was for what she'd done to Beau. "I'm not sure if you want the details . . ."

"I do."

"Well, when you came back for Elsie's funeral I had just missed my period and knew nothing for sure. I did think about telling you, but we weren't friends anymore, and besides, I was in denial. I was sure I'd missed my period because of the stress. I had heard somewhere that could happen."

"You could've taken a pregnancy test to find out for certain," Donovan accused.

"*Yeah. Sure.* Like I could've walked into the Hungry Bear to get one without half the town hearing about it. Or even worse, I could've gone to the clinic." She looked in the direction of town and could see in her mind's eye the clinic with its now boarded-up windows. "I know what I did to you and Ella is reprehensible, keeping you two apart. I'm sorry. It's all my fault."

Donovan just stared at her, as if he agreed one hundred percent. Couldn't he see that her heart was breaking all over again, just being around him?

"Can I ask a question?" she said. *Just this one thing.* "Do you want to be a father to Ella?" *Or is it too late?* He didn't answer immediately and something snapped inside Hope.

"Do you already have children? Forget it. Sorry I asked! None of my business. You're leaving soon!"

Anger flashed in Donovan's eyes and she knew she never should've come back here tonight.

"Hell, no!" he said.

Hope didn't know which of her questions he was referring to. She opened her mouth to ask, but Donovan was halfway through the door.

Come back, she wanted to cry out. But he was gone.

She'd gotten what she deserved. She'd left Donovan hanging for so many years and now it was his turn to do the same to her.

She sat there for at least five minutes, trying to be patient, telling herself—*no, fooling herself*—that he'd come back. That he'd be sorry for leaving her—now *and* then. But he didn't. Finally, Hope rose and snuck out through the door in the garage, unable to face any of them.

She drove back to town, wanting desperately to get Ella and take her home with her. She didn't want to be alone tonight. But Ella wouldn't want to be with her either. Ella would probably want to live at Lacy's trailer forever.

Hope parked her car and saw that next door, Bill's light was still on. For no reason, she started walking to his cottage. But she hadn't made two footfalls when the lights went out. Feeling paranoid, she wondered if the news had spread of how she'd treated Ella and Donovan, keeping them away from each other.

She turned around to head back to her place, except a moose had wandered near her minuscule porch, nibbling the branches she should've trimmed in early fall.

"Come on!" she said to the moose. "Give me a break!"

But he just stood there, taunting her, glancing over at her every now and then, as if to say, *I've never given you a break before. Why should I start now?*

It felt as if everything was coming to one defining point. Donovan back in town, Ella finding out that he was her father, and now the moose. Just as she was ready to sit down in the snow and cry, the moose wandered back into the woods behind her house.

She scrambled for her door, slung it open, then shut herself inside.

She was too tired to wash up the few dishes in the sink, though to her credit at least she thought about it. Instead, she went into her room and dressed for bed. She was miserable. This evening couldn't have gone worse.

She stopped in the middle of pulling on her nighttime kuspuk. *Yes, tonight could've gone worse.* She eased the nightshirt the rest of the way.

She didn't do it often, but now she got to her knees, leaned her elbows on her bed, and then properly thanked God for watching over Ella tonight, keeping her safe. Now, if only the Big Guy Upstairs would make her daughter see the light and forgive Hope for what she'd done. And make Donovan forgive her, too. While she was at it, she asked if He could help Ella stop drinking this very instant to keep from killing off more brain cells than she'd already done. But those were only pipe dreams. Tonight, she'd settle for Ella being okay.

Hope shut off the light and climbed into bed. But sleep wouldn't come. Her brain buzzed with anxiety.

Losing Izzie had set a certain standard for Hope's life. Hope was constantly telling herself that her troubles were nothing compared to Izzie dying. *It could always be worse* had become her mantra.

"Hope," Izzie said, making Hope jump. Apparently, she had fallen asleep, because Izzie was sitting cross-legged at the end of the bed, looking like a yogi, or the young child that she'd been. "I know you're thinking about me and I don't like that you use me that way."

"What way?" Hope asked, feeling too tired to fess up and too tired to hash out the evening with her little sister.

"You're being morbid," Izzie chastised. "Maybe, instead of saying that things could always be worse, you should start a gratitude journal."

"What do you know about gratitude journals?"

"I know things," Izzie said. "I know you have a mess to clean up from tonight."

"The dishes?"

"Don't be funny."

"I'm not. I just don't want to talk about it."

"But you have no choice. I'm here, so we're going to talk."

"It's simple, really. I've lied to my daughter since the day she was born. And I never told Donovan that he has a daughter. I think that covers it."

Izzie hung her head back and looked up at the ceiling. Either she was frustrated with Hope or she was conferring with someone up there.

Her silence propelled Hope to continue. "As you said, I messed up tonight."

"That's not what I said. I said you have a mess to clean up. I think it was a good start being grateful that Ella was safe."

"That was private," Hope complained irrationally, especially since this was just a dream.

"It's going to take some time, but I'm certain things are going to work out."

"How can you be sure?" Hope asked.

Izzie gave her a look that said she had to have the patience of Job when it came to dealing with her older sister. She sighed heavily. "I told you, Hope; I know things."

Chapter 9

FOR EIGHT DAYS straight, Hope woke up feeling hungover. It always took a minute to remember why her heart was heavy and why her emotions were spent. Ella was giving her the silent treatment—the teenage version of a toddler holding her breath. But at least she was home. Hope would just have to wait it out.

Then there was Donovan. Hope hadn't seen him since the incident at the lodge. *Incident* was a polite way of putting it; *train wreck* was more accurate. But Hope had seen Rick, as he'd been in the Hungry Bear often, mostly to pick up Sparkle, or to return her. But no Donovan. Hope wanted to inquire after him, but she held strong. She was, after all, born and raised Alaskan. Tough. Able to withstand anything. But not seeing Donovan was unbearable and felt like some painful déjà vu.

She crawled out of bed and headed for the shower. As she passed Ella's room, she couldn't miss the new sign posted on her door—*Keep Out*.

Hope gave it a sad smile. Today's silver lining . . . at least her daughter was communicating again.

In the shower, Hope stood under the hot water until the

tank nearly ran out. She felt guilty for that, too. Wasting hot water wasn't a luxury she could afford.

She quickly dressed, wrote a list for Ella of things she'd like done around the house—though it might be in vain—and then hurried to the Hungry Bear to open up. Before she had even unlocked the door, trucks started pulling up. People who worked on Saturdays wanted to pick something up for lunch. An hour later, Piney came downstairs.

She had been acting strange all week and this morning wasn't any different. She'd looked worried—and Piney never looked worried.

Hope checked out the last customer and went to the back. "Is something going on that we need to talk about? Are you unwell?" She'd tried every day to get Piney to talk, but Piney was mum. Which was so out of character for her. But maybe Hope was to blame. A lot of people weren't speaking to her now.

The chime over the door rang.

"Go take care of Miss Lisa up front," Piney said, chewing her lip. "I promise we'll talk. Just not now." Which was more than she'd said all week.

Hope had a sinking feeling that whatever Piney had to say wasn't good, but she hurried to help Miss Lisa pick out the best two bananas in the produce section and to bring a quart of milk to the front for her.

While Hope was handing Miss Lisa her sack of groceries, Rick arrived.

"Sparkle should be down at ten," Hope offered.

"Thanks. How are you this morning?" Rick had been asking this same question with the same concern each time he came in. He certainly hadn't forgotten the dramatic reveal at the lodge.

"I'm okay," Hope said, trying to deflect him with a perky employee-of-the-month act. "Can I help you find anything while you wait for Sparkle?

"Actually, I need to speak with Piney about hanging

something on the bulletin board." He held up a sheet of paper. "For Donovan," Rick clarified.

Hope didn't even try to look at what he had in his hand. She couldn't care less. Donovan coming back to town had upended her family, and neither he nor his poster deserved her notice. If she had been sleeping a little better, and if her daughter were speaking to her, Hope might feel more generous toward Donovan. But none of these things were the case.

"Piney's in the back."

"Thanks," Rick said, before walking down the aisle.

A few minutes later, he reappeared with a frown on his face and headed for the bulletin board.

"I have pushpins at the register, if you need them."

He nodded silently and hung up the piece of paper. Then he turned back to Hope, looking utterly miserable, nothing like the ultra-positive Rick.

"Can I help with anything else?" Hope asked.

Rick looked around first, as if to make sure they were alone. "How about some advice?"

"That depends," Hope said guardedly, in case Rick wanted to talk about Donovan.

"Piney seems to hate me. How do I get on her good side?"

Suddenly it all snapped into place—why Piney had been acting weird all week, and what she probably wanted to talk about. She was worried about Rick's intentions toward Sparkle. Which made perfect sense. After all, rumor had it that Piney had fallen for a good-looking, sweet-talking oil worker who didn't stick around . . . Sparkle's dad. Though she didn't normally show it, Piney must have had some pretty hard feelings about him taking off the moment Piney told him she was pregnant. But Hope couldn't tell Rick any of that. It wasn't her place. "There's only one thing you can do. Be a good man and don't mess with Sparkle's emotions."

"I'm not messing with Sparkle. I really *like* her," Rick said. "It's strange. The second I saw her, I knew I wanted to be near her."

Just the way Hope felt when Donovan had moved in next door.

"Love at first sight," she murmured.

Rick smiled eagerly, as if to say, *You get it.*

Hope wanted to quash that smile, tell him that love at first sight was bogus. That she was living proof of that.

"Piney seemed to dislike me from the get-go," said Rick. "I don't understand it. I've been polite, respectful. I'm a nice guy. Ask anyone." He didn't say Donovan's name, but he didn't have to. "Tell me what I gotta do."

"Don't keep Sparkle out all night, would be a great place to start!" Piney huffed, startling them both. "Sparkle is still healing from surgery. Did you know it takes twelve to eighteen months to mend internally after being cut open?"

Rick had it right. Piney didn't like him.

"Two o'clock in the morning," Piney muttered.

"Sorry, Ms. Douglas. It won't happen again." Rick looked genuinely contrite. "I was going to take her to a play tonight in Anchorage . . . *The Little Mermaid.* But I'll cancel."

Piney rolled her eyes. "Fine. Take her to the play. Sparkle doesn't get a chance to do many things like that. Get her a hotel room *of her own.* And have her go there *alone* at a decent hour."

Hope didn't think Piney could have much control over the hotel situation. But then she kept talking.

"I'm only going to say this once. If you get my daughter pregnant, I promise you that you'll regret it. I'll make sure your nuggets are hanging above the door next to the chimes. Am I making myself clear?" Piney never made threats, but Hope believed her now.

Rick's expression said he believed her, too. "Yes, ma'am." He paused for a second. "I really like your daughter." He looked as if he were going to say more but stopped.

Piney stared at him for a long moment. Then she scoffed, "We'll see."

Hope intervened. "Rick? Can I get you a cup of coffee and maybe a cookie to go with it?"

He smiled at her gratefully. "That would be nice. Thanks."

She led the way to the diner and poured him a mugful. "Hang in there," she told him before she headed back to the grocery side.

When Sparkle came down the stairs, Rick stood up. But Piney intercepted her at the bottom of the steps.

"You're going to take the day off. Rick is here to take you to Anchorage."

Sparkle smiled at Rick over Piney's head.

"You have to promise me that you'll get plenty of rest."

Sparkle hugged Piney. "I will."

Suddenly Piney spun around to address Hope. "We're going to have our chat now," she said.

"O-okay."

Piney glanced over at Rick and Sparkle in the dining area but lowered her voice to be doubly sure they wouldn't be overheard. "Hope, I hate to do this to you, but I have no choice. Sparkle's medical bills are piling up. I'm just not sure what I can do about them." She paused, looking pained. "I'm so sorry, but I'm going to have to let you go."

"What?" Hope had worked at the Hungry Bear for seventeen years, even through the decline of Sweet Home. "What am I going to do for a job?"

Piney reached over to the bulletin board, pulled down a sheet of paper, and handed it to Hope. "Your answer is right here."

Hope looked down at the advertisement—Home Sweet Home Lodge was looking for a housekeeper. The hourly wage was higher than Hope was making now, but there was no relief in what she was staring at. There was no gratitude. "I can't do that."

"You don't have a choice, buttercup," Piney said firmly. "When God shuts a door, He opens a window. In this case, the window leads to the lodge."

"And begging Donovan for a job?" The paper crumpled as she shoved it back at Piney. "No, thanks." There had to be some other way out of this predicament.

"What did I tell you years ago?" Piney said. "You've got to pull your big-girl pants up and do what has to be done."

"That's all I ever do," Hope complained. It had been one bad break after another . . . the accident, Izzie and Beau dying, getting thrown out of the house, Mom and Dad's divorce, the constant worry about money, Ella's drinking. And now, Hope was out of a job.

Piney looked at her with pity in her eyes. "Do you want me to talk to Donovan for you?"

Hope crossed her arms over her chest. "Absolutely not." Why couldn't her life be like a romantic comedy—like *Sparkle's*—where some rich guy stumbled over her doorstep and they ended up happily-ever-after, with three kids and a dog? Nope, Hope's life was more like a Greek tragedy.

Piney smoothed the paper, laid it out on the counter, and pulled out her phone. "I'll dial him for you."

"No!" Hope reached for the phone, but Piney slipped behind the counter.

"Hello, Donovan. This is Piney." She smiled over at her, as if Hope hadn't hit an all-time low.

And then Piney did the most awful thing. "Hold on," she said. "Hope wants to speak to you."

Hope stepped back, but the magazine rack stopped her and Piney caught up. Hope fumbled with the phone and thought about hanging up . . . accidentally-on-purpose. But she had no choice, did she? She had to take care of her daughter. They had to survive. She shoved her pride down, one more time. She was pretty good at it by now.

"I see you need a housekeeper." No hello, no greeting at all. She wasn't in a hi-how-are-you kind of mood.

The silence on the other end went on for so long, Hope began to wonder if Piney was just pulling a prank on her. She held the phone away from her ear. "So, all this is some kind of joke?" she said to Piney.

"Hope?" came Donovan's deep voice.

Hope rolled her eyes, put the phone to her ear, then turned her back on Piney, as if to have a private conversation.

"What?" She wasn't feeling very pleasant and was sure her tone conveyed it.

"I hesitated because I need someone full time at the lodge. As much as I'd like to give Ella a job, I need more than someone after school and on weekends."

This was pure torture. Her pride went down in one large lump and she wasn't sure she was going to be able to speak. But she did. "Not Ella. Me."

"Don't you already have a job?" Donovan asked.

Hope looked over her shoulder and glared at the woman who'd been a surrogate mother to her for the last seventeen years.

"Nope. Not since ten seconds ago. Piney fired me," Hope said.

"Laid off," Piney shouted so Donovan might hear.

"Po-tay-to, po-tah-to." Hope was still out of a job and would have to grovel to Donovan to get a new one. Everyone knew there were no jobs available in Sweet Home, the reason the place was pretty much a ghost town.

A thought hit Hope. *Izzie was right.* Maybe this wouldn't have happened if only she'd been grateful for all her blessings last night . . . like having a job. And not having to beg Donovan for a chance to be his housekeeper!

"Well?" Hope said. "Can I at least interview for it?"

"Hope," Donovan said on a frustrated sigh, "I don't want to hire you to clean up after me and the guests who stay here. It's beneath you."

Oh, that got her riled. "Nothing is beneath me! I think you've forgotten that here in Alaska, we have to suck it up and do what has to be done." She had an idea. "And just so you'll feel better, how about you give me the job, and I promise *not* to clean up after *you*. You'll have to pick up your own clothes off the floor until you leave. Do we have a deal?" It felt like she'd stuck out her hand for him to shake.

"Sure," he finally said, not sounding at all happy about the arrangement. "When can you start?"

Hope hesitated. Was she really doing this? Apparently she

was. Piney was gathering up Hope's coat and holding it out to her.

"Hope? Are you there?" Donovan said.

"I guess I can start right now."

DONOVAN HUNG UP and looked around the lodge, then down at his feet. Boomer was tugging on his shoelace. He reached down and picked up the furball. "Wow. I didn't see that coming. What a strange turn of events, buddy."

He wished Rick hadn't gone into town. It would be nice to have him as a buffer when Hope got here. Or for Donovan to have someone to talk to until Hope arrived. He didn't know what he was going to say to her, even after eight long days of dwelling on little else.

For the past few days, he'd spied on Ella—*his daughter.* He still wasn't used to the word. He'd found out when school started and ended and had sat outside Sweet Home High . . . to see evidence that she belonged to him.

But there was no denying it. The second Hope confirmed it, Donovan knew in his gut that Ella was his. She had super blue eyes, just like him, Dad, and Beau. Her hair was dark blond, just like his, too, not dark brown like Hope's.

He took Boomer into the kitchen and sat him down in front of his water dish.

"Maybe I should just give her all the cash in my wallet when she gets here and send her on her way. We have too much history between us for her to work for me."

But another thought hit him. Working at the lodge would serve her right for what she'd done to his family. But then Donovan remembered his promise to Beau, how he would forgive Hope. He could almost hear the universe laughing. *Good luck with that!*

Donovan frowned at the list he'd started of things to be done around the house and cabins.

"But she'd said she wouldn't pick up after me."

Boomer looked up at him.

"Yeah. I don't blame her either."

He needed to find a way to deal with her being here. "Maybe I'll start her working on Wandering Moose Cabin. The farthest one from the lodge."

Boomer whimpered and Donovan picked him up. "You know, if you didn't need so much attention, maybe I wouldn't need help at all."

Boomer licked Donovan's hand and Donovan lovingly scratched his dog behind the ears. "You're a lot of trouble, but I'm glad you're here. You're a good listener."

There was a knock at the door. Donovan trudged toward it, surprised Hope had gotten here so quickly.

He opened the door. *Courtney!* He looked past her but didn't see Hope's car on the road leading up to the lodge. He should get rid of Courtney quickly. He had a feeling it wouldn't be a good idea to have her here when Hope arrived.

But then, he thought, *Why should I care?*

"Hey, Courtney, what's going on?" he said.

She smiled brightly. "I was in the neighborhood and thought I'd stop by." She hefted a rather large purse and leaned in, as if she were ready to walk over the threshold. "I have some things to show you."

"Sure. Why not?" *Why not* pulled in behind Courtney's red Volvo.

Courtney turned around and squinted. "Is that Hope Mc-Knight?"

"Yes." He didn't have to explain to either woman why the other was here. Heck, he didn't even know why Courtney was here.

He held the door wide and Courtney glided in. He didn't wait for Hope to come to the door, but left it open a crack.

Courtney had made her way into the dining room and was spreading tile samples out on the table. She looked over her shoulder at him. "When I was in Fairbanks, I picked these up for you." She smiled as if she'd done him a favor. "I thought we could get started on the floor right away."

Hadn't he covered this with her already? He didn't want her help decorating.

Before he could answer, the front door creaked open and Hope stood there, frowning at the sight of him leaning over Courtney's shoulder.

Hope had no smile for him. Nor was she dressed to the nines like Courtney in a winter-white coat and a blood-red dress underneath. Hope had on jeans, a secondhand-looking brown parka, and of course, her wary stare.

"Hey, Hope," Courtney said brightly. "What brings you out to the lodge?"

Hope's lips formed into a straight line as her eyes flashed murder at him. Finally, she spoke. "I'm the new house-keeper."

He had to give her points for owning it. "Why don't you start on Monday?" Donovan wasn't completely insensitive.

"I'm already here."

"What about the Hungry Bear?" Courtney said. "Are you just working here at the lodge for extra cash?"

Hope grunted noncommittally and then said to Donovan, "Where am I starting? Do you have a list of what you want me to do?"

Donovan ignored the list on the counter. "Give me a minute, Courtney. I want to get Hope started and then I'll be right back."

He left both women standing in their corners—so to speak—as he rushed to the utility closet and pulled out all the cleaning supplies he'd bought, including a bucket and a wet-dry mop.

As he walked back toward Hope, he felt sorry for her. She was acting brave and stoic, but it had to be humiliating to have Courtney witness her relative downfall.

He handed Hope the wet-dry mop. "You're going to start in Wandering Moose Cabin." He slipped out of his moccasins and started pulling on his boots.

Without waiting, Hope turned for the door.

"See you later, Hope," Courtney said cheerfully. She had

a lot more to be cheerful about than Hope. Courtney wasn't going to have to pull down cobwebs, mop floors, and swab toilets.

Hope just gave a wave as she walked out the door.

When Donovan caught up to her he said, "I didn't know Courtney was coming by." He didn't owe Hope an explanation, yet he kept going. "She just showed up out of the blue."

"Sure." Hope didn't say it sarcastically, but he wouldn't blame her if she had. It seemed too coincidental for Courtney to be there, even to him.

"She brought tile for me to look at," he added.

"Oh, then you did find an interior decorator. Good for you." She patted him on the arm, this time being sardonic.

"No." He rolled his eyes, trying not to let it register that Hope had touched him. Through his coat, he could still feel the weight of her hand. "Courtney's okay, but she's the last person I'd want to decorate the lodge."

When was the last time Hope had touched him? He pushed the thought from his mind. Shoved it hard . . . like thinking about Hope's touch could be contagious.

They'd made it to Wandering Moose Cabin. The tiny porch was rotted, more so than the back porch of the lodge. "Be careful." And to make sure, he took Hope's elbow to keep her from falling through the steps.

She looked up at him, clearly insulted. "I'm not an invalid."

"I know. I'm just not sure what the insurance covers." Which was something he'd better find out.

He pried open the scratched and broken door, then went in first in case something was waiting for them. "Well, here it is."

The place was in utter disarray. The beds were tossed and the table toppled as if Papa Bear had been there, something he'd have to ask Mr. Brewster about. Everything was coated in dust, a broken window let in the cold October weather, and there was a hole in the floor where animals had certainly crawled through. The bear probably scared them away. This was too much for Hope to handle on her own, something he should've bothered to check sooner. The structure seemed sound, but the place needed a lot of work. He would have to hire a professional to put the cabin back to rights.

"Here." She took the bucket from him. "You have a guest. I'll be fine on my own."

Donovan, not in a hurry to get back to Courtney, pushed open the bathroom door, thinking he could stall a bit longer. He jumped as a squirrel scampered through another broken pane. He slammed the door shut. "Don't worry about the bathroom right now. I'll have to get that window fixed first." He'd ask Rick to pick up panes at the hardware store while he was in Anchorage. Back in the day, Donovan would've had to travel no farther than Sweet Home to get a window-pane from A Stone's Throw Hardware & Haberdashery. But that was the past.

"What happened in there?" Hope asked.

"A bear might've broken it," he mumbled, not wanting to admit that a squirrel had frightened him. But mentioning the bear reminded him. "You will be careful while you're here, won't you?"

"A few rotten boards don't frighten me," she said.

"I'm talking about the wildlife," he clarified.

"You really have been away too long. You've forgotten that Alaskans deal with wildlife on a daily basis, especially us out in the bush."

"Maybe." Or perhaps he'd worked hard over the years to block out his life in Alaska. If he was being fair, the past hadn't been all bad.

"What do you want to do about the beds?" Hope said. "I assume you'll be getting new mattresses."

"Yes. A complete overhaul. The beds have seen better days."

Hope had rescued a dirty quilt from the floor and was folding it. "I'll drag the mattresses to the end of the road and clean up in here." Before he could comment, she was pulling the corner of one of the full-size mattresses.

"Here, let me help." He grabbed another corner and they tugged it from the frame out to the porch. "I'll get it to the end of the road later."

He followed her back inside and saw that on the floor, underneath the bed frame, was a Hot Wheels car.

Hope picked it up. "One of Beau's?" She handed it to Donovan.

"Yeah." Donovan's chest squeezed uncomfortably as he gazed down at the Trans Am. "When we were little, Beau hid cars all over the lodge and cabins, thinking if we ever got snowed in, he'd never be bored."

"He loved cars and had a great imagination."

"Yes," Donovan said. "So full of life." And like that, the spell of happy memories was broken. "I better get back."

"Sure. I'll be here." Hope kept her eyes down, not meeting his.

Donovan picked up the mattress and carried it back to the lodge. He didn't want to deal with Courtney right now. But he went inside anyway. She was still at the dining table, but sitting down now with her knees crossed. She had legs that went on forever. But he wasn't a leg man.

"Listen," Donovan said. "Something's come up."

Courtney looked disappointed, as if she had drawn some conclusions.

"I need to head out," Donovan clarified.

"Should I take the tile with me?" she asked all doe-eyed.

"No. Leave them. I'll take a look later." But he already knew he would never swap the hardwood floors for tile.

"You have my number. Give me a call later?" Courtney said with her eyebrows raised.

He didn't respond but looked around searchingly. "Where's Boomer?"

"Oh, he was whining, so I let him out," Courtney said.

"What? Alone?" What had she been thinking? Boomer was helpless and a perfect-sized snack for a wandering bear.

"I set him out front. Didn't you see him when you came in?" She was acting like it was Donovan's fault.

He hurried out front. "Boomer! Boomer!"

Hope ran out of Wandering Moose Cabin. "What's going on?"

"Courtney let Boomer out on his own," he hollered back. "Help me find him."

But she was already coming his direction, looking between the other two cabins as she ran.

He noticed that Courtney had come out on the porch, but she just stood there. She wouldn't be any help anyway in her heels.

Hope caught up to him. "Have you looked around back?"

The river! If Boomer fell in and got trapped under the ice . . .

Hope squeezed his arm. "We'll find him."

They both ran behind the lodge. He didn't see Boomer. He hurried to the water's edge and looked at the ice on top and the river current roiling beneath.

But Hope was no longer at his side. Her legs were sticking out from under the shortest part of the deck. She was on her belly.

"What are you doing?" he said, hurrying over to her.

"Shh," she said. "I thought I heard something." She scooted farther under.

He heard it, too. There was a faint whimpering.

"I've got him," Hope said. Then there was a pause. "I can't move with my arms full. Donovan, you're going to have to pull me out by my legs to get me and Boomer out of here."

"Hold on." He latched onto her ankles and gently tugged. He could hear her making cooing noises to Boomer to calm him down until he finally pulled the two of them to freedom.

She rolled to her side and lifted Boomer up. "Go to Daddy."

Donovan took Boomer and held him tight. "You scared me, little buddy. But I'm glad you hid under there, where you were safe."

That was when Donovan realized Hope wasn't wearing her coat! Her sweatshirt and jeans were covered in leaves, dirt, and snow, and her face was smudged as if she'd rolled around under there on purpose. But she was grinning at him, and the sight of her was the best thing he'd seen in years. He couldn't help himself; he hugged her, the puppy between them. Then he did the stupidest thing. He kissed her. Just a thank-you kiss. But instantly it felt like so much more.

Familiar. Like sunshine. Or hot cocoa on a cold day. But most of all, goodness.

Kissing Hope felt more right than any other kiss he'd had in seventeen years. But Hope had killed Beau, tilted Donovan's world out of place to the point he hadn't recognized it. How could kissing her now make his world click back into place? Wonderful memories . . . and pain. The good mixing with the bad.

It was wrong on so many levels to kiss Hope now. Beau's laughter was gone. His grandmother's loving smile, too. Donovan awkwardly pulled away. Hope touched her lips, looking uncomfortable.

He focused on the one thing that would save him from this moment: *Boomer is okay!*

"Thanks for saving him." He rubbed Boomer's head, avoiding her eyes. "I've really gotten attached to the little runt."

"You always did love Berners." She shivered.

Donovan put his hand to her back. "Go. Get inside and get warmed up by the fire."

She must've been freezing because she hurried away. When they came around the corner, Courtney was almost to her car with her designer purse looped over her arm. She halted. "Hope, good lands, what happened to you?"

"She rescued Boomer from under the back deck," Donovan said proudly.

Courtney looked repulsed. "You're a mess."

Donovan didn't care what Hope looked like. He couldn't help himself; he picked a leaf out of her hair. "Get inside, Hope."

He turned back to Courtney. "I'll talk to you later."

He didn't wait to see if she had more to say, but instead followed Hope into the lodge.

Those few steps gave him a short moment to reflect, but it wasn't enough time. He didn't know why he'd kissed Hope. Surely it was a knee-jerk reaction. He should've stepped away after the hug.

But Hope had found Boomer! And he'd lost so much . . . *just like her* . . . which was something he'd never thought of before.

Chapter 10

HOPE STOPPED JUST inside the doorway and spoke to Donovan without turning around. Without gazing at his face.

"Look, just give me a moment to warm up. Then I'll get back to work on Wandering Moose Cabin."

She still couldn't believe he'd hugged her. *Kissed her!* Of course, it was for no other reason than she found Boomer. But apparently, her pounding heart believed what it wanted to believe and hadn't gotten the memo that Donovan didn't want her anymore.

It had been so long since she'd been in a man's arms. *This man.* The only one she'd ever loved, the reason her heart was doing triple time now. Her body remembered Donovan and had wanted to mold herself around him. But Donovan wasn't hers anymore.

"Go back outside and catch Courtney." Hope picked up Boomer as the puppy was trotting for the kitchen. She needed someone to calm her down, and Boomer would do. "I know you two have business to take care of. I'll be out of here in a second."

She started to walk toward the hearth, which was putting off plenty of BTUs. But she was stopped when Donovan laid both of his hands on her shoulders and spun her around.

He bent his knees so he could look into her eyes. Was he trying to slay her right here? It certainly felt like it.

"Warm up, then take the rest of the day off," he insisted.

She shook her head, kind of mesmerized.

"Full pay, of course," Donovan said. "You deserve it for what you just did."

He let go of her and removed Boomer from her arms. "Boomer probably needs a big gulp of water after the harrowing experience he just went through." Donovan rubbed his face into Boomer's neck. "Poor little guy. But you're safe now. Thanks to Hope." Then he set the puppy on his feet.

She couldn't stop staring at Donovan. In this moment, he was the boy from her past who loved Bernese Mountain Dogs. The boy she'd sworn to love for all eternity.

Donovan pointed to the hearth. "Go. Get warm."

She scurried to the hearth, putting her hands out to soak in the heat roiling off the fire.

"Marshmallows or no marshmallows?" Donovan called from the kitchen. Apparently, he'd forgotten how she liked her hot cocoa.

"Marshmallows, please," she said.

But she felt jumpy and knew she couldn't stay near him any longer. The hug—oh my gosh, the kiss—had been more than enough *sugar* for one day! She hurried to the kitchen. "You know what, forget the cocoa. I'm fine now. I'm heading back to the cabin."

Donovan was there instantly, shrugging out of his own coat. "You're still as stubborn as ever. At least take my coat," he said, holding it out to her.

She pushed it back. "I can't. I'm filthy. It's only a short jog to the cabin. I'll be fine."

Just then, the Hot Wheels car tumbled from his pocket, making them both go still. Making them both remember that Hope was the one who'd ended Beau's life. At least that was how Hope saw it.

She slipped past Donovan to the other side of the living

room, to the door. He didn't say another word to stop her. As far as she knew, he might still be staring at Beau's car.

As Hope ran to Wandering Moose Cabin, she brushed off her arms and chest as best she could. She probably should've taken Donovan's coat, because she was going to be dirtying up her own coat pretty badly. And it was the only coat she owned. Donovan probably had a closetful.

Back inside the cabin, she was thankful it was semi-warm, thanks to the baseboard heaters. She took off her sweatshirt and shook it outside, wearing just her thermal top. Then she grabbed the broom and vigorously swept the floor, counting on the exertion to warm her up. She had just begun to whisk the dirt into the corner when she heard a car leaving. She pulled back the dusty curtains, which nearly disintegrated in her hand, and saw Donovan's SUV pulling away from the lodge. For some stupid reason, it made her feel lonely. She thought about running back to the lodge to get Boomer, but knowing Donovan, he'd taken his dog with him.

Unfortunately, being alone made her mind wander to places it shouldn't. Even though she tried to put Donovan behind a *Do Not Disturb* door, she couldn't stop from peeking in, thinking about all she'd lost because of one awful moment long ago.

By noon, Wandering Moose Cabin was still a wreck but cleared of debris. Hope headed home for lunch, something she never had to worry about when she was working at the Hungry Bear. Now, she'd have to remember to pack a lunch every day. Just another reason it sucked that she was stuck working for Donovan Stone.

Once at home, she took a quick shower to get the rest of the dirt and leaves out of her hair. She blow-dried it quickly, dressed in a clean sweater, and then had the last spoonful of leftover soup and a few crackers she found in an open baggie at the back of the pantry. On the way home from Donovan's today, she'd have to run by the Hungry Bear and get her unpaid wages to buy some groceries. She wished she'd thought to ask Donovan how often she would be paid. Something a smart single mother would've done before she'd accepted the job.

Because there was still time left, she dug around in her fabric stash, which was tucked away in her closet, looking for something to replace the old curtains in Wandering Moose Cabin. She noticed something wedged between the box and the back wall, and was shocked when she pulled out the moose print fabric she hadn't seen in years. She'd bought it to make pajama bottoms for Izzie for Christmas, but she'd procrastinated too long. She'd decided she'd give Izzie the pj's for her upcoming birthday. But there had been no more birthdays for her sister. She remembered now that when she moved she'd tucked the fabric in the back of the closet so it wouldn't be a reminder of the moose that had snatched Izzie's years away from her.

Hope had a feeling that if she didn't do something constructive with the fabric now, Izzie would nag her in her dreams tonight. Her sister would play the dead card and say that Hope shouldn't bury the fabric . . . especially since she knew what it felt like to be buried. It wouldn't be the first time Izzie had gone there. To avoid her sister's chastisement, Hope spread out the fabric and measured. "Just enough to make the curtains and maybe a small throw pillow, too." Donovan's interior designer was probably going to hate it, but Hope decided to take the fabric back to the lodge to show him, assuming he had returned by the time she got there.

When she pulled into Home Sweet Home Lodge, Donovan's car was there, alongside Rick's. Rick had probably come back to pack a bag. If it had been any other two people, she'd have been sure they were yucking it up at her expense. *Hope McKnight the housekeeper.* She knew they weren't mean like that, but Hope felt humiliated anyway.

She grabbed the moose fabric from the back seat and went to the lodge's front door and knocked.

The door opened, and she smelled . . . was that pizza?

"Hey." Donovan seemed in a better state of mind than when he'd left her earlier.

"A couple of questions," she said. "First, what is it you want me to do this afternoon?" Hope couldn't stop her mouth from watering at the scent of garlic.

"Come in."

"In a second, I will." She wanted to ask this next question in private. "Your flyer listed the hourly rate, but it didn't say when or how often payday was." She tried to sound casual. Tried not to sound desperate.

"I don't know. What do you think?"

Daily! "Weekly would be fine," she said.

"I'll tell you what. Speak to Rick about whatever works for you. He likes to feel needed." This last part Donovan said loudly over his shoulder.

He clearly had no idea how embarrassing all of this was for Hope.

"Don't look like that," Donovan said. "It's Rick's job. For the life of me, I don't know why he gets a kick out of W-9s and such."

"Okay."

Donovan stood back and Hope stepped inside.

Rick came out of the kitchen carrying a pizza stone and set it on the dining room table. "Hope, join Donovan for lunch. I'm leaving in a moment and our boy here hates to eat alone. Especially since he went to all the trouble to make this marvelous pizza."

She couldn't stop herself from angling to the side to get a better look. It really was a masterpiece: sausage, pepperoni, and black olives piled high with oozing strips of mozzarella layered on top, and spinach leaves perched around the circumference of the pan. The man should open a pizza parlor in Sweet Home.

"There's plenty," Donovan offered.

Hope stopped staring at the pizza and held up the moose fabric, trying to ignore her stomach's rumblings. "I brought fabric from home for Wandering Moose Cabin. That is, if you want it. I don't know if you noticed, but the curtains have outlived their usefulness. I can make the curtains tonight and bring them back tomorrow. With your approval, of course."

Rick beamed. "See! What did I tell you? Hope is our girl!"

Hope wanted to say she hadn't been anyone's girl in a long, long time.

Donovan touched the fabric. He was probably thinking of the accident, too, and gave her a sad sort of smile. "I think it would be great. You don't mind using your own fabric for the curtains?"

"Not at all."

"You can't make them on your own time, though," Donovan decreed. "I bet one of the sewing machines in Nan's studio still works. If not, run home and bring your sewing machine back here. You sew on *my* time."

Donovan fingered the fabric. "I really love the idea of decorating each cabin according to its name. Do you have any more of the moose fabric, enough for a quilt?"

She shook her head.

Rick was standing at the table, cutting up the pizza. "Don, you should take Hope to Anchorage or Fairbanks to pick out fabric. Get the lodge fixed up right."

"No," Hope said. She couldn't believe Rick had put Donovan in that situation. He wouldn't want to take her anywhere. "Really, I don't mind making the curtains at home tonight with what I have."

"If it's for the lodge, you do it here during working hours," Donovan said firmly.

"Well, I'm outta here," said Rick as he put two pieces of pizza on a paper plate and laid foil over the top. "My lady is waiting."

"Bye," said Hope. "Have a good time."

"Text when you get there," Donovan added.

"Will do." Rick picked up the duffel bag at the door with his free hand. "Hope, we'll get all your paperwork squared away when I get back." With that he was gone, leaving Hope and Donovan alone.

• • •

"WE NEED TO talk." With Rick gone, Donovan felt awkward, but there were things he and Hope needed to discuss. Not about the lodge, but more important things.

He took the moose fabric from her and set it on the arm of the couch.

"Talk about what?" Hope seemed as cautious as a mother deer.

"Come get a plate. And tell me what you'd like to drink," Donovan said.

"Water." Hope followed him into the kitchen.

He pulled two of his grandmother's stoneware plates from the cabinet, handing them to her, and then poured two glasses of filtered water for them.

In the dining room, he took his seat, deciding to start the conversation with something benign. "I know you said that you wouldn't clean up after me, but I was wondering if you could fix up Nan's studio this afternoon, since you refused to take the rest of the day off. Or at least start on it?"

"You're the boss," she muttered.

Donovan nodded to the food. "Dig in. I can't eat it all myself." Which wasn't true. Cold pizza for breakfast was one of his favorites. He took two slices and set them on his plate. "While you're cleaning up the studio, can you make a list of things that might spruce up the space?"

She stared him down. "I doubt the new owners will want to have a large sewing room."

True. "Well, I'd like to make the studio into something that Nan would be proud of." Ugh, he was being sentimental. "Courtney has some ideas about what to turn the space into."

Hope didn't look happy about the prospect of involving Courtney. The truth was that he didn't want Courtney involved either.

"Eat up," Donovan said, before he took his first bite.

Hope covered her unhappiness by taking a piece of pizza.

He wanted her to take a few bites before he delved into the other reason he needed to talk to her.

They both ate in silence. He wished Rick had started some music before he left. The air was heavy with unsaid words. Disjointed thoughts weighed heavy on his mind. But he chose to focus on the tangible. Boomer was lying by the fire. The sky clouded up outside. And the grandfather clock had just chimed two.

Donovan looked down at the envelope that Rick had left on the table. When Hope had nearly finished her slice of pizza, Donovan picked up the envelope and set it beside her.

"I know this won't make up for not being in Ella's life," he said, "but here's a check for back child support. Rick did some research and came up with a fair number."

Hope looked horrified . . . and speechless. Finally, she said, "I don't want your money!" and pushed the envelope back to him. "I just need the job here. Until I can find another one."

"Take the money, Hope. It's for Ella, anyway, not for you."

"No. And don't even think about trying to give it to Ella. I've raised her to take care of herself. You flashing a bunch of cash in front of my daughter will only confuse her."

Yeah, he didn't like how Hope kept saying *my daughter*. He'd have to make her see reason. "What about incidentals for Ella? A little walking-around money?" As Nan used to call it. He had to do something. He just couldn't sit around while his daughter lived in poverty. "What about clothes? A car?"

"No! Ella doesn't need a car." Hope looked infuriated. After a minute she sighed and said, "Okay, I will accept child support going forward. You could pay for her phone and her school clothes."

"I will absolutely take care of those. What about groceries?" he asked.

"We're *fine*."

He could tell he'd better back off.

"I just want to be clear, I'm talking about going forward," she said. "No back support. I mean it. What's done is done."

The way she said it made him think that was her mantra.

Well, he'd give in now, but maybe he could provide support for her and Ella without Hope knowing. "What about a college fund?" he asked. "Does Ella have one?"

Hope sighed heavily. "There's no fund."

"Does Ella want to go to college?"

"I would love her to go."

He could almost hear what Hope didn't say: *I would love for Ella to have the college experience that I never had.*

"Would you let me set up a college fund? I'll make sure it's fully funded—books, tuition, room, and board." He wanted to invest in Ella's future because he hadn't been part of her past.

Hope shook her head and looked up as if she were complaining to the ceiling.

"What's wrong?" he asked.

"Ella's *my* responsibility!"

"It took both of us to make her."

"Yeah, except . . ." She sighed. "I can't lie, you helping with college takes a huge load off my shoulders." But she didn't look happy about it.

"Then what?"

"I don't take charity."

"It's not charity, Hope. She's my daughter, too." To him, his voice sounded like stone. He hoped Hope heard it, that he wasn't budging.

"Fine. Help with college, then." She still seemed conflicted, but he didn't care. If nothing else, his money would buy Ella a future.

Hope looked as if her brain were spinning. "But let's not say anything to Ella yet."

"Why?" Was Hope trying to keep him and Ella apart? "While I'm here, I want to get to know my daughter." And after he left, he would make sure that he came back often to see her. And she could come to Florida and visit him and her grandfather, too. "What's your reasoning behind not letting Ella know that I'm going to be part of her life going forward?"

She rolled her eyes. "Good grief, Donovan, it's not personal. Ella is trying to come to grips with having a *living* father. I want to be the one to talk to her about college and everything." Her frown deepened. "And she's not necessarily speaking to me at the moment," Hope said, almost to herself.

"Can I do anything to help?" Donovan asked.

Hope scooted back her chair. "No. All I wanted was my assignment for this afternoon and you've given it to me."

HOPE SNATCHED THE moose fabric from the couch and headed down the hall to Elsie's sewing studio, feeling even more humiliated than she had this morning, when she'd been forced to take this job. How was that even possible?

Donovan and his damn envelope had caught her off guard. And then on the opposite end of the spectrum, she was still reeling from the kiss this morning. She swore her lips were still tingling.

Someone was following her down the hall. Girding herself, she spun around, but it was only Boomer. She scooped him up and held him close. "I'm glad you're here, cutie. Your owner is driving me crazy!"

She walked into the studio and scanned the room, which she hadn't seen since she brought in the firewood. A new wave of nostalgia hit her. It was as if the Sisterhood of the Quilt had just stepped out to have a bite to eat at the dining room table and would be right back to their cutting and sewing. She could almost feel the love—the love they poured into their quilting projects and the love they had for one another. The love seemed to overflow from the studio to the lodge and into Sweet Home itself. The studio made Hope remember everything good, everything right with the world. Now there was just a void, an emptiness that had never been filled, keeping her from feeling whole. She quashed the sadness. Now wasn't the time to feel sorry for herself; now was the time to work.

Hope took a critical eye to everything she saw. The room

was large, bigger than the expansive living room. But instead of bear rugs covering a wood floor, this one had worn linoleum with spent threads everywhere, as if Elsie had been sewing only this morning. Design walls were hung on three sides with pins still stuck in them. Bolts of fabric stood upright on a specialty shelf, and there was fabric stretched across the long island in the center of the room, where irons were evenly spaced along the homemade ironing board.

"The first thing to do is to sweep the floor." Hope set Boomer in the chair in the corner and grabbed a broom. "I'll let you roam as soon as I get these threads up. Otherwise, you'd track them all over the house."

"Are you talking to me?" Donovan said, startling her. He was leaning in the doorway.

"I'm talking to your dog," she said.

"Listen, Hope, I didn't mean to upset you by trying to give you money. Never my intent. I just thought I should—"

"Be the *big man* and point out how I haven't made anything of myself?" she finished for him.

"No. That's not it at all. Ella is entitled to her father's help." He walked farther into the room and picked up a rotary cutter from the cutting mat. He stared directly at the tool but clearly wasn't seeing it. "I hate that I've been a deadbeat dad."

Do not feel sorry for Donovan, she told herself. She forced a roll of her eyes. "Please. You had no idea that Ella existed." What made her want to lay a hand on his arm to soothe the hurt expression on his face? She stayed rooted to the spot, not trusting herself to move closer to him.

He took the broom from her and began sweeping the threads into a pile. She watched for a second—maybe longer than that, actually—then left the room to find the Windex and the paper towels from under the kitchen sink.

When she got back, Donovan was scooping the threads into a dustpan. Hope went to the first window without a word.

They proceeded to work in silence, doing a strange dance

as they straightened and cleaned his grandmother's beloved room. It was almost hypnotic, and for once, the nagging voice inside Hope's head quieted.

At four thirty, she received a text from Ella.

When are you coming home?

Hope looked over at Donovan, who was dusting one of the tabletops, and found that he was staring back.

"Is everything okay?"

"Yes." Hope hated to do this. "Do you mind if I leave now? I'll work extra tomorrow. The text was from Ella."

"Not tomorrow; it's Sunday."

"Right."

"Go on home." He gave a little *scoot* gesture. "Let me know if you come up with ideas for updating this room or any of the other rooms on the property."

"I will." Hope scratched Boomer behind the ears and stepped outside, where she texted Ella that she was on her way. Hope's heart was racing and for a change it had nothing to do with Donovan. *Ella is looking for me!* Maybe Ella had forgiven her.

But Ella only wanted to borrow the car.

"Lacy and I are going to Tyler's house to decorate for his Halloween party."

Hope gestured at the calendar hanging by a nail on the kitchen wall. "It's a little early, isn't it?"

"Geesh, Mom. The party is next weekend. We have a lot of exams next week so we thought we'd get started on it now," Ella said.

"Is there going to be a keg at Tyler's party?" Hope knew this direct question would certainly provoke Ella's anger.

Sure enough, Ella glared. "Can I have the car or not? Lacy's mom has theirs. Apparently, Aberdeen's date tonight isn't able to drive."

Hope didn't ask Ella what that meant but instead handed

her the keys. "Don't have a drop of alcohol or your driving privileges will be revoked. *Forever.*"

Ella rolled her eyes and walked toward the door without a word.

"I want you home before midnight," Hope said. Sober, unharmed, safe.

Ella only grunted before slamming the door behind her.

Hope walked into the living room, feeling defeated. She was too tired to make dinner and wished she'd nabbed some of Donovan's pizza before leaving the lodge. If she'd known why Ella wanted her home, she could've made a pit stop at the Hungry Bear first. They needed milk, canned tuna, and bread, at the very least. She shoved her stocking cap back on her head and headed off for the store on foot. If she hurried, she should make it before it closed. But if not, she still had the key in her coat pocket and she would use it this one last time.

Ten minutes later and a bit winded, Hope got close enough to the store to see Piney locking up for the night. But the weird thing was she was outside the store, instead of in, and holding several bulging Hungry Bear shopping bags.

Hope hurried across the street. "Closing up a few minutes early?"

Startled, Piney spun around. "Oh, it's you. I was just coming to your place."

"To see Bill?" Hope asked. Piney never came to see her, so she must mean Bill.

Piney held up the bags. "A grocery delivery for you."

Oh, heck no. Hope didn't want charity. "You don't need to give me groceries. I came to buy my own."

"They're not from me, buttercup. I got a telephone order to send groceries to your house."

"Who was it?"

"I don't know," Piney said.

"How can you not know? You know everyone in town." But Hope had a sneaking suspicion of who it might be. "Male or female?"

"Um, female." Piney seemed a little rattled.

"How did this woman pay? With a credit card?"

Piney looked downright agitated. "Stop asking so many questions and help me get these bags into Betsy." Betsy was Piney's Volkswagen Beetle. "The milk is heavy."

Hope took the bags from her. They really were stuffed. "What's in here?"

"Milk, bread, meat. Just everyday items," Piney said.

Hope waited while Piney opened the car door. "Oh, fine, but tell Donovan not to do it again." He'd certainly worked fast. He must've called Piney before her car was out of the lodge's driveway.

"No one said it was him," Piney said stubbornly. "I don't know who it was."

Hope put her hand in her pocket and pulled out the key to the Hungry Bear. "Here. I also came to return this. I don't need it anymore."

Piney gaped as if Hope were handing her a beating heart. "K-keep it," the older woman said, fairly choked up. "In case of emergency."

Hope continued to hold it out to her.

Piney clasped Hope's hand, closing her fingers around the key. "You're still my backup, buttercup. What if I have to rush Sparkle to the hospital again?" Piney gave her a sad smile. "What if you have a hankering for mint chocolate chip ice cream in the middle of the night?"

"I won't—" Hope began.

"Keep the key," Piney said firmly.

Piney was family when Hope didn't have any. She couldn't let this one thing with the Hungry Bear ruin their relationship. "Fine." Hope felt like she was doing a lot of giving in tonight.

"That's my girl," Piney cooed. "Now get in Betsy and let me give you and your groceries a lift home."

When they got to Hope's house, Bill came out onto his porch and waved.

Hope said good night and trudged to the house with her

groceries in tow. When she got inside her empty cottage, she wanted nothing more than to collapse on the couch and close her eyes. But she had food to put away.

"I guess I'll have to thank Donovan—right before I tell him to mind his own business," Hope said, as she methodically shoved the food into the fridge.

When she was done, she pulled out her sewing machine to work on the curtains for Wandering Moose Cabin. It was a small act of rebellion, since Donovan wanted her to make the curtains during work hours at the lodge. "This should make up for the groceries he bought me."

As she pressed the fabric, she visualized the cabin on a bright summer's day, the breeze blowing the curtains, making the cabin feel fresh and light. Guests would certainly enjoy the Alaskan flavor of the fabric . . . Her smile faded. The curtains would soon be replaced by his interior decorator. The thought stalled her pressing and she switched off the iron, frowning. She shouldn't be waxing poetic about the lodge. She didn't have a stake in it. Or in Donovan, for that matter. She shouldn't be putting the smallest piece of her heart into the lodge when it was only going to be sold off soon.

She went to the pantry and pulled out the peanut butter and bread. But after fixing a sandwich and sitting in front of the TV to eat, she wasn't in the mood for a sitcom *or* a drama. Her life seemed full of both right now—her daughter's drinking problem, getting laid off from the grocery store, and having her emotions unreasonably wrapped up in Donovan Stone . . . again. Not even Hollywood would pick up a story as outlandish as hers. She ate her sandwich with the wind howling outside the window, and when she was done, she stretched out on the couch to wait up for Ella.

She must've fallen asleep because Izzie cleared her throat. Hope opened her eyes and saw her sitting on the armrest at the end of the couch.

"So, you got fired from the Hungry Bear?" Izzie said gleefully.

"I didn't get fired. I was laid off. There's a difference."

"Either way, you no longer work there," her sister said. "I'm glad. You needed a change of pace."

"Should I say I have a new job or do you already know that?"

Izzie stroked her chin thoughtfully, as if she were an old man smoothing down his beard. "Hmm . . . Donovan as your boss? How's that going?"

Good and bad. But Hope wasn't in the mood to confess that it hadn't been as horrible as she'd expected.

"He's going to pay child support," Hope reported instead.

"That will make him feel better, knowing he's helping Ella. And helping you," Izzie said.

"I'm so confused," Hope admitted. She still loved Donovan. And there was nothing she could do about it. Time and distance hadn't diminished her feelings. Chastising herself hadn't worked either. Every time she banished him from her mind, his image would somehow weasel its way back into her soul and put down roots . . . deeper than before. Should she accept that she would always love him like this, be in this much pain?

"I know you're confused. And conflicted," Izzie said, leaning her head against the cushion while gazing at Hope.

"Having Donovan here has turned everything upside down—" Hope started.

"Mom?"

Hope came awake.

Ella stood in the opened front door, looking at Hope as if she'd lost it. "Who are you talking to?" Ella scanned the room. "Is someone else here?"

Hope sat up. "No," she said honestly as Izzie faded away.

"But you were talking as if . . ." Ella trailed off.

"Come sit here, Ella. I have some things to tell you about myself."

Chapter 11

HOPE PATTED THE couch beside her. "Shut the door and then sit next to me."

Ella froze, looking worried. "Are you sick?"

What could Hope say, that her heart had been broken a long time ago and never healed? "No, honey, I'm not sick. I'm as healthy as ever." Now, her mental health, well, that was a different story.

Ella settled in beside her and Hope wrapped an arm around her shoulder. It felt good to have her daughter relax into her like she had when she was little.

Hope smoothed down Ella's hair. "Sometimes, when I'm stressed, I dream about your Aunt Izzie. I tell her what's going on with me, you, Piney . . . everyone."

"Does she talk back?" Ella asked.

Hope nodded. "Yes." She sighed, thinking about Izzie's sage advice and the sharp words that usually went along with it. "I know I'm dreaming, but it feels so real. I'm sure it's a defense mechanism to help me deal with my day. She helps me sort through what's bothering me, especially if something unexpected happens."

Ella turned her head up and stared into Hope's face. "What happened? What's bothering you now?"

Hope ripped the Band-Aid off. "The Hungry Bear. I no longer work there. Piney laid me off."

Ella pulled away. "She can't do that! You've been there forever. You practically run the place."

"That's an exaggeration, Ella." Though Piney had relied on Hope to take over for her on many occasions. "It wasn't personal," she said soothingly, trying to pacify Ella and to calm herself as well. "Sparkle's surgery cost a lot of money."

"What are you going to do for a job? Are we going to have to move to Anchorage like Wes Splitlinger's family, when his mom lost her job?" Ella teared up. "I don't want to move. I want to graduate with all my friends at Sweet Home High."

Hope put her hand on Ella's arm. "We're not moving, sweetie. I already found a job." More like the job found her.

"Where?"

Hope knew the relief in Ella's voice would be erased with her next words. "I took a job at Home Sweet Home Lodge."

Ella stared at her as if she didn't understand. "The lodge? Why? Are you trying to get back together with *him*? Or are you trying to force me to like him?"

"Heavens, no! You know why I had to take the job. I have to work. To pay for rent, utilities, food."

"So that's why you were talking about . . ." Apparently Ella couldn't say her father's name.

"Donovan," Hope provided. "Yes."

"I don't want you working there! He never made an effort to get to know me, so why should I want to know him?" Ella started to stand, but Hope gently gripped her arm.

"Sit back down. There are things I have to tell you. I've known Donovan my whole life, and I've loved him that long, too. From the moment he moved in next door."

"Loved him? How old were you?" Ella asked, almost accusingly.

"Six years old."

"No one can fall in love when they're six."

"I would certainly agree with you if it hadn't happened to me."

"And what about him? Did he fall in love with you then?"

"No. But we were great friends. I'd even call us best friends if he and his brother Beau hadn't been so close."

"Beau?" Ella said, surprised.

"Yeah, Beau," Hope said, watching as Ella clicked the pieces into place.

"Okay. Now I get the *Beau* thing."

Hope had given her daughter the middle name Beau. *Isabella Beau McKnight*. Which wasn't common knowledge around Sweet Home. If they did know, they would only think it was because Beau died in the car along with Izzie that snowy night.

Ella continued on. "But if Donovan was your best friend, does that mean that you talked to him like I talk to Lacy? Like, about everything? That seems crazy."

"Oh, yes. We were always together. We played all the time. Ran in the woods and fished in the river behind the lodge." It all came back to Hope, their magical childhood. She wondered if Donovan remembered it as she did. Running wild and exploring the world. "Although it all changed when we hit high school," Hope said quietly.

"How did it change?" Ella asked. "Is that when he turned into a jackass?" She looked as if she had firsthand knowledge of how boys could do that.

"Hormones," Hope said truthfully. "Girls. Donovan was very popular. Star quarterback. Good looks."

"So the jerk started ignoring you?" Ella asked.

"First of all, Donovan isn't a jerk. And no, he didn't ignore me," Hope said. "He just continued to treat me like his pal and tell me about his exploits."

"Like I said—a jerk!"

"In his defense, Ella, he had no idea I cared for him in that way. Then . . ."

"Then what? Did you finally tell him that you loved him?"

"He woke up when I told him I didn't want to hear about his dates anymore. That I would no longer give him advice,"

Hope said. And he certainly didn't like it when she'd finally accepted Jesse Montana's invitation to go out with him.

"But how did . . . *I* happen?" Ella asked with a grimace.

"You were not a one-night stand, sweetheart, if that's what you were thinking. I admit, you weren't planned, but your dad and I were going steady by then. We had plans for a future together. College. Marriage. Kids. The whole nine yards."

Ella stood, her face turning red and angry, her hands curled into fists. "Did he leave you when he found out you were pregnant with me?"

"Calm down. You were at the lodge—you saw that Donovan had no idea he had a child."

"Then what happened? Why didn't you tell him about me?" Ella asked, her voice pitched higher than before.

Hope wrapped her hand around Ella's hand and stood, too. "Izzie wasn't the only one who was in the car with me that night, when I . . . when I'd been drinking."

"Who else was with you?"

Hope's stomach lurched. "Donovan and his brother Beau."

"So what does that have to do with him not knowing about me?" Ella asked.

"Beau died in the accident along with Izzie."

"His brother?" Ella looked stunned.

"Yes. I killed Donovan's brother." Hope wrapped Ella in a hug. "Donovan was very, very angry. He left Sweet Home and never returned." Until now.

"But you loved him." Ella began to cry.

"Yes, and I'm sure Donovan loved me." This next part would be the hardest, being truthful about something that hurt so much. "But, Ella, sometimes love just isn't enough."

"Mom, I'm sorry I ruined your life!" Ella sobbed into her shoulder.

"Hush, sweetheart. You did *not* ruin my life." Hope's vision became blurry with tears. "I've been lucky. So lucky. Because I've had you all these years." She suddenly realized the depth of what she'd done to Donovan by not telling him the truth. He'd missed out on the most precious thing in life . . . his daughter. "I love you, Ella."

"I love you, too."

Hope stroked her daughter's hair. "Now that you know everything, will you give your dad a chance?"

"Mom, I don't want to talk anymore."

Hope wanted to say more. Wanted to ask if Ella finally understood why she had to stop drinking, because alcohol ruined lives, irreversibly. But Hope didn't want to chance pushing Ella away. The last eight days had been hell. She had to hold on to this moment, hold on to her daughter for just a little bit longer.

DONOVAN TRIED TO settle in for the night but he felt jumpy. He never should've agreed to have Hope work at the lodge. The scent of her damned flowery shampoo was everywhere. Finally, he put on his coat, picked up Boomer, and grabbed his keys from the counter before heading for the door.

"Yeah, I know you don't like the dark, Boomer," Donovan said, "and I know you just want to climb into my bed and go to sleep for the night. But we're going to take another drive." To take his mind off Hope. To leave the day behind. To forget kissing her and holding her in his arms.

He drove with no destination in mind but ended up at the entrance to the cemetery again.

He looked down at Boomer. "I didn't plan it, but I guess you and I are going to visit Beau." It was strange. This was Donovan's third trip to the cemetery since coming back to Sweet Home. Yes, he'd thought about Beau throughout the years, but he never imagined he'd spend so much time at his grave.

Also strange? That being here was comforting.

Leaving the headlights on, he climbed out of the car and walked with Boomer over to Beau's headstone. Donovan laid the red Hot Wheels car atop the grave marker. "I thought I might hang on to this, but I think it belongs here with you, Beau."

He crouched down and set Boomer next to him.

"I'm trying to forgive Hope, I really am, but I might not be able to. I hope you understand, Beau." Donovan sighed deeply. "I'm still wrapping my head around it, that I have a daughter. You know I always wanted kids . . ." His voice quavered and fell silent. He wiped dirt from the stone. "So, Hope came to work at the lodge today." Donovan looked off into the darkness. "We should never have worried about Hope being fragile. The way she's raised Ella all alone, she's got plenty of grit."

Boomer reached up and put his paws on Donovan's thighs. He picked him up and stood. "I know I gave Hope the job, but I'm not sure I can let her keep it. Not sure I can be around her day in and day out." He looked up at the sky and tried to put his feelings into words. "She's gotten under my skin again. Loving her before took everything away from me . . . you and Nan. I can't go through it again. I just can't. I'm not sure I'm that strong."

From nowhere, a piece of paper glided in on the wind, as if it were a message from above, and landed at Donovan's feet. He looked around at the trees surrounding the cemetery. A moment ago, there hadn't been any breeze at all. Donovan picked up the paper. It was a list of chores and errands— *sweep entryway, stock pantry, clean out garage,* and so on. Donovan broke into a smile, then gazed at the gravestone. "Brilliant. I knew I could count on you, little brother. Thanks for the idea."

He looked down at Boomer. "I think we can go home now. What do you think?"

Boomer looked up at him and Donovan could've sworn the puppy smiled.

AFTER ELLA WENT to her room, Hope got into bed, but she couldn't sleep. It was probably because she'd had that nap earlier, and not because she couldn't stop thinking about how comfortably she and Donovan had worked alongside each other in his grandmother's studio.

Hope climbed out of bed and went to the kitchen, thinking she might have a snack. But the moose fabric called to her from the ironing board and sewing won out over snacking. It wouldn't wake Ella; her daughter was a hard sleeper and had grown up with the late-night whir of Hope's sewing machine.

She set up her machine and began stitching. Normally, sewing was absorbing, but tonight, her mind was on something else. Someone else . . . Donovan. She kept reliving the kiss over and over again. He'd stirred her comatose insides back to life. And not in a good way. It was uncomfortable loving him the way she did. The wound had reopened, making the pain fresh. But ohh . . . it had been wonderful to embrace him once more. At the same time she was truly frightened of what would certainly happen . . . she was going to experience the heartache of losing him all over again.

"It means nothing," she said to her idle sewing machine. "Donovan was grateful, that's all. Now get back to work."

An hour later, the simple curtains were done and Hope crawled back into bed. As she pulled up her quilt, she said, "Izzie, if you're around, can you let me sleep?" Finishing their conversation from earlier could wait. "There's lots to talk about, but I'm beat. I hope you understand." Hope closed her eyes and slept soundly.

The next morning when Hope strolled into the kitchen, Ella was eating a bowl of cereal at the table.

"Who are the curtains for?" she asked.

"The lodge," Hope answered. "Wandering Moose Cabin."

"I see." Ella gave her a look as if the curtains meant something. But at least Ella was back to speaking to her.

"Why are you up so early?" Hope asked. These days it was unusual to see Ella dressed on a Sunday morning.

"I don't know. I thought maybe I'd go to mass with you." Ella lifted her eyebrow in warning, as if to tell Hope not to make a big deal out of it.

"Sounds good." Hope went to the coffeemaker, trying to contain the high five she wanted to give herself. Ella hadn't been to St. Ignatius since the funeral. Hope hadn't forced it. She understood Ella's grief. And the way church could emphasize the hole in their hearts that would probably never heal, the place in her heart where Hope's dad had been.

An hour later, they left the house in their warm clothes to walk to church. Others were walking along Main Street to St. Ignatius as well. The Baptist church had just let out and Ella waved to Lacy and Aberdeen as they passed on the other side of the street. Hope was still ticked at Aberdeen but decided to let it go. After all, Ella seemed to be on the road to forgiving Hope.

All felt right with the world.

That changed only a block later, when they entered the church and found themselves the object of stares. What was that about? She and Ella weren't late. Hope looked down to reassure herself that she'd dressed appropriately. *Why all the gawking?*

Then it hit her. The news must've spread that she'd been laid off from the Hungry Bear. This was probably the juicy tidbit that had the townsfolk turning and murmuring to one another as she and Ella walked down the aisle. Hope's name even rose above the crowd of whispers a couple of times. Just like when she was pregnant, she went to her old mantra: *Let 'em stare. Let 'em gossip.* She loved Sweet Home, but she certainly didn't like how everyone butted into everyone else's business.

But then a few steps closer to the altar, she saw it . . . the reason Sweet Home was all a-twitter. Donovan Stone was sitting in their pew! Hers and Ella's! Did Donovan have a sixth sense and know that was *their* place? Hope had claimed that pew when her mother kicked her out of the house. Third row from the front, on the left. Back then, even though shame at killing Izzie and Beau had been crushingly new, and her pregnancy had started to show, Hope had refused to hide in the back of the church. She figured God could see her no matter where she sat, so why not let everyone else see her, too. And as her belly had grown, Hope had become even more defiant, refusing to answer anyone who fished for answers about the father of her baby.

But now her baby daddy was making a spectacle of them all and Hope wanted to hide. No, she wanted to turn around and hightail it home. Escape. To Antarctica, maybe. Until Donovan Charles Stone left Sweet Home for good.

Apparently, Ella hadn't seen him. She kept walking toward their pew, oblivious. Hope didn't know what to do. If it wouldn't draw more attention to the impending catastrophe, she would dive for Ella and tackle her before she made a monumental mistake. Ella couldn't sit beside her father! She just couldn't! They weren't one big happy family.

And Ella was a wild card, without a reliable filter. She might yell at Donovan for trying to displace them. Or accuse him of trying to insinuate himself into their midst. For sure some kind of scene would break out. And it would fuel Sweet Home's gossip mill until at least the end of winter.

Suddenly Ella stopped short. *Thank goodness,* Hope thought.

But then Ella spun on Hope and glared at her as if she were in charge of the church's seating chart.

Hope pointed to the pew off to the right, away from Donovan, hoping to put away the dirty laundry that they'd hung out for Sweet Home to see.

Hope slipped into the safe-haven pew. Ella followed with a huff and dropped beside her.

"You could've let me know you asked him to sit with us at church," Ella hissed. Hissed loud enough that passersby outside the church could hear.

Donovan turned and looked back at them. Once again, Hope wanted to make a run for it, this time from his piercing eyes, which didn't miss a thing. "I didn't ask him to church *or* to sit in our pew."

"Then what's he doing there?" Ella said angrily.

"Communing with God?" Hope feebly offered. Even

though Donovan had been a hellion in his youth, he had never missed mass.

To Hope's relief, the processional music began and the congregation stood and opened their hymnals. But she couldn't help glancing over at Donovan every other stanza.

Ella put her hand over the page, glaring at Hope. "Stop it."

She was right. Hope was pitiable. Especially since Donovan didn't look at her once during the service. The first half of Father Mike's sermon was on the power of forgiveness, while the second half covered the harm of gossiping. He had certainly tied Hope's troubles up with a nice neat bow. *Thanks, Father Mike.*

After church Piney stopped Hope as she was trying to hurry out the door.

"Come by and eat with Bill and me. Family dinner, you and Ella."

Ella held out her phone, demonstrating that she'd been texting since the moment church was over. "I'm headed to Lacy's."

Piney nodded. "Then you, Hope. You'll come?"

Out of the corner of her eye, Hope saw Donovan shaking hands with Father Mike. She turned to Piney. "I can't, I have too much to do." *Run!*

Piney took her hand. "It's not because you're upset with me, is it?"

Yes! Partly. "No. I'm too busy. I have to get ready for next week."

Piney squeezed her hand. "If you change your mind, we'll be at my apartment."

Trying to put on a brave front, Hope smiled before removing her hand from Piney's. "Thanks." She turned to Ella. "Don't be late."

Ella nodded and hurried for the door. Hope followed close behind, not to keep up with her daughter but to avoid Donovan. And to avoid the curious stares from the folks of Sweet Home.

But once Hope was home, she didn't want to do laundry

or mop the floor or make a menu for next week. She looked around her empty little house, feeling lonely, until her eyes landed on the Rubbermaid container in the corner, the one holding Izzie's Memory Tree quilt. She took it into the kitchen and gradually lost track of time as she cut Izzie's clothes into blocks and strips. When Ella got home around five, she pulled a container of fish soup from the freezer, dumped the contents into a pan, and set it on the stove. Hope returned to cutting out pieces while the soup heated, then scooped up two bowls.

"Sit with me," Hope offered.

"Nah. I'm going to eat in my room."

Fine. Hope would just keep working on Izzie's Memory Tree. By the end of the evening, the blocks had been organized, the cut pieces placed in baggies and tagged. She felt good about what she'd accomplished. Somehow, working on Izzie's quilt had given Hope a reprieve from worrying over Donovan.

But as soon as she fell into bed and closed her eyes, Izzie was there.

"So, you told my niece about you and me having our little chats," Izzie said.

"I'm lucky she didn't call the head of the loony bin to have me committed."

"It's good you talked about it . . . and other things. But you didn't tell her about the kiss," Izzie said, singsonging *kiss* like the middle schooler that she'd been.

"I don't want to talk about the kiss." How could she, when she still didn't know how she felt about it? "There's nothing to talk about, anyway. It was just a thank-you kiss. No big deal."

"No big deal? I think Donovan still loves you and wants to get back together," Izzie said, acting the wise woman that she wasn't. "And you still love him."

"Stop it! I think the afterlife has demented your brain." But it was actually Hope who was demented. Who else, besides her, talked to their dead sister?

"Hope, he was sitting in your pew at church. That could not have been a coincidence," Izzie said.

"And yet, it was," Hope insisted.

"Well, tomorrow you should talk to him."

"Of course I'm going to talk to him. He's my boss now."

Izzie gave her a look, the same one their mother gave Hope when she was disappointed in her. "Don't be obstinate. I mean talk to Donovan about your *feelings* and how you'd like to rekindle the old flame."

"Don't be ridiculous. I am not doing that." But the truth was, Hope was very curious to find out how that theoretical conversation might go. "Good night, Izzie. I'm going to sleep."

The next morning after getting Ella off to school, Hope drove out to the lodge with butterflies attacking her stomach. Had Izzie been right about Donovan? Did he still have feelings for her after all these years? Answers would have to wait.

When she arrived, Donovan's car wasn't at the lodge. But he must've been there. The old clothespin attached to the front door from the Charles and Elsie days held a piece of paper. Hope pulled the note from the door. But it wasn't a note at all.

It was just a typed list of chores for Hope to complete. *Depressingly impersonal.* It was demoralizing how much she'd been anticipating seeing him today. While if the note was any indication—and it was—he hadn't wanted to see her at all.

She held the list up. "Izzie, if you're listening, you were wrong. Donovan doesn't have feelings for me. He only wants me to clean his toilets."

Chapter 12

FOR THE NEXT week, the same awkward dance was afoot. Hope would drive to the lodge, hoping to see Donovan's car, but it was never there. The only thing that awaited her was that darned typed chore list clipped to the front door. The chores were easy and only took her a couple of hours to complete.

She was starting to go a little batty from the mystery of *Where is Donovan?* And how did a chore list miraculously appear on his door each morning? On Wednesday night, day three of Donovan's disappearance, she drove back to the lodge at eleven p.m., looking for signs of life. The place was dead. No cars. No lights. Abandoned, as it had been for seventeen years. She was certain he was gone for good, but the next morning, a new chore list was on the door. If she had the money, she might have bought a wildlife camera to capture him sneaking back at night. The only thing she knew for certain was that he was avoiding her.

Hope even felt desperate enough to go to the Hungry Bear to ask Sparkle if Rick might've mentioned where Donovan had gone. But only Piney was there, slicing bologna for Paige Holiday.

"I'm busy," Piney said. Sparkle was nowhere in sight. "Do you mind checking yourself out at the cash register?"

"Yeah, I can do that." Hope bought a loaf of bread before leaving for home without any answers.

She gave up expecting Donovan to be home. She deep-cleaned Black Bear Hideout Cabin and pulled the swayback mattress, with a lot of huffing and puffing, to the end of the driveway, for Dewey Winkle to haul away. Having new mattresses delivered to Nowhere, Alaska, would cost a fortune, but that was what Donovan wanted. Curse the guy! She missed working cozily beside him in his grandmother's studio or moving things around in Wandering Moose Cabin. She was a team of one now. All day long, she stopped herself from speculating where Donovan had gone off to and when he might return. Or at least she tried. She hated that she'd run him off, kept him away from the lodge and from Sweet Home.

Friday's chore list came with no chores at all, just a typed instruction: *Take the weekend off.* She went home and started her own list. A list of possible jobs to check out. She couldn't work for Donovan another week. She couldn't stand how she was pining for him all over again. She even considered looking for work on the North Slope. Housekeepers were always needed there and the pay was more than she could make in Sweet Home. But Hope knew she couldn't leave Ella to fend for herself, as she had been forced to do. Besides, since the debacle at church last Sunday, Ella was drinking even more than before. Hope was beyond knowing what to do at this point. It hadn't worked to ground her and it wasn't safe to take away her phone. The phone was Ella's only lifeline if she ended up in a car crash like Hope had at nearly the same age.

She wondered if it would have been better if Donovan had never come back. Any more contact with him and Ella might really go off the deep end. Also Hope's yearning heart was in danger of not surviving if he returned.

She sat at her kitchen table, staring sightlessly at the list in front of her. The last note on the door hadn't mentioned anything about getting paid. She wondered if Donovan had forgotten about paying her weekly. But not ten minutes later, her phone dinged with an email from PayPal. The subject line read *Money is waiting for you*. Hope bristled; she'd told Donovan she didn't need his charity. Then she saw the note inside: *Payday. Includes signing bonus.*

The amount was triple what she expected for a week's work.

"Signing bonus, my foot," Hope sniffed. But she really couldn't afford to turn it down. Ella needed new gloves and new boots.

Hope decided, for her daughter's sake, that she'd swallow her pride this time. She rationalized that money for boots and gloves was really child support. "When I see Donovan at church on Sunday, I'll give him back the rest of the bonus."

But Sunday morning, he wasn't there. Continuing to read her mind, Father Mike preached a sermon about patience, about letting go and letting God. Patience was not her strong suit. Neither was leaving things to chance.

But the sermon tugged at Hope. Self-reliance hadn't really gotten her anywhere. Maybe just this once, she *should* turn things over to a higher power and see what He could do with her mess of a life. She bowed her head and prayed for Ella to stop drinking. She prayed for her friends Piney and Sparkle, thanking God for putting them in her life. While she was at it, she asked God to forgive her for being angry with Piney. Then Hope did the unthinkable. She prayed for Donovan—with no strings attached—asking God to shower goodness on him now that he'd left Sweet Home for good.

DONOVAN RACED TO Sweet Home with his sleeping dog beside him in the front seat. Apparently Boomer didn't have the same worries that humans had. Donovan hadn't slept well in a week, not since leaving Sweet Home. He hated knowing that he'd *run* again, just like before. And just like his mother had when he and Beau were kids.

He was glad to be reunited with Boomer. Donovan had

boarded him at a loving, run-free establishment in Anchorage . . . five stars on Yelp. Boomer looked well-fed, healthy, and happy. It was clear that Donovan had missed the dog more than he'd been missed.

He glanced at the dash clock and cursed the stupid flight delay in Florida. He was late, really late, for the monthly town council meeting. He pressed the accelerator harder.

It had been a nice visit, but he was taken aback to find his father preoccupied with a new girlfriend, Rose, who'd apparently moved in two weeks ago. Dad seemed eager to meet Ella, but mostly he was immersed in his new relationship. Donovan was glad his dad had finally found someone after all these years with whom to share his life.

Yes, it'd been an impromptu trip. *No*, he hadn't given his dad any warning. It was just that Donovan had been looking for a break from Sweet Home, a break from all the emotions that being there had stirred up. What he especially needed was a break from Hope.

At least the trip had been illuminating. Ever since Grandpa's death he'd been so worried that his dad needed him to move to Florida right away. Instead, he'd only felt underfoot, with Dad and Rose acting like a couple of honeymooners.

One thing he did right was to tell Piney where he was going, and ask her to print out his emailed list of chores every night and stick it to the lodge's front door.

He glanced at the dashboard clock again. Seven o'clock already. No time to head home, shave, and change first. He pulled into the Baptist church parking lot, grabbed his leather portfolio with his notes in it, clipped on Boomer's leash, and headed for the meeting. Boomer had other ideas—he needed a break and apparently another few minutes to sniff around after that. When Donovan finally walked into the church, Leaky Parks was at the lectern, the meeting in full swing. The rest of the room turned to look at Donovan as he pulled the creaking door closed behind him.

Leaky motioned to someone in the front row as Donovan strode with Boomer up the aisle, taking in the faces all around him. Some he didn't recognize, but most he knew from his youth. The one face he wasn't prepared to see was Hope McKnight's as she stood and turned around.

She stared at him, looking utterly speechless. Then she opened her mouth as if she was going to ask him where he'd been, but apparently she decided otherwise, because she clamped her lips tight together.

It was Piney's loud throat clearing that brought Hope back to her purpose, because Hope nodded at Piney.

"As head of our local chapter of MADD," Hope started, "I just want to remind everyone about MADD's Halloween watch on Thursday."

Donovan's stomach clenched. *Hope volunteers with MADD?* Why hadn't Piney said something when he'd mentioned petitioning the council? Even better, why hadn't he stayed in Florida and left Sweet Home to deal with Sweet Home?

Hope was still talking. "We have several teams who will patrol the streets to make sure we have a safe trick-or-treating for the kids this year."

Leaky moved back in front of the lectern as Donovan took a seat.

"Thanks, Hope, for the reminder. If you have questions about your time slot, or still need to sign up, see Hope afterward."

Hope stood again. "We do have a couple of openings, so please sign up tonight."

Leaky pointed to him. "Donovan Stone has asked to speak tonight. Donovan, would you like to come forward?"

Donovan made his way to the front to stand before the council, who sat at a makeshift dais. He passed handouts to each member.

"I know most of you remember my grandparents, Elsie and Charles Stone. I'm here to petition the council to lift the dry decree for one night to revive one of my grandmother Elsie's favorite traditions, the Wines of Alaska wine-tasting party to kick off Sweet Home's Christmas Festival." He could feel Hope's disapproving frown without even seeing it, and he understood. His proposed wine tasting was in direct conflict with Hope and her cause.

"I don't know if you know this or not," Leaky said to Donovan, "but Sweet Home's Christmas Festival has been gone for many years now. There just wasn't enough interest. Or for that matter, a large venue like the lodge or the hardware store for people to gather."

Which didn't ring true—the elders of Sweet Home and a good number of its citizens were gathered here in the church tonight. And St. Ignatius was even a bit bigger than the Baptist church. It was as if a domino effect had started the night of the accident that killed his brother and Izzie, which eventually killed off the town, too.

"I know Sweet Home is dry now. I also understand that Alaska has a crisis of addiction." He didn't want to reveal personal details, but it looked as if he was going to have to, especially since the council members were staring at him as if they'd already made up their minds. "I know firsthand how destructive alcoholism is. You see . . ." He paused. "I'm an alcoholic."

There were many startled faces, but his gaze narrowed in on Hope. For some reason he feared her judgment above everyone else's. For a split second he thought he saw sympathy on her face, but then it was gone.

Piney pointed at him. "It's not surprising. You were a tippler even in your teens. You take after your mother," she said bluntly.

He couldn't deny it. It was the main reason his parents had gotten a divorce. "I'm lucky, though," he said. "I found AA and have been in recovery for years."

Hope stood, and he had the irrational expectation that she'd say she was proud of him. But that wasn't what happened. "Then why are you doing this?"

Donovan knew how painful this must be for her. Her past had been a particular kind of hell.

But he had a strong urge to honor his grandparents this

one last time. "I think reviving the Christmas Festival will help Sweet Home. And Nan always said that there'd be no Christmas Festival without first kicking it off with the Wines of Alaska."

Leaky didn't look convinced. "We remember the devastation our town endured when we lost Isabella, Beau, and then your grandmother . . . all because of alcohol. You should remember it, too, Donovan Stone. I think you came up with this cockamamie idea so you can sell the lodge for a higher price."

Sweet Home had always been able to see through him. "Yes, true, I originally saw bringing the lodge back to life as a way to boost the sales price. But I came to see the wine tasting as a tribute to my grandparents. I'm sure you heard that my grandfather passed away last month?"

Everyone on the council nodded.

"Then you must understand why this is so important to me. Also, a successful wine tasting could inspire the new owner to support the town."

"So you already have a buyer?" Leaky asked, hopeful.

"No. But my business manager and I are putting together a business plan for whoever ends up with the lodge. Remember my grandmother's café? One of our ideas is to open it up again for lunch, say five days a week, like Nan used to do. We're already fixing up the cabins so they can be rented." He felt guilty for using the proverbial *we* when it had been Hope who was doing the lion's share of the fixing. He couldn't help but glance at her and he got what he expected—a glare. He continued, "I'm confident of finding an investor who wants to revive the lodge with so many possibilities. But in the short term, think of the influx of money the Christmas Festival could bring in *this* season. The holiday jobs it could provide. There's still plenty of time to promote it." Though October was winding up in a couple of days.

"Give us a minute to talk among ourselves," Leaky said, before turning to huddle with the rest of the council.

Boomer whined and Donovan picked him up, catching a

glimpse of Hope in his peripheral vision. Her back was nee-
dle straight and it was obvious she was fuming. He wanted
to go to her and explain, to win her approval. But it was so
hard to explain why this wine tasting had become so important to him. His feelings about Sweet Home and the lodge
were a jumbled, tangled mess, like Christmas lights that had
been thrown haphazardly into a storage bin.

Hope stood again. "If I may say something?"

"Go ahead," Leaky said.

"Donovan could do all those things he mentioned without
lifting the dry decree."

Donovan gazed at her, trying to convey how sincerely he
wanted to help the town. "You know how much the wine
tasting meant to my grandmother and the Sisterhood of the
Quilt."

"But—" Hope started.

Leaky cut her off. "It doesn't matter. We've come to a
decision."

His face held no clue as to which way it was going to go.

"I'm sorry, Hope," Leaky said. "We've decided to look forward instead of backward. We approve Donovan's petition."

"But—" Hope tried again.

Leaky held up his hand. "We hear your concerns." He
looked over at Donovan. "The decree will be lifted for one
day, but that's only if you agree to all our stipulations."

"Certainly," Donovan said. "What are they?"

"First, only the Alaskan sweet wines your grandmother
served. No beer or hard alcohol."

"That's the plan," Donovan agreed.

"No minors."

"Of course."

"Keys will be collected at the door. You'll need to set up
a system to get everyone and their cars home afterward."

That would be easy. Donovan could hire two people—
one to drive the attendees home in their cars, another to follow them and drive back to the lodge for the next group.

"The wine must be served with food," Leaky said.

"All of this is doable." Donovan felt tremendous relief. He hadn't even realized how invested he was in the Christmas Festival and the wine tasting. Up until now he thought it was about missing his grandparents. But something had shifted, and his vision expanded. Suddenly he could picture a vibrant Sweet Home, the way it had been seventeen years ago. He felt like he could really help the town before he sold off and left Sweet Home forever. But even as he had the thought, his future life in Florida was becoming blurry.

The one thing he saw clearly was an image of the lodge restored to its former glory and then some. He had the means to make the lodge bigger and better than it was before. It all must've been rolling around in his brain since he arrived back in Sweet Home because the vision became clearer. "If it helps," he interrupted the council, "my grandfather had plans drawn up to add more suites to the lodge and more cabins to the grounds." His grandparents had always wanted to expand but never had the energy to do more.

"Yes, yes, that's a fine idea. But there's one more thing," Leaky said, pulling Donovan back to the present.

"Yes?" Donovan smiled, feeling victorious. "Anything."

"The final stipulation is that you have to fix up and reopen A Stone's Throw Hardware and Haberdashery in time for Christmas."

Donovan was dumbstruck.

"Your trap's hanging open," Leaky said.

"But I'm not going—"

"I told you this was an all-or-nothing deal, Donovan. Reopen the hardware store or your Christmas Festival wine tasting is a no-go."

Donovan took his seat, feeling dazed, angry, dismissed . . . even cornered. He hadn't been prepared for this scenario. And he was always prepared. Didn't they know that he could just pick up and leave Sweet Home and let the lodge rot?

But he couldn't do that. His grandparents would be so disappointed in him if he didn't see this through. He'd be disappointed in himself if he ran. Again.

Restoring the hardware store to its previous charming state was an impossible task, especially with such a short deadline. Getting the lodge up to snuff by the weekend before Christmas, when the Christmas Festival took place, was going to take every minute of his time, plus Rick's. Donovan did have some help—Hope. But the three of them couldn't do it alone. With the hardware store added to the agreement, there was no way he could get it all done.

In dismay, he stared at the back of Hope's head, musing that the old Hope would've jumped in and saved him. She would've explained to the town that the lodge was enough. But *this* Hope just sat, staring straight ahead, as if Donovan weren't there. Just a ghost.

Maybe he *was* one.

He was shocked that he didn't matter to her anymore. Shocked by how much it hurt. He longed for their old closeness. Which was something he never expected, not in a million years.

PINEY WAS FEELING pretty pleased with herself. It had been her idea to make the hardware store part of the deal and she didn't feel one bit guilty about it either. The extra money wouldn't put a dent in Donovan's net worth, but it could literally mean life or death for Sweet Home.

If only she could come up with a way to bring Hope and Donovan together, some neutral ground away from the ogling eyes of Sweet Home, where they would have a chance to recapture the love of their youth. She put the idea out there, knowing the universe would provide.

Chapter 13

DONOVAN, WITH BOOMER in tow, left the Baptist church only to have his arm tugged, pulling him to a stop.

Hope had fire in her eyes. "How could you do this to us?" It was clear she felt personally betrayed.

Yes, it was personal for Hope. And, he guessed, personal for him, too. The loss of Beau, his grandmother, and Izzie all felt fresh.

That look on Hope's face made him regret not giving her a heads-up about speaking to the council tonight.

"Tell Leaky you've changed your mind." Her words were almost a plea.

"I can't do that." Donovan felt an overwhelming need to make things up to his grandparents for running out on them when Beau died.

"If you can't do it for me, then do it for your daughter."

"What are you talking about?"

Hope pulled him over to the side of the road; apparently she didn't want the rest of the town to hear them as they piled out of the meeting.

She dropped her hand from his arm and her eyes darted self-consciously to several people who were openly staring at them. Hope took a deep breath before bringing her eyes back up to meet his. "Ella has a drinking problem."

No! Why couldn't he have passed on his ability to throw a hundred-yard pass? Or that he could code like a son of a gun? He'd wanted to pass his strengths to Ella, not his biggest flaw—the family drinking gene.

But maybe Hope had it all wrong. "Tell me what's going on." Ella might have caved to peer pressure at a party sometime, but that didn't mean she had a drinking problem at all.

"Ever since my dad died, Ella's been drinking a lot. I think she's self-medicating with booze, trying to dull the pain. She and my dad were close. He lived part time with us from the time she was little." Hope choked up a bit. "We both miss him."

Donovan wanted to wrap her in his arms and comfort her. But he couldn't. He'd only just forgotten how good she felt in his arms the last time. Well, he was only kidding himself about that, too. He could never forget how she felt. She was imprinted on him as surely as if her heart were carved into his own.

But she wasn't the old Hope, and he wasn't the screwed-up kid who'd left Sweet Home at eighteen.

"What have you done to help her?" he asked.

Hope looked around as if the answer were off in the bushes or in the street. "I don't know. I've tried everything—grounding her, lecturing, watching her every move. I even told her the whole truth about Izzie"—her voice hitched—"and Beau."

"Where is she right now?" Donovan asked.

"This very minute? I don't know. I asked her to come with me tonight but she said she was going to Tyler's and afterward, Lacy's." She dropped her head and shook it, looking wary. "Aberdeen said she was going to lock up the liquor but I doubt that she did."

Donovan took her arm. "Come on."

Hope pulled away. "Where are we going?"

"To find our daughter." Donovan hoped he was doing the

right thing. In his gut, he felt it would help Ella to see both of her parents working together for her good.

"Aberdeen lives down the road from my rental."

"We'll check there first. If she isn't at Aberdeen's, then we'll drive out to this Tyler person's house."

Hope nodded and they hurried to his car. The council members and attendees all stopped to watch as he opened the passenger door for Hope.

"Ignore them," he instructed.

"Easy for you to say." Hope slid into the car. "You don't live here."

He set Boomer in her lap before going around to the other side and getting behind the wheel. He didn't want to talk about leaving Sweet Home, so he changed the subject. "What the council is asking me to do—reopening the hardware store by Christmas—is impossible."

"Good." Her happy tone wasn't encouraging. She pointed at the signpost. "Turn right at the stop sign. Aberdeen's is the first trailer on the left."

Donovan did as she directed. When he turned the corner, Hope sucked in some air.

"My car isn't there."

"Don't panic. Where does Tyler live?"

"Out on Cemetery Road."

A road Donovan had traveled several times since he'd returned to Sweet Home.

Hope guided him to the boy's house, but Hope's car wasn't there either and all the lights were out.

"No one's home. Where is she?" Hope asked worriedly.

"Text her," he said. "Just to make sure she's all right."

"I already did but she didn't answer."

"Does this happen often—you know, where Ella goes off on her own and makes you worry?"

"Unfortunately, it comes with having a teenage daughter."

That certainly rang true. He'd only been a father for a short period of time and he was so anxious he was having trouble concentrating on the road.

"What next?" he asked.

"Home. I'll go home and wait for her to return. I seem to be waiting for her a lot lately," Hope said resignedly.

"If it's okay, I'd like to wait with you," Donovan said.

"You don't have to," Hope insisted.

"I know. But I want to anyway. For Ella's sake." And his own.

Ten minutes later he pulled up in front of Hope's tiny house. It was almost small enough to fit inside his living room back in San Jose.

He grabbed Boomer and followed Hope up the shoveled walkway, thinking she really did have her hands full—keeping up with a house, a job, and an unpredictable teenager!

She unlocked the door, turned on the light, and he stepped in after her—straight into a puddle.

"What the . . ." Hope's words died as she ran to the room at the back—looked like a kitchen—water splashing beneath her feet.

He set Boomer on the love seat. "Stay!" Then Donovan rushed after her . . . Boomer did, too, getting all wet. Nothing he could do about it now. Donovan hurried to Hope. "What happened?"

She was reaching under the sink, pulling out a wrench and muttering to herself, "A pipe must've broken. Or the water heater. Bad luck follows me around."

"Hand over the wrench and tell me where the shutoff valve is."

"I've got it—"

"Don't make me wrestle you for it. I'm a half foot taller." He gently touched her arm. "Let me do this one thing for you."

"You already did one thing for me . . . the signing bonus, remember?" She fired her words as if she were at target practice and his face was the bull's-eye. She frowned and then handed over the wrench. "The shutoff valve is in the dungeon."

"Dungeon?"

"The basement. It's a cellar, really. I certainly don't go

down there unless I have to. Here." She went to the corner and scooted an area rug away with her foot, revealing a metal ring that was flush with the water-soaked hardwood floor. "You'll need a light. There's no electricity down there." She opened a drawer, uncovered a flashlight, and held it out to him.

"Where is the shutoff valve?"

"About three feet up on the south wall." She pointed south.

He'd never liked dark enclosed spaces, but he would do this for Hope. And for Ella.

"What are you doing?" he asked as Hope grabbed a broom.

"Sweeping what water I can out the back door. Or else I might as well turn this place into an ice rink."

It did seem unusually cold in the house. "Did the furnace go off, too?"

"No." She looked defensive. "I turn it down when we're out. Conserving energy. Saving the planet. I'm a good world citizen."

He'd forgotten how it could be. He hadn't grown up with much, like most people in Sweet Home. They were all used to getting by on little, even the essentials . . . like heat. Suddenly he was grateful he'd had Rick send Hope that bonus.

Hope was glaring at him with her *Don't you pity me* face with an extra *I'm fine!* in her eyes.

"I'll be right back." He reached down and yanked open the door in the floor, flipping on the flashlight before descending the steps into what looked like hell. As he did, water splashed into the hole. Hope was quite possibly sweeping the water on his head on purpose.

He shone the flashlight side to side, illuminating a basement so empty and musty that rats, spiders, and ghouls would find it too spooky. No wonder Hope never came down here. He went to the south corner, located the valve on the wall, and shut it off. "All done!"

Hope cried out, and he nearly tripped up the stairs, afraid something had happened to her or Boomer.

"What's wrong?"

He found her in the small coat closet near the front door, trying to pull out a wet box. Boomer was in one arm, wrapped in a towel, looking confused.

"Here, let me," he said.

Hope moved out of the way and he stepped in, carefully lifting and maneuvering the soggy box out of the closet.

"Support the bottom. It's Izzie's things," Hope cried. "Her trinkets and artwork."

Donovan remembered Izzie's talent for art. "Where do you want me to put it? Kitchen table?"

"Yes. It won't hurt the Formica."

But once in the kitchen, he set the box on a chair. He took Boomer. Hope pulled out two stuffed bears and a small jewelry box. He leaned over as she opened it and saw the cross necklace.

"It's from Izzie's first communion," she said hurriedly. Finally she pulled out the box from the very bottom.

"No!" she cried in dismay. Water was dripping from it.

It had to be the artwork. "Let's spread them out on the table and the counter. If we can get them dried quickly, maybe it won't be so bad." He knew of a good art restoration firm in California.

"The house is waterlogged. There's no chance that they'll dry out at all," Hope said, sounding defeated.

"Okay. Then we'll take them to the lodge and spread out the artwork on the cutting table in Nan's studio." Then he'd call that restoration firm . . . anything to keep the wobble out of Hope's voice. "But first, let's get them out of this smaller box." Then he thought of something else. "Is there anything in Ella's room that might be getting damaged?"

"Aside from the clothes she leaves all over the floor? I'll go check."

As soon as she left the kitchen, he pulled out his phone. Rick picked up on the second ring. "Can you and Sparkle come to Hope's house right away? Bring a bunch of empty boxes from the Hungry Bear."

"What's going on?" Rick asked.

"Hope and Ella are moving in with me."

"WHAT?" HOPE WAS this close to blowing a gasket. "Are you crazy?"

Startled, Donovan turned around but then spoke into the phone. "I'll tell you everything when you get here. Hurry."

She slammed her hands on her hips. "Call back whoever that was. I'm not moving in with you!"

"It was Rick. We're going to get your stuff out of here. Tonight."

Hope's mind was spinning. Maybe Piney had room for her and Ella. But who was she kidding? That apartment was tighter than Hope's minuscule house. "Just give me a minute to think."

"Okay." But his voice sounded as if her taking a minute wasn't going to change his mind.

He had most of Izzie's drawings spread over the counter—the fairy world Izzie loved to jabber about, the secret woodland home for animals who spoke, and drawings of a magical kingdom with a whimsical castle.

"What's the damage in Ella's room?" he asked.

"It may be a total loss."

"Really?"

"Her clothes are soaked as expected. I'm going to have to reintroduce that girl to her dresser drawers and closet and what they're used for. But I did find the culprit . . . the water heater. The ceiling has partially collapsed, making it a complete disaster."

"What about her schoolwork? Is it okay?"

"I didn't see any papers or books on the floor. Her desk is piled high so I assume everything is there or with her."

"Do you have any trash bags to put Ella's wet clothes in? We could get them in the washing machine as soon as we get to the lodge."

"I really don't think it's a good idea," Hope said weakly.

She could feel herself beginning to cave—just like the ceiling in her daughter's room. She didn't have any other options. There was no hotel in Sweet Home, and even if there were, she didn't have the cash for a room anyway. Plus Ella had school in the morning. "I guess we could stay at the lodge for one night. But not in the main house."

"You'll have to stay in the lodge, it's the only place with beds. Unless you didn't throw out the other mattresses this past week?"

Which reminded her that he'd left and hadn't said a word. How many times in her life had she told herself to quit worrying over Donovan Stone? *Too many!* "Yeah, I lugged the mattresses to the road for Dewey Winkle to pick up over the weekend." Thinking about Donovan's absence this last week reminded her of something else. "You need security cameras at the lodge. You never know who might be lurking about when you're not there." *Like someone clipping a note on your door!*

"That's a good idea. I want to make sure you're safe when I'm not around."

That wasn't the point.

"So you're okay with staying at the lodge?"

Ella wasn't going to like it. She'd probably want to stay at Lacy's until their little home dried out. Yet again Hope felt like a failure as a mother. "We'll stay." What other choice did they have?

There was a knock on the front door, and then Rick and Sparkle came in, their arms loaded with boxes. They both looked aghast at the waterlogged floor.

"What happened? A tidal wave?" Rick gave her a sympathetic smile.

Hope pointed up. "The water heater. It's in the attic. Totally dumb, as it flooded the house." She looked back into the kitchen to see Donovan carefully repositioning Izzie's pictures. She knew it was silly but those pictures meant a lot to her. She was kicking herself for not framing them long ago and hanging them on the wall.

"Where do you want us to start?" Rick asked.

Hope pointed to Ella's bedroom. "Ella's desk would be great. I'm going to collect some trash bags to put all her wet clothes in."

"Is there someone I should call about getting things repaired?" Rick asked.

"Thanks, but no. I'll have to email the owner. He moved to North Carolina six years ago when his wife passed away. With the time difference, it's too late to call him now." For all the good it would do. True, Mr. Morse was obligated to pay for a new water heater, but how soon would he send the money? And she didn't have spare funds to replace all the stuff that was ruined.

Rick gave her a concerned look. "Well, just know that I'm here to help. As an employee of Stone Enterprises, I'm completely at your disposal."

Sparkle beamed at her man before taking a box into Ella's room.

Hope only nodded. *Stone Enterprises*, indeed. She wasn't used to having any backup besides Piney and Sparkle. Her mother, the town, and even Donovan had shown her their backs. She was alone in this world and she was scared to death of letting anyone in. Especially Donovan.

Before she could get to the kitchen for the garbage bags, Donovan appeared, holding them in his hand. "I found them under the sink."

Hope took them as graciously as she could and was proud for not barking at him that she could've handled it herself. "I'll get started."

"Do you want help?" Donovan asked.

"I've got it."

As boxes were filled, Donovan and Rick carried them out to their cars. Hope made sure to carry the box with Izzie's Memory Tree pieces herself. When she started to drag Ella's wet clothes to Donovan's car, though, he reached to take them from her. She wanted to snap that she wasn't helpless, but they were in a hurry. The temperature was dropping and the bags would probably freeze if they waited much longer.

Within about an hour most of their things were packed.

"Hope and I will head to the lodge to start washing Ella's clothes," Donovan said.

"No worries," said Rick. "Sparkle and I will be right behind you, after we pack up the fridge."

As Hope slid into Donovan's car—ready to text Ella—Ella pulled up in front of them and hopped out.

"What's going on?" she asked.

Hope rushed over to head her off at the pass. "The water heater broke and flooded the house."

"So where are you going? Why are you leaving?" Ella looked panicked, as if Hope were abandoning her.

"You and I are going to stay at the lodge for a little while."

"No! We should stay with Piney," Ella argued.

"Sweetie, there isn't room. You know that," Hope said.

Ella looked over at Donovan, her expression guarded. "I don't want to live with him. It'll be weird."

"You'll be with me. I promise it won't be weird at all. And as soon as the new mattresses arrive, we'll have our pick of cabins to live in." Of course, after the windows and holes were fixed. And the plumbing and electrical were checked.

"How soon will that be?" Ella looked as if she were working out the upcoming negotiation in her head. "How soon until we have our own cabin?"

"I don't know, but I'll ask him to put a rush on it, okay?"

"All right, I guess."

"I'll ride with you," Hope said.

"No. I've got my stuff all over the front seat. I'll meet you out there."

But when Ella pulled out, she kept driving straight instead of turning left toward the lodge.

"What's the matter?" Donovan said, making Hope jump.

She frowned. "Don't sneak up on me." She pulled out her phone. "Ella said she's going to the lodge, but my car just drove past the turn."

"Maybe she's taking a different route," Donovan speculated.

"Going down the wrong path is more like it." Hope speed-dialed her daughter but it went to voice mail. She sighed into the phone as the message played and beeped. "Where are you headed?" And then, "Call me!" Hope hung up.

"Give her a minute," Donovan said. "I'm sure she just needs time to absorb this. She'll probably beat us out to the lodge."

But Donovan was wrong. Ella wasn't waiting for them. Hope left two more messages before she put the first load of Ella's clothes into the washer. Rick and Sparkle carried the boxes to the hallway upstairs.

As promised, Donovan spread out Izzie's drawings on the large table in the sewing studio and brought in a fan. Hope headed upstairs to unpack. She took her old room—the one she always used when she stayed over at the lodge—and she put Ella's things in the bedroom next door.

Finally she headed downstairs to put in another load of laundry.

"I'll do that," Donovan said. "You go to bed."

"No. I'm going to wait up for Ella." Hope texted her again and then went to the living room to sit on the couch and gaze out the picture window, which gave her a view of the driveway. She stared at it for a long time while Donovan sat in his recliner across the room.

"Do you need anything to eat or drink?" he asked.

"No. I'm fine." But Hope was a big liar. Where was she going to get the money to fix her house? Yes, it was Mr. Morse's responsibility to fix things, but he had done little for repairs over the years and she had gotten used to taking care of things herself. She closed her eyes and said a prayer, but she wasn't sure if God was listening, as He certainly had more pressing matters. Like always, Hope was on her own.

"Hope? Hope?" Donovan was nudging her awake.

But she was exhausted and just wanted to sleep. "What is it?" she murmured, not opening her eyes.

"It's Ella."

Hope shot up. "Is she hurt?"

Donovan grabbed her arms, steadying her. "I'm sure she's fine. I woke you because she's been sitting out in the car for at least ten minutes. Should I go get her?"

"No. I'll do it."

Donovan walked her to the door. He pulled her coat from the old coatrack and handed it to her without saying more.

Hope hurried out on the porch and headed down the stairs. As she rushed to the car, she saw Ella through the foggy window tipping back a bottle, and not a soft drink bottle either. It looked like a full-size cheap chardonnay.

Hope slung open the door. "What are you doing?"

"*Not* drinking and driving." Ella grinned lopsidedly. "You should be proud of me, Mom."

Hope stretched out her arm. "Give me that."

Ella jerked away playfully, sheltering her bottle, then took another quick swig before finally handing it over. "Sorry. It's all gone." She giggled. "You'll have to get your own."

"Where did you get the wine?"

Ella twisted her fingers in front of her mouth, locking her lips.

"Get in the lodge. You have school tomorrow."

Ella slid out of the car, giving new meaning to the word *tipsy*.

Donovan held the door open for them and Hope handed him the empty wine bottle.

Ella looked up at him as she passed. "Hello, *Father*," she said sarcastically.

Donovan gave Hope a questioning look but she had nothing for him. Not even a sliver of bandwidth. He'd have to come up with his own way to deal with his surly teenage daughter. But then she remembered he wouldn't be here long enough to have to concern himself with the *joys* of parenting.

"Just help me get her upstairs and into bed," Hope said as Ella sagged against her.

Donovan supported her other side and together they lugged her upstairs. After they got Ella settled on the bed, Hope dismissed him with "I've got this." She was used to taking care of her daughter by herself. Donovan left as she unlaced Ella's boots.

"I'll need to get a rag from downstairs," Hope muttered to her unresponsive daughter, "to clean up the mess from your boots." Snow could ruin the hardwood floors.

After Ella was tucked in, Hope stepped into the hall and was surprised to see that Donovan was wiping up the floor. He stood and gently pulled Ella's door shut, whispering, "Is this typical?"

"Don't judge me, Donovan." She'd told him she'd tried everything she'd ever heard that could help teens stop drinking. None of it had worked.

She slipped past him and down the stairs to get a glass of water to put beside her bed. She wasn't going to talk anymore tonight.

Once back upstairs, she checked in on Ella to find her snoring quietly.

God, please help her. This had become Hope's constant prayer.

Hope dragged herself to her bedroom, quickly donned warm flannel pajamas, and climbed into bed, deciding to leave the lamp on. She was so exhausted from the emotional upheaval of the evening that she assumed she'd pass out as soon as she snuggled under Elsie's Flying Geese quilt that she had loved so much.

But for several moments, she was wide awake, listening. Was she waiting to hear Donovan's footsteps on the stairs? *Ridiculous!* No, pathetic. At first there was silence but then she heard quiet male voices. Either Rick had come home or the master of the house was talking to himself. As the deep voices drifted through the floorboards, Hope was lulled to sleep.

She came awake suddenly, knowing someone was there with her. She rolled over and saw Izzie sitting at the small wooden desk, tapping her fingers.

"How did you get here?" Hope asked.

Izzie frowned. "How do you think? You're here, so I'm

here." She smiled at Hope mischievously. "So, big sister . . . shacking up with Donovan?"

"It's only temporary until I can get the house fixed."

"But you're in your old room," Izzie argued. "It must feel nostalgic."

"The lodge only has a couple of rooms decent enough for visitors. This just happens to be one of them."

Izzie looked around. "Lots of memories in here."

"I know. I'm trying not to think about it." This room was where Ella had been conceived. That snowy night when Hope slept over at the lodge and Donovan had snuck in to keep her warm. He'd held her close and lovingly gazed into her eyes, saying he was looking at the woman he was going to spend the rest of his life with. Everything had happened so naturally between them. She'd never regretted that one perfect night. That was the last time she'd stayed here, just days before the accident. Which should have been ancient history by now, but it felt like it was yesterday.

Hope changed the subject. "I'm extremely worried about Ella. Staying here at the lodge seems to have exacerbated the situation."

"You know what I think?" Izzie said.

"If I say no, are you going to tell me anyway?"

Izzie gave that tinkling laugh that always reminded Hope of bells. "Of course I'm going to tell you. I think you should ask Donovan what you should do."

"That's crazy. I know Ella better than anyone," Hope said, incredulously.

"Yet he's the recovering alcoholic."

"Oh."

"Yep. You're going to have to team up with your baby daddy." Izzie grinned. "Who better than her father to help your daughter with her drinking problem?"

Chapter 14

DONOVAN SCRATCHED BOOMER behind the ears while he sat in the old recliner. There was nothing like the unconditional love of a dog to soften his troubles.

"So the town council has demanded the impossible," Rick said. "We're smart guys. We'll figure out how to get six to eight months' worth of work done in seven weeks." He flipped open his laptop. "We'll start from scratch. You know how much I dig Gantt charts."

"Freak," Donovan kidded him. He set Boomer on the floor and went to the dining room table to join his friend.

"We all have our thing. Mine just happens to be spreadsheets," Rick said, not offended at all. "I think you're the freak because you're all about coding."

But no computer code was going to fix this mess or carve an escape hatch into the wall Donovan had been backed into. Maybe rebooting the Christmas Festival's Wines of Alaska was a dumb idea and he should cut his losses. Hope certainly thought so. She would probably be happier if he just winterized the lodge and left town until spring, when he could put it on the market.

"What should we tackle first?" Donovan asked.

"Open up the pictures you and Courtney took of the hardware store and show me what needs to be done. Tomorrow, I'll drive into town and take a look myself. With Sparkle as my tour guide, of course."

"Of course." Donovan stared at him for a long moment. "I have to say that I've never seen you like this."

"I know. I'm besotted."

"I can't believe you used that word. You're sounding like a girl."

Rick shrugged, not threatened. "I'm *feeling* like a man who's found his one and only. And you?"

"Let's get down to work."

They stayed up half the night, drinking coffee and planning, but the deadline was still out of reach.

"There's no way we can get it done," Donovan concluded. "Even with the four of us—you, Sparkle, Hope, and myself—working twenty-four hours a day.

Rick glanced up from his laptop. "We will. I'll hire workers in Anchorage or whatever big city is the closest."

Donovan shook his head. "But how are you going to get them here on such short notice? According to your Gantt chart, you needed a crew here four weeks ago." Donovan felt defeated.

"Don't worry about it. I'll take care of the details. The good news is that you know how to swing a hammer. I bet Hope and Sparkle do, too." He held up his hands. "I'm much better at typing but I'll do what I can. You go to bed. I'll stay up a while longer and order supplies."

"I can help with that," Donovan said.

"No. Sleeping Beauty is getting cranky and should get some rest." Rick gave him a concerned look. "I promise it's all going to work out."

"I doubt it." Donovan pushed back his chair. "I'll see you in a few hours." He grabbed Boomer and headed upstairs.

Once he got to the top landing, he glanced at Hope's door for a second longer than he should've. He couldn't believe the crazy mess that had brought her here but was glad that she was. He went to his room and settled Boomer at the end of his bed. But when he lay down and stretched out, he couldn't sleep for thinking about the impossible deadline. Or was it the four cups of coffee keeping him awake. Or it might be that his houseguests—Hope and his daughter—were sleeping soundly across the hall. Like a strong wave taking him unaware, he was hit all over again. He and Hope had a daughter! The thought was overwhelming, yet he was pleased to no end. Ella was a mixture of energy, sass, angst, and joy, especially when she played with Boomer. She reminded him of his grandmother. Of Hope. Of Beau. And the best of him. God had dropped a miracle in his lap and Donovan was grateful.

Yet he was aware that if he hadn't come back to Sweet Home, he might never have known about Ella. Anger at Hope welled up again. But Father Mike had said not to expect forgiveness to be a one-and-done. Forgiveness was a process. Which required patience and lots of practice. The payoff was relief from the pain of the past.

Donovan finally dozed for a couple of hours before his alarm went off. He was so wiped out he was sure no amount of coffee would fix the problem. Once again, he considered putting Sweet Home in his rearview mirror. But the thought of leaving Ella when he hadn't even gotten to know her had him rolling out of bed. He couldn't immediately fix what was troubling his daughter, but he could tackle today's to-do list that Rick had put together.

When Donovan stepped into the kitchen, Hope was already there, looking in the cabinets. She must've set her alarm to early o'clock, too.

"Coffee's up there," he said, pointing.

She jumped and grabbed her chest. "You did it again. Don't scare me like that. Especially when I'm not fully awake."

"How'd you sleep?" he asked.

She paused before answering. "Fine. You?"

"The same," he lied.

She went back to making coffee. "I'll get this started and

then I need to get Ella's clothes in the dryer so she'll have something to wear to school."

He shook his head. "I finished her clothes last night."

"You what?"

"I hung up a bunch of her things since I wasn't sure if they went in the dryer or not. Go take a look in the laundry room. You may need to pop something into the dryer."

"You didn't have to do that." She sounded almost angry.

"It's no big deal. I was awake." *And she's my daughter, too.*

Hope turned on the coffeemaker and huffed from the room.

She was back in a few minutes. "Um, thank you for taking care of her things. Sorry, you know, for how I acted. I'm not used to getting help and it kind of freaks me out."

He raised an eyebrow and grinned. "Have you thought about therapy for that?"

"Like I could afford it," she muttered.

He pulled down a couple of coffee cups for them. "Should I get a mug down for Ella, too? Does she drink coffee in the morning?"

"Goodness, no. She already drinks too much soda with caffeine as it is."

"What does she like for breakfast?" he asked. He genuinely wanted to know.

Hope scanned the room. "If it's okay, I'll make French toast, her favorite. I want to do something special to make up for her having to stay here."

His defenses went up but he settled them down. He remembered being a teenager and how even little changes could set him off. "Make yourself at home." He pulled all his thoughts together and tried to form them into words. "You know, I'm not sorry that your water heater flooded your house."

"What? That's a horrible thing to say—"

He blew out some pent-up air. "Sorry. Not what I meant. What I'm trying to say is that I'm glad you're here."

Her eyes flicked wider in . . . surprise?

He had to set her straight. "I'm glad for the chance to get to know Ella."

"Yes, well, that's good. I'm glad you want to know her." But judging by her tone she wasn't completely on board. "She's a great kid." Hope poured her coffee, not meeting his eyes. "I assume, since I'm your employee, that I'll have to help you get ready for the wine tasting?"

"Yes. If that's okay."

"What if I say no?"

"You can't, Hope. It's all hands on deck. And then some, if you're up for it."

She turned around suddenly, her face expectant, her coffee nearly sloshing over the side. "Do you mind if Ella helps out, too?"

"That would be great." He should've thought of it, another chance to spend time with his daughter. "We can definitely use all the help we can get." Now he had five people on the team.

"I think an after-school job would be good for her, help her to work through her grief over my dad." Hope opened the fridge and pulled out a carton of eggs. She paused for a second. "You said at the town council meeting that you're a . . . recovering alcoholic?" She looked embarrassed to have said it aloud.

"I am. What do you want to know?" he asked.

"I was wondering if you have ideas on how to get Ella to stop drinking. How did you stop?"

This was the first inclusive thing Hope had said to him concerning Ella.

"The military helped a lot," he responded readily. Being in the service gave meaning and purpose to his life and helped him through his darkest days of losing Beau. "There's nothing like Uncle Sam bearing down on you to make you get out of bed in the morning." The military had also given Donovan a career path. He served his term of service, got his GED, went to college, and then started his own software company. Last month, days before Grandpa died, Donovan had exited the company, setting himself up financially for years to come. Or at least he'd thought so. Now a lot of the profits would be going toward the lodge and the hardware store.

"I'm not sending Ella off to military school, if that's what you're proposing," Hope said.

"I was just telling you about my first wake-up call. AA is what saved me," Donovan clarified.

"There aren't any AA meetings nearby. I've checked." Her expression was thoughtful. "But there should be. We have a real problem here in Sweet Home."

Donovan wondered what he could do to bring AA here. But Rick had made it clear last night that they already had their hands full with the lodge and the hardware store. It didn't matter. "We'll think of something for Ella," he promised. Donovan would do anything for his daughter.

"Think of what for Ella?" Ella stood in the doorway. Her eyes were scrunched together as if the kitchen light were actually causing her pain.

Hope set the eggs on the counter and hurried over to her, pushing her hair back from her face. "I'm making French toast. I hope you're hungry."

Donovan would bet that Ella's hangover would keep her from eating. He opened the pantry and pulled out a bottle of Advil. "I've got something for that headache."

Ella looked too miserable to argue and dropped into a chair.

"Most of your clothes are in the laundry room down the hall," Hope said.

"Why?"

"A consequence of leaving them on the floor. They all got wet," Hope reported. "Everything is washed, thanks to Donovan, but you might need to throw something into the dryer."

"I'm supposed to be at school early this morning."

"What for?" Hope asked.

"Makeup exam," Ella answered.

"Makeup for what?" Hope's pitch had risen.

"Chemistry." Ella held up her hand. "Do me a solid. No third degree this morning."

Hope sighed. "Fine. We'll talk after school."

"I'm busy after school." Ella dropped her forehead to the kitchen table.

Donovan set a couple of crackers, an Advil, and a glass of water in front of her. "Eat the crackers, then take the pill. It should help."

Wordlessly, Ella looked up at him with bloodshot eyes.

"I promise it'll make you feel better," he said.

Ella put her head down again. "I don't need a father," she said into the table.

He tamped down his hurt. "How about a friend, then?" For as long as he was here, he was going to be parental backup for Hope . . . if she'd allow it. Maybe he and Ella could grow into a father-daughter relationship. It was going to be hard since he was leaving soon, but he was going to try.

Hope cracked eggs while speaking over her shoulder. "Whatever you have going this afternoon, Ella, you need to cancel it."

"Why?" Ella groaned as if the single syllable took too much effort.

"You're starting your new after-school job."

Ella glared at her. "What are you talking about?"

Donovan jumped in. "We're going to revive the Christmas Festival here in Sweet Home. We're on a tight schedule and we could really use your help around here."

She stared at the crackers as if they were poison. "What if I don't want to?"

"Non-negotiable," Hope said with mock cheeriness as she dipped the bread in the whipped eggs.

Donovan was in awe of Hope's patience and even keel with Ella . . . and he wanted to participate. "Did I mention, Ella, that I pay my employees pretty well?"

"Well, that's something." She picked up a cracker and nibbled at it.

Boomer wandered in. As if Ella had puppy radar, she popped up and grabbed him. "You are so stinking cute!" Her transformation from moping teen to happy kid was evidence that Boomer cured hangovers.

"Can you take him outside?" Hope asked. "Donovan needs to fill me in on what needs to get done today. Wear my boots. They're by the front door."

Ella didn't need to be told twice. She took the dog and Donovan couldn't help but follow, just to watch his daughter. He was in awe of her, too.

She put Boomer down for just a moment while she slipped on Hope's boots, all the while chatting with his dog about how *cute* he was.

When she opened the door, she stopped short and turned back to Donovan, a quizzical expression on her face.

"What is it?" he asked.

"I'm not certain. But I think you have company."

Donovan stepped in front of her and peered out, unsure of what he was seeing. At least half a dozen vehicles were packed into the lodge's driveway, with more idling in the road. "What's going on?"

"I don't know. Mom?" Ella yelled over her shoulder. "Come see this."

Donovan slipped on his boots and stepped outside as Mr. Brewster got out of his truck carrying not a new puppy this time, but a notebook. Donovan met him halfway. "'Morning, sir."

"We've been waiting for you. We figured you'd be up early. But"—Mr. Brewster checked his watch—"I guess we were wrong." He glanced at the door and then grinned at Donovan.

Donovan looked behind him to see that Hope was standing in the doorway, and then she disappeared. Ella had gone into the yard, her attention absorbed by the dog.

Mr. Brewster nodded toward Boomer. "I see that runt is thriving."

Donovan had no interest in changing the subject. "I'm confused. Why is everyone here?"

Mr. Brewster motioned to the cars. "This is your labor for the repairs on the lodge." He handed over the notebook. "I've made a list of workers and what you're to pay them given their different skills and experience." He passed him a second notebook. "This is an itemized list of the repairs that need to be made to the hardware store. I have other workers meeting me there in an hour. I figure you have the lodge under control, so I appointed myself foreman of the hardware store remodel. You know, I worked there part time for nearly twenty years. I'll even stay on to stock the shelves for you so you'll be open in time for the Christmas Festival."

Donovan was speechless. He couldn't believe Mr. Brewster had pulled this together overnight, while he and Rick had been spinning their wheels.

"I don't know what to say," Donovan finally sputtered.

"But, just tell me you have a list of things that you want done here at the lodge. Otherwise, all these people came here for nothing."

"Yes, I have a long list ready."

"I hear Hope is going to decorate for you," Mr. Brewster said. "It's good to see you two back together." The old man gave him a stern look, as if a firm talking-to were coming. "But you two really should be married first before living together." He nodded toward Ella. "It doesn't set a very good example for little Isabella."

"We're not—" Donovan started.

But Mr. Brewster was already heading back to his vehicle.

HOPE FLED TO the kitchen, her cheeks blazing. Everyone in Sweet Home knew she was "shacking up" with Donovan Stone! She rifled through the cabinets, looking for a stainless-steel carafe to put hot coffee in so she could start a new pot. Elsie used to have one here.

Something was burning. She turned off the French toast.

Ella came back into the kitchen. "Where's the laundry room?"

"Down the hall, last door on the right," Hope answered. "How about some regular toast instead?"

"I'm not hungry." Ella grabbed a cracker on her way out while Hope tossed her burned breakfast in the trash.

Donovan came into the kitchen, still looking shell-shocked. He took a slug of coffee before asking, "Why are you hiding?"

"I'm not." She opened the fridge and stuck her face inside, hoping to cool it off. Also, she had a good reason for looking in there. "I'm checking if we have enough food to feed everyone."

"Place a quick order with Piney and then I need your help picking out paint, tile, and furniture online."

Hope turned to face him. "You can't pick out furniture online. You have to sit on a couch or test a mattress to see if it's comfortable."

Donovan opened his mouth but didn't get a chance to answer as Rick ambled in with a pleasant grin on his face.

"What's going on?" Rick asked.

"Unexpected visitors," Donovan said.

"Who?"

"A crew to start repairs on the lodge."

"Really?"

"Did you call Mr. Brewster and set this up?"

"Who's Mr. Brewster?" Rick asked.

"He's an old friend of the family who's appointed himself foreman of the hardware store," Donovan answered.

"Then who's foreman here?" Rick asked. "If I get a vote, I vote for you."

"I'm delegating. I think you should oversee the lodge repairs. We should take advantage of all this labor while we have it."

"Okay, I'll take care of ordering lumber for the lodge and the hardware store. Then what are *you* going to do?" Rick asked.

"After I put in some online orders, I'm heading to the

hardware store. It's going to take a lot more effort to get the store up and running by Christmas than the lodge."

Hope's stomach fell. Which was crazy. She shouldn't care if Donovan was here, there, or in Timbuktu. Making Rick foreman for the lodge, though, felt as if Donovan would do anything to keep from being near her. But he wasn't wrong. The hardware store was a mess. To begin with, it needed a new roof, according to what Leaky Parks had told her a while back.

Hope grabbed the notepad on the counter and took it to the table to start the grocery list. Unfortunately, instead of helping with the repairs, she would be spending her morning cooking for the crew.

There was a knock at the door and then a "Hello." It was Piney and Sparkle laden with grocery bags. "We come bearing gifts."

Rick hurried to Sparkle and gave her a quick kiss on the cheek, but instead of lightening her load, he relieved Piney of her bags. *Clever move.*

Sparkle blushed.

"What's in the sacks?" Hope asked.

"Lunch for the workers and food to stock Donovan's pantry. I figured since he was gone for a week his refrigerator would be empty."

Hope's ears perked up. Piney sounded as if she knew where Donovan had been. Hope would be doing some arm-twisting later to find out what she knew.

"Can you help me put everything away?" Piney asked.

Hope asked her own question. "Who's watching the store?"

"Bill is manning the cash register," Piney said.

In all the time that Bill had been in Sweet Home, Hope had never known him to work at the store.

"I'm headed right back but I needed to speak to you first," Piney said.

"Oh?"

"You need to measure all the windows for new curtains here in the lodge and the cabins. Then look around and decide what furniture would look best."

Hope was torn. On the one hand, she had a definite vision for the lodge, but it might not match Donovan's, which meant working closely with him. She dreaded being near him . . . and at the same time, she longed for it.

"I see that look on your face," Piney said. "But you're the best one to bring this place into the new millennium. You've always had such great decorating sense. Look how you've kept the Hungry Bear's front window looking so charming and up to date all these years. You yourself have said how much you've always loved this lodge." She looked beyond Hope. "Donovan, what do you think?"

He came into the dining room. "I agree. I can't do it all, Hope, and it would be great if you oversaw the decorating."

"The lodge is yours," Hope protested. "It should reflect who you are and what you like."

"My taste isn't the issue," he said quickly. "I just want to spruce up the lodge to sell it. Don't forget, I'm not staying . . ." Was she imagining it or did he look a little uncertain? Conflicted, too? Her heart fluttered.

Stop it! Hope told herself. She needed to make *He's not staying* her new mantra. He probably wished he'd never even brought up the Christmas Festival to the council. Well, she didn't need him here. What she needed was Donovan gone so things could get back to normal. But maybe she shouldn't rush him; without him here, she would be without a job and no place to stay.

Boomer looked up at her with big sad eyes.

"I bet you'd like some breakfast, wouldn't you, little guy?" she said.

Donovan pushed away from the counter, but she held up her hand. "I've got it." She poured Boomer's dry food into a dish and filled his water bowl.

"All I care about is that the lodge should look Alaskan," said Donovan. "And not *old* Alaskan like it does now."

Piney nodded. "Then it's settled. You and Hope will work together to put the lodge and cabins to rights. Take your measurements, and then you both need to head to Anchorage. After you pick out furniture, hit the quilt shops for fabric for both the window treatments and the quilts."

"What?" Hope's brain was buzzing as she tried unsuccessfully to block Piney from shoving a pad of paper at her.

"Bill and I put together a list of possible quilts and the amount of fabric needed for each."

"Quilts? Seriously, Piney, you and I barely have enough time to make curtains." *And you're nuts if you think I'm going to Anchorage with Donovan!*

"Good lands!" Piney said. "We won't be doing this alone. We'll enlist the help of the others in Sweet Home who can sew."

Hope knew her mouth was hanging open. "Well, I can't—"

Ella rushed in with her backpack dangling from her hand. "Mom, can I take the car to school?" She knelt down to kiss Boomer on the head.

Hope was still staring at Piney. "I can't go to Anchorage today. I have to take care of Ella."

"Hogwash!" Piney exclaimed. "Ella will come here after school and help Sparkle. Have no worries, buttercup. I'll stay at the lodge with Ella until you get home." Piney smiled at Ella as if she had a secret. "Ella has me and her dog to keep her company this evening, right?"

"Mom, I'll be fine. I don't need a babysitter. Boomer and I can hang." Ella had her hand out. "Now, can I have the keys?"

"They're in the basket by the front door." She turned to Donovan to see what he thought about Piney's steamrolling, the impromptu trip to Anchorage, and his reaction to the two of them obviously being thrown together.

Donovan stepped into the fray. "Listen, Piney, I don't have time to make a trip to Anchorage. Why don't you take her? You and Hope can make a day of it. Besides, what do I know of curtains, fabric, and decorating?"

Piney dropped her hands to her hips. "I can't traipse off

to Anchorage. I'm going to recruit people to sew. And besides, I have the Hungry Bear to manage as well." She peered at him sternly. "I'd think you'd want to do whatever you had to for the sake of Elsie's Wines of Alaska wine tasting."

He frowned at her for a long moment, an intense staredown. Finally he caved. "Fine. For my grandparents."

Hope, completely unhinged from the exchange, followed Ella to the front door. "Are you sure it's all right if I go to Anchorage?"

"Mom, *you do you*," Ella said snarkily. "I have to get to school."

Hope was sure Ella didn't approve of her and Donovan going off together. She wanted to shout that this wasn't a date, not by any stretch of the imagination.

As Ella pulled on her coat, Hope said, "Text me when you get home from school. Come directly to the lodge so you can help."

"Keep track of your hours." Donovan had followed, too, and pointed his thumb over his shoulder. "There's a notebook on the table where everyone is going to log in and log out. Just add your name to the list."

"Sure." Ella squatted down to give Boomer one more kiss on the snout. "I'm outta here."

Hope felt a twinge of fear. What if Ella didn't come home after school? What if she went out drinking instead?

"Don't worry." Piney squeezed in beside her and patted her back. "I'll look after her. I'll text her when school lets out and have her run by the store to get something for the lodge . . . like lettuce. Something that might freeze in the car. That'll get her here quickly." Piney wrapped an arm around her shoulder. "Go. Have fun in Anchorage. You never let yourself do anything because of that sweet cabbage of a girl. But you ought to be able to get out of Sweet Home now and then."

Yes, but this was different. Going to Anchorage with Donovan meant spending long hours in the car with him. Close quarters. She wasn't sure her heart could take it.

Piney didn't seem to notice Hope's apprehension and the fact that she was rattled. "I know you value your self-reliance, but we're all here for you. I've told you a million times that it takes a village, Hope. It's time you tap into your resources. We love you and Ella."

"I know you do," Hope said. But the rest of Sweet Home could be a bunch of gossiping ninnies. Or at least that was what she'd thought at seventeen. But now—well, look how Sweet Home had pulled together for Donovan, the prodigal son. Momentarily, it made her heart full. "I better measure the windows. Donovan, do you have a tape measure?" she said over her shoulder.

"I can do better than that." He went to the small desk in the corner and retrieved a stack of papers. "You won't need to measure anything. Courtney did it in preparation for listing the lodge. She gave me a copy of all the measurements *and* a layout of the lodge so it will be easier to pick out furniture. I'll have Rick call ahead to the furniture store so they can have an experienced salesperson ready."

It was only eight o'clock in the morning but Hope already felt worn out. Plus her nerves were frayed at the prospect of spending the day alone with Donovan.

"Let me get ready." She'd need an extra notebook and sketching pad if she was going to make design decisions for the lodge. She also needed to pack an extra set of warm clothes, a blanket, and a few other items. "Donovan, you might want to bring along an extra set of clothes."

His eyebrow hitched up and she blushed.

"In case of emergency," she said firmly. She wanted to tell him to take his mind out of the gutter, but hers seemed to go there repeatedly where Donovan was concerned. "You can't have forgotten that here in Alaska we have to be prepared for anything."

"Yes, right," he said, chagrined.

Piney hung her coat on the rack. "Before I head to the store, I'll pack your food for the road." She glanced at the clock, frowned, and then looked back at the both of them.

"On second thought, don't even think about coming home tonight. You have too much to do. I'll definitely stay here with Ella, that is, if it's okay if Bill comes out here for dinner with us."

"Make yourself at home." Donovan patted Piney on the shoulder. "Thank you for everything, especially for looking after Ella."

Hope felt three emotions at once. First, resentment that Donovan would presume to thank Piney for looking after *her* daughter. Second, anger at Piney for insisting they stay the night in Anchorage . . . *together.* Third, complete and utter panic. What if being stuck in the car with him was too much for her? What if her emotions got the best of her and she told Donovan how she'd missed him all these years? How her heart was bursting with joy to have him back in Sweet Home? How it'd been so wonderful for him to hold her and kiss her again? And that she'd like to do more of it?

She needed to get a grip. In the meantime she went to pack.

Within the hour, they were climbing into Donovan's SUV with their emergency gear and overnight bags.

"Rick gave me a list of stores to hit. I guess I'm going to be the assistant to the interior decorator today."

Hope shook her head. "I'm not the interior decorator. I'm just helping out . . . *a friend.*" It was a ballsy remark. She even dared to glance in his direction, only to be rewarded with a confused frown. *Well, I won't try that again.* They weren't friends anymore, only thrown together through circumstance. Oh, how her heart longed to be his again. But her good sense knew better.

While he drove, Hope drew sketches and made notes of things the lodge needed, from towels to linens to wall décor. Anything to keep her mind off the chauffeur.

"I have a question about the hardware store," she said all businesslike, trying to come back from her earlier faux pas. "Are you going to put the quilt shop back within the store, the way Charles and Elsie had it?"

"Mr. Brewster's drawing does include that," Donovan said.

"I feel a *but* coming."

"There's not enough time to order fabric, at least enough to make it look like it did before. Maybe the new owner will revive the quilt shop and bring the hardware store back to its former glory." Donovan looked contrite. He probably didn't know any more than she did what the new owners would do. But the quilt shop within the hardware store had been a real draw to their quirky, charming town. Visitors from all over had come to see it . . . and to shop. The thought made her sad, to come this far and not go all the way with the restoration. She realized that she'd even been imagining the revival of the Sisterhood of the Quilt.

"Speaking of fabric," Hope said, changing the subject, "did it register that Piney expects us to pick up fabric to make quilts for each of the cabins and the B-and-B rooms? It's going to be expensive, you know."

"I think it's a great selling point," Donovan said. "If we can make this a turnkey operation, buyers should be lining up when I put it on the market."

There it was again. The one thing Hope was scared of— *Donovan leaving*—and at the same time, she was worried he would never go. She was in serious danger of falling for him so deeply that she would never recover.

She tucked her fear away and concentrated for the rest of the trip on how to optimize their time in the city.

When they pulled into Anchorage, it was midafternoon. "Big things first," Donovan said. They headed to the furniture store.

There they tried out every large comfy sofa for the living room, the gathering spot for the B-and-B guests and the cabin dwellers alike. The salesman assumed they were a couple and Donovan didn't correct them. Her stupid heart played along, too. Picking out furniture for the cabins was easy, the same items for each one. Hickory log bed frames, side tables, and dressers provided the Alaskan flair Donovan was looking for. Plush hotel mattresses would give the feeling of luxury out in the wilderness. The bedrooms in the main building would have a more substantial feel, with cedar log beds, something the two of them decided upon together.

"What about the non-B-and-B bedrooms?" Hope asked, referring to the family's living quarters and feeling more than a little awkward when asking. It wasn't like they were building a home together. "Do you want to do the same cedar log beds for those?"

"No. I think we should differentiate the living quarters from the guest quarters, don't you? Something more upscale?"

"It's your dime," Hope said.

"Come help me find what will work." Donovan strolled over to the luxurious bedroom sets as if they were a staple in his life. Not the same boy she knew, who loved to camp under the stars and run wild through the woods.

He insisted Hope try out each bed, lying side by side, deciding on the perfect firmness together. Where he was being practical, she was imagining choosing mattresses for the two of them. After testing nearly every one—and her nerves frayed beyond repair—they picked out the furniture for the family bedrooms, different styles for each. For Ella's room, she indulged her whimsy and chose two wooden sleigh beds, something she'd always dreamed of having as a kid. For her room, she chose a more sophisticated look, a cream leather upholstery bed, one that would look great with a Barbara Lavallee–inspired quilt laid over a reading chair in the corner. For the master bedroom Donovan chose a massive four-poster bed that looked fit for a castle. The carved posts stood at attention like four turrets guarding the bed. Perhaps an extra loft quilt would work best with that one.

"Now that we're done here, let's go buy the soft furnishings for the rooms," Donovan said.

Hope looked at her watch. "If we're going to get fabric, we better do it now before they close."

"Remember my grandmother's Sisterhood of the Quilt

wall hanging?" Donovan asked. "Would you be willing to duplicate the quilt and update it with new fabric?"

"Absolutely not. It's your grandmother's quilt." The wall hanging looked like an aerial shot of a group of quilters' hands as they worked on a simple quilt. It was one of a kind, special. And Hope had no right to change any of it.

"I thought I might send the original to my father to hang in his home in Florida."

Hope felt foolish. "Oh. That would be nice. I'm sure your dad would cherish it. But maybe you should get Piney, Bill, or one of the other quilters to work on it. Someone who's a better quilter than me."

He shrugged. "I want you to do it." He had a sad smile but seemed determined.

His insistence was really messing with her. And she tried not to read any more into it. Tried not to think that Donovan cared about her and wanted her to do this one special thing.

"Okay, I'll make it." *For you.*

"Thanks."

As they drove to the first quilt shop, Hope sketched the Sisterhood of the Quilt wall hanging and did some quick math to figure out how much fabric it was going to take. The way they were blowing through money, Hope was sure Donovan was going to max out his credit cards soon.

"How about we hit two shops today and then a couple on our way back tomorrow?" She checked his expression before saying the rest. "I know I mentioned this before but you do understand that the fabric for the quilts isn't going to be cheap, right? We could buy some inexpensive comforters at Walmart that would look great."

"I know that would be fine, but it's not just about selling the place, Hope. I have a vision for it, something my grandparents would be proud of if they were here."

"As long as you're aware."

At the quilt shop Donovan stood close while Hope pulled bolts and had the sales help start cutting while she went to get more. Her bank account would never allow a shopping spree to buy any fabric she liked without concern for cost. And she loved every second of it. The store clerks seemed excited to get such a large order so late in the day. Donovan didn't even flinch when he was told the total, but instead gave a friendly smile to the cashier as he handed over his credit card.

They arrived at the next quilt shop just as it was closing. Hope was almost giddy when she found the Barbara Laval-lee Arctic Wonders fabric and took it to the cutting table. She pulled out her phone and turned to Donovan. "Look at this. Isn't this quilt so Alaska?"

The shop owner peeked over Hope's shoulder. "Oh, that's the Arctic Adventures pattern from Patti's Patchwork. We have that one. Let me get it for you."

Donovan smiled at the picture. "That quilt will look great in your bedroom."

"That's what I was thinking. But it's not my bedroom. Just a place I'm staying for now."

He gazed at her as if they'd never been apart and all their history was shared. "*Your bedroom*, Hope. Nan always insisted you should call the lodge home."

"Yeah, well, that was a long time ago." Why did he have to look at her that way? Stir up old feelings? She could feel her cheeks getting warm and she grappled for something to say. "Elsie would be tickled that there are going to be special quilts in every bedroom. I remember her talking about doing it herself." Hope had already bought moose fabric, bear fabric, even Highland cattle—Highland Coos—fabric for the cabins. Tomorrow, she'd look for some buffalo plaid for the boys' rooms. "So . . . do you know what you'd like for the master bedroom?" It was awkward for her to ask. It wasn't as if they'd ever share the room together but her mind went there anyway.

It had been one heck of a day, with her feelings going haywire. Out of control . . . Frazzled! Excited! And at the same time, she knew she was getting all worked up over nothing.

"I don't know. What do you think?" Donovan said, bringing her back to center.

"Honestly, I think you'll need to tone down that bedroom set with something more delicate." She held out some fireweed and forget-me-not fabric. "Something like this."

"I like it. Let's get it while we're here."

Hope picked out the coordinating fabric but knew she'd want to speak with Bill and Piney before cutting into it.

"We can come back here in the morning and get more fabric, if you need to," Donovan suggested.

"That's okay. I think this is it for here."

After a shopping trip that was more fun than Hope had dreamed, they drove to a restaurant down the street, where Rick had made them a reservation.

The restaurant was thronged with diners in nice clothes, clinking glasses and making a din. She'd been in Anchorage with her dad, of course, but she'd never been out on a date there. *Not that this was a date!* She laughed to herself . . . as if she'd know what to say or do on a date. Hope tried not to feel embarrassed when Donovan slipped an extra bill to the maître d'. Was it because the maître d' was staring at Hope's old brown parka and secondhand black skinny jeans? She could dimly remember a time when clothes had been important to her, but that was before she had rent, car payments, and a child to raise.

Hope tagged along as Donovan was led to an intimate table in the back. She almost wished they'd been placed at the bar because sitting across from him was almost too much. This table for two was meant for holding hands and gazing into each other's eyes. She was happy when the menu was set in front of her. Even happier when the food arrived quickly so she could focus on it instead of how blue Donovan's eyes were. And how those eyes used to be filled with love for her. He was so good-looking and so generous with his smiles for others . . . and today he'd been generous with his smiles for her, too.

The seafood was fantastic and Hope ate heartily; shopping, plus being near Donovan all day, had worked up her appetite. When the waiter brought their decaf coffees at the end of their meal, Donovan scooted closer, making her world tilt a little. If it'd been another time, she would have leaned over and kissed him. Laid one on him because that was what the moment called for. And what her heart wanted to do.

"Is your notebook in your purse? I thought of a couple more things we should do before we head back tomorrow."

Like make out? But that was her adolescent brain rearing its silly head. Her single-mom brain told her to move away from him and get a grip. *Put a lid on it.* Treat Donovan like he was a stranger and not like she'd loved him all her life. "Yes. Right." Besides, they weren't a couple. He was her boss and she was the hired help. She reached in her bag, pulled out the old composition notebook that Ella had used last year in natural sciences, and flipped to a clean page. "Go ahead."

He listed several places to visit and then the waiter brought the check. Hope got a glimpse of the total; her bank balance couldn't even afford the tip. "Thanks for dinner. And for picking up the hotel."

"It's a business expense."

"But still . . ." Hope hadn't eaten out in forever. The truth was that tonight would be her first night in a hotel since Ella was born, while for Donovan it was probably old hat.

He reached over and touched her arm. "Ready to head out?"

She gazed at his hand, wondering at the solid touch of him, and she felt light-headed.

He immediately dropped his hand, and once again, she felt awkward, self-conscious. She looked down at the notebook on the table and couldn't, for a second, remember why it was there. But then she got it together. "Some stores are open until nine. We should take care of the towels and linens. Don't you think?"

"Agreed," he said.

An hour and a half later, with the car loaded down, they headed to the hotel. Hope stayed in the car to call Ella while Donovan checked them in.

"Hey, Mom," Ella answered, giggling.

Oh, no! Had she been drinking?

"Where's Piney?" Hope asked.

"She's at the front door, telling Bill good-bye," Ella said, barely able to get the words out.

"What's going on there?" Hope asked sternly.

"I'm on the floor and Boomer won't stop jumping on me and licking me like I'm a dog lollipop." Ella gurgled with laughter. "Stop it."

"How was school today?"

"The usual."

"How did the makeup exam go?"

"All right, I guess."

"You're going to have to buckle down, Ella. College applications are right around the corner."

"Come on, Mom." Ella huffed like college was light-years away.

"I miss you," Hope said, trying to counteract the nagging. "I wish I were there."

"So you could be on my case even more?"

Hope sighed. "No. What did you do at the lodge this afternoon? Organize the garage?"

"Nah. Piney had me sew up a dog bed for Boomer."

Hope rolled her eyes at the phone. She'd have to talk to Piney about spoiling Ella. "You know you're going to have to do manual labor like cleaning, right?"

Ella ignored her. "I like Piney's sewing machine. The thread doesn't get knotted up every other second like yours does. When are you getting home?"

"Hopefully early evening. I'll send you a list of things to do tomorrow."

"Okay." But it sounded like *Whatever*.

"Can you tell Piney to give me a call?"

"She's right here." Ella must've handed her the phone because she said, "It's Mom."

"Hey, buttercup, how goes the shopping?" Piney chirped.

"A whirlwind. Donovan has bought out Anchorage. But

we need to talk about you coddling Ella. She's nearly grown and she understands she needs to work."

Piney ignored her and whispered into the phone, "So how are the two of you getting along? Two peas in a pod, eh?"

"No. Just a boss and an employee." Hope saw Donovan coming out of the hotel. "Take care of my girl. I'll text when we leave the city tomorrow."

Piney laughed. "Don't do anything I wouldn't do."

Hope hung up. That innuendo wasn't helping her already frayed nerves. Didn't Piney understand how being cozied up in the car all day, and then shopping with the sexiest guy Hope knew, was pure torture? Delicious torture. The kind of torture that had Hope wishing for a good-night kiss . . . and possibly more.

Hope jumped as Donovan opened his door.

"We're all set," he said. "Our rooms are near the back entrance." He handed her the key envelope. "Room 129."

She didn't say anything. Couldn't say anything for fear of saying something suggestive. Something like . . . *Let's share a room and save the expense of two.* But her living in a fantasy world had to stop. He didn't feel about her the way she felt about him.

When he parked, she pulled out her small duffel bag and nearly ran for the door. But he beat her there and scanned his key card and held the door open for her.

"Thanks." Her room was the first one on the left, and she knew she'd be able to breathe any minute . . . once she got in her room with the door closed behind her. And when she did, she was going to give herself a stern talking-to about not reviving her crush on the man who'd broken her heart.

She scanned her key card, then reached for the knob, knowing peace and calm were only feet away. But as she pushed her door open, Donovan gently grabbed her arm, stopping her.

"Wait," he said.

She turned to find him gazing at her, his eyes searching hers.

"Yes?" Or was she saying *yes!?* Her body certainly felt like molding itself up against him. Maybe even purring a little, too, because the way he was looking at her was making her heart pound faster.

"I want to thank you." He let go of her arm. "You've been a real trooper today."

Her outlandish expectations plummeted, fell to the hallway carpet with a splat. Donovan wasn't going to pull her into his arms and kiss her passionately. How could she be so incredibly stupid!

"Oh, something else," Donovan said, awkwardly this time. "There's one more stop we need to make tomorrow. We need to hit up a clothing store before we head back to Sweet Home."

He had great clothes. Why was he acting weird?

"What are you needing?"

"Um, it's not for me." He cleared his throat as if trying to select his next words carefully. "You need to *up* your wardrobe, Hope. As hostess for the Wines of Alaska, you'll need a cocktail dress of some kind."

"Are you out of your mind? Your grandmother never wore a cocktail dress. Probably in her whole life. Donovan, this is Alaska."

"I'm trying to attract a certain type of buyer."

She frowned at him . . . no, glared. "Fine!"

"And while we're at the mall, I'd like you to get some other new clothes for yourself."

As she opened her mouth, he put his hand up.

"Before you argue, it's not a handout, it's business. You're the housekeeper, a representative of Home Sweet Home Lodge, right?"

She was fuming now. "I'm not wearing a housekeeper's uniform, if that's what you're getting at." He'd probably want her decked out like a French maid.

He shook his head. "That's not what I'm thinking. I'm thinking something like a concierge's dress."

"A dress and heels for the housekeeper of an Alaskan

lodge? Yeah, right. Traipsing through the snow between the cabins and the lodge in my kitten heels, then scrubbing floors in a stylish dress? Quite the picture."

"Just some nice slacks and a blouse, then," he countered.

"I don't have that kind of money—" She was going to add *you egotistical idiot*, but she made herself stop before she got fired.

"I'm buying. Maybe while we're at the mall, you can pick up a couple of things that Ella needs, too."

So Donovan was embarrassed by both his daughter and his daughter's mother. *Great!*

"Good night, Donovan!" She tried to escape inside, but he wedged his foot in the door.

"Don't be mad." Just like that, a wave of memories came flooding in, until she felt as if she might drown. How many times had he said that to her when they were teenagers and in love? She'd been a ball of hormones then, taking things wrong, reading things into his words that weren't there, not realizing that boys didn't think things through before opening their mouths. *Apparently, men didn't either!*

"I'm not mad, Donovan; I'm furious. Now you can leave. You've insulted me enough for one evening, don't you think?" How could she have allowed Donovan Stone to wound her again?

To his credit, he looked ashamed. "Sorry. I didn't mean to." He let go of the door and it shut.

But a second later, there was a knock.

"What?" she barked.

"I'm going out for a while," he said through the door.

It was late. Where could he be going at this hour, besides a bar? Which he shouldn't be doing. Had she driven him to drink?

"I'm going to a meeting," he explained, as if reading her mind. "Text me if you need anything."

"Okay," she said quietly. She was alone. Which was how it was supposed to be.

She padded across the modern room, slipped her shoes off, and flopped onto the king-sized bed, burying her face in the pillow. Well, a few words from him had straightened her out. She'd spent the day thinking he might like her again, be attracted to her, but apparently, he'd just been biding his time, trying to figure out how to tell her that she dressed like a hobo. She kept replaying every moment of the day and it still ended with him calling her a *trooper* and then telling her that she needed new clothes. She was an idiot.

"Hey," Izzie said. "You want to talk about it?"

Hope turned over to see Izzie stretched out on the other pillow as if she were luxuriating in the room.

"You know he's kicking himself for how he handled it," Izzie said.

"I doubt it. When he gets back, Scrooge McDuck will probably toss his hundred-dollar bills on the bed and roll around in them."

"I don't think so. You know he just wanted to do something nice, to help, something you really need, too. He just went about it the wrong way."

"Because he's ashamed of me."

"We've talked about this before. He feels bad. He has so much and, let's face it, you could be the poster child for welfare."

"Thanks for the reminder that I'm nearly destitute."

Izzie rolled over and faced her. "But you're not. It could always be worse." She sounded just like their mother.

"What am I supposed to do?" Hope asked. "Say thank you for the handout?"

"You're going to be gracious. You're going to let him buy clothes for you and Ella. You're going to allow it because it will *bless him*. What is the little prayer that you say every morning?

Hope didn't want to repeat it but Izzie was waiting, giving her that pursed-lip look.

Defeated, Hope sighed. "Please let me be a blessing today."

"That's the one. It's a fine prayer. It's a perfect way for you to give to others—"

"Because I have nothing else to give," Hope finished. She offered Izzie a smile, though it was sad. "Thanks."

"Sleep well. Tomorrow you'll have a chance to be a blessing again."

Chapter 15

HOPE STARED SILENTLY out the window of Donovan's car as they drove back to Sweet Home. Despite Izzie's admonition to be gracious, Hope had been sullen all morning while Donovan dragged her around the mall from one clothing store to the next. She really tried to be open to his charity but she'd had a lot of practice in making it on her own. When he saw she was in the same mood that he'd left her in last night, he must have figured there was no point trying to cajole her into a happy-to-shop-with-you mood, but that certainly didn't stop him from buying her several dresses, two pairs of sensible pumps, four pairs of slacks, two sweaters, and five blouses. She half expected him to pick out some underwear and socks for her, too.

Yeah, he must've thought he was being sly when, behind her back, he took a winter coat to the counter. She'd looked down at her brown puffy coat and thought, *There's nothing wrong with this*. It was still functional and only had one small rip in the sleeve. She was already planning what to do when he presented her with the coat. She'd nod, then give him his money back . . . somehow.

But Hope was happy that they'd found some nice things for Ella. She had never had the cash to do a traditional back-to-school shopping spree, which was what this haul felt like. Ella would be thrilled.

Donovan broke the silence as he pulled into the parking lot of a small-town grocery store. "I need to stop for coffee." So apparently he'd slept horribly last night, too. "Do you want me to get you some?"

"Thank you, I can get my own," Hope said evenly, as if she were the queen of Cool, Calm, and Collected.

Although she was none of those things.

The quirky two-story grocery store was fairly empty. She browsed every snack aisle while he ordered his coffee from the only worker in sight. Hope grabbed a small bag of chips and then headed upstairs to see what was there, stalling until Donovan was done so she could order her coffee without him nearby.

Last night had proven she should put the dream of him out of her mind forever. He was nothing but her employer, who wasn't even going to be in Alaska much longer. He was a stranger to her now, not the boy she'd loved for most of her life. Perhaps she'd never loved him at all, but had made it up, a romantic fantasy. Sure, they'd played together as kids, but that was the only truth she believed in now. She would be cordial, because he was her boss, but she would no longer be looking for signs that there was still something between them. Last night he'd confirmed it. *Trooper!* He might as well had called her a pal.

After she made a quick tour of the camping gear, board games, and clothing upstairs, she heard Donovan thank the cashier and knew it was safe to head back down. She kept her eyes on him while he pulled out his phone and made a call. *Probably making a date with Courtney, the way he was grinning.*

Where had that come from? Hope wasn't supposed to care who he dated, or who he kissed. She was supposed to have a new mind-set—one that didn't include pining over him.

She was almost to the bottom of the stairs and working really hard to keep her emotions in check. Why had Donovan so inconveniently come back into her life? It was infuriating. And infuriating that he could still affect her this way.

She went for the last step and somehow she missed it. The next moments happened in slow motion. Her ankle rolled, and she fell forward. Donovan turned. Rushed to her. Slipped his arms around her. Caught her. Stopped her, by mere inches, from making a full face-plant, although her outstretched hand still crushed her chips as they hit the floor.

The pain in her ankle was so immediate that she was barely aware of Donovan holding her—at first. In the next second, she was fully aware she was crushed against him. Someone should bottle Donovan's embrace for the masses—it was a natural painkiller.

"Are you okay?" he asked, his minty breath sliding past her cheek.

"My ankle," she gasped. "I think I sprained it." Tears were misting her eyes, so maybe being in his arms wasn't the cure-all, after all.

"Can you get me some ice?" he called to the young woman behind the counter. Then he turned back to Hope, "We need to find you a doctor."

"No! I'm fine." Her whole adult life, she'd never had health insurance. "I just want to get back on the road."

He nodded. "I'll get you to the car and come back in for the ice and our coffees. Cream and sugar?"

"Yes." She felt stupid for falling off the last step, and even stupider being carried to his vehicle. *Insult to injury*—literally—he was even buying the coffee that she'd insisted she could get on her own.

"Come on, gimpy, let's get you settled in the car." He started them toward the door.

She glared at him.

"Too soon?" he said.

"Yeah."

"What about ibuprofen? Do you have any with you?" he asked. "You're going to need it."

"I don't know." She, who prided herself on being prepared! But pain and proximity to his beating heart were fogging her brain so she couldn't think.

"No worries," he said. "I'll get some."

It was pure bliss—*and utter agony*—to be held against Donovan, his arm around her waist as he helped her to the SUV. And he smelled so good! It almost made her forget that her swelling ankle hurt like a son of a pipefitter. He was affecting her in ways that could be dangerous to her wellbeing, so she conjured up unwashed laundry, last Sunday's crossword puzzle, and roadkill.

None of it worked.

He opened her car door and helped her inside. But he seemed unsatisfied. "You should be lying down with your foot up. I'll rearrange things."

"No. I'm fine."

"At least let me dig out one of the new pillows for your foot. Maybe two."

Donovan leaned across her to start the engine to get the heater going. Which got *her* heater going, too. She was both saddened and relieved when he left her to go back into the store.

While he was gone, Hope gingerly pulled off her boot, exposing her fat ankle and fat foot. "How am I going to work now?" Who knew how long it would take for the swelling to go down? "My life is a hot mess," she moaned. "One disaster after another."

Before her pity party was completely over Donovan was back with two paper sacks and two coffees.

"Your ankle looks bad." He reached for the door handle as if to leave again. "I'll ask inside if there's a doctor in town. I'd feel better if you got an X-ray."

She laughed mirthlessly. "Look around . . . a town this size? I'll be fine." *It's my own dang fault*. She should've been watching where she was stepping instead of dwelling on him. A life lesson she wouldn't soon forget. As if her ankle would let her anyway.

"We're not leaving until we get you squared away." He held out one sack. "Your ice."

She took out the ice pack and positioned it on her ankle while he dug around in the second sack. He pulled out a new bag of chips and a banana, holding them both out. "Here's your chance to make good choices."

She was way beyond *making good choices*. "It's no contest." She grabbed the chips and set them in her lap.

"You have to eat before taking an anti-inflammatory."

"Yes, *Mom*," she said.

Next he produced a humongous bottle of Advil.

"That's enough to keep a grizzly pain-free for a month," she grumbled.

He glanced at her ankle again, his brow furrowing even more. "Stop complaining and take your meds."

"You're as bossy as Piney."

"Well, somebody has to push back against your stubbornness. I'm glad you've had her all these years," he said.

He had no idea how much he'd hit it on the head. If not for Piney, Hope wouldn't have had anyone.

He pulled out a bottle of water. "To stay hydrated. The coffee is just for fun." He passed that over to her, too, and then put the car in gear.

Hope ate a few chips, took two Advil, and then leaned her head back, closing her eyes. The throbbing in her ankle matched her heartbeat, not letting her forget what a fool she'd been. It was also a great reminder to put Donovan and her attraction for him in a box and leave them there. She felt satisfied with her resolve and drifted off to sleep.

Hope woke up as Donovan pulled into the lodge's driveway. She sat up and looked around, noticing that the driveway was empty. Surely the crew hadn't finished for the day.

"Where is everyone?" she asked.

"Look behind you," Donovan said. "Most of Sweet Home is parked out on the road. They must've thought we'd need the driveway to unload." He smiled at her. "They were right."

The lodge's front door opened and Rick and Sparkle appeared, slipping on their coats.

"Sit tight," Donovan ordered. "I'll come around to get you. You can't afford to slip and hurt your other foot."

He has that right. The image of two casted feet had Hope staying where she was.

Sparkle was beaming at Hope. "Perfect timing. We just got here. I see the car is loaded down." Her expression turned puzzled. "What's wrong?"

"Twisted my ankle," Hope said glumly.

"How?"

"Paying attention to things I shouldn't," Hope admitted cryptically.

Donovan got to her side of the car. "She fell walking down the steps at that funky grocery store a couple hours ago. Rick, can you get on the other side of Hope and we'll get her inside?"

Rick seemed amused. "Nah. You carry her in and I'll unload the car."

Donovan didn't even give Hope a chance to protest as he knelt down and scooped her out of the car, his arms under her legs, like a twenty-first-century Rhett Butler.

"No!" But it was too late. He had her halfway to the door.

That was when she noticed all the people around, some with tools in their hands, some with cleaning supplies.

"Stop thrashing about," Donovan complained. "You're making a spectacle of yourself."

"Put me down. This is the last thing I need." Hope hated being helpless, but what she hated even more was *looking* helpless. This was giving everyone the wrong idea.

Donovan easily carried Hope over the threshold while she cringed at the image they'd produced for onlookers. *Just what the wagging tongues of Sweet Home needed.*

"What time is it?" she asked.

"Five o'clock," Piney said, coming out of the kitchen. She looked as amused as Rick had. "Is there something you need to share with me?" She had a did-you-elope-in-Anchorage twinkle in her eyes.

Hope glared at her. "Stop smiling. I sprained my ankle. And it hurts." Then she turned to Donovan. "Okay. We're inside now. So put me down!"

"Take her to Elsie's studio," Piney said. "We have a surprise for her."

"What surprise?" But Donovan was on the move again, hauling her away, and Hope couldn't keep Piney in her line of sight.

He used his foot to push open the studio door and Hope saw it. Saw *them*. All of them. It was as if she'd been transported back in time. A familiar gaggle of women were setting up their sewing machines, chatting away . . . until they saw Donovan holding her like a bride. The Sisterhood of the Quilt had somehow been revived and—even more surprising— they were speechless.

"How? Why?" Hope sputtered.

But they were all gawking at her.

She glared at her transport, then spoke to the room. "Donovan was just helping me into the house. I sprained my ankle." Then to Donovan she whispered, "Put me down!" and pinched him to let him know she meant business.

"Ouch," he said, but he didn't budge.

Miss Lisa moved a sewing bag off the couch and onto the floor. "Donovan, be a dear and set Hope here on the sofa."

Aberdeen grabbed a pillow for Hope's foot as Donovan gently eased her to the cushion.

Paige Holiday picked up Boomer and set him in Hope's lap. "Some extra love to help heal your foot."

"Do you need anything else?" he asked Hope.

Yeah. Erase everyone's memory of the last minute.

But she only mustered up, "I'm fine." She'd been saying that a lot lately, although it wasn't remotely true.

"I'm going to help unload the SUV," he said. Several women followed him out, apparently to help, too.

"What is everyone doing here?" Hope asked Aberdeen, who was still fussing with her pillow.

"We're here to sew quilts for the lodge." Aberdeen was beaming as if Christmas had come early. "I took off work so I wouldn't miss anything. I loved coming here with my mom when I was a girl."

"Yeah, me, too," Hope said. Everyone seemed to be feeling the same . . . nostalgic.

Donovan walked back in with an ice pack in one hand and the bag of Barbara Lavallee fabric in the other. He laid the ice pack over her elevated ankle and said, "I made sure your new pattern is in the bag with your fabric."

The Sisterhood gave a collective sigh. Hope was mortified at all his attention. "Thanks," she finally mustered.

"Donovan," Piney said, "tell Hope how it was your idea to bring us all together."

His gaze traveled to the Sisterhood of the Quilt wall hanging. "I thought it would be a nice way to honor Nan, having you all here again." He paused as if he'd run out of things to say. "I'll get the rest of the bags."

Hope couldn't stop herself from being affected by Donovan's act of kindness. To bring the Sisterhood together was beyond thoughtful. How was Hope supposed to keep her emotional distance if he kept doing nice things?

Well, she just had to. She didn't have willpower when she was a teenager, but she was a grown woman now. A woman who had learned how to survive. She didn't need a man, which meant she didn't need him.

As soon as Donovan left the room, Miss Lisa struck. "Does this mean that you two are back together?"

"Heavens, no!" Hope exclaimed, then tried to change the subject. "I can't wait to show you the Barbara Lavallee fabric we got in Anchorage."

"He's being awfully sweet, though," Aberdeen chimed in, as if ringing the gossip bell for all of Sweet Home.

"Not sweet," Hope argued. "He needs the lodge's housekeeper to be in tiptop shape, is all." What if Donovan had to give her job away to someone with two functional legs? What would she and Ella do then?

Piney appeared, followed by Bill, who was carrying both his and Piney's sewing machines. Piney pointed to her old spot by the window. "Set them over there. And, Lisa, everyone, back up and give Hope some room to breathe."

Miss Lisa smiled at Hope as if she couldn't wait to get on the phone to share the big news.

Piney held up a sheaf of papers. "Bill's spent all day figuring out how we're going to get all the quilts done by the Christmas Festival. He's broken it down into steps and we've decided who's going to do what." She glanced around the room. "Get those worried looks off your faces. Aberdeen, you won't get stuck pressing all the fabric, just some of it. Lolly, you'll only have to cut some fabric. I've also taken your work schedules into account so there are no worries there." Piney started passing the papers around the room. But she didn't hand one to Hope.

"Where's my assignment?"

"You'll be busy with decorating the lodge."

What Piney didn't know was that Hope was going to make the Barbara Lavallee quilt and the new Sisterhood of the Quilt wall hanging.

Donovan returned with bags loading down his arms.

"Just set them on the cutting table," Piney said. "We'll get them sorted."

Donovan nodded and did as he was told. He turned to Hope. "Need anything?"

Not to fuss over me so much would be nice! But instead she said, "No. I'm good."

He left without saying more.

Hope turned to Piney. "Where's Ella?"

Aberdeen answered. "Lacy and Ella had to run out to Tyler's house. He's throwing the Halloween party tomorrow night."

"A school night? I thought the party was on Friday," Hope said.

"Something came up and it was moved." Aberdeen didn't seem shaken up about the switch.

"Who's chaperoning?" Hope asked.

"I assume Tyler's parents."

Darn Aberdeen for being so nonchalant! Hope would have to get to the bottom of this. But first, she pulled out her phone and texted Ella: I'm back at the lodge. When are you going to be here? For dinner? Hope hit send.

Ella wrote back. Late. Don't wait up.

But that was exactly what she was going to do. Hope texted a reminder. Be home by 10:00. You have school tomorrow.

The women got busy divvying up the fabric and refining the schedule as delicious smells from the kitchen floated into the room.

Donovan stuck his head back in. "Rick and I have started dinner—spaghetti. Just wondering if that's okay with everyone?"

"Yes" went up around the room.

"What about you and Ella?" he asked pointedly. "Are you both fans of spaghetti?"

Once again Hope blushed. Why did he keep singling her out?

"Ella won't be here. She's at Tyler's getting ready for the party tomorrow night," Hope said.

"On a school night?" he asked incredulously.

At least she and Donovan were on the same page . . . on this one topic. "Don't worry about dinner for her. She'll be late."

Donovan did a quick head count. "I'll let you know when it's ready."

"I'm going to go help," Miss Lisa said, and she left with Donovan.

Hope called Piney over and spoke quietly so the others couldn't hear. "Can we send Sparkle to get Ella? I just have a bad feeling."

Piney nodded. "Sure thing, buttercup. Do you want Bill to go along as reinforcement?"

"I think Sparkle can handle it."

"Where do you think Ella is?" Piney asked.

"Try Tyler's house first. If not, then she'll probably be at Lacy's," Hope said.

Piney squeezed her hand, then went to Sparkle and whispered in her ear. A moment later, Piney gave Hope an it's-all-handled nod. Sparkle brushed a hand across Hope's shoulder as she made her way to the door.

But as Sparkle walked out, Courtney Wolf strutted in, immediately coming to a full stop. Her long-lashed eyes flitted from Hope's face to her propped foot to the dog in her lap, then back to her face. She plastered on a cheery smile. "Hey, Hope," she said lightly, "what's going on?"

Hope wanted to ask if she was here to win Donovan's heart *and* his bank account. But people might think Hope wanted Donovan for herself. Besides, nobody in a two-hundred-mile radius could measure up to Courtney, Miss Alaska second runner-up. And if Hope was being fair, Courtney wasn't really all bad.

Hope finally answered, "You know me, Courtney, just lazing around."

Courtney's perfect lipsticked mouth transformed into a pout. "Are you all right?"

Piney stepped in front of Courtney. "Hope's fine. Are you here to help? If I remember right, you were quite good with a sewing machine. The outfits you made in high school were good enough for the runway."

Courtney didn't look pleased to be reminded of her poor beginnings and being forced to make her own clothes. Now, she was haute couture, especially for the wilds of Alaska.

Piney's expression turned soft as if she regretted what she'd said. "We could really use your craftmanship. Have you ever made a quilt?"

"No." Courtney looked uncomfortable, as if she knew she didn't quite belong here.

"Then stay. I'll show you," Piney said.

Courtney sneezed. "I can't." She glared at Boomer. "I'm allergic."

"Can you take the pup out to Donovan?" Piney asked Aberdeen.

"Sure." Aberdeen scooped the little dog from Hope's lap and she instantly felt cold. She pulled the quilt off the back of the couch to wrap around her.

Big mistake. The quilt sparked a memory Hope thought she'd snuffed out.

This was the quilt she and Donovan had cuddled under on the back porch and sometimes in his car. The first time they held hands had been under this quilt. Their first kiss, too.

Hope pushed the quilt away. She couldn't afford these memories. Not anymore.

Thank goodness Paige diverted Hope's attention. "Piney, are we to take the fabric home and work on it there?"

"Heavens, no. We'll piece the quilts here." Piney glanced up at the wall hanging of the Sisterhood of the Quilt, as if she were getting marching orders from it. "To honor Elsie." She paused for a long moment. "It's been a long time since we came together here and we may never get this chance again."

But Piney's demeanor was in opposition to her words. Her cheerful expression said this wasn't an ending at all, but a beginning, that the Sisterhood would be together for years to come. Hope knew that look—Piney's I-have-a-plan look—and worried they might be in for a wild ride.

"WHO WAS THAT?" Lacy asked.

Ella rolled her eyes and put her phone away. "Mom. She wants me to come home. If you can call it that." *The lodge isn't home.* Why couldn't they just move back into their house and make everything go back to the way it was before . . . before Donovan came to town?

"I bet it's weird," Lacy said.

"What?"

"You know, your dad." Lacy had a dreamy look on her face. Gross. She needed to quit acting like Ella's biological father was *hot*.

"He's not my dad," Ella insisted. "He's just someone my mom slept with." *Yuck!* "Do you have anything to drink?"

"Soda or something stronger?"

"Stronger." Ella put her hands to her head and squeezed. She just wanted *it* to stop. But how could it? Life was so messed up.

Lacy went to the kitchen, where Aberdeen kept the alcohol. "Mom told me to stay out of it, you know."

"I know." But Ella needed something to take the edge off. Something to give her clarity. She did know one thing: she didn't like Donovan. If Grandpa were around, Ella could talk to him about Donovan, how he'd shown up out of nowhere, how he was screwing up her life. But Grandpa was gone. And Lacy was being no help.

There was a knock at the door. "Do you want me to get it?" Ella hollered.

"Yeah," Lacy said.

Ella rolled off the couch and went to answer it. When she pulled it open, she couldn't believe her eyes. Standing there were Sparkle and Rick—with Donovan right behind them!

"Um, what's going on?" Fear gripped Ella. "Is Mom okay? Did something happen to her?"

Sparkle took Ella's hand. "Your mom's fine."

"Then, why?"

"Time to come home for dinner," Rick said cheerily.

"I told her I'd be home later." Ella hated that her mom would pull this crap, sending someone else to do her dirty work. And to send Donovan? *Unforgivable!*

"I could use some help with Boomer," Donovan said, holding up the dog for her to see. Until that moment, Ella hadn't realized that the puppy was in his arms. "With so many people at the lodge, I'm afraid he's going to get trampled. Seriously, we need you to come home because Boomer likes you best."

It was pure blackmail, but Ella couldn't resist. "Give him to me." She knew there was a tone in her voice, but she didn't care. Donovan handed over the dog. "Let me get my coat."

But as she turned, Lacy was there. "What's going on?"

Ella sighed heavily. "Do you want to come for dinner?" If she had to go, then she was bringing a friend with her.

"Let me dump these in the sink first." *The drinks.* "I'll need to text my mom at work, too."

"Don't worry about it," Donovan said. "Your mom's already at the lodge."

"Why?" Lacy asked.

"Because the Sisterhood of the Quilt is back," Sparkle announced.

"What's the Sisterhood of the Quilt?" Lacy asked.

Ella knew. Her mom talked about them when she told stories about Aunt Izzie. "All these old ladies used to sew at the lodge together and called themselves the Sisterhood of the Quilt." She set Boomer on the couch and slipped on her coat. "Mom talks about it as if it was special, but it sounds boring to me."

"Come on, you two," Sparkle said, "so you can see for yourself."

MISS LISA WAS draining the spaghetti when Donovan returned to the lodge and his duties in the kitchen. "Are you ready for me to take over?" he asked the elderly woman.

"Yes. I'd like to start cutting out the Highland Cow fabric. I'm making a Snowball quilt design for the Highland Coos Cabin."

"I'll join you," Sparkle said.

Donovan peeked into the living room and saw that Ella, Boomer, and Lacy were sitting in the beanbag chairs. "Ella, can you do me a favor?"

"Do I have to?" she shot back in typical teenage fashion.

"I would appreciate it," Donovan said.

"*Fine.* What is it?"

"Can you go to the sewing studio and ask the ladies and Bill what they'd like to drink with dinner?"

She didn't bother to reply, but with much groaning, she put Boomer on the floor and she and Lacy got to their feet.

Donovan pulled the Parmesan cheese from the fridge, but his curiosity was too strong to resist. He handed Rick the pot holders. "Take the bread out. I'll be back in a second."

He headed down the hall but didn't go into the studio. Instead he listened from just outside the door.

"Good grief, Mom," he heard Ella say. "Did you buy out the store?"

"Several stores," Hope replied. "Listen, would you and Lacy like to make a quilt for one of the cabins?"

Piney chimed in. "We could really use you girls' help. How about Wandering Moose Cabin? It's a Rail Fence quilt. Not that hard. It won't take you long with the two of you working together."

"I guess," Ella said. "I'm loving the moose fabric."

"Me, too," Lacy squealed.

It was working, just like Piney had predicted. He was sure that if Ella would just get involved, the Sisterhood of the Quilt would provide some stability for her. Give her a life raft in a sea of teenage angst.

Chapter 16

HOPE WOKE UP in her lodge bedroom to the smell of coffee brewing downstairs. She felt groggy from her throbbing sprained ankle. She'd been lucky last night that Donovan hadn't insisted on carrying her upstairs. Instead Rick and Sparkle had come to her rescue and helped her up to her room. But Hope couldn't shake how good it felt yesterday to be cradled in Donovan's arms. She squeezed her eyes shut, disgusted with herself.

She would do better today, she promised herself. Besides, she had a lot to occupy her mind if she was going to have everything decorated in time for the Wines of Alaska event. She put her feet over the side of the bed and took a second to strategize how best to get to the coffee. She hopped and hobbled to the door, then fumbled her way downstairs as quietly as she could, though her ankle hurt like crazy. As she neared the kitchen she heard, "Do you want me to fix you eggs? Bacon?" Donovan sounded as eager as Boomer begging for a treat.

"No. I'm good," Ella said sharply. She sighed. "Mom said I need to thank you for the new clothes."

"No problem. Do you need a lunch for school?"

This was painful. Hope decided to help him out. She plastered a smile on her face and hopped into the kitchen, hoping pain didn't register on her face. "So how is everyone this snowy morning?"

Ella rolled her eyes. "I assume you don't need the car today. Can I take yours?"

"Yes, as long as you come straight home after school."

"What about Tyler's party?"

"You have to get your homework done and have dinner here before you go." Hope went on, hoping to defuse the argument that was coming. "Bring Lacy with you after school. I bet Aberdeen will be here and we can have a family dinner."

Ella's gaze flitted to Donovan, then back to Hope. "No family dinner. Lacy and I can eat in the room I'm staying in. Speaking of . . . when are we moving into the cabin like you promised?"

Hope opened her mouth, but Donovan jumped in.

"It would be better for your mom if she stayed here until her ankle healed."

"Yeah. Sure. Mom can stay here," Ella said firmly, "but I'll go stay in one of the cabins."

"Nope," Hope said. "You and I stick together."

Ella threw her half-eaten toast in the trash, mumbling under her breath, "Unless I'm staying at Lacy's."

Hope decided to ignore it. "Have a nice day at school."

Ella harrumphed, then turned to the dog at her feet. "Come on, Boomer." They left the room.

"Aren't you worried she'll follow through?" Donovan asked.

"Not this time."

"But you didn't tell her not to," Donovan said.

"It's best not to engage when she's being snotty. Can I give you a piece of advice when it comes to Ella?"

"I guess so."

"What you're doing is not how you *do it*," Hope said.

"Do what?" Donovan asked.

"The eggs, bacon, and lunch thing. You can't get Ella's affection that way. You're going to have to be cool."

"I *am* cool," Donovan said, but there was a bit of questioning in his voice.

"Maybe you were cool in high school, but this is a different kind of cool. I've had years of practice and I still blow it all the time. Just be chill and let her come to you. It's like holding out your hand to a dog to let it know you first, instead of running straight to the dog for a big old hug. You're likely to get bitten."

"What can I do?"

"Just be there for her. Be present but don't hover," Hope offered, though she could think of a million times when she hadn't struck the right balance. "The goal is to not act overeager. Teenagers easily pick up the scent of *desperate*."

"I wasn't acting overeager—"

But Hope cut him off. "Yeah, you were."

"Fine, I'll do better. But only if you sit down and put your foot up. I'm going to hunt down some crutches for you today."

Hope put herself into a chair and lifted her leg to rest in another one. "Crutches would be appreciated."

"Don't worry about working. You have sick days."

Hope scoffed. "I've only been working for you for a short while."

"We're waiving the probation period." Like she was part of Stone Enterprises, Inc. He stared her down. "You were hurt on the job. Period."

"No. I was a klutz at that grocery store," she said.

He poured a mug of coffee and set it in front of her. "Eggs? Bacon? Do I need to fix you a lunch?"

She threw a napkin at him. "*I* don't like *desperate* either."

"Good to know." He popped a bagel in the toaster. "Breakfast will be ready soon."

When the bagel was done, he set it in front of her with a container of whipped cream cheese. "I'll be back."

Piney showed up just as Hope finished her coffee and bagel and helped Hope to Elsie's studio. "I know you want to start decorating today, but I feel like you should rest your ankle."

Hope sighed. "You're probably right." The rest of the day was a blur as she first read the directions for the Arctic Adventures pattern, then worked out the details on how to redo the Sisterhood of the Quilt wall hanging. She also took time to make a project list of what needed to get accomplished in each room and each cabin to get all the decorating done in time. Izzie's quilt pieces sat untouched in the box in the corner, but Hope knew that she would eventually get to them when the other work was done.

From what Hope could ascertain, several older women of Sweet Home were taking over her tasks as the lodge's housekeeper. When she tried getting to her feet to find out what they were working on, Miss Lisa reminded Hope, "If you allow your ankle to heal properly, you'll be back to work sooner." But from her place on the couch, she was able to direct others on where to hang the new items on the wall after the paint was dry, what towels were to be stored for the cabins, and what linens were to go to the living quarters upstairs.

At some point, Donovan deposited a set of crutches next to her. But then she didn't see him the rest of the day, not even when Sparkle announced that dinner was ready. But at least Ella showed up after school with Lacy in tow. With help from Piney, the girls quickly got to work cutting out their quilt for Wandering Moose Cabin. When it came time to go to Tyler's party, they both seemed reluctant to leave their project. Ella even said she wouldn't be gone long as she kissed Boomer's nose. Two hours later, Ella and Lacy were back.

"We just want to work a little more on the quilt. Aberdeen said it was okay if Lacy stayed the night."

"That's fine by me." Though her daughter hadn't asked permission. Hope was just thrilled that Ella hadn't come back drunk. "If you want, Sparkle just made hot cocoa. It's in the kitchen."

Ella picked up Boomer, who was really getting too big to lug around, and took him with her. When she and Lacy went

to bed, Boomer went with them. Stoically, Hope made it upstairs by herself. Everyone had left and Donovan hadn't returned from the hardware store.

Feeling lonely, Hope considered stealing Boomer from
Ella, but the truth was that cuddling a dog wasn't going to fix
the problem.

FOR THE NEXT several weeks, Donovan worked night and
day at the hardware store. He usually arrived home late to a
quiet house and barely saw Hope at all. He glanced in the
bathroom mirror and wondered what she thought of the
Alaskan-man look he was sporting. He'd stopped shaving, to
save time, and he'd needed a haircut even before coming
back to Sweet Home.

He finished up in the bathroom and walked into the hall,
wondering if Hope would be at breakfast this morning. But
he knew the answer: she wouldn't. She must be making herself scarce on purpose, while he had breakfast alone with
Ella. If only the city council hadn't forced him to fix up the
hardware store he'd have more time to get to know his
daughter. He wouldn't be in Sweet Home forever. The good
news was that Ella didn't seem to be nearly as angry at him
as she'd been. He'd done what Hope had suggested—
basically played hard to get—and it seemed to be working.
Ella had loosened up, talking to him about Boomer and how
to train dogs. It was a start. He'd have to thank Mr. Brewster
for giving him a job with dogs when he was a kid.

What he really needed to thank Mr. Brewster for was all
he'd done to renovate the hardware store. The old man had
really pulled everyone together, putting the right person in
the right job. Donovan still wasn't convinced it would be
ready in time for the Christmas Festival, but everyone sure
was trying. He was so incredibly grateful for the town's help.

As he walked down the stairs, he pondered the logistics
for Thanksgiving. While everyone took off for the long
weekend, Donovan planned to work as much as possible,

especially since Ella wouldn't be around. Hope had said she took Ella on a turkey camping trip every year, where they brought a turkey roast and baked it over the coals. He wished Ella would come help him at the hardware store over the weekend, or it might have been nice if he'd been asked to go along on the camping trip, too.

But maybe it wouldn't have been the best to be camping with Hope again, which would dredge up the old feelings and bring back the good times they'd had together. He already had enough recent memories to deal with . . . like holding Hope in his arms. And how it made him feel both vulnerable and invincible at the same time. Though she could take care of herself, holding her made him feel fiercely protective, and in those seconds, he wanted to be her man always. Even more unnerving, and frightening, was that those few moments with Hope had been the first time he'd felt *right* in close to two decades.

In the kitchen he found Ella sitting quietly at the table. "You're up early."

"Yeah." She didn't even look up from her phone.

Donovan started the coffeemaker, then pulled down two boxes of cereal—Ella's Lucky Charms and Life for him.

"So," Ella started, still concentrating on her phone. "In the trophy case at school, there's two pictures of you, holding trophies."

"Yeah. State football champs, junior and senior year."

"So you were a real hotshot, huh?"

"Not all that impressive, since our division was super small. Everyone had to play to make up a team."

"Quarterback?" she asked, looking up this time.

He nodded. "I could throw."

"Were you a jerk to the girls? Acted like you were *all that*?" There was something in her voice—she seemed . . . hurt.

"What's his name, Ella? If someone is treating you badly, I'll take care of it!"

She jumped to her feet, grabbing her phone. "It's nothing.

It's none of your business anyway. Stop acting like you're my dad!" She stomped from the room without pouring one ounce of cereal.

So much for the headway he'd made.

"Did I hear Ella?" Hope asked.

"Yeah. I screwed up again."

Hope patted his arm as she limped by. "Not your fault. She didn't come with an instruction manual."

It was nice that someone knew how he was feeling.

"How's your ankle?" he asked. "I noticed your crutches have gone missing."

"I'm glad to be rid of those devil sticks. My ankle's fine."

"Your limp speaks volumes. I hope you're staying off it, letting it heal."

"I spend most of my time at my sewing machine or guiding others on what piece of furniture needs to be put where. Speaking of sewing, you should peek in your grandmother's studio when you have a minute, to see how the quilts are coming along."

"I'll do that." He gazed at Hope for a long time and wondered what it would be like to have days like this on a regular basis. Passing in the hallway, feeling her touch, moments of him sharing his life with someone like Hope.

She gazed back, but finally broke the spell. "How's the hardware store coming? I hear bits and pieces from the Sisterhood of the Quilt. I'd like to hear it from the horse's mouth."

"It's coming along well. In fact, I think I can start spending more time helping here." He was hoping that if he was around more, he could navigate Ella with more finesse. "Besides, someone needs to take Rick's place here at the lodge. I understand he's taking Sparkle back to Louisiana for Thanksgiving to meet his family."

Hope's smile lit up the kitchen. "Those two are something."

"Yes, they are. I don't know about Sparkle, but for Rick it was love at first sight."

Hope blanched at his words. "Yeah, well, that happens sometimes." She stood. "I better get to work."

"What about breakfast?" he asked, not sure what he'd done to run her off.

"Maybe later," she said. "I have no appetite now." As she shuffled to the doorway she tossed over her shoulder, "Just to keep you in the loop, Ella and I are moving into Wandering Moose Cabin today."

"Why? You both are so settled here."

"We need our own space. According to Rick, the cabin's ready."

Why couldn't they stay here with him? And why did Rick have to be such a blabbermouth? "I don't understand." Then he grasped a straw to stop them from leaving. "What about Boomer? He's gotten used to sleeping with Ella, and I think she'll be disappointed if he's not with her."

Hope tilted her head. "Disappointment is part of life. It's better to learn that disappointment can be around any corner, instead of being blindsided when the rug gets pulled out from under you."

Okay, he got that she wasn't talking about Ella and Boomer. But what had he done to disappoint Hope?

"I really think staying here would provide stability for our daughter."

She raised an eyebrow and stared him down for a long moment. She didn't need to say what she was thinking. *My daughter! Not yours!* Then without a word, she walked from the room.

He put his mug down, hard. He'd messed up with both of the McKnight women this morning and his coffee mug had more of an idea of what he'd done wrong than he did.

HOPE WAS FURIOUS at Donovan and at herself. He'd never loved her the way she loved him and that made her a chump. Chumps believed in love at first sight. And falling in love with him at six years old made her the biggest chump of all.

She needed the job here at the lodge, but she didn't need to live under the same roof as him. As soon as she saved up enough money to fix her house, she'd get back to her small, uncomplicated life.

Hope didn't go to the studio. Instead, she limped her way back up the stairs to pack. Ella met her coming down.

"Have a good day," Hope said, trying to muster up some genuine cheer.

"Yeah, like that's going to happen."

They were both in miserable moods.

"I need you here right after school. We have a lot to do."

Ella grumbled as she left the lodge.

Since Hope's ankle had left her pretty much out of commission for the last three weeks, Ella had been helping with the housekeeping, and some evenings, she stayed in and sewed with the Sisterhood of the Quilt. When she did, Hope was optimistic that things were going to be okay. But just as often, Ella would go out and come home drunk, making Hope feel helpless. A failure. She wished Donovan had been around more to help. Like for the past seventeen years.

When Hope was done packing her room, she went to Ella's and filled a laundry bag full of her daughter's clothes. Outside, she heard cars pulling up, alerting her that workers were arriving for the day. Careful not to do more damage to her ankle, Hope dragged Ella's laundry bag downstairs. As she hit the bottom step, Jesse Montana walked in the front door.

"Morning, Hope." He gave her a friendly wave. "I hope it's okay but Piney told me to just come on in and find a task to do in the notebook. On the dining room table?"

"Yes, that's fine." Hope waved him over. "Can you help me get my stuff over to Wandering Moose Cabin first?"

"I thought you lived here now," Jesse said.

"Ella and I were just waiting on the new mattresses and they arrived yesterday. But I can't wrangle our things down the stairs and to the cabin with my ankle still out of whack."

Suddenly she noticed Donovan in the kitchen doorway,

taking in their exchange. By the glower stretched across his face, he wasn't happy.

Jesse turned to look at Donovan, too, as if asking for permission.

"Do as the lady wants," Donovan said in a harsh tone.

She pointed upstairs. "My bedroom is the first one on the left. Ella's is next to mine. If you could get her stuff, too?"

She started for the laundry room, dragging Ella's laundry behind her. Suddenly she was relieved of her load. "Hey—"

"I've got it." Lugging the laundry, Donovan passed her but kept talking. "And before you say *she's* my *daughter*"— he used a high-pitched voice, as if Hope sounded like that!— "let me remind you that I'm Ella's parent, too."

"Fine!" Hope reversed direction and, snatching her coat off the coatrack, hobbled out the door. A moment later, she heard the door open and close again. Sure that it was Donovan and worried he might scoop her up and carry her the rest of the way to Wandering Moose Cabin, she sped up, slipping as she went.

"Be careful, Hope," Jesse hollered.

"Oh." She slowed down to let him catch up. "It's just that it's cold out . . . the reason I'm hurrying."

He was carrying two boxes but he extended his elbow toward her. "Hold on to my arm," Jesse said. "I can get you to the cabin safely."

"Thanks. I'm okay." Jesse, who had been working construction all around Alaska for the past several years, was nice to her in high school, one of the few people to treat her with kindness instead of making fun of the preggo. "When did you get back?" she asked. Since leaving the Hungry Bear, Hope had become a little disconnected from the daily gossip.

"Two days ago. I don't know if you heard but my mom's sick."

"I had heard. I'm so sorry." Patricia was battling cancer, and Hope had no words to comfort him. "I think I will hold on to your arm, if that's okay." She hoped her touch could take away some of the sadness in his eyes. "Tell me what Shaun is up to? The last I heard he was working for an oil company in Texas."

"Yes, the bro's still in Houston but he'll be here for Thanksgiving."

"Your mom told me that he was engaged," Hope said.

"Not anymore. They broke up," Jesse said.

Hope heard footsteps crunching in the snow behind them and turned to see Donovan carrying her old-fashioned suitcase in one hand and Ella's laundry bag in the other.

"Hold up," he called.

They stopped and waited for him, though Hope wanted to keep going.

"So Mr. Brewster just called and he needs able bodies to help at the hardware store today. Do you mind?"

"Sounds good," Hope piped up.

Mr. Grouchy gave her a look. "I'm not talking to you."

Jesse grinned at their exchange. "I'm glad to do it. As long as I can check in on my mom now and then."

"Absolutely. As much as you need to," Donovan said. "Here, I can take those boxes."

Jesse transferred them. "It was good to see you again, Hope." He gave her the same kind smile he'd given her when they were young, but now he was a man.

"We should catch up while you're home," Hope said deliberately. Yes, it would be nice to visit with Jesse for a while, but what she really wanted was to see the flash of anger ignite in Donovan's eyes. *Good.* He deserved it.

Hope watched Jesse walk away.

"Come on." Donovan waited until she turned back around before he started walking again.

"You two seem very friendly," Donovan said. "After I left, did you and he start dating again?"

"Why do you care?"

Donovan's jaw clenched and the vein on the side of his neck bulged. "Never mind. Get inside. You need to get off your foot."

Hope hobbled up the new solid steps, opened the red-painted door, and walked inside. Wandering Moose Cabin had been transformed from a ramshackle hut to a cozy hideaway. The hole in the floor had been fixed and the hardwood had been polyurethaned to a glossy shine. The walls had been dusted and the small café table in front of the window had been painted a wilderness green. New headboards, new mattresses, and new sheets adorned the extra-long twin beds. Hope was pleased that she'd donated Izzie's moose fabric to the cause because the window coverings pulled the whole room together.

"Since the quilts aren't ready yet I'll make sure some blankets are brought down to the cabin." The offer was generous but his tone wasn't.

"Bill said the quilts are nearly ready to come off his long-arm machine." Hope opened the bathroom door and peered inside. It had had a makeover as well.

"What about putting a microwave, mini fridge, and a coffeemaker in here?" she asked.

"No, not this cabin," he said firmly. "Meals will be eaten at the lodge."

"Don't you think guests will expect those amenities?"

"You're not a guest. You're—" He stopped himself, then started again. "Ella is family."

"Don't you think, then, that she ought to be able to keep Boomer with her at night?"

That seemed to quash his machismo. "Yes. You're right. But let me be the good guy and tell her, okay?"

"Sure."

They stood there for a few moments in awkward silence. Finally, Donovan said, "Are you sure you won't reconsider and stay at the lodge?"

"We'll be happy right here," she said, praying it was true. At least Ella would have Boomer to keep *her* warm at night.

But what about Hope? Donovan was standing right in front of her. But he wasn't smiling. He didn't love her like

Boomer loved Ella. He was just glaring at her like Hope had made a big mistake.

Yes, Hope was already regretting her rash decision to move out of the lodge. But that regret was just her heart wanting more from him, which wasn't going to happen. She'd gotten used to living without him once before. She could do it again.

Chapter 17

AT NOON DONOVAN sat down in his grandfather's office and opened the security camera app on his computer to see if everything was operational. Everything looked good . . . until he got to the video from the wine cellar.

"Hey, can you . . ." Hope was standing in the doorway. "What's wrong?"

"Come see for yourself." She might as well see the truth with her own eyes. "The wine cellar, last night."

Hope walked in and stood over his shoulder as he replayed it. "What am I looking at?"

"Wait for it." Donovan watched again as Ella keyed in the security code for the cellar and went in. Less than a minute later, she reemerged with two bottles of wine.

"No. How could she?" Hope whispered. In the next second, she said, "She's in so much trouble."

No. She's a troubled teen. But Donovan didn't say it. Instead, he reached up and took Hope's hand. "Can you let me handle it?"

"I'm her mother. It's up to me to lay down the law." She sighed. "I don't want Ella to see you as the enemy. I'll take the heat."

He didn't like it. Didn't like the worry lines between

Hope's eyebrows. Didn't want her to go through this alone. He squeezed her hand. "Okay. You can let her know she's busted. But, Hope, we're in this together. Tell her that she's in trouble but let me dish out the consequences."

"I don't think that's a good idea."

"She stole from the lodge. It should be me who gives out the punishment."

"Seriously, Donovan, she'll never want anything to do with you if you play the heavy." Hope let go of his hand. "What do you have in mind?"

"Something to help Ella."

"You're not going to tell me?"

"I think you should remain in the dark. You don't want to be complicit, do you? Ella can't blame you if you don't know."

Hope gave him a hard glare. "It better not be corporal punishment! I won't allow it."

"Of course it's not corporal punishment. Nevertheless, she is not going to like it. I know I wouldn't if I were in her shoes." Since he'd found out that Ella might have a drinking problem, he'd been thinking about a way to help. Now was his chance.

"I'm just so angry," Hope said. "Other things, too. When your kid is in trouble, you're hit with a mixture of embarrassment and heartbreak. And guilt, too."

He took her hand again, expecting her to jerk away, but she didn't. "You know, Hope, this isn't completely her fault. I'm the one who passed my drinking problem to her." Bad genes. "She inherited a tendency to addiction. But we can give her tools to overcome it."

"I hear what you're saying, but it's hard for me to believe I'm not responsible. I'm the one who raised her. I've done the best I can, but our life hasn't been easy."

Donovan pulled her in for a hug. "I'm so sorry. I know I'm responsible for that, too."

For a second, they held each other. He was overwhelmed with emotion and kissed the top of her head, wishing he'd been here to help Hope. Help Ella. For no other reason than he wanted to, he tipped Hope's face up and kissed her, trying to erase the furrow between her brows. Trying also to ease the panic within him. And it worked. Until she pulled away and slipped from his embrace before he was ready to let go.

"I have work to do . . . sewing, decorating." She left the room.

That afternoon when Ella arrived home after school, he watched Hope follow her upstairs. He wasn't proud of himself, but he quietly snuck upstairs, too, to listen outside Ella's bedroom door.

"First," Hope said, "do you have any homework?" Apparently, the Inquisition could wait until after schoolwork was done.

"I finished it during free period."

"Good. Now hand them over," Hope said.

"Hand over what?"

"The bottles of wine you stole yesterday."

"Oh." Ella's attitude deflated. "How did you know?"

"I'm your mother. I know everything," Hope said with convincing bravado.

"There's only one left," Ella said.

"Get it for me," Hope said.

"I don't have it. I took it to Lacy's."

There was silence. "Fine," Hope finally said. "I'll drive over and get it."

"Don't! I'll get it. It would be so embarrassing, Mom, if you went over there."

"You should've thought about that before you took something that didn't belong to you. Plus, it's illegal for a minor to be in possession of alcohol." Hope was quiet for a moment, then she made an audible sigh. "Fine. Text Lacy and tell her that you'll be over within the hour to pick up the wine. I'm driving you. And just so we're clear, you're grounded."

Donovan thought it was generous of Hope to help Ella save face.

"There's more," Hope said. "You'll have to work off the bottle you stole."

"What's it worth? Twenty bucks tops?"

"I don't think it's the amount that's the problem. You broke our trust."

"What, are you and *him* a team now?"

"Yes." Then Hope hesitated. "We're your parents."

"He's not my father. He's just the sperm donor."

That hurt.

"First, watch how you speak to me," Hope said firmly. "Second, there will be consequences for what you've done. What they are is up to Donovan."

"Consequences? More than one?" Ella complained.

"I don't know. He'll have to tell you. He wouldn't share them with me."

"Great," Ella said. "Punishment from *dear old dad*."

"Scoot over."

He heard the mattress squeak.

"When you see him, you're going to have to apologize."

"I know."

"And you're going to have to mean it," Hope said.

Donovan had heard enough, and he really needed to break the habit of eavesdropping.

Quietly, he walked downstairs and back to his grandfather's office, remembering his past, feeling thoughtful and ashamed of the things he'd done as a kid. He pulled out his phone. "Hi, Dad," Donovan said when his father picked up. "I wanted to wish you an early happy turkey day, and well, I want to apologize for all the trouble I got into as a kid."

"Awww, don't worry about it," his dad said good-naturedly. "You were just rambunctious."

"I banged up the car. I drank all your beer. I was a pretty wild kid. You can't deny it," Donovan said.

"You were perfect," his dad insisted, which made tears spring to Donovan's eyes. Father Mike had talked about God's unyielding love and forgiveness. Donovan decided his own father must take after Him.

"I'm trying to make amends once more for all I did," Donovan said, feeling as choked up as he had the first time. "I'd like to hear again that you forgive me."

"Of course I forgive you. I'm your dad."

PINEY WALKED INTO Elsie's study and immediately knew something was wrong with Hope. She was upset.

For a few moments she studied Hope and wasn't feeling good about what she saw—no twinkle in her eyes, only worry. Things weren't progressing with Donovan the way Piney had planned. Even though Donovan carried that girl in so lovingly from the car, Hope had been acting like he meant nothing to her at all.

Hope had lived at the lodge for a month and she and Donovan weren't any closer to matrimony than the day she moved in. Things actually were worse, since apparently Hope had moved out to one of the cabins.

Something more had to be done! Maybe Piney needed to set Hope up with Jesse. That should shake things up, make Donovan get off his butt and marry the girl before it was too late.

ELLA LAY ON the bed in her lodge bedroom, staring at the ceiling and trying not to cry. Her life sucked so hard. This wasn't even her bed. It was some fancy sleigh bed with some fancy mattress in some room she'd been forced to stay in. At least the quilt was old and worn . . . and warm. She crawled underneath it, not wanting to ever come out.

She hated herself for what she'd done. She'd never stolen anything before in her life. Not even gum from her mom's purse. She didn't know what had come over her. She'd needed a drink and she'd seen the cellar's password hanging from the magnet on the refrigerator. It was just that sometimes it was all too much . . . *Life*. Drinking helped to dull the pain. But now, drinking was going to force her to apologize to Donovan. Her *dad*.

Ella buried her face in her pillow, feeling horribly embarrassed. He probably hated her now and would tell everyone that his daughter was a thief. And then everyone would know what a loser she was. They would think she didn't know right from wrong.

There was a knock on the door. "Ella?" her mom said. "It's been fifteen minutes. The pity party's over. I need help in Elsie's studio."

She wished her mom would leave her alone. "I have homework to do."

"You told me you finished it," her mom said.

"Fine." Ella sat up. "I'll be down in a minute."

"And, Ella?" Her mom's voice was muffled, like she had leaned her head against the door.

"What?"

"You might as well get it over with. He's in the garage."

Great. Ella was so looking forward to it. "Fine." She crawled out of bed, blew her nose, and opened her door, expecting her mom to be standing there, tapping her foot impatiently. But the hallway was empty.

She walked down the stairs and past Elsie's studio, where her mom and a lot of the other women from town were working and laughing like crazy. At least someone was having fun. She exhaled and marched on. The doorway at the end of the hall led to the humongous garage.

She didn't see Donovan at first. But then she spotted him in the corner, pulling boxes down from a shelf. For a fleeting moment, she wondered if maybe she could just skip this part; her mom would never know.

But I would.

"Hey, can I talk to you?" Ella said quietly.

He didn't turn around. "Sure. Come help me with these."

She walked down the four steps into the garage. "What are you doing?"

"Just checking out the Christmas decorations. Rick bought a bunch of new stuff while we were in Anchorage but I wanted to use some of my grandparents' too."

All of a sudden it hit her that he was talking about *her great-grandparents*, part of her family. A whole family she knew nothing about. "What were they like?"

Donovan looked over his shoulder, a warm smile on his face as if he was remembering something nice. "They were the best, the most welcoming and patient people I've ever known. Nan seemed to always have home-baked cookies in the oven and Grandpa was always whistling while fixing something around the place. Your mom could tell you. She loved it here. We used to have so much fun, playing in the woods and fishing in the river. You should ask her about it." He turned back to his boxes. Ella thought he was done talking but then he said, "Have you ever been ice fishing?"

"Yeah. Mom takes me a couple times every winter," Ella said, coming closer. She picked up a glass bauble that had a poinsettia on it. "It's usually a lot of fun."

He didn't look up but had stilled. "Would you go with me while I'm here? I haven't been since I was about your age." He seemed frozen, waiting.

"Sure," Ella said, feeling weird about this. "Can we bring Mom along?"

"I don't think so, not with her bum ankle."

"Listen," Ella said, not wanting to talk about ice fishing, "I'm sorry I took the wine. Mom said you were going to dish out the punishment because it's your lodge and all. And I doubt ice fishing is the consequence for what I did."

He faced her then. "Ella, I'm an alcoholic." His expression looked worried. "I started drinking heavily when I was about your age."

She put the ornament back in the box. "Well, I'm not an alcoholic and I don't drink heavily, if that's what you're getting at."

"I don't think you're the kind of kid who steals either. Yet you were reckless enough to take wine that you knew you shouldn't take. And you knew that we'd installed security cameras all over."

She hated that he was right on all counts.

"You're a smart young woman," he continued, "yet the siren call of alcohol had you doing something that you have to admit was uncharacteristic of who you are. It's a slippery slope, Ella. If you're not careful, booze can turn you into someone you don't like." No one had ever talked to her like this: serious, but not stern, not judgy. If anyone else said this to her—like her mom—Ella would stomp out of there . . . but Donovan had a calm way of making sense.

"You've probably heard that alcoholism is a disease," he said. "Even though there isn't a specific gene that causes alcoholism, some people do have a genetic predisposition to addiction, which explains why alcoholism often runs in families. My mom was an alcoholic. Her father was an alcoholic. And I'm an alcoholic. I just want to spare you the misery that the rest of us have gone through."

Ella looked away as the stupid tears were coming again. She had to swipe at her face a couple of times before she could speak. "What am I supposed to do? How am I supposed to not become one?"

"I thought you could join AA with me."

"I don't want to," she said. "Besides, Sweet Home doesn't have any meetings like that. And I can't go all the way to Anchorage or Fairbanks all the time." Wasn't there a quick fix? "What if I just decide that I won't drink anymore?"

"That might work. I don't know," he said. "The truth is that life is hard. And when things get tough, I still want a drink, I mean *really* want a drink. When that happens, I call my sponsor. His name is Mark and he lives in San Jose where I go to meetings." He gave her an encouraging smile. "Sweet Home needs a place for alcoholics to meet, a place to help them get sober and stay sober. I propose that you and I work on finding that place and setting it up. As a punishment it fits the crime, don't you think?"

But I'm not an alcoholic! she wanted to say. "If I help you, does that mean I'm not grounded?"

He laughed. "Oh, you're still grounded. I know better than to overrule your mom."

"But you and I will, you know, be cool, if I help?" She wanted to ask if he could forgive her, but she just couldn't bring herself to say it.

"Listen, Ella, you said you were sorry and I've forgiven you. You're my daughter and I want us to be friends. I want to get to know you. Ice fishing might be a good way to start, don't you think?"

"Yes." It was the least she could do. He hadn't yelled at her, and now that he'd talked to her honestly, like she was an adult, too, she didn't believe he would out her to everyone as a thief and tell them to lock up their silverware. "We can go ice fishing. But when are you going to have time? From what Mom and Piney say, even with all of us working, the lodge and the hardware store still might not be ready in time."

He handed her a box. "You're important to me. I'll make the time."

The waterworks started again and her shaky hands weren't even free to wipe away the tears. The rest of her was shaking, too. It was dumb but apparently she'd always wanted to hear those words from her dad.

"Take those into Nan's studio and show them to your mom. It'll be a walk down memory lane for her."

"'Kay." Hurriedly, Ella left the garage, trying not to cry like a stupid baby. She really needed a drink.

Oh, crap! Maybe Donovan was right. Maybe she did have the disease, too.

HOPE KEPT ONE eye on the fabric she was cutting and one eye on the door of the studio, waiting, knowing Ella had gone to the garage. The seconds went by slowly, minutes torturing her by inching along. Finally, Ella came into the studio, her eyes red, her lashes tinged with tears.

"What's wrong, cabbage?" Piney asked from behind her sewing machine.

Hope gave Piney a don't-coddle-her look. "She's fine.

Ella, can you help Miss Lisa cut out the blocks for the Highland Coos Cabin quilt?"

"Sure, Mom." She set the box down on the table. "Donovan wants you to look at this."

"What is it?" Hope asked.

"Old Christmas ornaments, I think."

Hope reached out and grabbed Ella's hand and squeezed, searching her eyes, whispering, "Are you all right?"

"Yeah."

"Good." Hope gave her a quick hug. "The fabric is all pressed and ready at the mat." Ella didn't go to the cutting table, but stayed beside Hope as she pulled back the lid on the box. "Oh."

"What is it, Mom?"

"Some ornaments we made when we were kids." She pulled out something that looked like a teddy bear made from dough.

"I remember Elsie nearly buying me out of flour that year," Piney said. "She said you and Donovan wanted to make one for everyone in town."

"I think after we made a treefull for the lodge, we lost interest, but it certainly brings back memories."

Ella took out another ornament. "What's this one, Mom? It looks like a Hot Wheels car."

"It was my brother Beau's," Donovan said from the doorway. Hope's stomach did an excited flip-flop.

He walked farther into the room. "Your uncle Beau loved cars more than anything else in the world, Ella. Hot Wheels, when he was a kid, and real-life Camaros when he got old enough to dream of driving. He always said it would be the first car he would buy when he had enough money."

The whole room had gone quiet. No one expected to hear Donovan say Beau's name ever again, but even more surprising was that he'd publicly acknowledged that Ella was his daughter. And it made Hope beyond happy.

Piney headed toward Donovan, making shooing gestures with her arms. "You, Hope, and Ella take the box into the living room and go through it together. That way Ella can hear all the shenanigans you hellions got up to as kids."

"But the quilts have to get—"

Piney cut Hope off. "We can handle it for a few minutes, buttercup. Besides, the Highland Coos fabric looks wrinkly to me. I'll give it another press while the three of you visit. And bond."

Hope was a little embarrassed by the last remark, but Donovan didn't correct her, so he must have been okay with it. He grabbed the box and left for the living room.

Hope took Ella's arm and followed. He set the box on the couch. She and Ella sidled up beside him.

"Did Unele Beau really hang the Hot Wheels on the tree?" Ella asked timidly.

"You bet. Even when he no longer played with cars." Donovan cleared his throat. "IIis last Christmas, when he hung the car on the tree, he said that by the next Christmas he'd have his own."

Donovan gave Ella a sad smile, then leaned over the box. "He was sixteen."

Hope laid a hand on Donovan's back with the hope of comforting him. He didn't pull away.

Ella moved closer, too. "What else is in there?" Which was the perfect thing to say.

Donovan pulled out a small quilted patchwork ornament. "Nan made one of these for each of us." He turned it over. "She stitched our names on the back." He looked at it and then passed it to Hope. "This one is yours."

She took it and ran her finger over the embroidered name. "Yours was a quilted wolf block, wasn't it?"

He pulled out three more and spread them out on the couch. "Yes. And Beau's was a fox. Grandpa had a bear."

It was always so sweet that Elsie included her in the family. Which made Hope wonder if she could've foreseen the future.

Ella reached in the box this time and retrieved a porcelain cardinal. "What's special about this?"

Hope and Donovan shared a look while he carefully took the ornament from Ella. Hope let him explain.

"That was Nan's. Her grandfather gave her that bird ornament when she was a girl. It was her prize possession. It was always the first ornament to go on the tree." He stared at the ornament, cradling it. Then he turned to Ella, holding it out to her. "I think it should be yours now. Nan would've wanted her great-granddaughter to have it."

It was a moment of reverence as the heirloom was passed from father to daughter. Hope discreetly swiped at a tear. But when she glanced up Donovan was staring at her. His look should've held hate or blame. But he was gazing at her with what might have been acceptance in his eyes.

Chapter 18

DONOVAN WOKE UP early Thanksgiving morning. He wanted to get to the hardware store to prep and paint the break room while everyone was off. It hadn't been easy to turn down Piney's Briny Tofu Turkey invitation—well actually, the non-turkey was easy to turn down—but it would've been nice to be with people he cared about today.

Especially Hope and Ella.

His family.

The thought blew his mind. Well, he could get something done at the hardware store and keep busy while they were on their camping trip.

As he entered the kitchen, Ella held up a box of Life cereal in offering.

"Thanks. That would be great. Do you want me to start some water for hot cocoa?"

"Yeah." She pulled down two bowls.

He cherished this nearly choreographed time with Ella in the mornings. "So where did you two decide on?"

"I think Lake Bend. But you know Mom; she could change her mind again." Ella rolled her eyes. "She wants to make sure that I try out some new skills."

"How many Thanksgivings have you been doing this?"

"All of them. As far back as I remember." Ella pulled the milk out of the refrigerator and handed it to him.

"Can you do me a favor?" he said. "Can you run into my office and bring me the box on my desk?" It was weird that he'd called the office *his* and not Grandpa's.

Ella gave him a look. "Do I have to *run*? Can I *walk*?"

"You must be wide awake if you can sass me so early in the morning."

She smiled and strolled leisurely from the room.

Donovan watched her go, smiling just because he had a daughter.

Ella returned, holding the box. "So what's this?"

"You tell me," Donovan said.

Ella flipped it open. "It's a cell phone."

"Correction, it's a satellite phone."

"What's the difference?" she said.

"Satellite phones don't rely on cell towers; they bounce off satellites."

"And you have this why?"

"It's a gift for you and your mom to take on your camping trips. I know your mom is hell-bent on teaching you survival skills. I want to contribute to your camping safety."

Hope appeared in the doorway. "I'm hell-bent on what?"

Ella used the phone to point at him. "Donovan got us a satellite phone."

Hope frowned and opened her mouth, but he cut her off before she could complain.

"You're welcome." He took a seat across from Ella.

Hope strolled over to the coffeemaker. "Are you sure you don't want to go to Piney's?"

He thought she was about to ask if he wanted to come along on their camping excursion. He recovered quickly. "I'm sure. I heard what was on Piney's menu. It makes sense now why you have a standing date to get out of town and go camping on Thanksgiving."

Ella laughed. "Don't worry about missing out. There'll be leftovers."

Thank goodness a new garbage disposal had been installed last week.

"What are you going to do for food today?" Hope asked.

"Don't worry about me. I have an important date with a paintbrush. I'll make a sandwich and take it with me."

"If you're sure . . ." Hope said.

"I'm sure."

"Ella, hurry up and eat your breakfast so we can get going," mother said to daughter. "I want us to get our camp settled while it's still light."

They were gone within a half hour. Donovan didn't dally either and was gone shortly afterward with his lunch and a thermos of coffee for his day alone at the hardware store. On his way into town he called and wished his dad and Rose a happy Thanksgiving. Yes, he felt a little alone, but he was looking forward to getting the break room painted as a surprise for the workers who would return on Monday.

The day flew by and only once or twice did he think longingly about Hope and Ella. He pictured them catching a few fish to add to their turkey roast on the coals and making s'mores over an open fire. He hoped they were staying warm.

Just as he was cleaning up his paint brushes around five, he received a text from Piney informing him that there was an emergency at the lodge.

He threw the dirty paintbrushes in a bucket and rushed to his vehicle. As he sped to the lodge, he tried to get hold of Piney. And when he got no answer, he called Hope's new satellite phone. No answer from her either. Had Hope and Ella been in an accident? He drove faster.

Cars were parked along the road as if it were a normal workday at the lodge. He pulled into the driveway, and before he could turn off the vehicle, Ella and Hope stepped out on the porch.

"What's going on? Why are you back?"

"We decided not to go."

"Why?" He looked around. "And why is the whole town here?" At least it looked that way.

"Talk to Ella," Hope said.

"Dinner's ready." Ella went back inside but Hope stayed where she was.

He searched her face but he didn't see any sign of distress. "Tell me."

"It's a surprise Thanksgiving dinner for you."

"I don't understand."

"It's to thank you for remodeling the lodge and hardware store. For bringing jobs back to town. For giving them hope."

But what he was doing wasn't altruistic. He was doing this to honor his grandparents . . . and to make a buck.

Hope studied him for a long moment. "Just so you know, it was Ella who suggested this whole thing. Apparently, she overheard a couple of workers saying they were going to have a better Christmas because they'd been working at the hardware store."

"Ella?" he said in wonderment.

"Yeah, your daughter. You better come inside and say hello to everyone. And just so you'll be prepared, Piney brought you a hefty dish of her tofu turkey."

"Thanks for the warning." But he had a stupid grin on his face, one he was sure wouldn't leave for the rest of the day. He held the door and they stepped inside.

It was like stepping into the lodge twenty years ago. So many smiling faces, especially the familiar smiling faces like Mr. Brewster, Miss Lisa, Aberdeen, even Jesse Montana and his brother Shaun . . . It was so surreal; Donovan wouldn't have been all that surprised if Nan and Grandpa walked through the front door and knocked snow from their boots. With everyone here, a piece of his youth had returned—the loving arms of community—and he hadn't realized until this moment how much he'd missed it. He hadn't experienced real community—*Sweet Home, Alaska type* community—since the day he'd left.

Men slapped him on the back and women squeezed his arm. Cries of "Happy Thanksgiving" created a racket. Oh, how he wished his grandparents were here to see this.

Hope laid a hand on his back. "Go sit. The food's on the table."

Piney appeared with Bill by her side. "Bill is mighty glad for this shindig. He's fond of a real turkey leg."

Bill—always a man of few words—gave a slight nod.

Ella appeared again, this time with Lacy at her side. "Boomer keeps sniffing around in the kitchen. I bet he can't wait for scraps."

Aberdeen carried in the monster-sized turkey and shyly set it on the table to a round of applause. "I was glad to do it."

"Make room," Piney commanded. "Donovan has to be hungry after working all day."

When everyone was gathered around the table, they joined hands.

"Donovan, you say grace," Piney said.

Donovan obediently bowed his head. "Father, we thank you for this meal we are about to eat, for good friends to share it with, and for our time together." That nearly encompassed all the warm feelings he was having, so he continued, with the blessing he'd said around this table as a child. "Bless us, O Lord"—others joined in with him—"and these Thy gifts, which we are about to receive from Thy bounty. Through Christ, our Lord. Amen." Donovan finished with the sign of the cross, as others did as well.

They all tucked in to the turkey, moose ribs, and smoked salmon pâté. It was a noisy affair and so much more fun than coming home to an empty house.

Donovan stood and raised his glass. "I'd like to propose a toast. To Sweet Home. For sharing this marvelous food." Everyone raised their glasses and drank. Donovan remained standing. "It wouldn't be a proper Thanksgiving if I didn't share how thankful I am for all of you." He glanced over at Hope and Ella, mentally giving thanks specifically for them. Though Hope said this was Ella's idea, he knew it was Hope who had pulled it off. Later, he would get her alone . . . and thank her properly.

Piney stood next. "To our loved ones lost. To Charles and Elsie Stone."

"To Charles and Elsie," the crowd said.

Donovan added his own private toast, *To Beau and Izzie*. He couldn't help but glance at Hope, wondering if she could read his thoughts. She was staring at him until his eyes reached hers and then her gaze darted away.

Mr. Brewster stood next. "To Donovan . . . for coming home."

"To Donovan," the crowd said cheerily.

They were acting like he'd come home for good. But Alaska wasn't his home anymore. He would have to let it slide today, but as soon as he could, he was going to have a serious conversation with Mr. Brewster again, and make him see the truth.

When the pumpkin, salmonberry, and blueberry pies were served, Piney called out to Donovan, "Your grandfather Charles always cut down his Christmas tree the day after Thanksgiving. Do you remember?"

"Yes." He and Beau always went along, even before they were old enough to hold the handsaw.

"I assume you'll carry on the tradition?" Piney looked pointedly from him to Ella.

"Ella, would you like to go with me to get the tree?" he asked.

The panicked look on her face said he shouldn't have put her on the spot, in front of everyone here.

"And your mom, too?" He made it sound like a question.

Hope turned to her daughter. "If you want me to go, I can go." But she didn't sound too enthusiastic.

Ella glanced at Lacy.

"Lacy and Aberdeen are welcome, too," Donovan offered.

"I have to work tomorrow," Aberdeen said. "But Lacy can go if she wants."

"Sounds like fun," Lacy said. "As long as your mom can bring some of her famous hot chocolate along."

Hope looked at Ella, who nodded. "I can absolutely make hot chocolate. I think we're out of cocoa so I'll have to run to the Hungry Bear tonight."

After dessert—Donovan had tasted each pie and couldn't decide which he liked best—he noticed several of the women rise and start to clear the dishes.

"Sorry, folks. There is a rule here at the lodge, a new rule," he clarified. "The people who prepare the home-cooked meals get to relax afterward. Everyone else cleans up." He stood. "Like me. Anyone else?"

Lacy pulled Ella up. "We'll help."

Jesse rose, too. "Shaun and I are heading home. Mom texted that she's awake."

Piney hurried from the table, speaking over her shoulder as she went. "I made Patricia a plate to take to her."

"Thanks, Piney."

Miss Lisa got to her feet and reached for two plates. "Cleaning up is part of Thanksgiving."

"Nope. Please go relax in the living room," Donovan said.

Bill stood and joined the kitchen crew.

"I thought you made the moose ribs," Donovan said.

"I'll load the dishwasher." Bill's tone brooked no argument.

"Thanks." Donovan gathered more dishes from the table and took them into the kitchen, glad they'd installed two new dishwashers.

Hope gathered dishes, too, and joined them.

"Out," Donovan said. "New house rules, remember?"

"I didn't do much," she said.

"Can I talk to you for a minute?" He pulled her into the hallway and from there toward his office. Once they were inside and the door shut, he said, "I'd like to come along to the Hungry Bear after the crowd thins. I could use your help picking out snacks for the tree-hunting expedition, things Ella and Lacy might like."

"Okay," she said dubiously. Clearly she meant, *That's what you wanted to talk about?*

"Listen. I want to thank you for today. Everything you did."

Hope acted like a caged animal. "I told you. It was Ella."

"And she had no help pulling this together?" He reached out and started to pull her in for a hug. But gently squeezed her arm instead. "You're a good person." He wanted to tell her more, like how she'd grown into an amazing woman and had raised an amazing daughter. But he couldn't. She'd get the wrong idea. He was leaving and he didn't want to lead her on. "Thanks for everything."

He walked out of the office and back to the dishes, leaving her behind. But he didn't think that was going to stop the stirring inside—the old feelings, how it'd been between him and Hope . . . *the longing*. He worried he might never be the same again.

WHEN THE KITCHEN and dining room were cleaned up, Hope didn't go hang out with the others in the living room. Instead, she headed upstairs to Ella's old room and knocked. "Donovan and I are heading to town to get snacks for tomorrow from the Hungry Bear. Anything special you want?"

"I'm too full to answer right now. You know what I like." A week ago, Ella might've complained, not wanting Hope to spend time with Donovan. "Lacy and I are going to work on our Wandering Moose Rail Fence quilt, if that's okay?"

"Absolutely. You two are part of the Sisterhood of the Quilt and you can work in the studio anytime you like . . . as long as your homework is done first."

Ella hugged her and then turned back to Lacy. "Come on. Let's head downstairs."

Smiling, Hope savored the hug, not wanting to go downstairs and make small talk. *Maybe I can sneak off to the Hungry Bear without Donovan seeing.* But that wouldn't be nice. And although he said she was a good person, she was still making up for what she'd done to him.

But when she got downstairs, people were pulling on their coats.

"What's going on?" Hope asked Piney.

"Most everyone wants to get a good night's sleep so they'll be fresh for tomorrow morning."

"Is there something I don't know?"

"The lot of them are planning to be back at work on the lodge and the hardware store first thing."

"But it's a holiday weekend. Donovan doesn't expect anyone to work," Hope said.

"Yes, but everyone's concerned that the businesses won't be up and running by the Christmas Festival."

Hope nodded. "There's still so much to be done."

"You don't worry about a thing. You and Donovan pick out a tree tomorrow. The Christmas tree is one of the important items on the to-do list." Piney gave her a hug. "This Thanksgiving potluck was such a good idea. It really brought the community together, especially the people who live alone, making sure they weren't left out this time of year."

"It was Ella's idea," Hope reiterated for the hundredth time. But she had been the one to organize it. "I'm happy we'll have the Christmas Festival this year. It's another way to bring everyone together."

"I'll see you here, tomorrow, after your Christmas tree adventure. The Sisterhood of the Quilt will be working feverishly."

Donovan came into the entry as Piney was pulling on her boots.

"Hope, are you about ready to go?" he asked.

Piney's eyebrows shot up. "Where are you two going now? A date?"

Hope glared at her. "Donovan wants to pick up snacks for the tree hunt tomorrow. I told him he could tag along with me to the Hungry Bear."

Donovan frowned at Piney as if she were being ridiculous. Hope agreed. It wasn't a date and Piney better quit suggesting that it was. Thank goodness Piney didn't know about the kisses they'd shared!

Chuckling, Piney walked out the door.

Donovan pulled Hope's new coat from the hook and she automatically slid her arms into the sleeves.

Hope muttered at the shut door, "I don't know why she keeps doing that." *Keeps thinking there is more going on between us than there is.* She glanced down and realized that Donovan was zipping up her coat. She didn't make a fuss, and she didn't stop him either. For her, it felt like one of the most intimate moments they'd ever shared. She took that second to gaze upon him, marveling at him being so close.

"Let's get going," he said huskily, which made her wonder if he felt the buzz between them, too.

Or had her imagination gone off the rails? *Yes, most definitely!* She'd killed his brother and he could never feel anything for her again.

Yet there was . . . something there. Something different. Instead of avoiding her, he seemed to actually like spending time with her now. Was it possible Donovan was beginning to forgive her? The thought threatened to bring tears to her eyes. She wanted his forgiveness. Actually, she wanted more from him. Much more. Could they ever go back to where they'd been in high school? Probably not. But that didn't keep her from wanting him. In the moment she decided to admit to herself that she still loved him. Not the love of a teenage girl for a teenage boy . . . but the love of a woman for a man. It was deep and real and she was going to own it. Whether it was good for her or not.

But was she going to act on it? Absolutely not.

She opened the door and rushed out to the car. She had to break the mood, make things normal between them— *employee and boss.* She spoke over her shoulder. "Did you know that the group here tonight—maybe the whole town— plan to be back at work tomorrow?"

"Yeah." He opened her car door and then hurried to the other side.

"Should we postpone the tree-hunting trip?"

"According to Mr. Brewster, he has the hardware store under control and everyone at the lodge knows what they're doing, too." His voice grew softer. "Besides, Ella's all set to go, and I want to strike while the iron is hot."

"You're right." Something had changed. Hope was no longer wishing Donovan would leave so her heart wouldn't be in danger. It was too late for that and she'd have to deal with the emptiness when he left. The real issue now was that she'd kept Ella away from him for too long. He deserved to spend time with his daughter. To build memories . . . *for when he was gone*. She didn't trust herself to think further than today or to say more.

They drove the rest of the way in silence. When they arrived at the Hungry Bear, Hope pulled out her key and unlocked the door, knowing she had only a few minutes to disable the old-fashioned sound-activated alarm, first the alarm itself and then the control panel at the back door.

She moved as quietly as she could to the meat counter, where the alarm sat. Donovan followed her, standing so close behind her in the darkened store that she could smell his minty breath. She turned to face him, intending to ask for some space, but she couldn't get her lungs to work properly; her breathing was too shallow. His chest rose and fell in time with hers, breath for breath. She felt like she'd entered into a dream. He tenderly hooked her hair behind her ear and searched her face in the shadows. Then his gaze fell to her lips. She lifted her head, and as if in slow motion, he leaned down and kissed her. Or maybe she met him halfway. The kiss was hesitant, tender, questioning. And then, as if a switch had been flipped, Donovan pulled her into his arms, molding her to the length of him, pushing the limits, the kiss going from innocent to igniting with passion. Electricity flowed between them in the safety of the darkness, making her ache, hoping it would never end. She turned off her brain and threw everything she had into kissing him back. He lost his balance a little, rocking backward into a display of stacked cans. She didn't care. *I'll pick the cans up later.* But as they clattered to the floor, the alarm blared and the alarm light strobed. The whole thing screamed, *Danger, danger!*

She jumped away from him.

The alarm was right; this moment had been full of danger. Her heart was a weakling—fragile as a crystal bulb—and couldn't take Donovan's kisses. He tried to keep hold of her, but she pushed him away.

"I have to shut it off," she yelled above the blaring noise, as if that were the sole issue. How could she admit that she wouldn't survive having her heart broken again?

She hit the switch on the alarm and then went to the control panel. Once she entered the code, she turned on the overhead lights, bringing the world into clearer focus.

She went back to where the cans had been scattered, but Donovan was nearly done rebuilding the display. He glanced up at her, then looked away. "Sorry."

She didn't know if he meant sorry for the kiss or sorry for the mess . . . and she was too afraid to ask.

"I'll get a cart."

DONOVAN SHOULDN'T HAVE kissed Hope. It was wrong to . . . to start something, when it was almost time for him to leave Sweet Home. But that was his brain talking. His heart couldn't dig up a good reason why he shouldn't pull Hope into his arms again. It wasn't just old times; this was new, powerful. A pull so deep that he couldn't name it.

Awkward silence settled over the Hungry Bear as they loaded the grocery cart with snacks for the girls and lunch fixings for the workers who were going to be at the lodge tomorrow. Hope's stiff movements made him wish he hadn't kissed her. They'd started to become friends again and now he'd probably ruined it.

She rang up the groceries and he handed her his credit card without a word. They drove back to the lodge and he carried in the groceries while she put them away. When she was done, she went down the hall to the studio. He was left alone in the kitchen staring at nothing.

Finally he pulled out his car keys and headed out for a

drive. Not far from the lodge he realized he should've thought this through first, as snow was starting to come down hard. He pulled into the cemetery and parked. He sat there for a couple of minutes before tramping through the fresh snow to Beau's grave.

"Oh man, you're gonna laugh. I did something really stupid tonight," he said to Beau, dusting snow from the tombstone even though it was immediately covered again. "Hope and I were at the Hungry Bear, and it was dark, and it was right after she'd organized this amazing Thanksgiving dinner." The wind blew even harder, swirling snow all around him as if to say, *Get to the point.* "I kissed her. I mean I really kissed her, like she was still mine and we were going to be together forever."

He traced Beau's death date on the headstone, though it felt impossible that his brother was really gone. "I'm a complete idiot. I don't know what to do."

He looked up but couldn't see the sky, only snow. He wasn't going to get an answer from Beau this time. The answer was really inside himself but he didn't want to pull it out and examine it. He might have to let go of the past if he did.

He returned to his car and slid behind the wheel but didn't want to go home just yet. Hope would be there. Though he'd made his decision, he wasn't certain he could keep from pulling her into his arms again. Instead he drove into town to check if the paint had dried in the break room. Then he paced the aisles, remembering how he'd followed his grandpa around the hardware store as he helped customers, until he was old enough himself to help customers find what they needed. Some of his best lessons about human nature came from working at this store. Donovan settled in behind the old cash register—which they were keeping for nostalgia's sake—and thought about the countless hours he'd spent checking out items for the citizens of Sweet Home and the tourists who came to see the eclectic hardware store. Donovan longed to go back to those days, when Beau was alive and this town was their home. Finally, around midnight he put his memories away and drove back to the lodge.

The second he walked in the door, Hope—with Boomer in her arms—jumped to her feet from her place on the couch. She had such a worried look on her face that panic made his heart pound.

"What's wrong?" he asked.

"Where were you?" she said. "It's snowing."

"Did something happen to Ella?"

"Ella's fine. She went to bed. I didn't know where you were."

"I went for a drive."

"But the weather is horrible!" She turned away as if she were composing herself. "Boomer was worried. Ella asked after you, too."

Boomer must have heard his name. He wiggled to get down, and she set him on the floor and released him. He scampered across the hardwood and slid to a stop at Donovan's feet.

"Come here, you good-for-nothing ragamuffin." He leaned over and ruffled his furry head.

Hope walked toward Donovan with a pad of Post-it notes and a pen in her hand, holding them out.

"What's this for?"

"Ella and I have this system," Hope said. "We leave a Post-it on the microwave telling the other person where we are."

Yes, he'd seen their notes to each other stuck there.

Hope didn't look him in the eye. "It's a simple courtesy, letting everyone know where you are. *And* when you might get home." She gave him a pointed look. "It's what people do, so others—especially dogs and children—don't worry about them."

His chest warmed unexpectedly. *Hope worries over me.* It was dumb that it pleased him so. And frightened him. "I'm sorry."

"It's okay. Just don't do it again." She turned away. "It's the snow, you know?"

He did know. A heavy snowfall would naturally frighten her more than the average Alaskan. When others saw snow as a nuisance, she would see mangled bodies and death.

He put his hands on her shoulders and pulled her back a little so she could lean against his chest. He wrapped his arms around her. "I'm truly sorry."

She relaxed and suddenly he didn't feel the need to apologize for the kiss at the Hungry Bear. He just needed to make sure he didn't hurt Hope.

"Are you going to be okay?" he asked.

She slowly moved away from him. "Now that you're home safe and sound, I'll head to bed."

"Good night, Hope. I'll see you in the morning."

She said nothing more as she slipped on her boots and her coat, grabbed a thermos, and went out the door.

Two seconds later, he realized he still had Boomer. And he'd made a promise to his daughter. He put on his coat and his hat and he and Boomer went to Wandering Moose Cabin. He knocked lightly, not wanting to wake up Ella if she was already asleep. Especially if it meant he could steal a kiss from Hope out here on the porch.

But Ella opened the door. "Oh! You brought me Boomer!" The cabin smelled of hot cocoa.

"He likes sleeping with you." Donovan looked inside. "You know, we'll need to get you a bigger bed soon. It won't be long before that dog won't fit in a twin, even by himself."

Hope stepped into Donovan's line of sight. "It'd be cheaper to get a dog bed."

"Mom, if he wants to buy me a bigger bed, you should let him."

Donovan smiled. "I'll let you two work it out." He wished they'd invite him in for cocoa. If only they were still living at the lodge, he wouldn't have been excluded. But as it was, this was their space and he was intruding. "Well, good night."

He made his way back to the lodge alone. The house was empty and made *him* feel empty, too. As he turned out the lights downstairs, he couldn't help but relive the kiss at the Hungry Bear. *She kissed me back. I didn't imagine it.* When he'd come back to Alaska, he never dreamed he would find Hope, let alone kiss her. Or that kissing her that way would feel so right that he'd want it to go on forever. But it couldn't. His Sweet Home expiration date was approaching. Approaching too fast. He'd be taking advantage of Hope if he kissed her again. He couldn't hurt her more than he already had. He was leaving after the Christmas Festival. But he was already feeling homesick for Sweet Home, missing Hope and Ella, even though he hadn't left yet.

He woke earlier than usual and sat sipping his coffee as he tried to concentrate on drawing up a to-do list for the lodge workers today. He didn't get far before Hope came into the kitchen.

"Morning," he said. "Coffee's ready." He went back to his list, not knowing how he was supposed to act around her today. He couldn't let himself fall for Hope all over again. But right now, his whole body wanted to give her a kiss that would last them the whole day. "Where's Ella?"

"Sleeping in. She and Lacy were texting late last night. I finally got tired of telling her to get off her phone and went to sleep myself."

"If you two were back here in the lodge, you both could have your own space," he argued logically.

"My dad always said that love grows better in small houses."

"The offer is always on the table," he said.

But she gave him a look and he knew exactly what it meant: *There's no such thing as always, Donovan Stone. You're selling this place, so stop offering anything!* Yes, it was one hell of a look.

Chastened, he went back to his list.

Thirty minutes later, Ella rolled into the kitchen, looking tired but not unhappy about the day ahead.

"Do you know where we're going to look for a tree?" she asked.

He nodded. "Where my grandfather—your great-grandfather—always took me and Uncle Beau. Do you know the rules for cutting down trees in a national forest?"

"It depends on the forest," Hope piped up.

"True. But in a nutshell, we can't use a chain saw. We have to use hand tools and only cut down one of the skinnier, less healthy trees, leaving the best trees for the forest. Also, we can't down a tree within two hundred feet of the road or a body of water."

"Have you been Googling the rules?" Ella asked, laughing.

"Maybe." Donovan killed the apps on his phone. "Can you be ready in thirty minutes? I want to get an early start. Short days and all," he said.

"Spoken like a true Alaskan," Hope observed.

"Old habits die hard." He turned to Ella. "What about Lacy? Can she be ready to go soon?"

"Lace isn't going with us. She texted this morning to say she might be getting sick. I'm pretty sure she's just allergic to the cold."

Donovan looked at Hope and Ella, feeling a surge of happy anticipation. Their first outing together, as a family.

Chapter 19

WITH HOPE AND Ella with him in the cab of Mr. Brewster's truck, Donovan pulled onto the snow-covered road to access his grandfather's secret tree-hunting spot. He'd been worried there for a few minutes that he wouldn't be able to find it because the terrain had changed so much. He glanced down at Hope's ankle and decided they wouldn't be able to trek far once he parked. "Hold on, ladies. We're going off road." He made a sharp right from gravel road onto uneven ground.

Ella squealed delightedly as they bounced their way across the field toward a stand of smaller trees.

"Does this bring back good memories?" he hollered to Hope.

"Yeah, I guess. But I must've enjoyed whiplash then." But she was smiling and it pleased him so.

"We're almost there." He pulled up and parked, giving them room to down a tree that wouldn't crush Mr. Brewster's truck in the process.

They all got out of the vehicle. Ella held up her phone and took a picture. "Let me send this to Lacy first." But two seconds later, she was complaining. "I don't have service."

"Good." Donovan pulled a saw from the back and held it

out to his daughter. "You won't have time to mess with your phone anyway. You have a tree to fell."

She shot him a couple of daggers but took the saw. He grabbed the ax from the bed of the pickup for himself.

Hope leaned her back against the truck and looked up.

"Which one do you think?" Donovan said.

"Either number one or number three?" Hope said.

"They're both the right size, I think." He turned to Ella, who was pocketing her phone. "You decide. One or three."

"Let's get number three. It's the skinniest," she said.

"And will be easier for you to cut down?" he teased.

"I had a feeling I'd be doing all the work." Like a soldier who didn't mind doing her duty, she marched toward the tree.

Donovan joined Hope at the truck. "Should I really let her do it by herself?"

"She knows what she's doing. My suggestion is to let her get started, then give her a hand if she wants it."

Ella circled the tree and at the same time examined the terrain.

Donovan wasn't as calm as Hope and couldn't stand by without saying something. "You do know that the tree is going to fall in the direction of the side that you saw."

"Duh," she answered back. She chose her spot—away from them and the truck—and started sawing.

He could only keep quiet for one minute more before heading toward her. "How about I swing the ax a couple of times to get started? I haven't had my workout today."

Ella stopped sawing. "Yeah. If you want to."

Donovan tramped through the snow, not feeling a bit of the cold, because he was going to cut down his first Christmas tree with his daughter. He turned back to look at Hope, who had her phone out and held up, apparently taking pictures. He had the urge to run back, take her in his arms, and spin her around like he did when they were young. But he kept walking toward Ella. Man, he couldn't remember the last time he'd been this happy.

Together, he and Ella cut down the nine-foot spruce and got it to the truck under Hope's direction. The three of them started to tie down the tree but Ella bailed after getting her end secured.

"I'll warm up the truck." She was inside the cab before they could say anything.

Donovan went to Hope's side to help her. But when he got near, he noticed how wild and lovely she looked with the forest as her backdrop. He wanted nothing more than to snuggle his hands inside her coat and ravage her mouth . . .

Instead he wrapped her in a bear hug. "This was fun," he said into her hair. "Thanks." He let go and quickly went to his side of the vehicle and opened the door, not wanting to gauge her reaction. A couple of moments later, she got in the truck, too.

"Mom, are you all right?" Ella asked.

"I'm fine. Let's get home."

Donovan smiled and put the car in gear.

Back at the lodge the three of them got the tree inside, once again with Hope directing.

"Ella, keep your end up. You don't want to scrape the floors."

He and Ella set the tree on the tarp he'd laid down before they'd left. He went back outside to wind up the rope and grab his keys from the ignition.

"Hey, Don," Jesse said. Shaun was with him, his tool belt loaded. "Did you find the tree you were looking for?"

"Yeah. Just got it into the house. How did things go here?" He'd left enough food to feed an army, so he knew that was okay.

"We just finished up with the Highland Coos Cabin. Anything else you want done for today?"

"No. That should do it." Even though he was paying double for the holiday weekend, Donovan didn't care if they knocked off early. He knew the brothers were going to check in on their mom. Donovan was just so grateful for everybody's efforts. "See you tomorrow at the hardware store?"

He couldn't help it, he just didn't like Jesse working at the lodge with Hope around. Especially if Donovan wasn't here to monitor.

"Yeah. Have a good evening." Jesse and Shaun waved as they walked toward their cars.

Donovan headed back into the lodge. Christmas music was playing quietly as Ella—still red-cheeked from the outdoors—dug through one of the ornament boxes he'd brought in from the garage. "Where's your mom?"

"Making cocoa. It's tradition." Ella grinned and he realized not for the first time how much he'd missed out on.

Hope came in with a tray. "Get it while it's hot."

"Can you hold the tree while I put it in the stand?" Donovan asked.

"Not yet. We have to make a cocoa toast first," Ella said.

"Another tradition?"

"Yes. Mom does the toast," Ella said, informing him of protocol.

They all raised their mugs and Hope, the eloquent toastmaster, declaimed ceremoniously, "To a day of goodwill, cold weather, and warm hearts."

"Amen," Donovan said as they clinked their mugs together. An image of the Three Musketeers came into his head, and his emotions threatened to overwhelm him. "That was lovely, Hope."

Ella whispered loudly. "Don't get too excited. She gives the same toast every year."

Donovan beamed at Hope. "Well, I think she nailed it."

Hope held the tree while Donovan guided it into the stand. When he was done, he lay on the floor for a moment longer, listening as Ella sang along to "O Holy Night." Then he joined Hope and Ella in wrapping the lights while they sang "White Christmas." It was sweet, heartwarming, and mostly on key. He and Ella started on the ornaments next, while Hope decorated the living room with the Christmas items Rick had picked out in Anchorage. When she was done, she, too, chose ornaments and they found the perfect home for them on the tree. He was having a ball, his own Norman Rockwell Christmas. He never imagined he'd have this kind of Christmas again.

"Are you ready for ice fishing in the morning?" he asked Ella. "And by that I mean, are you ready to leave your cell phone at home so you won't be disappointed when there isn't any service?"

Ella gave him an *oh, Dad* look, which pleased him to no end. She turned to Hope. "Are you going with us?"

"If it's okay, honey, I'm going to pass. I have a lot to do around here," Hope said. Donovan expected she needed to rest her ankle after today's trek through the woods.

Ella shrugged. "I guess it's just us, then."

But when Donovan woke the next morning, a winter storm was raging outside. Ella came blowing in the front door, pulled off her snowy boots, and joined him in the kitchen.

"Mom says ice fishing is off for today." Ella sounded peeved and disappointed, as if it were her mother's fault.

"Too dangerous," Donovan concurred.

"Yeah, I guess." Ella plopped down in her chair. He had already set out the cereal and milk for her.

He shouldn't have been glad for her disappointment but he was . . . because it matched his own. He would make certain to fit in their fishing venture before he left. He pulled his laptop over and opened the lid. "How about you and I work on getting an AA meeting in Sweet Home?"

She frowned but dutifully pulled up a chair. "Okay. But I've been thinking Sweet Home is too small to have its own group."

"Not true. According to this, it only takes two or three people to start one." He showed her the screen. "Plus a meeting place, a coffeepot, and some AA literature."

"I guess we could get the word out to the other small towns that we're starting one up."

"That's a good idea," he said. "Let's get our application in."

"But what about the meeting place?"

"We better make some calls, don't you think?"

For the next several hours they worked alongside each other to bring an AA meeting to Sweet Home. Afterward he made them cocoa and they drank it at the table, with everything feeling comfortable between them.

"I need to check on things at the hardware store," he said. "I was wondering if you'd like to do a project for the lodge." The box of supplies had arrived yesterday, ahead of the storm, thank goodness. "Could you paint new signs for the cabins—Wandering Moose, Highland Coos, and Black Bear Hideout? I've seen your drawings, Ella. I think they're really good. Also, I'll need new signs for the B-and-B rooms upstairs—Eagle's Nest, Lone Wolf Den, and Caribou Cove."

"Are you kidding me?" Her eyes were bright and eager. "You want me to make signs, like a professional?"

"You're on the payroll, aren't you? The lodge would be lucky to have your artwork on the doors," Donovan said. Plus, it thrilled him that Ella would put her mark on the lodge. But then reality set in . . . the lodge would be sold soon and belong to someone besides him.

"I think I have some acrylics in one of my boxes in the cabin." Ella started for the doorway.

"Stay put and eat your breakfast. I'll be right back." He went to his office and returned with the box. "If you don't have everything you need in here, let me know." He set the box in front of her.

She looked in as if Christmas were inside. Then she excitedly pulled out paintbrushes, palettes, and tubes. Finally, her gaze came up to meet his. "Are you sure?"

"Of course I'm sure," he said. "You have talent. Just like your Aunt Izzie." Before Donovan could feel a pang of sadness, Ella jumped up and hugged him, taking him completely off guard. But it made him so happy!

Immediately she pulled away. "I won't let you down. I promise."

"I know you won't." There was nothing she could do that would make him love her less.

Realization hit. He did love her. His daughter, Ella. He cleared his throat, because it was a little tight. "Seriously"—he sounded choked up even to his own ears—"let me know if there's anything else you need."

She didn't seem to notice as she kept going through the art supplies. "I can't wait to tell Lacy."

For the first time, he felt like a real dad. And he'd gotten a real dad hug, though he doubted Ella would ever call him that or see him as her father. But it didn't matter. He would treasure this moment, hold on to it for the rest of his life.

Donovan's cell phone rang. "It's my dad," he said to Ella. "I'll be right back." She would have to get to know her grandfather in due time, too.

He walked into the hall to answer it. "Hey, Dad, what's up?"

"Hi, son." Dad sounded down, more down than Donovan had heard him in a long time.

"What's going on?"

"Oh, it's just . . . Rose moved out," Dad said.

"What happened?" Donovan asked, immediately calculating how quickly he could get to his dad. An impractical task. It wasn't just the winter storm either. There was so much left to be done here.

"Her ex-husband wants to get back together," Dad explained. "I understand, you know. They have five kids, a history, but he'd kicked her out of the house and left her with nothing. I don't know how she can even consider going back to him."

"Women are forgiving." Donovan looked up as Hope came through the front door. He gave her a sad smile. "Dad, what can I do to help?" His father shouldn't make the trip to Alaska as he was still recovering from back surgery.

"Nothing, really, son. Just wanted to see how things were going there."

But Donovan knew the house must be quiet with his grandfather gone. "I don't have a date yet, but I'll get to Florida as soon as I can." Donovan was conflicted, eager to be with his dad but reluctant to leave Sweet Home. Yes, it was something he'd known all along, but still . . . "I'll get back to you. Let me see how the next several weeks go, okay?"

"Don't worry about me. I'll be fine," Dad said stoically. "I just wanted to let you know about Rose."

"I'm glad you did." Which solidified Donovan's plans. "I'll talk to you soon." He hung up.

Donovan shoved his phone back in his pocket, feeling more torn than he had in his whole life. Dad needed him in Florida, but Ella was here in Alaska. Hope, too! He'd only just found her again and he wasn't ready to leave her just yet. Then there was Piney, Mr. Brewster, and hell, all of Sweet Home, the people who'd stepped up to help him out.

It was an impossible situation with no easy solution in sight.

OVER THE NEXT three weeks, Ella went ice fishing with Donovan—twice. It was fun, though he'd been kind of a dork about it, acting too excited. Donovan must've forgotten what a blast it can be to fish in Alaska.

Mostly Ella used her free time to work on the signs for the cabins and B-and-B rooms. Now she sat at the dining room table finishing the last one—Lone Wolf Den. She was sad her last sign would be finished soon. Although . . . Piney had said she wanted a couple of new signs for the restrooms at the Hungry Bear, and Miss Lisa wanted a *Welcome* sign for her front door. Maybe more people in Sweet Home would want Ella's help, too, after she finished those requests.

She hadn't felt this okay in a long time. She still felt sad about Grandpa dying and wanted to drink every day. But she hadn't had a drop since she and Donovan had been going to the new AA meetings at the Catholic church. It had been embarrassing at first but now it wasn't so bad. More people had shown up each time, even some kids from high school.

Mom cranked up the music in the kitchen. She was singing, actually singing. Ella had never seen her so relaxed, even happy. She wondered if it had to do with her dad being here in Sweet Home. She'd never call Donovan Dad to his face, but she'd been trying it on for size . . . just for fun. Ella guessed he wasn't so bad and maybe she should ease up on him. Besides, he'd been pretty good to her, allowing her to use his SUV a few times to drive to Lacy's trailer and back.

Ella glanced at the text that had just come in. "Mom? Can Lacy, Uki, Annette, and Ruthie come over and sew?" It was cool that her friends had agreed to try quilting. Donovan had told her that her great-grandmother Elsie said her female friendships were the most important thing in her life. He was always saying corny stuff like that, but Ella didn't mind. She loved hearing about her family.

A moment later, Mom appeared with a spoon in her hand. "Do you really have to yell? I'm just in the kitchen."

"Can my friends come over?" They'd been calling themselves the Chicas of the Quilt, as they were all in Spanish III together and not a bunch of old ladies like her mom.

"Sure. As long as you clean up after your friends. To be clear, this time you'll be the one to collect the dishes around the house."

"I promise," Ella said, putting the final touches on the wolf of Lone Wolf Den.

But last time, she'd seen how her dad and mom had laughed together while picking up after the Chicas, like they were having the time of their life. It was weird. But just remembering made Ella smile.

FOR THE FIRST time in Hope's adult life, she had leisure time, or maybe it was spending long hours with the Sisterhood of the Quilt, sewing in Elsie's studio, that made work feel like play. And decorating the lodge wasn't really a job but a fun pastime. Everything felt so right these days. Sweet Home had pulled together, as if the Sweet Home of her past had returned. Or maybe it was just having Donovan home.

He hadn't tried to kiss her since the alarming episode at the Hungry Bear, and Hope hated to admit that she was disappointed. It was like being told she couldn't have her favorite ice cream anymore. Or that she couldn't breathe air again.

But at least the awkwardness between them was gone. Something was up with Donovan, though. He seemed sad, and when she asked him what was wrong, he gave a noncommittal grunt.

She finished the last stitch on the binding of the new Sisterhood of the Quilt wall hanging, left Ella and her friends, and went in search of Donovan for quilt show-and-tell. As she walked toward his office, she overheard Rick.

"You told me to keep you updated on the finances and it's not looking good. You've sunk a lot more money into the lodge and hardware store, nearly double what we expected."

"What's the plan, then?" Donovan said.

"Stop spending money."

"But the job isn't done yet."

"You need to raise more capital," Rick said. "Do you want me to sell some stocks? You'll pay more in taxes due to short-term capital gains."

"No. Sell my condo in San Jose instead," Donovan answered.

Hope's foolish heart soared and sang out, *Donovan's staying in Sweet Home!*

"There's no problem with selling your condo and making a profit. Does that mean that you're going to stay here as I suggested on our first day? And that's even before I knew you had family here . . . and Hope . . . ?"

"No. The plan's the same. I'm moving to Florida, near Dad. He needs me."

Hope squeezed the quilt tight to her chest. *But Ella needs you. And I need you, too.* She couldn't draw enough breath to walk away and regroup. As if regrouping was really going to fix her breaking heart.

Donovan cleared his throat. "Just tell me that the proceeds from the lodge and hardware store will be enough." His words sounded like they were strangling him.

"Sure, it'll be enough." Rick paused. "But is that what you really want to do?"

"Just sell the condo." There was a scraping noise.

Hope didn't realize until too late that it was Donovan pushing back his chair. He bumped into her outside the office and had to grab her arms to steady her.

He looked more upset than she'd seen him since returning. "What is it that you want?"

She might have answered with her immediate desire: for him to admire the quilt in her arms—but all she could think in that moment was her secret desire: a happily-ever-after . . . with him. And *that* she could never say.

She shook her head and walked away, willing her wobbly legs to get her to the kitchen, and hoping he couldn't tell from her gait that she was dying inside.

Donovan is leaving. True, he'd never told her different, but she'd started to hope he'd change his mind. Now she was devastated. Hope's heart was breaking all over again, for herself and this time for her daughter, too.

Ella needed to know, to be prepared. And Hope had to tell her.

She'd raised Ella to live in the real world, with all its hardships, disappointments, and heartaches. This would truly test her daughter's abilities. Hope knew . . . because it was testing her own.

DONOVAN WATCHED HOPE walk away. For the life of him, he couldn't remember where he'd been going when he bumped into her. He went back into the office, trying to stop his pounding heart. But it was impossible. Hope made him weak. He couldn't wait to get out of Sweet Home.

"Did you forget something?" Rick asked.

Yeah. My good sense. But he didn't say so. "No."

"Listen," Rick said, "I want to talk more about this, but I

told Sparkle I'd run into town and get her so she can sew with the Sisterhood of the Quilt tonight."

"Okay." But it wasn't okay. Donovan was between a rock and a hard place. What was he going to do about his dad? What was he going to do about Ella? And what the hell was he going to do about his pounding heart?

Donovan waited until Rick vacated his office before he slumped into his chair. He pulled open his grandfather's desk drawer and took out the envelope with *For Donovan* written in Grandpa's handwriting. Donovan had only opened it once and had ignored it since. He pulled it out now and looked at his grandmother's engagement ring and wedding band. What the hell was he supposed to do with those? He shoved the envelope back in the drawer and shut it.

What he had to do was stay busy. He scooted his chair up to his laptop to do the final upload of Home Sweet Home Lodge's website. He needed reservations—lots of them—to make the books look good before he put the lodge up for sale. And to make all of this worth it.

Rick was right; the lodge could once again be profitable, and the hardware store, too. The sad truth was that the new owner would reap all the benefits of the hard work that Donovan and the town had put into the establishments.

On the computer, Donovan finished his last round of tests and then published the site to the web.

He wished real life were more like programming. Coding was straightforward—either right or wrong, it worked or it didn't—whereas life was just messy and complicated. He had no idea how he was going to continue his relationship with Ella and still keep his commitment to his dad. Maybe fly back once a month to see Ella? But he knew enough now about teenage girls to realize that even if he did come back, Ella might be too busy with her friends to spend time with him. He was in a no-win situation. And that wasn't even putting Hope into the equation, or the rest of the people of Sweet Home. He'd loved working alongside the people he'd known when he was a kid, his old friends . . . with the exception of

Jesse Montana, who was way too friendly with Hope for Donovan's liking. He wondered if Jesse and Hope would hook up after he left. Which would really piss him off.

Trying to calm down, Donovan opened his email to read the latest from his dad. Though he didn't come out and say it, Donovan knew he wanted him to come to Florida now. Donovan hit reply and started typing, assuring his dad that he'd be home by Christmas Day. But the word *home* didn't feel right so he backspaced through it and typed *in Florida*. Home had once again become Sweet Home. And the thought made Donovan miserable.

He left the email unfinished, scratched a message on a Post-it, and grabbed his car keys. On his way out, he slapped the note on the microwave, glad he didn't see Hope on his way out.

Chapter 20

WITH HER ARMS full, Ella piled all the empty soda cans into the kitchen sink for rinsing. Her mom stood next to the refrigerator, watching, as if making sure she was following through now that her friends had left. "Geesh, Mom. I told you I'd clean up after them. I just needed a few minutes to finish the block I was working on."

"That's not it," her mom said. "I need to talk to you. Just leave those for now."

Her mom's tone was scaring Ella. She left the cans and tried to prepare herself for bad news. It felt just like when her mom told her that Grandpa had died.

"I'll make us some hot tea, okay?" her mom said.

"Just tell me."

"All right." Her mom sat at the kitchen table. "Come sit with me."

Ella took her normal spot, across from where her dad sat. "Where's my—um, Donovan?" Shouldn't he be here with them for this? Her mom looked so serious.

"He went for a drive." She pointed to the microwave, which had a Post-it with his handwriting on it.

"Then what's going on?" Ella held her breath.

"I'm worried. I'm afraid you're getting too attached to him," her mom said.

"What?" Ella had to calm her heart down. "What are you talking about? I thought you wanted me to get to know him. I thought that was the reason you made sure that we had breakfast every day, just the two of us."

"I do want you to know him. I just want you to be prepared," her mom said.

"Prepared for what?"

Her mom reached out and took her hand. "He's not staying in Alaska, sweetie."

Ella jerked away. "He is, too. You're just saying that because you're jealous."

"What? I'm not—"

But Ella cut her off. "You are! You're no longer the only parent. There's someone else to boss me around and you don't like it." Except Donovan never bossed her around. He just liked spending time with her. Ella glared at her mother.

Her mom stared back for a long moment. "Okay. Maybe you're right that I don't completely like sharing you. But you have to know that I'm thrilled that you and Donovan are getting along so well."

"Then you just need to stay out of it, okay?" Ella jumped up from the table, wishing her dad were home so he could tell her that it wasn't so . . . that her mom had it all wrong!

Ella went down to his office to wait for him. She sat in his chair and spun around until she got bored. She decided to check her email on his laptop, since she'd left her phone in the studio.

She shook the mouse and his laptop woke up, displaying the Home Sweet Home Lodge website. She clicked through all the links and looked at all the photos. When she was done, she looked at the other opened windows. She shouldn't have been snooping, but it was all boring business stuff: a spreadsheet of items stocked in the remodeled hardware store, accounting software, and his email app. For no reason at all, she clicked on the app and read the email in progress.

Subject: Moving to Florida

Dad,

Just wanted to let you know that I'm wrapping things up here in Alaska. I'll be in Florida by Christmas Day and ready to look at houses. You can count on

The note stopped there, but to her he'd said it all. She re-read it to make sure it was true. Her mom was right. Dono-van was leaving and Ella couldn't understand what all this had been about. He'd worked so hard to make her love him and now he was ditching her to move as far away as possible!

"What are you doing at my desk?" Her dad's booming voice made her jump.

"I-I . . ." She tried to pull it together. Then she glared at him. "I was finding out the truth."

"Were you going through my desk drawer?" He seemed super mad but she didn't care.

"You know, it's going to crush Mom that you're not stick-ing around!" She wouldn't admit it was going to crush her, too.

"What's going to crush Mom?" Her mom appeared be-hind Donovan. "And why are you yelling at Ella?"

"Because she should know better than to snoop through my desk."

"I wasn't—"

But he cut her off. "I am really disappointed in you, Ella! My gosh, you're nearly an adult."

Ella's cheeks were burning up and tears started running down her face, which was really pissing her off. She had to get out of there.

Her mom started yelling at Donovan, and Donovan yelled back . . . and Ella was to blame. She fled the office and ran down the hall, stopping in the dining room where she'd left her backpack earlier. Several bottles of wine sat there, ready for the upcoming wine tasting. She grabbed one and shoved it into her backpack. Then she pulled on her boots and coat and ran out the door.

She sobbed into the night, not caring that it was snowing hard. *I've been so stupid! The three of us aren't a family!* Four of them, if she counted Boomer. For a second, she thought about turning around to get the dog, but she couldn't go back. Ever. She ran for the path in the woods that was a shortcut into town. Maybe she could hitchhike from there to make her way to Anchorage.

She could hear her mom and Donovan calling out to her but she kept running, which wasn't all that easy in the snow.

Maybe a few minutes ago she was nearly an adult, but by walking out, she'd crossed over and was a full-fledged grown-up now. She would get a job in the city. *No more painting signs for fun!* That thought made her cry harder. From now on she had to make her own way in the world. Fine. It was what her mom had been preparing her for, her whole life. And it wouldn't be in Sweet Home. She had to escape to anywhere but here.

She wound her way farther into the woods. This path would take her back out to the road about a half mile from town, the perfect place to hitch a ride. But the reality was that Sweet Home was off the beaten path. Not many cars driving by this time of night. Maybe a snowplow, but that wouldn't get her to Anchorage. At least she had her backpack, which was full of essentials like extra gloves.

She ran faster and cried harder until she could no longer hear her parents hollering. She slowed her pace then and searched in her backpack for tissues. She pulled her hood over her head and started walking again, trying to figure out what she was going to do.

One thing was for sure . . . she wasn't going to be a stupid kid anymore and believe in happy endings ever again.

"WHERE CAN SHE be?" Donovan stood next to Hope in front of Wandering Moose. He shouldn't have yelled at Ella.

It wasn't until she ran off that he realized what Ella had been doing—reading his email, not looking at the engagement ring hidden in his desk drawer. He'd been rash, panicked. He should've been calm and talked to her, instead of . . .

He tried to keep the fear at bay but he couldn't. They'd been calling for Ella for the last twenty minutes. They'd checked all the cabins. They'd walked to the road and didn't see her. *God, let her be all right* was the only prayer he could think of. He couldn't lose Ella now. She meant so much to him. "Hope, the snow is really coming down hard." What if they didn't find her soon?

"I know. I'm worried, too. At least she didn't take the car." Hope was eerily calm. The only other time he'd seen her like this was when Izzie and Beau died.

"Did you notice that Ella nicked a bottle of wine from the table?" It was his fault. He should've locked up the wine the second he arrived home. Alcohol lowered the core body temperature, making alcohol and cold weather a dangerous combination.

Ignoring his question, Hope asked, "Do you have your keys on you?"

"Yeah."

"Let's hurry and drive to town to see if we can find her along the way. By now, Lacy could've picked her up and the two could have gone off together."

With the bottle of wine! He didn't say it, didn't want to alarm Hope further.

They rushed to his vehicle and got in. The second Hope was latched in, he peeled out, buckling his seat belt as he sped out of the driveway.

The car slid this way and that on the snow and ice as he raced to town. He had to get to his daughter! He had to fix everything.

"Donovan! Slow down!" Hope yelled. "Getting us killed won't do Ella any good."

But as soon as the words were out of her mouth, he hit another patch of ice and careened off the road, down an embankment, the vehicle bouncing, jerking them around. Out of nowhere a tree appeared, as if sprouting suddenly from the ground. *Bang!* At the instant of impact, the airbags exploded. He was dazed for a moment, then—"HOPE!"

She didn't answer him. He reached for her, pushing the airbag away, checking for signs of life by the dashboard lights. Her eyes were closed, but she seemed to be stirring.

"Hope! Hope! Are you all right?" He couldn't pull her closer as the steering wheel had pinned him in and his leg was hurting like crazy. *Probably broken.* "Talk to me, Hope."

"I think you took a wrong turn," she said, her eyes fluttering open.

"Are you injured?" he asked.

"My right arm. I can't move it. And my head. I think I banged it against my window. It really smarts."

"Oh, Hope, I'm sorry!" But he was relieved she was conscious. "You were right. I was driving too fast. Sweetheart, can you ever forgive me?"

Her laugh was strained. "Accidents happen. I promise that as soon as the headache subsides, I'll forgive you." She groaned. "Well, maybe."

He took her hand and kissed it, laughing. "I'm never letting you go. You know that, don't you?"

Gingerly she turned her head to look at him. "What?"

He should've realized it sooner. "Hope, you've gotta know that no one has ever occupied this heart of mine but you. I love you." It felt so good to say it.

"I must be in worse shape than I thought." She closed her eyes again. "I thought I heard you say you love me."

"You heard right," he said. "And it's way overdue. I love you, Hope."

Hope opened her eyes, stunned. "Really?"

"Really."

She smiled, her eyes glistening with love for him, but her furrowed brow showed she was still in pain.

"Please forgive me for running away after Beau and Izzie died. I had to blame someone, so I blamed you. I'm so sorry."

"You're forgiven," she said.

"Thank you." Although he was pinned in the car, a huge weight was lifted, like an elephant had been hoisted off his chest. He kissed her hand again. "I love you so much."

"Does this mean that you're not leaving?"

"I'm not leaving you and I'm not leaving Ella. Ever." And he had to find Ella. "I'm sorry I screwed everything up. I'd give anything to keep you and Ella safe."

Suddenly a light shone in his window, a very bright light. But he wasn't going toward it, even if St. Peter himself were there to take him away! Because he finally had Hope back.

Hope squeezed Donovan's hand. "It's Ella!" The exclamation made her wince.

"Ella!" Donovan tried to open his door, but he couldn't.

A second later, the back door was yanked open. Ella climbed in and latched onto their shoulders. "Mom? Dad? Are you okay?" She was out of breath.

She'd called him *Dad*!

"You scared me! I saw you run off the road."

Hope unlatched her hand from Donovan, reached back, and clasped Ella's hand. "We're banged up but we're going to be fine."

"Your mom was knocked out for a second. She may have a broken arm and I think I have a broken leg." Donovan desperately needed to get Hope to the hospital to make sure she was going to be all right. He was frustrated that he couldn't move.

Ella took a deep breath as if centering herself. She let go and rummaged through her backpack, then leaned over the front seat with a penlight. "Mom, let me check your pupils." She flashed it in both of her eyes. "She might have a concussion; I'm not sure. We can't let her go to sleep, okay?"

"I'll do my best," Donovan said.

Again, Ella dug around in her backpack. "Here. It's Advil to help you with the pain for your leg." She handed over a couple of pills, plus a bottled water. "After you take that, I need to fix the gash on your forehead."

"I'm bleeding?" he asked.

"It's pretty gnarly," Ella said.

From nowhere, it seemed, wet wipes appeared and soon she was bandaging his head.

"Mom, you awake?" Ella asked.

"Yes."

"Good. I'll be right back."

Before he could tell Ella to stay put, she was gone.

"Where's she going?" Hope asked.

"No clue," he said, taking Hope's hand again. He had to keep her awake and talking. "I hate to pressure you, but do you have something you'd like to say back to me?"

"What? About the weather?" Hope asked. "Or about how you should sign up for a course on how to drive in winter weather?"

He sighed with relief, so happy she had her wits about her . . . a good sign. "No jokes right now. You know what I want to hear. I said I love you but you didn't say whether that was good news or bad." A moment ago, he'd been sure she loved him back, but now a niggle of worry came over him. Maybe the concussion had caused her eyes to glisten. Maybe she didn't love him at all.

Hope laughed. "You should see yourself right now. Stop panicking. You have to know I love you, too. There's never been anyone in my life but you. It's always been you, and I don't want to scare you, but it's always going to be you. What is that you used to say to me? Oh, yeah, *You rock my world*."

Though it hurt, he stretched over and kissed her on the lips. This moment felt more intoxicating than any whiskey he'd ever drunk.

They were interrupted again by the back door opening and Ella sliding in once more. "I made a flag of sorts by tying my orange hunting vest to a post, marking where you ran off the road. And, Dad, thanks for the satellite phone. I used it to call for help. I could've hiked into town from here but there was no way I was going to leave you two."

"Speaking of *leaving*—" Donovan started.

But Hope took over. "Isabella Beau McKnight, if you ever scare us like that again by running away, I promise you'll be grounded for life . . . and then some."

"Beau?" he asked.

"Yeah. Ella needed to have your family in her name, too."

"That's nice." Donovan's throat was tight.

"You know I really loved Beau," Hope said.

"I know," Donovan answered, all feeling of blame gone with love taking its place.

Ella laid her hand on his shoulder again as if she were connecting to him and his family.

He took hold of Ella's hand. "Your mom's right. You can't ever run away again; you really scared us. Really scared me." He wasn't sure when his heart rate was going to return to normal, if ever. He kept telling himself that Ella was okay. "You're my daughter and now that I've found you, I can't lose you. I'm sorry I yelled. In the future, I'll do better and try to explain first, instead of raising my voice. As far as the email you saw, I'm not going to send it. I'm not selling the lodge or the hardware store. There's no way I can leave you and your mom. My dad will just have to move to Alaska, or at the very least, spend his summers here with us."

"I'd like to get to know him," Ella said.

"He's eager to know you, too," Donovan said.

"And, Hope." He paused. "If I could get down on one knee, I would ask you to marry me." He already had the perfect ring to give her.

Ella gasped and Hope laughed but stopped. "Ouch, that hurts."

"Well?" he asked expectantly.

"Oh, was that a proposal? Then I accept."

Ella put her arms around them and gave them a gentle squeeze. "I'm so happy." She giggled. "Does this mean I get a car? Aberdeen said you're loaded and that I'd probably get all kinds of stuff."

Donovan was so happy that he started to say yes but Hope beat him to answering.

"Absolutely not!" Hope said. "You get two parents instead."

Ella leaned her head against Hope's. "I can live with that."

For the next twenty minutes, the three of them talked about nothing and everything.

"I guess this means you'll be moving back to the lodge," Donovan said, knowing he would rest easier when they were all under the same roof together again.

"Not until we're married," Hope answered.

He squeezed her hand. "It's going to be a very short engagement, then."

"Fine by me," Ella said. "I'm tired of traipsing back and forth between Wandering Moose and the lodge." Suddenly she stopped talking and turned left and right, searching the back seat.

"What are you looking for?" Donovan asked.

"Where's Boomer?"

"We left your dog back at the lodge," Donovan said.

"Are you kidding me?" Ella was incensed. "What would've happened to him if I hadn't saved you two?"

"Another reason you better not run away again," Donovan said.

A second flashlight shone in the window.

Ella cracked open her door to the man standing outside.

"Are you folks all right?" he said. "I saw the orange flag from the road."

"I already called 911," Ella responded confidently, "but could you wait at the road to show them where we are?"

"You bet. Can I do anything else for you in the meantime?" he asked.

"No," Ella said. "We're going to be okay."

Chapter 21

TWO DAYS LATER, Hope and Donovan were recovering on the couch, watching as the Wines of Alaska tasting kicked off the Christmas Festival. Jesse had hung all of Izzie's artwork, making the lodge feel that much more like home. People—Sweet Home residents and visitors from other towns joining in the celebration—packed the living room, dining room, and kitchen . . . just like the old days.

"I feel like a couch potato," Hope said a little glumly. She was used to staying busy and it was downright painful sitting here—though leaning against Donovan's strong body was heavenly.

"Really? I'm quite enjoying it." Donovan had his broken leg propped up on a chair. "You know, doctor's orders specifically included couch potatoing until your concussion heals. Try to enjoy the break. We'll be busy soon enough. Rick said reservations are pouring in on the website. Besides, it's nice to just sit here with you next to me." He wrapped his arm around her.

Hope smiled. "I am relishing in that part of the recovery." She played with the ring on the chain around her neck. It was like back in high school, but instead of Donovan's class ring, it was his grandmother's engagement ring. They hadn't told a soul yet, so she dropped the ring back inside her shirt and went back to scanning the happy faces around them. "They really didn't need *us* to bring the Christmas Festival back to life."

He kissed her forehead. "Yeah, they did."

Hope understood. Miss Lisa had let it slip about Piney's plan to get her and Donovan back together . . . which in a way had brought the town together, too.

"I'm really grateful," Hope said, "that the Sisterhood of the Quilt swooped in and took over. Everything looks great." She touched the bandage on his forehead. "If it's okay with you, I hope it leaves a scar. Scars can be sexy. You know, like Poldark."

"Stop fantasizing about other men," he said with good humor.

"I'm not. It's just that Poldark . . ." She sighed. "But I've never seen you look more handsome and rugged."

He laughed. "I think either the concussion or the painkillers have gotten to you." Then he got serious. "How are you feeling? Maybe it's time for you to lie down and rest."

"I'm good. With you by my side, everything feels perfect."

Ella joined them. "Can I sit for a minute?" She squeezed between them, laying her head on Hope's shoulder.

"Good," Hope said. "I'm glad you're here. I was just getting ready to talk to your dad about the hardware store."

"I bet I can guess," Donovan said. "You want to talk about the quilt shop."

"You know me so well."

"Just get with Rick and have him set up accounts at the fabric companies," Donovan said.

"Can I work the counter, cutting fabric?" Ella asked. "I'm pretty good at it."

"Of course you can work the quilt counter," Donovan said. "In fact, if you want, I'd love for you to learn all aspects of the hardware store. It's in your blood, you know. We've all worked there—your great-grandfather and great-grandmother, your grandfather, your uncle Beau, and me." He paused. "And half the town has worked there, too."

"I can't wait. But what are you going to do about tomorrow, Dad?" Ella pointed at his cast.

He wrapped an arm around her. "The ribbon-cutting ceremony at the hardware store?"

"Yeah."

"I'm going to send *you* to cut the ribbon," he said.

"Really? That's so cool! But are you sure?" Ella asked.

"Yes, I'm needed right here to take care of your mom."

Ella guffawed. "Yeah, right. I've seen you with those crutches. You're so clumsy I thought you were going to break your neck when you were getting the marriage license on the way home from the hospital."

"Shhh," Hope said. "It's a secret between the three of us."

Ella sighed. "Don't you think there's been enough secrets, Mom?"

"Our daughter has a point." Donovan sounded more and more like a proud father. "Let's share the good news."

Hope gave a little shrug, which apparently was all the encouragement Ella needed. She jumped to her feet.

"Can I get everyone's attention, please?" Ella said above the noise. "I have an announcement to make."

Gradually the room was hushed.

Ella turned back and beamed at her parents before pushing on. "I just wanted to let you all know that you're invited to a wedding. My mom and dad are getting married!"

The room was stunned for a moment, then clapping broke out. Above the din Piney shouted, "It's about time!"

Donovan pulled Hope closer and they stared into each other's eyes for a long moment.

This time Ella plopped down beside Donovan, lighting up the whole room with her delighted grin. "That was easy."

Hope nudged Donovan. "Have you ever seen a happier kid?"

"Never." Donovan kissed her temple, then kissed Ella on the head.

People came over to congratulate them and Hope had never been happier either. When it calmed down, she said,

"You know, this rush wedding that you want is going to require a lot of work. I'm sure we can arrange to be married at the church, but I'm not sure what we can do about a reception, especially with the two of us banged up."

Sparkle and Piney appeared, squeezing in on the couch on either side of the trio.

Piney pulled out a notebook. "You don't need to worry about a thing. Sparkle and I have it all planned out."

"What? It was just announced," Hope said.

Sparkle laughed. "Mom and I made the lists a month ago. We've even got some of the food made; it's in the freezer at the Hungry Bear." Rick came up behind Sparkle and laid a hand on her shoulder, making Hope wonder when the two of them were going to tie the knot.

"I'm confused," Hope said. "I didn't even know there was going to be a wedding until a few days ago."

Piney reached over and squeezed her hand. "Buttercup, haven't I told you a thousand times that I can predict the future?"

"Yes, well, you haven't always been correct with your predictions," Hope said. "What was it, fifteen years ago when you predicted I'd no longer have to worry about money? That I'd go on an exciting journey? That I'd settle in with the love of my life?" Suddenly Hope was gobsmacked. All of those things had come true.

Piney laughed. "My predictions always come true . . . eventually."

Boomer wandered over and jumped up, putting his paws on Ella's knees. She picked him up, setting him on her lap. With the growing pup the couch was at more than full capacity.

Sparkle smiled up at Rick, then back at Hope. "All of us had more than an inkling that there was going to be a happy ending here. You and Donovan are meant to be together."

"I concur," Donovan said. "It just took me seventeen years to come to my senses."

• • •

THE NEXT FEW days flew by, and with each one, Hope felt better, more like herself. Plus she was eager to be married to the man she'd loved her whole life. It was decided they would marry at midnight mass on Christmas with the big wedding reception set for New Year's Eve, exactly eighteen years after Izzie and Beau's death. Hope was immediately against it when Ella made the suggestion, but Piney assured her it would be good karma for her and Donovan to make happy memories on the anniversary of the accident. She claimed her tarot cards agreed.

Christmas Eve morning, Hope, Donovan, and Ella rose early for breakfast and quiet time before the whirlwind of activity began. Boomer was in rare form, running around as if he knew something exciting was going to happen that night.

"Are you sure we can't open presents now?" Ella sounded like she was six again.

"Nope," Hope said quickly, before Donovan gave in to her. "In the morning."

"But you'll sleep in, especially since the wedding is so late tonight."

"We promise to get up." Donovan winked at Hope. She still couldn't believe she'd caved and let him buy Ella a used Subaru Outback, which Jesse and Shaun Montana had promised to drop off early in the morning. The speed at which Donovan found and bought the car made Hope wonder if he'd lined it up beforehand. She had come to appreciate that he didn't want to spoil Ella, just relieve her hardships.

Using her good arm, Hope poured another cup of coffee. "Piney says she's going to be here at noon to make sure we have a little food prepared for the day," Hope said to Donovan. "I insisted she didn't have to do that."

Ella put down her mug. "Yeah, I told her I was capable of opening a can of soup for you two."

"There's no stopping Piney," Donovan said. "She's a force of nature. However, I'm not sure she'll be able to control the size of the New Year's Eve reception. Jesse said he heard a couple from another town telling someone at the Christmas Festival how they planned to come back for the New Year's Eve bash. I guess they felt welcome here in Sweet Home."

"Yes," Hope said. "Rick said all three cabins are booked."

"Really?" Donovan said. "I wonder why he didn't tell me."

"Maybe he's concerned about you wobbling out to do one last check on the cabins," Hope said. "Maybe your wife-to-be gave him a heads-up to that fact."

"Oh?" Donovan didn't sound affronted.

Ella got into the game with a rib. "Dad, we're seriously worried about you breaking your other leg. We'll all feel better when you stop using those crutches."

Hope turned to Ella. "I know Wandering Moose is all packed, except for our shower stuff. Do you mind taking care of it this morning?"

"Okay, Mom."

"Hold up," Donovan said. "I'll shoot Jesse a text to see if he and Shaun can run by to do the actual moving."

"Dad, I can do it," Ella insisted.

"Don't argue with me. I'm getting married today." He delivered it with a tease and a smile while pulling out his phone. "Besides, you're busy. You do remember that you'll be standing up with us tonight, right?" Sparkle and Rick, too.

"Yeah, I remember," Ella said, giving him that same smile back.

"And that Boomer needs to have a bath today," Donovan reminded her. "The ring bearer has to smell good. I promised Father Mike."

Ella hugged Boomer. "He'll smell like a rose. Promise."

At noon exactly, Jesse and Shaun showed up, and right behind them was Piney. But not just Piney, the whole Sisterhood of the Quilt—the Chicas included.

"What is this?" Hope asked. "Are we going to have a sew-in?"

"No," Piney said. "We're going to have a wedding shower. We're armed with food and maybe a present or two."

"I don't know what to say," Hope said.

"Don't say anything. We're on a schedule. Donovan is only giving us an hour."

"Donovan?" Hope said.

"Yes. Your groom is pretty good at keeping a secret, I think," Piney said.

The girls and women ventured into the studio, which looked sharp with a fresh coat of paint, the reinvented Sisterhood of the Quilt wall hanging, and updated window coverings.

Hope noticed as she stood in the doorway that the women were all gathered in one corner of the room.

"What are you all doing?" Hope asked.

"Wait a second," Ella said from behind Hope. "Dad said to wait up. He's having trouble getting down the hall."

Hope looked over her shoulder, and sure enough, Donovan was gimping toward her on his crutches.

"Donovan, what's up?"

"It's your wedding present," he said. "Tell them that I said you can see it now. I'm almost there."

Hope glanced back into the studio as the women parted, revealing a sewing machine with a large white bow on top, right in the spot where her old sewing machine usually sat.

She turned back to Donovan, who was coming up behind her. "How?"

"The Sisterhood of the Quilt selected it, I ordered it, and Jesse picked it up and slipped it in here a while ago," he said.

"But Jesse just got here," Hope said.

Donovan smiled mischievously. "Then he did a good job of sneaking in through the garage undetected."

Hope wrapped her good arm around her future husband's neck—careful not to knock him off his crutches—and laid a passionate kiss on him, while the Sisterhood of the Quilt made catcalls.

"Mom! PDA! There's children present!" Ella scolded.

292 • Patience Griffin

"Okay, get out of here," Hope said to Donovan. "It's girl time."

As he turned to go with a big grin on his face, she patted him on the butt. She still couldn't believe that she could kiss Donovan Stone anytime she wanted now.

"Hurry up, Hope," Piney said. "I told you we're on the clock."

"What clock? The wedding isn't for another twelve hours," Hope said, so happy the Sisterhood of the Quilt was here.

"Donovan's worried we're going to wear you out with our carrying on. He wants you well rested for tonight." Piney gave her a wink, then turned to the others. "Aberdeen, help Ella and Hope get settled on the couch. Lacy, Uki, and you other girls, pour the punch in the plastic cups we brought and pass them around. After that, give out the snacks."

"Excuse me." Donovan was back, this time with Jesse.

"What is it?" Piney asked with a little irritation in her voice. "You're cutting into our time."

"Jesse forgot Ella's present," Donovan said.

Jesse maneuvered carefully past Donovan, holding another sewing machine, this one with a pink bow on top.

"Sorry about that, kiddo," Jesse said, placing Ella's machine next to Hope's.

For being so thoughtful, Hope needed to give Donovan another kiss—a mind-blowing one—but she guessed that could wait until they were alone tonight . . . after they were married.

Ella jumped up and gave her father a hug. "Love you, Dad," she whispered. But Hope heard her and it melted her heart.

"Love you, too," he said back hoarsely. Then he disappeared from the doorway again.

"Okay, now for the main attraction," Piney said. "Lisa, you go first."

The women lined up behind Miss Lisa. Ella's friends lined up next to them.

"We didn't have time to make you a quilt," Piney said. "I

apologize. I should've had everyone working on these from the start, instead of just focusing on the food."

"Working on what?" Hope noticed everyone was holding a tissue-wrapped something in their hands.

"Go ahead, Lisa, show her," Piney said.

Miss Lisa came forward and handed the present to her. "We all saw your Izzie Memory Tree quilt drawing the first day we met here."

"Actually, Bill made sure they saw it," Piney chimed in.

Miss Lisa acted like Piney hadn't admitted that part and continued. "Since you were laid up with your hurt ankle, and then busy with decorating and the other quilts for the lodge, we thought we would each make a block for you to give you a head start on Izzie's quilt. I hope it was okay that we got into your Izzie fabric."

"Of course it's all right," Piney said. "We're family. Now open it."

Hope gently pulled back the tissue paper to reveal a moose block for the upper right corner of the quilt. Miss Lisa had embellished it with two of Izzie's buttons. Hope pushed herself off the couch. "Oh, Miss Lisa, it's beautiful." She hugged the older woman.

"Stop all that hugging," Piney said. "We'll never get through everyone. Now, Hope, sit back down." Piney pointed to Lacy. "It's your turn."

Lacy came forward and handed Ella her tissue-wrapped package. "You're my best friend, Ella, and I'm so happy you've got a dad now."

Hope knew this was hard for Lacy; her parents were divorced when she was two, and her father wasn't involved in her life.

Lacy went on. "Each of the Chicas has made a block, the start of a Friendship quilt for you. Open it. Look, we've all signed our blocks."

Ella pulled back the paper to reveal a Log Cabin block with Lacy's name stitched in the middle of one of the logs. "Look, Mom."

Hope examined it, and then Ella held it up for everyone to see.

One by one, everyone—Aberdeen, Lolly, Paige . . . even Courtney, whose wolf block was a work of art—brought up their blocks and gave them to Hope or to Ella.

Hope was overcome with joy and love for these women. When she woke up that morning she hadn't believed her heart could handle a smidge more emotion, but she was wrong. She was flooded with happiness.

Piney was the last one to come forward but carried a much larger package than the others. A box, actually. "This is from Bill. I tried to get him to join us, but apparently he's too much of a man to attend a girly wedding shower." She passed Hope the plain box. "He didn't just make you one block for Izzie's Memory Tree. You better open it up and take a look to see what's inside."

Hope pulled off the lid to reveal a stack of blocks—some houses, some trees, and some traditional blocks—none of which were in her design. "What's this for?"

Piney handed her a piece of paper. "He took liberties with your original design and expanded it to include all of Sweet Home."

Hope studied the paper and saw that Bill hadn't just expanded her design, he'd made it a work of art.

"The fabrics in his blocks are from each of our own stashes," Aberdeen explained. "See, my block shows my trailer, and is made from my own fabric."

"My house is from my fabric, too." Miss Lisa said.

All of them began talking at once about what fabric was used in their house or trailer block.

"Settle down now," Piney said. "Bill wants you to know that you're not obligated to use his design or any of his blocks."

"I'm overwhelmed," Hope finally said. "Of course I'm going to use his design and his blocks . . . all of your blocks! This is the best gift I've ever received." Even though she cherished her new sewing machine and couldn't wait to learn how to use it, the blocks from all these women and from Bill represented a priceless gift: her community. And she knew if Donovan were standing here, he'd agree.

"But here's my question," Hope said. "How could Bill have made all of these blocks in the last few days?"

Piney gave a dismissive wave. "For all Bill blusters about not believing in my powers, he certainly trusted me this time. He's been collecting fabric and sewing blocks since that first night you took Izzie's tree design over to his cabin."

Hope would have to get Bill alone to give the grizzly old man a bear hug, the big softy.

She beamed up at Piney, at all of them. "Thank you so much for making these blocks for me. For us! If Izzie were here, I know she'd love them, too." What a tribute to her little sister and a tribute to Sweet Home.

"Okay, everyone, have fun for a few minutes before I kick you out of here," Piney said.

Ella grabbed her blocks and joined her friends in the corner—chattering and laughing.

Piney sat next to Hope and laid a little package in her lap. "I didn't want to give you my block in front of the others."

Hope's brow furrowed. "Why not?"

Piney gathered her hand and patted it. "Look at the block and you'll see."

Hope couldn't imagine what could be wrong with it. She tore away the tissue to reveal a square block with a heart in the center.

"Just like Sparkle, you're my heart, Hope. But I didn't want the others to know that I play favorites." She wrapped her arm around her. "There's nothing in the world I wouldn't do for you." She paused for a long moment, frowning. "Just so you know, I'm sorry."

"For what? It's been a wonderful day," Hope exclaimed.

"About letting you go from the Hungry Bear."

"Oh, that," Hope said.

"It was for your own good. I hope you can see that now."

Hope rested her head on Piney's shoulder. "I get it. But you know, laying me off could've backfired."

"No, it couldn't have," Piney said with confidence. "I told you I knew everything would work out." She scooped up the quilt blocks from Hope. "You need to have something to eat and then lie down for a while, okay?"

"I will." But Hope just wanted to sit there for a little longer. "I love you, Piney."

"I love you, too, buttercup."

After Hope ate, she did as she was told and went upstairs to lie down while the Sisterhood of the Quilt cleaned up the studio. As soon as she fell asleep, Izzie came to her . . . and she wasn't alone.

"Mom?" Her mother was wearing a white, gauzy dress, as was Izzie, and they were holding hands. Hope had seen them holding hands a million times before, but this time it seemed as if Izzie were the adult and her mother the child.

"Go on, Mom," Izzie said. "Tell her."

Mom reached out as if to stroke Hope's hair. "I'm so sorry for how I acted over the accident. The truth is, underneath all my anger, I really blamed myself. It was my job to keep Izzie safe and it was my fault she died."

Izzie rolled her eyes. "It's no one's fault. It was an accident, and accidents happen, right?"

With earnest, Penny looked at her younger child. "I'm still coming to terms with it."

"Okay. We can accept that," Izzie said. "Tell her the rest."

Penny nodded. "I hope you can forgive me for how I behaved."

Hope's eyes filled with tears. "Yes. Of course." Motherhood had given Hope insight into a lot of things, but mostly into the past. When Mom shunned her seventeen years ago, it wasn't because she didn't care for her anymore; Mom was just drowning in grief.

Izzie cleared her throat. "You know, big sister, that forgiveness brings healing."

"I know that." Hope was counting on it, too.

"Thank you, Hope," Mom said.

"And?" Izzie prompted their mother.

Penny gave Hope a sad, expectant smile. "Please, darling, know I've always loved you."

Those words meant the world to Hope. "Yes. I know."

Her sister walked closer and cocked her head, as if ready to impart some final wisdom. "Mom and I think you can handle it from here."

It was true. Hope was coping better than she had her whole adult life. "But my wedding's tonight—"

"Mom and I will be right beside you when you walk down the aisle." The little imp glowed.

The thought of them being there filled Hope with peace, love, and tranquility.

"Even when we don't see each other," Izzie said, "you know that I'm always with you, right?"

"Yes, I do."

"Right here." Izzie laid a hand over her heart, just as Hope did the same.

Epilogue

ELLA AND HOPE walked back to the SUV while Donovan watched from the back seat. His leg prevented him from driving, forcing Ella to be the chauffeur.

He'd given his two girls time alone to add things to Izzie's tree at the edge of the forest. Besides, there was no way he was making it up the hill on his crutches. He scratched Boomer behind the ears as the dog stretched out on Hope's side of the back seat. "Next stop's the cemetery."

He and Hope had been married a week, the best week of his life. He still couldn't believe that Ella wanted to add his last name to hers—Ella McKnight-Stone. They'd forgone the honeymoon for now, because Ella needed them. He only had a year and a half left with her before she'd be off to college, probably art school. His daughter had so much talent.

For the millionth time since returning to Sweet Home, he wondered what it would have been like to have had *this* all these years. But then it occurred to him that the separate journeys he and Hope had been on—concerning Beau, Izzie, and the accident—was part of *their* story. Maybe if they hadn't gone through the things they had, this moment wouldn't have been so sweet. What if he'd stayed in Alaska and hadn't had the military to help him get sober? Would his drinking have driven him and Hope apart? The answer was unequivocally *yes*. She would've been smart enough to dump him and never look back. For the first time, he was grateful for it all—the good, the bad, the time away from each other. Moving forward, he'd never take his family for granted; he'd only appreciate his one great love, Hope, and his wonderful daughter, and how good life could be with them in it.

The ladies opened their car doors and got in.

"Boomer," Hope scolded. "Get back up front with your sister."

He did as he was told, especially with Ella's coaxing, "Come on, good boy. Come on."

Ella got Boomer situated and herself buckled in. "Are you ready back there?"

"Wake me when we get there." Hope laid her head on his shoulder.

"It'll have to be a short nap," he told Hope. "We're only a few miles away."

Hope sighed. "I'm exhausted from the wedding reception last night."

They all were spent—in a good way—from their crazy, wonderful New Year's Eve soirée.

"Best party ever!" Hope reached over and took his hand.

"It was," piped up the peanut gallery in the front.

Donovan kissed Hope's hair. "We couldn't have asked for better." He caressed Hope's shoulder, so grateful to have her near. "The town was in rare form, and many of the visitors announced they were coming back every year for Sweet Home's New Year's Eve party."

"A new tradition?" Hope asked.

"Sounds good to me."

Piney had been right about having their reception on New Year's Eve. Their perceptions of the past had changed.

Five minutes later Ella pulled into the cemetery. "Dad, are you sure you want to get out of the car?"

"I'll be fine." He might not be . . . but he had gotten marginally better on the crutches, especially on flat ground.

Ella and Boomer got out and raced each other across the snow.

Hope slid out and hurried to the other side to help him.

"We're quite the pair, aren't we?" he said.

She pulled out the crutches and held them with her un-casted arm. "I think we're perfect," she said, smiling.

Ella ran back toward them with Boomer on her heels. "Hurry up, slowpokes. We have to get back in time. Mom, you're the one who said you were eager to put together Izzie's Memory Tree quilt today."

"I know."

They'd reached Beau's grave.

"Take all the time you need," Hope said, kissing him on the cheek.

He reached in his pocket and pulled out the new car he'd picked up at the Hungry Bear. He tore open the package. Then, careful not to knock himself over, he leaned down and set it on the top of Beau's tombstone. "I bought you a new car. A Ferrari. Thought you might like it." He looked over to see his wife, child, and dog at Izzie's grave and realized he wasn't alone anymore in his pain. "Listen, little brother," he said to Beau, "I just wanted to stop by. It's a new year and all." *A better year.* "I've got everything I've ever wanted . . . and needed. You were right. You let me know that first day that I had to forgive Hope. I love her so much, you know? And Ella, too. I'm such a lucky man." A breeze whipped up the snow in reply. "I miss you, Beau."

"Dad?" Ella yelled as she ran to the car. "Are you ready to go?" She looked down at the dog, who was running beside her. "Boomer's cold."

"I doubt that," Donovan hollered back. Berners were born for this weather. Donovan was, too. "I'm coming."

Hope came up beside him and they kissed for a long moment, something they'd been doing a lot since he'd come to his senses.

"Break it up," Ella hollered. "You're the ones who said how important today was. You said the Sisterhood of the

Quilt always used to come over on New Year's Day. A big sew-in is what you said. The Chicas are probably already there!"

Donovan reluctantly pulled away from the kiss. "We better go." His grandmother would be so pleased that the New Year's Day tradition was continuing. "Back to real life."

"And what a wonderful life it is!" Hope said, beaming up at him.

Donovan couldn't help himself and kissed her again until his kid started yelling. *His kid! His wife!* He still couldn't believe it. "I owe you everything, Hope."

With her hand gently touching his arm, she walked beside him while he hobbled, both of them looking forward.

Acknowledgments

A published book does not come about by one person alone but is created by a team of people. First and foremost, I want to thank Tracy Bernstein for the amazing edits and lasting friendship. Thank you, Claire Zion, for making the back-cover copy sing and choosing the happy couple for the front cover. Thanks to Michelle Kasper and Amy Schneider and all the people at Berkley who brought *One Snowy Night* to life. Thank you to the quilt shops in Alaska who were so kind to speak with me, and to Kris Hansell for your invaluable input. As always, thanks to Kevan Lyon, my faithful agent. And last but not least, to Kathleen Baldwin for being a most wonderful friend in life and in writing.

Turn the page for a preview of

Once Upon a Cabin

Coming from Jove in December 2021

VICTORIA ST. JAMES gripped the chair in the lawyer's office as she and her sister McKenna glanced at each other nervously.

Terrence, their great-uncle's lawyer, opened the door and wheeled in a big-screen TV.

"Please tell us what's going on," Victoria implored. "Is Uncle Monty okay?"

"Montgomery is well." Terrence plugged in the television.

"Then why all the secrecy?" McKenna asked. "Why were we summoned?"

The sisters feared the worst. Uncle Monty was their last living relative. Having him meant more than the large inheritance they were to receive when he passed away.

"All will be revealed on the recording," Terrence said calmly. He stood back and hit play.

Uncle Monty appeared on the screen. "Hello, girls."

They were hardly girls. Victoria was twenty-eight and McKenna was twenty-nine; they were only eleven months apart.

"I've made plans for the both of you," Uncle Monty continued.

Victoria's worry turned to excitement. The last time Uncle Monty made plans, she and McKenna were whisked off to Monaco for a month.

"I've sublet your condo. Make peace with it," Uncle Monty said.

"Wait a minute." Victoria was confused. This wasn't the uncle they knew. "Pause the video."

Terrence clicked the remote.

"Is our uncle ill?" McKenna asked.

"He doesn't seem like himself," Victoria added.

"He's fine and of sound mind," the lawyer said. He turned the video back on.

But Uncle Monty looked a little pale. "I've decided it's time you two stood on your own two feet."

"I bet it was *Peggy* who decided," McKenna said under her breath. Peggy was Uncle Monty's new girlfriend. At least she was a fiftysomething hussy instead of the thirtysomething hussies he usually dated. Peggy had been shocked when she found out that the St. James sisters didn't work. *And why should we?* Victoria thought. Uncle Monty had the means and allowed them to enjoy life without bounds.

On the screen Uncle Monty was wearing a stern expression she'd never seen before. "You both need to change. This is your notice: I've put your trust funds on hold."

"You've what?" McKenna complained to the screen. "I have a climbing trip at the Grand Canyon all planned."

"Go home and pack," Uncle Monty said. "You'll need clothing for four seasons but especially for cold weather. No Dallas winter for you girls this year. You're headed for Alaska."

"Well, that's not so bad," McKenna said, smiling. "There's plenty of outdoor activities there."

Victoria frowned at her sister. "Sure, Alaska is great for you. But what am *I* supposed to do?"

Uncle Monty continued, looking increasingly grim. "I really hate to do this to you girls, but I'm going to split you up. One in the city, one in the wilderness."

"Sounds good to me," McKenna said cheerfully.

This time Victoria glared at her. "I don't think Anchorage, Fairbanks, or Juneau is the size of Dallas. They probably don't have a single Galleria among them."

"And here's the hardest part," Uncle Monty said. "I've tied all this to your trust funds, credit cards, and inheritance. If you complete your respective stays, the money will be yours. Terrence has your assignments."

The lawyer passed a folder to each of them. Victoria flipped hers open but couldn't believe what she was seeing. "One year on a homestead *in the middle of nowhere*?"

"He can't put me in a *bank* in Anchorage and expect me to survive," McKenna said at the same time.

Monty was talking again. "You've both heard me speak about my time as a young man living in Alaska near the small town of Sweet Home. Well, I've spoken with Piney at the Hungry Bear Grocery-Diner and she's found some gentlemen to help you adjust to Alaska."

But Victoria wasn't really listening at this point. "Why is he doing this to us?" she asked Terrence. "The Spring Gala is next week and I have responsibilities. I'm on the hospitality committee!"

Uncle Monty was waving. "I'll see you both in a year." The screen went blank.

"This is a disaster," Victoria grumbled.

"He can't split us up, Tori," McKenna said fiercely.

McKenna had always watched out for Victoria, as she was the younger and weaker of the two. The word everyone used to describe her was *fragile*. Just like their mother, who had died during an asthma attack, Victoria had weak lungs, too.

She looked back at the screen, but it was blank; their uncle was gone.

As if choreographed, she and McKenna pulled out their phones at the same time.

"It won't do any good," Terrence said, pointing to their cells. "Monty is on a trip around the world for the next year. You are welcome to email him, but he'll only have limited access."

"He can't do this to us!" Victoria wanted to scream. "He can't make us go to Alaska!"

"True," Terrence said. "Neither of you has to accept your assignment."

"Really?" McKenna said.

"Yes. You can stay here. Get jobs and pay your own way in the world."

He didn't say the rest, but Victoria could read his expression. *Pay your own way, just like the rest of us.*

Terrence continued. "All assets are frozen except a modest allowance for incidentals, nothing like the unlimited access to cash and credit you had before."

"What about Tori's medication? Her inhaler?" McKenna looked as worried as she always did where Victoria's breathing issues were concerned.

"Of course," Terrence said, giving Victoria a pitying glance. "I'll have all of her prescriptions mailed to Sweet Home."

McKenna didn't look satisfied.

"Fine," Victoria said, tired of always being the sickly one. "We'll do it."

"We will?" McKenna said. "We'll stay here and get jobs? Do it on our own without the trust fund? Okay, but I don't think your master's degree in ancient literature and mine in parks and recreation are going to pay enough to feed us, let alone make rent on the condo."

"No, silly. We're going to accept the challenge and go to Alaska. Uncle wants us to get out of our comfort zones, and we will."

McKenna shook her head. "Alaska is a good fit for me but I don't think it's a good idea for you. Remember when I dragged you to Thailand? You didn't exactly love roughing it."

Victoria was determined to prove her uncle—and that snooty Terrence—wrong. "Come on, sis. We can do this. A year will go by quickly," she added comfortingly, but she didn't believe it. The year would drag on. It would be miserable.

• • •

SIX DAYS LATER, Victoria and McKenna were on a plane to Anchorage, both of them still shell-shocked from uprooting their life in Texas. When the pilot announced they would be landing soon, they reached for each other's hand and held on tight. Not because they were afraid of a bumpy touchdown but because they would soon be separated.

"We've never been apart for more than a few days," Victoria whispered.

"I know." McKenna's voice was filled with worry. "Did you pack your nebulizer?"

"You've asked a million times. And yes, I have it packed. Along with my EpiPen."

"I can't stand it that I won't be there with you," McKenna said.

"Stop worrying." Something Victoria said often to her overprotective sister. But then it all overwhelmed her again. "A homestead! It sounds dreadful. Like living in *Little House on the Prairie*." It rang of hard work and broken nails. She glanced down at her perfect manicure, knowing it might be some time before her hands looked this nice again. Glancing out the window, she saw her reflection. "No highlights or shopping malls." She knew most people saw her as pampered and shallow, but she wasn't as spoiled as she let on. Not even McKenna knew the joy Victoria got from shopping for the women's shelter. After all, every woman—homeless or not—deserved to look good when interviewing for a job! Victoria's other clandestine pastimes? Stocking the local food pantry and paying random people's utility bills through the Pay It Forward Organization. Why did Victoria keep her charitable acts a secret from everyone, even her sister? A long time ago, Uncle Monty gave her some sage advice: *When you do nice things for others, do it anonymously, never toot your own horn.*

How was she supposed to do those things when her accounts had been frozen and she was banished to a homestead? She had no idea.

"Tori," her sister said, squeezing her hand. "Don't worry. It's all going to be okay."

Victoria just gave her a sad smile.

When they got off the plane, Victoria headed straight to Starbucks.

"What are you doing?" McKenna said.

"Getting my last latte for a year!"

Surprisingly, McKenna ordered a drink as well instead of rushing her like usual. They took a couple of sips and headed for baggage claim. When they arrived there, two rather attractive men—one in a suit, the other in jeans—were holding up signs with their names. As expected, the suit was holding McKenna's name, and the mountain man was holding Victoria's. The girls turned and frowned at each other.

"Let's get this over with so we can get back to our normal lives," Victoria said firmly. She set her sights on Mr. Mountain Man, walking straight to him. "I'm Victoria St. James."

His eyes widened in surprise. "Jesse Montana." He scanned the sleek black dress she'd bought at Nordstrom's. He took in every inch of her with his eyes, and seemed to be appreciating the view, and at the same time, he looked like he might be biting his tongue. To top it off, he glanced over at McKenna and nodded as if to say *she* knew how to dress properly. McKenna was wearing her L.L.Bean flannel shirt, Levi jeans, and Merrell hiking boots, looking like the next wholesome cover model for an REI ad.

Victoria bit off her next words. "Is something wrong?"

"You do know, don't you, that I'm taking you to a cabin in the woods?"

"Of course," she said, steeling her eyes and maintaining eye contact.

He broke away first and gestured to McKenna's handler, Mr. Business Attire, Victoria's kind of guy. "Okay, well, this is my friend Luke McAvoy. He works at First National Bank here in Anchorage."

Luke gave her a sparkling smile. "Nice to meet you, Victoria." His voice was deep and rich. She couldn't help but smile back.

But the frown on McKenna's face displayed her unhappiness. Not because Victoria was smiling at him, but because she was stuck with a banker, dashing though he might be.

The baggage claim horn blew, and the conveyor belt motored on. Jesse tilted his head toward the carousel. "Let's get your bags."

Victoria stared at him for a moment. If there was any way she could get by without Uncle Monty's Gold Card, she would've grabbed her sister and hopped on the next flight back to Dallas.

Jesse raised an eyebrow. "Point out your luggage. We'll follow you."

McKenna looped her arm through Victoria's and leaned over. "What if we just switch places? No one would ever know."

"Yeah, but we would," Victoria said with a sigh.

"I know."

As luck would have it, their luggage was first—McKenna's brown duffel bag and Victoria's three oversized Louis Vuittons. "That's McKenna's and those are mine." Victoria stood back and waited. McKenna reached for her duffel, but Luke grabbed it first.

When the men had their luggage beside them, Jesse nodded to Victoria. "Say your good-byes."

Victoria thought she might cry, which would be utterly humiliating.

McKenna hugged her. "I need you to take care of yourself, Tori." She squeezed her tighter. "I'm going to miss you so much!"

"I'm going to miss you, too." She didn't want to let go, but she finally stepped away. "I'm going to text you a thousand times a day."

"You better!"

Reluctantly, Victoria walked away with Jesse. "What was that all about?"

"What?" he asked.

"I saw that look you and Luke gave each other."

"Yeah, well, texting your sister a thousand times a day won't be possible," he said, looking down at the tile floor.

Victoria clutched her bag with her cell inside. "I won't let you take my phone!"

"Calm down. That's not it." He motioned with his hands as if tamping down her distress. "Where we're going there's poor cell reception."

Tears threatened once again. She followed him with her rolling carry-on, trying to pull herself together. He might be right, she might not be up for the challenge, but that didn't mean that she had to show how weak she was in front of this mountain man.

When they walked outside, she glanced around. "No limo?" she joked.

"Not where we're going, princess," Jesse replied without a hint of humor. "Four-wheel drive will work better."

A dark cloud settled over Victoria. *And so my year of misery has begun. Yippee.*

"CHEER UP." JESSE felt sorry for Victoria. She clearly didn't belong in the wilds of Alaska; she looked more suited for the concrete jungle of New York, L.A., or some other big city. He'd bet his hard-earned money that she wouldn't make it a week in the little cabin outside Sweet Home.

Victoria straightened her shoulders and stared him straight in the eyes, which was a little unnerving since her eyes were a vivid green. "I'm fine," she declared.

"Wonderful. I just hope you have some good utility clothes in these suitcases." He glanced at her cute black dress, tights, and silly short boots one more time. When they arrived at the homestead, she should soak her sophisticated clothing in kerosene, light a match, and incinerate them to a crisp in the burn barrel. "What you're wearing isn't going to work for homesteading."

"McKenna packed some of her jeans and a couple of chambray shirts in my suitcase."

"Good. Would you like to stop at Walmart on our way out of Anchorage, just in case? If not, the hardware store in Sweet Home might have your size."

She huffed. "No, thanks. Neiman Marcus is more my style."

"Then you're out of luck." For his peace of mind, he hoped the other clothes in her suitcase didn't hug her body the way this dress outlined her curves.

He pointed to his new red Ford F-150. He glanced over at Tori, but she didn't seem keen to climb up into the cab. "Meet Ruby."

"Hm?" she answered distractedly.

"My truck. Her name is Ruby." He opened Tori's door and pointed out the running board. "Use the step to climb up." She was tiny enough for him to lift her into the cab, and for a second he wondered if he shouldn't speed up the process with a boost. She was probably hesitant because her dress was so short. He looked away as she maneuvered her way up and inside.

He went to the driver's side and climbed in, trying to put himself in her place. *Displaced.* Piney had recommended Jesse for the job, and he appreciated it. But he hadn't known, until he'd talked to Luke, what his new employer—Montgomery St. James—was up to. Jesse actually felt bad for both Tori and McKenna. And he was worried for himself. This was going to be one tough job. Maybe he should ask the old man for a raise now!

He put the vehicle in gear and drove out of the parking lot, deciding to give Tori the three-cent tour before taking her to the boonies. "Hey, look at that." He pointed to the moose in a crop of trees as they left the airport. "I bet you don't see that in Texas."

Her mouth formed into a surprised O, making him glad that he'd taken this route. She was more suited to delight than sadness. He began a running commentary on the highlights of Anchorage, starting with a drive by Lake Hood as two seaplanes took off. She looked at everything with interest, and he was glad to see her so animated.

"I've been working on your homestead this past week," he told her. *Trying to make it livable.* "The old place has been empty for as long as I can remember." But he was proud of the headway he'd made and wished he'd taken *before* pictures. "I had Piney, the owner of the Hungry Bear, stock your shelves with some staples."

She gaped as if he were speaking a foreign language. "Oh, I don't cook," she finally said. "I usually order in or eat out."

He was definitely in over his head. "You do know what a homesteader does, don't you?"

She gave him her stubborn stone-face. Was it really up to him to make her understand?

He sighed but continued anyway. "Homesteaders live off the land. Grow their own food in the garden and either hunt for meat or raise cattle, goats, and chickens. Then they preserve their food for when it's not in season. As a homesteader, you don't necessarily earn money; your job is to keep you and your family alive. That's it." He glanced over at her astonished face. "So you see, eating out or ordering in isn't part of the deal."

She was frowning now, and looked like she might be about to cry.

"Your uncle's homestead is eight miles outside Sweet Home, so it's not conducive to eating out at the diner every day anyway." Especially since she wouldn't have a vehicle, but he decided not to mention that tidbit. "You really don't know how to cook?"

"I know how to work the coffeemaker, if that counts as cooking," she said with a hint of sarcasm.

What could he say to that? He went silent then, deciding to not explain anything more. Soon enough, she'd see what she was up against.

VICTORIA SHOVED JESSE'S comments aside and enjoyed the scenery. Everywhere she looked, there seemed to be mountains. She'd traveled plenty, though mostly to warm climates with beaches and lots of parties. But this view was breathtaking, and she could see why people might want to live in Alaska.

They drove for several hours, going through many small towns until finally they passed the city limits sign for Sweet Home, population 573.

"Sweet Home has the basics," Jesse said. "As I mentioned, it has the Hungry Bear. And here's the newly reopened A Stone's Throw Hardware and Haberdashery, where you can find just about anything you'll need . . . like sturdy clothing. At each end of the town, we have our churches—Baptist and Catholic. The schools sit behind the old medical clinic, which is shut down now. The bank is over there, but it closed for good last month."

By the time he finished saying these words, they had passed through Sweet Home and were looking at the wilderness again. *Who in their right mind would want to live in such a tiny village?* But she kept the sentiment to herself, especially since he seemed proud of his small town.

After a few minutes, Jesse made a right turn down a gravel road, and after another mile, he turned again and pulled between two trees, drove another two hundred yards over grass, and then stopped the vehicle.

"Well, we're here," Jesse said cheerily.

Victoria's stomach dropped. The log cabin looked smaller than the walk-in closet at her condo. If you could call it a cabin; it was as ratty as a shack. "You can't expect me to live here!" she cried in a high-pitched voice.

His pitying look really ticked her off. "It's not that bad. Don't worry. My job is to teach you everything you need to know about homesteading."

He got out and went to the back to retrieve her luggage while she sat there trying to absorb this fresh hell her uncle had banished her to. Jesse came to her side of the truck and opened the door. He might as well have dragged her out of the vehicle, for the look he was giving her.

He must've seen her gaze go to two buckets of water sitting by the front door. "I brought those from the spring this morning so you wouldn't have to schlep them yourself your first day here. Firewood is by the stove, too, so you'll be warm tonight." He set the luggage down on the porch and opened the door.

Toto, we're not in Dallas anymore.

Victoria felt like she was having an out-of-body experience but managed to say, "Water? Firewood?" She'd never given a faucet a second thought, but apparently here in Nowheresville, Alaska, running water was a luxury. And warmth? She'd been wearing shorts since early March, but with the temperature dropping, April here in Alaska felt like it could start snowing any second.

He held the door wide, and she walked into the eighteenth century, and not some English ballroom either. This place was Daniel Boone's cabin. There was no refrigerator, no cooktop, only two shelves with an iron skillet, a Dutch oven like she'd seen in *Julie and Julia*, and cans of food from this person Piney he'd mentioned. And wasn't Piney a strange name?

She spun on him. "You've got to be kidding me!" She was in shock. "If I *could* cook, there's no place to even do it."

He set her luggage by the bed and put his hands up defensively. "You'll use the woodstove."

That must be the cast-iron contraption in the corner.

He continued. "There's a small oven area and two burners on top. It should be plenty for you."

She choked back a sob. *What a nightmare!* "Uncle Monty can't expect me to live here. You have to take me back to Anchorage. To McKenna!" *Now!*

His face fell into a frown, as if he were concerned she might start wailing. Which she was trying really hard not to do.

"Let's get you settled in. I'll show you how to get a fire going." He pulled the quilt off the bed and wrapped it around her.

She hadn't realized she was shaking. She grabbed the edges and tightened them around her neck, burying her chin into the cotton blanket, seeking comfort. But this homestead had none.

Jesse went into action over at the woodstove, crumpling newspaper and shoving it inside. "You'll be an old pro at making a fire in no time. I'm using newspaper for tinder, but I'll show you how to find good tinder in the woods so you can make a fire by yourself anywhere." He pulled open a coffee can, retrieved a matchstick, and struck the match, lighting the paper in the bottom of the stove. "Next, you'll set a little kindling on the fire." He blew on the paper and twigs until the larger bit of wood caught fire.

"I hope there's a smoke detector," she said to herself, wondering just how safe it was to have a fire going when the place was made of logs!

"I'll let that sit for a second, then I'll set one of your logs on there." He pointed to the stack of wood.

And how sanitary was it to have part of the forest in your house? What about bugs? Spiders? And other creepy crawlers?

She was paralyzed. He was acting like she was really going to stay.

He stood, shoving his hands in his pockets. "I promise it's going to be all right."

Maybe, she couldn't help thinking, *if you'd take me in your arms and give me a mountain man hug!* But his body language said she was screwed.

She didn't have faith that she could survive here ten minutes by herself, but his lack of faith in her was making her mad—mad enough that she decided she'd have to prove him wrong! "Where's the restroom? I want to freshen up." She scanned the room for a second door but didn't see one.

He raised an eyebrow and tilted his head toward the door. "The outhouse is east of the cabin."

She was horrified but managed to square her shoulders.

"Thank you." She walked toward the door, but his words stopped her.

"Keep an eye out for moose, wolves, and you gotta know this is bear country, too."

She sucked in a breath and spun around to see if he was kidding.

"Just be careful," he said. He might as well have said, *Have you had enough?*

She gripped her hefty Louis Vuitton handbag, deciding it would make a good weapon, if it came to that. "I'll be back shortly." She marched out the door, her eyes darting this way and that, making sure some grizzly wasn't ready to pounce.

Once she was off the porch, she wanted to make a run for the outhouse, but first she turned back to make sure Jesse wasn't looking. But he was, standing there in the doorway with his arms crossed over his chest. She gave a little wave and then proceeded toward the toilet, forcing herself to walk with slow, even steps. But then something occurred to her and she turned back around.

"If there's no running water in the cabin, how am I supposed to take a shower?"

Jesse shrugged like it was no big deal. "There's a basin under your bed. You'll get water from the spring or the river and wash up that way."

She glanced down at her long hair, holding some up for him to see. "How am I supposed to wash this in a basin?"

"Oh," he said, as if only just noticing she had blond curly locks almost to her waist. "There is an option."

"I'm not cutting my hair!" Victoria said. Her hair was her best feature.

"You don't have to. Piney rents out showers at the Hungry Bear to homesteaders and truckers. I'll take you into town once a week, if you like."

"This just gets better and better," she groaned. Was this

part of Uncle Monty's plan? Did he want her to reek like an animal by the time she got her weekly shower?

She stomped the rest of the way to the outhouse, not caring in the least if some wildlife did surprise her on the way there. Maybe it would put her out of her misery.

Ready to find
your next great read?

Let us help.

Visit prh.com/nextread

Penguin
Random
House